The Fourth Beginning

By

Paul Gee

Published by New Generation Publishing in 2013

www.newgeneration-publishing.com

 New Generation Publishing

Contents

1 Questions

"It's perfectly simple," said Adam. "I want the truth."

"I seriously doubt that," the Storyteller replied.

"What does that mean?" asked Adam, somewhat taken aback.

"It means," the Storyteller explained, "I'm not at all sure you will want the truth even if we can find it. And if we do, I am absolutely certain it won't be perfectly simple – or simple, or perfect.

"Excuse me," said Adam testily, "but I think I know what I want."

"Really?" the Storyteller smiled. "Well answer me this. Which truth do you want? Mine, yours, his, hers? The truth of any of the world's religions or the truth of none? What kind of truth will satisfy you? Revealed truth, scientific truth, the truth of experience? Above all, the truth about what?"

"I want an answer to the question that every man asks," said Adam flatly.

"And woman," added Eve.

"Oh, that question!" said the Storyteller, with perhaps a hint of mockery in his voice. "And you are?"

"I'm Eve."

"Yes," Adam continued. "That question."

"So your name is Adam and her name is Eve," queried the Storyteller. "Is that supposed to mean something?"

"Only that their respective parents favoured archetypal biblical names," answered Luke.

"And who are you?" asked the Storyteller.

"I'm Luke – I'm the family dog."

"I was wondering if you might not be the serpent." The Storyteller chuckled.

"Or even whether, indeed, I might be," mused Luke. "Odd, isn't it! The sentence means the same whether the 'not' is there, or not. Either way, fairly obviously, I'm not a serpent; I'm a dog."

"A dog attracted by the finer points of linguistics and semantics," observed the Storyteller.

"And a highly articulate dog, except that people can't hear what I say," Luke added. "Can you be articulate, I wonder, if no one can hear you?"

"I can hear you," offered the Storyteller.

"That's because you're the Storyteller," suggested Luke.

"Well? What about our question, the question?" Adam persisted,

1

obviously oblivious to the conversation between the Storyteller and Luke.

The Storyteller adopted a most serious, almost intimidating, tone. "I tell you this, Adam. If you persist with your enquiry and if I were to agree to help you seek an answer, we would have a long and difficult journey ahead of us, a journey across vast continents and through interminable aeons of time, through the darkest passageways of the mind, on to the peaks of human imagination and, quite possibly, into the depths of hell. I cannot pretend the quest would be free of danger, nor can I guarantee it would be successful."

"So you advise against the venture?" asked Eve.

"Certainly sounds like it," said Luke. "Not the most appealing prospectus. Lots of danger; certain trauma; no guarantee of a safe arrival, success or even survival."

"This is not a package holiday," the Storyteller responded, dealing with Eve's question and Luke's unheard comment. "What we are considering is the journey of a lifetime. If you persist, I will take you. The real question is, will you come with me? Will you dare to come with me?"

"Why should I go with you on such a journey?" Adam probed. "You do not say where I will be going or what challenges I will face. Why should I go with you if there is such uncertainty and such danger?"

The Storyteller answered: "You should come with me because you ask 'why?'- and because you would like to know the truth; because there is a chance you will find it; because there is danger whether you come or stay; and because, in a sense, you have no choice."

"Then I will go," said Adam.

"Wait a minute," exclaimed Eve. "No discussion. You will go. What about me? Am I to stay? Or am I to go? Or doesn't it matter?"

"No, no, no," said Adam, hoping he had dealt with all her questions.

Eve probed: "'No' to what? No, I'm not to go. Or no, it doesn't matter. Or no to any discussion. You're always doing this."

"It seems we have the beginnings of a 'domestic'," the Storyteller murmured. Only Luke heard.

"I shouldn't worry," said Luke with the weariness of long experience. "They do this a lot. It's their way of communicating."

"Sounds more like arguing," muttered the Storyteller.

"What I meant," said Adam in an attempt to soothe his wife, "was 'of course we can discuss it'."

Eve remained unsoothed. "We can discuss it – but you've already made up your mind."

"Well," Adam sighed, "if you're convinced I've already made up

2

my mind, there is no point in discussing it."

"So we can't discuss it," challenged Eve.

"No," Adam responded, "I'm just saying that if we begin a discussion with you convinced I'm not prepared to have a discussion, any discussion we have is unlikely to be productive."

"So you're prepared to change your mind," Eve persisted.

"No, I didn't say that," said Adam defensively. "But I am prepared to discuss whether or not you come with me."

"So you can make a decision to go on your own," said Eve triumphantly, "but I can't make a decision without your help or your approval."

"Did I say that?" asked Adam, exasperated.

"Stop," pleaded the Storyteller. "I am inviting both of you. Each of you has a decision to make. You may make it alone or together. But what I said to Adam applies just as much to you, Eve. It is up to you."

"But, in the end, I have no choice," said Eve. "It's a funny decision where there is no choice."

"She really is quite argumentative," said the Storyteller to Adam.

"But right," Luke pointed out to the Storyteller. "If there is no choice, it's not really a decision-taking situation. And when you say there is no choice, what do you mean?"

"What I mean is very simple," said the Storyteller. "Each of us has an allotted span. You can sit still or you can run. You can sleep or you can stay awake all hours. You can let your brain atrophy or you can seek the truth every moment of every day. But whatever you do, the clock ticks, and it ticks inexorably in one direction. So, you see, you can make lots of decisions about how you spend your time but, at the end of the day, you take the journey. And, at the end of the journey, my friends, is the end of the day."

"Do you want to go?" Adam asked Eve.

"Apparently, I have no choice," Eve responded.

"Do you want to go?" Adam repeated.

"Do you want me to go with you?" Eve asked.

"Of course I want you to go with me," said Adam. "I was just worried about the danger."

"I think I can face danger just as well as you," said Eve. "In any case, as we know only too well, danger can strike anywhere at any time."

"Are you sure?" Adam asked. "We will be going into the unknown. We don't know the risks we will be taking."

"Neither do you," Eve pointed out. "I would rather share the risks than stay here worrying about the risks you were facing alone. In any

3

case, we can help each other."

"And me," added Luke for the benefit of the Storyteller. "You can't leave the family dog behind. Mind you, on balance I'd rather we all stayed here. From a canine perspective, this truth thing is much over-rated. A soft rug by a warm fire has the edge any day. But if you are going, then I'm going with you."

"Very well," said the Storyteller. "It's settled."

2 Before the beginning

It was three years since the accident. The family (Adam, Eve, daughter Bella and dog Luke) had gone to the park. It was Bella's seventh birthday and they had thought a walk in the park would help them to work up an appetite and possibly siphon off some of Bella's prodigious energy before the tea party they were giving her and her friends later. When they had set out, the sun had been shining.

In the course of their walk, clouds began to gather quite quickly; thick, dark, rain-laden clouds. Eve had suggested they return and Adam agreed. Bella wanted to carry on playing with Luke, who was an exuberant puppy, but her parents overrode her wishes. "Come on Bella," Eve had cajoled, "You'll catch your death of cold." "Your mother's right," Adam had added, in support of his wife. They turned round and began to retrace their steps. Half way back, the heavens opened and Eve suggested they should take shelter under a tree.

It was a fine tree, with a rich canopy and wide-spreading boughs. No one knew how old it was but it was certainly older than any living human. It stood there, proud and full, surely ready to take anything the elements threw at it.

It was just after they arrived that the lightning struck. Both Adam and Eve had replayed the sequence of events many times in their heads and yet it still remained chaotic. First, the flash of lightning blinded them. Almost at once, there was a dreadful cracking sound, drowned out by a thunderclap so loud that all three of them and the dog were temporarily deafened. With two of their senses impaired, neither parent saw the bough of the tree split from the dark trunk, swing downwards and kill their daughter.

3 In the beginning

It all began on a cold winter's evening in a comfortable house in a street lined with elm trees in Harrow.

Adam and Eve were relaxing in their sitting room, with Luke, their golden retriever, stretched out in front of a log fire, happily warming his white, fur-covered stomach. The wood crackled happily, as it morphed from fibre to flame. Adam was browsing the internet on a laptop. He was thinking of changing his mobile and was researching the latest smart-phones. Eve was flicking through a magazine, looking for colour schemes she might apply to the dining room when they next redecorated. Neither was watching the large plasma TV screen. It was an evening like many others, comfortable, mildly constructive, unexceptional.

oooOooo

Luke's ears pricked up. There was a knock at the door.

"Bit late for visitors," Adam observed, reluctantly setting aside his laptop.

"If it's Jehovah's witnesses," Eve speculated, "be polite. They mean well."

Adam grunted. Luke rose from his comfortable station in front of the fire to join his master. This was his job – watchdog, escort, guardian – and he rather enjoyed it. Adam opened the door.

"It's time," said the visitor.

Adam knew the man. "Oh! It's you," he said.

The visitor grinned. His piercing blue eyes, wreathed in laughter lines, twinkled. "Yes, it's me and it's time. Not that you should confuse the one with the other."

"It's time," Adam repeated. "Is that a call for action or the answer to a question?"

"And what question might it be the answer to?" the visitor asked.

"Well it could be the answer to many questions; 'What stops everything happening at once?' Or 'What allows us to distinguish between cause and effect?' Or 'What makes change possible?' Or…"

"Enough!" said the visitor. "It's time for action, not aphorisms."

"Who is it?" Eve enquired.

"It's him; it's the Storyteller."

"Well you'd better invite him in. You're letting all the warm air out."

Adam stood back from the door. The visitor entered. Luke, stern and unyielding defender of the household, wagged his tail vigorously and licked the hand extended to him. "Hello, Luke," the Storyteller greeted the dog. "How's tricks?"

"That's really not funny," Luke responded. "I don't do tricks. As you well know, I am not comfortable with such frivolity. I'm towards the thinking end of the canine spectrum."

"Doggedly intellectual, then? Sorry." The apology lacked sincerity.

The Storyteller entered the living room. He was of indeterminate years, certainly not young but not old. There were hints of grey in his hair, and his skin was wrinkled but more from exposure to the elements than from age. His physique was wiry, the kind of body that is far stronger than it looks.

"It's time," he said again, addressing Eve.

"What? Now?"

"Now is always best; it's all we've got."

"We'll need time to get ready, time to pack. We can't just leave."

"Yes, you can," said the Storyteller. "This is no ordinary journey – far from it. You need not worry about what you leave behind. It will all be here when we return or even if we don't, all here just as it is now."

"But...," Eve objected but was silenced by a wave of the Storyteller's hand.

"Come outside and I will show you how we are going to travel," the Storyteller paused, "unless you've changed your mind."

Eve followed the Storyteller to the door, with Adam close behind. Luke wove his way ruthlessly between human legs to reach the door first.

"What do you think?" asked the Storyteller.

"It's a camper van," said Eve, dismissively. The vehicle looked of middle years and in no more than reasonable condition. It had been sprayed bright yellow to cover any damage to the bodywork and now looked rather cheap and gaudy.

"It's a mobile home," said Adam, trying to be fair.

"It's an amazing piece of work," said the Storyteller. "And so is this man."

A small, slightly stooping figure stepped down from the driver's compartment. He wore a black beret which more or less contained his full head of white hair. His skin was brown, tanned, weather-beaten, his eyes a soft brown surrounded by deeply-etched lines. He was shifting nervously from one foot to the other.

"This," said the Storyteller, with a hint of pride in his voice, "is Gwoat."

"What kind of a name is that?" Luke asked. "It's virtually unpronounceable."

The Storyteller laughed. "Unpronounceable!" he minded to Luke. "That from a dog that only I can hear! Anyway, it's not that hard. There are other words that begin 'gw'."

"Name one," Luke persisted.

"I can see you are not to be put down," the Storyteller responded, with a turn of phrase that was certain to resonate with a dog. Luke chose to ignore the jibe. "Well, there's 'gwyniad'," the Storyteller hazarded, "a white fish found somewhere in Wales."

"Huh!" minded Luke. "Gwyniad! Not exactly an everyday word, is it?"

"And likely to become less common as sadly the gwyniad is threatened by extinction. But what about Gwen, then?" the Storyteller offered. "Or, if you're prepared to accept homophones, let's not forget the 'sanguine penguin'?"

"What sanguine penguin?" Luke asked.

"Never mind. There will be time enough to explore that possibility later. Thank you for reminding me," the Storyteller smiled.

"Gwoat," Eve mused. "That's an unusual name." She had heard none of the exchange between Luke and the Storyteller.

Gwoat seemed about to speak. Indeed he had been eager to tell them something from the moment they had met. But the Storyteller cut in. "Actually, it's not a name so much as an acronym."

"An acronym for what?" Adam asked.

"Homophones and acronyms," Luke mused silently. "What kind of an adventure is this going to be?"

"The Greatest Worrier Of All Time," the Storyteller explained. "We shall surely need his attributes on our journey."

Adam looked at the figure of Gwoat. The man looked more like a dilapidated French onion seller than a mighty warrior but he knew appearances could be deceptive.

"So we are to enjoy the protection of a hero?" Eve enquired uncertainly. She too had misheard the 'worrier' bit.

"Hero is over-stating it," Gwoat spoke in a slightly faltering voice, "but I will certainly help you to leaven courage with caution, to be sure."

Both Adam and Eve remained puzzled. "Oh, I see," the Storyteller laughed. "Worrier, not warrior. Gwoat has many virtues but his nervous disposition sadly precludes the heroic."

"It's all right," Luke woofed. "We've all got it. Absolutely flank-splitting."

8

"You're rather grumpy for a gifted golden retriever," the Storyteller chided. He turned to Eve. "Gwoat is our driver. He knows the bus inside out. He's the best."

"You mean we are to drive where we are going?" Adam sounded both surprised and disappointed. As someone who loved the hi-tech developments of the 21st century, Adam had been rather hoping the mode of travel would exceed his most extravagant technological expectations. This van was not it. "I thought you said we were going to travel through time and space."

"I did and we are," the Storyteller responded.

"I hope it's bigger on the inside than on the out," Eve offered, fearful that keeping such a vehicle tidy when occupied by four adults and a dog would be impossible.

"No, I'm afraid not," said the Storyteller. "In common with most things that have an outside and an inside, the van is slightly smaller inside than outside." He then added, "By the thickness of its walls."

Eve's brow wrinkled. In order to believe in any of this, she had assumed they were leaving the mundane world of common sense and reason and were embarking on an adventure into the limitless, unbridled world of the imagination, a world where anything was possible.

The Storyteller read her thoughts. "Don't worry. You won't be disappointed. You will meet gods and heroes and dragons. You will fly over mountains and into the bowels of the earth. You will see miracles performed. You will see death overcome. You will experience hope and fear, terror and love. All this you will have. But there are limits – and one of them is that the inside of something will never be bigger than its outside."

"Won't it be rather cramped?" Eve asked.

"No, it will be perfectly adequate," the Storyteller replied. "Only you, Adam and the dog will sleep in it, if the need arises. Gwoat and I have our own arrangements. Not that there will much time, if any, for sleeping."

Gwoat started to perform a jig. "He does that when he is bored, or nervous," the Storyteller explained. "And, since he is easily bored and habitually nervous, he tends to jig around most of the time when he's not actually driving. Sometimes even when he is," he added. "I suggest we get underway as soon as possible. When embarking on an adventure, there's no time like the present."

"And no time except the present," Luke added.

"Absolutely." The Storyteller gave Luke a congratulatory pat, as all of them climbed into the van.

"I'm really sorry but we can't go anywhere – at least not yet," Gwoat spoke. His voice was high-pitched and betrayed a faint Irish accent. He had been trying to speak for some time but he had been so agitated, he hadn't managed to get anything out.

"And why is that?" the Storyteller asked.

"We've been clamped," said Gwoat.

Before the party could express irritation, surprise or disillusion, a parking meter person, for such her uniform implied she must be, appeared at the back of the van. She was writing a ticket as she approached them.

"This isn't a restricted parking area," Adam spoke with authority. "You can't give us a ticket. And you certainly can't clamp this vehicle. We've never had any clamping in this area."

The parking meter person, a middle-aged, overweight woman, with dyed blonde hair and grotesquely heavy make-up, finished writing the ticket and handed it to Adam with a flourish. "I can and I have," said the woman. "You are causing an obstruction. So I can give you a ticket."

"And who is being obstructed?" Adam asked, clearly annoyed.

"Me," said the parking meter person.

"This is really silly. If we were causing an obstruction, which we're not, how would clamping help? That would simply mean we would be causing an obstruction for longer," said Adam, now angry.

"Not an auspicious beginning to the journey of a lifetime," Luke offered.

"Are you calling me silly?" shouted the woman. "It's my job to stop selfish, stuck-up, arrogant buggers like you from clogging up the capital's arteries with illegally parked cars which are clearly causing an obstruction."

Adam was spoiling for a fight but he knew the best way to respond was with cold, calm infuriating reason. "Let me explain, dear. This van, which incidentally is not mine but has come with my approval to pick me up, is parked outside this house, which funnily enough is my house. So how is a vehicle briefly parked outside my house to pick me up, how is that causing an obstruction? How else could it pick me up? And, while we're on the subject, where are the notices warning of any parking restrictions? Where are the yellow lines? Where is there any indication that vehicles cannot be parked here? My word! There are none. Could that be because this is a quiet residential area without any parking restrictions?"

"You think you're clever," sneered the parking person, "but obviously you are not clever enough to know the law. You can be charged with causing an obstruction anywhere on the public highway that someone in a position of authority," and the woman put heavy emphasis on the word authority, "considers you to be causing an obstruction."

"It won't work, Grimrose," said the Storyteller, addressing the woman by name. "You can't stop us. Clamping! That's a new one. Pathetic! You could have tried a thunderstorm, or an earth tremor, or a serious rip in the fabric of space-time. But no, you issue a parking ticket. It's insulting. This is a serious quest. If you want to impede it, try something a bit grander than a wheel clamp. And, by the way, you look ridiculous. Given you can appear in any form, this particular manifestation shows a serious lack of imagination and a deplorable loss of dignity."

For the first time the parking meter person looked uncertain. "You are picking on me because I am a woman," she said, and then sobbed.

Adam blinked. Grimrose was changing in front of him. In place of the noisy, boisterous, rotund bully was a thinner, younger but still deeply unattractive female. The uniform had morphed into a cheap frock and the peaked cap had become a headscarf, tied in the manner of a down-trodden housewife of the 1950s.

"We are not picking on you," the Storyteller responded with a hint of irritation seeping through the patient tone he had adopted, "and even if we were, it would not be because you're a woman. It would be because you are a bloody nuisance, and a terminal haemorrhoid – in short, an anal pain."

In response to this modest diatribe, the 1950s housewife began to age dramatically. In a few moments, she had become an exhausted, life-weary, older woman, with desiccated sagging breasts, creaking bones and a face that managed to combine a bland flaccidity with a network of lines gouged in her face by trouble, worry and the passage of time.

"Just because I'm old." Grimrose's tone conveyed a mixture of anger and resignation. "You think you can ignore me just because I'm old," Grimrose croaked. "Is this how you would treat your own mother?"

"Give up," advised the Storyteller. "It's not going to work and you are embarrassing yourself. Tell your master he will have to do better than this, a lot better. We will lose respect for him if he tries this sort of nonsense again. Now take your ticket and your clamps and that grotesque disguise (playing the poor old mother card, really!) and be gone."

Grimrose did and was.

4 The journey starts

The party boarded the camper van. Gwoat settled himself behind the wheel and, apart from an occasional nervous twitch, seemed almost calm.

Adam, still hopeful that their mode of transport was more than it seemed, waited for Gwoat to turn the ignition key. He half expected a panel full of winking lights to slide into view, accompanied by the whirring into life of an anti-matter thrust generator, or something of that sort.

Instead, the engine turned, struggled and died.

"Great," said Eve. "What a start to the journey of a lifetime!"

"Don't upset him," the Storyteller advised. "You'll set off one of his episodes."

Gwoat turned the key again. The engine seemed to fire but died.

"It hasn't had much use lately," the Storyteller apologised. "Not much demand for the truth in recent times," he mused. Then he encouraged Gwoat. "Try one more time."

For the third time Gwoat turned the key. There was no response, other than a faint hissing sound.

"I thought everything worked out on the third try," Eve addressed the Storyteller. "Isn't that the way it works? Try once, try twice, then third time lucky."

"This isn't about luck." The Storyteller seemed hurt. "Nor is this a fairy tale. And you had best prepare yourself for rather more drastic reversals than a flat battery."

"It's not flat," said Gwoat. "I charged it yesterday."

Without warning, the engine started.

"Well that's a bit of magic," Adam suggested.

"Let's go," the Storyteller, fearful the engine would stall, urged Gwoat. Gwoat slipped the van into gear and with a couple of jerks, they were on their way.

"Where exactly are we heading?" Adam asked

"A316 and then the M3," Gwoat answered.

"That's not quite what I meant," Adam returned.

"It will have to do for now," the Storyteller intervened.

They made good time. The roads were busy but the camper van seemed highly manoeuvrable and they cut through the traffic without any problems. At least, nothing impeded their progress.

"We'll stop at Fleet services," the Storyteller announced. "We need some fuel."

Eve frowned. None of this made any sense. The Storyteller had promised them a quest, a heroic search for the truth, a journey full of challenge and danger. But their mode of transport for this demanding venture was faintly ridiculous, their driver profoundly neurotic and unsuited to questing and their preparations evidently patchy. "Couldn't you have filled up before we left?" she asked of the Storyteller petulantly. He ignored her.

They pulled off the motorway at Fleet between Junctions 4a and 5.

"We should drive straight round to the petrol station," Adam suggested. He was keen to be back on the road.

Gwoat turned into the main car park and parked as close to the restaurant and shop buildings as possible. "He needs his bar of chocolate," the Storyteller explained. "He gets so fidgety without a chocolate burst he can scarcely drive."

"Well, he'd better stock up with bumper packs," said Eve, "because we can't stop every half hour for our driver to gorge himself on chocolate."

The party, excluding Luke, alighted and entered Fleet services. "Do you know, I fancy an all day breakfast," Adam confided to Eve.

"You can't," Eve responded. "You've just had dinner. And, in any case, it's not the right time for a breakfast."

"It's good at any time," Adam explained. "That's why it's called 'all day'."

Adam didn't press the point. He too wanted to resume their journey. Food could wait – except of course for Gwoat who emerged from the shop triumphant clutching a large box of assorted chocolate bars.

"Well, that should see us from here to eternity," Eve observed.

As they descended the steps of the shopping area, their attention was caught by a commotion from the disabled parking spaces close to the steps where a group of motor cyclists had gathered. Two or three of them were taking up the disabled parking spaces.

A youth, a thin and callow stripling, and a tall older man, wearing a porkpie hat with a rather sad, small, drooping, feather attached, appeared to be confronting the motorcyclists.

"Why don't you mind your own business?" one of the leather jacketed motorcyclists asked the youth.

"It is not permitted for abled people to park in these spaces," the youth persisted.

"That's an odd turn of phrase," thought Luke who, although left in the camper van, was close enough to hear the conversation through a half open window.

The older man, who could see trouble brewing, intervened. "Come now, Numpty, there is no need to explain such rules to these gentlemen."

"Numpty," the most voluble of the bikers exclaimed. "Numpty, that's a bloody good name for a fucking idiot."

"There is no need for such language," the older man objected.

"So you're another one telling us what to do now, are you?" enquired the lead biker, with more than a hint of menace. "I tell you what," he continued. "You fuck off or you'll both end up entitled to park here."

Several of the bikers laughed.

"How dare you speak to Uncle Rambler in such a way, and why do you use the word fuck so frequently?" asked Numpty.

"I've only used it twice, but I'll fucking well use it as fucking often as I fucking like," the biker shouted. "Now fuck off!" he concluded, giving the youth a shove.

The young man, whose bodily co-ordination was as doubtful as his mental cohesion, fell backwards to the ground. The bikers laughed. Numpty struggled to his feet and made towards his assailant, striking the posture of one about to engage in a bout of fisticuffs.

"This could be fun," sneered the lead biker, who had just unlocked the safety chain on his bike and was clearly considering other uses for it.

"Leave him alone," Eve spoke.

"Keep your nose out of this, bitch," snapped the biker. His fellow riders sensed that the situation was escalating.

"I'm calling the police," Eve responded.

"Call all you like. Those bastards are only interested in handing out speeding tickets. We'll be long gone and you'll still be waiting for an ambulance before the police get here."

Numpty took a swing at his tormentor, and missed. "There you are," quipped the biker. "It's never us that starts a fight. You saw him. This is going to be self-defence."

There was a murmur of laughter and jocular support from the other leather-clad riders.

"Stop this," said Adam.

"Not another one!" exclaimed the lead biker in mock exasperation. "Where are they all coming from?" With that, the biker swung the chain low, catching Numpty behind the knees and dropping him once again to the ground with a thud.

"What about you?" the biker addressed Adam. "Are you up for it?"

"Not here," Adam responded. "Let's take it somewhere quieter."

There was a collective 'Ooooh!' from the bikers, some genuine surprise mixed with the derision.

"What are you doing?" Eve asked.

"Leave him," the Storyteller intervened.

"But…," Eve's voice trailed off.

"There's a quiet space behind the petrol pumps, at the side of the buildings," Adam addressed the biker. "We can conclude our business there. By the way, I'd advise you to leave the chain here. If you bring it, I may be compelled to employ lethal force."

The biker was clearly stunned by this turn of events. Here was a well-dressed, middle-class plonker taking on a gang of hairy bikers on behalf of a retarded stranger. Not only taking them on but casually warning he might have to use lethal force. Doubt flickered in the eyes of the biker and then, instead of fading away, doubt took a firmer hold. 'I really can't back down,' he thought. 'So I'll have to go through with it. Just my luck to pick on some Armani-dressed ex-SAS, black belted psycho! So should I take the chain, or not? He's unarmed, as far as I can see, so the chain gives me a pretty big advantage. On the other hand, he's warned me that, if I take it, he might kill me. Why? Because to defend himself against a lethal weapon he might have to take lethal measures? Or because he'd be so pissed off if I'd used the chain, he'd kill me in a fit of pique?' Unable to determine which motivation was more likely but unhappy with both, he put the chain into one of the metal studded panniers on his bike.

"Let's go," said Adam, leading the way round to the open area between the restaurant/ shopping complex and the fuel station.

"Are you not going with your friend?" the Storyteller asked of the other bikers.

"He's not our friend. He just rolled up here a few minutes ago," said one of the biker group.

"Seems a bit of a nutter to me," offered another.

"Don't know him from Adam," remarked a third.

"What is going on?" demanded Eve.

"Don't worry," the Storyteller advised.

"Don't worry!" Eve expostulated. "Don't worry! Adam's a manager. He doesn't fight."

"Are you sure?" the Storyteller smiled. "You have to understand," he continued, "this is a quest for the truth. We will all have to fight, one way or another. More importantly, we will have to try to make sense of all that happens. Most of all, out of the chaos of events, we will have to make stories. This is our first opportunity. But don't be afraid for Adam. That biker is not a real threat. If you want to worry about someone, I should take a look at young Numpty. He struck his head on

15

the tarmac when he fell."

Eve hadn't noticed that the young fellow felled by the biker still lay where he had fallen. His companion, the older man with the sad porkpie hat, was kneeling beside poor Numpty, who showed no sign of movement.

oooOooo

By the time Adam and his adversary had reached open ground, the morning sun was blazing down. Adam wondered how it could be mid-morning when they had left home late at night and hadn't been on the road more than 45 minutes. He also thought, since it was evidently mid-morning, it was very much a good time for an all day breakfast.

Adam stopped and turned to face his opponent. He was surprised that he felt more excited than fearful.

"You can't hit me," said the biker immediately. Gone was the mean, aggressive, threatening yob.

"Why not?" asked Adam, understandably puzzled. "Didn't we come here to fight?"

"You can't hit me, because I am a woman," the biker explained.

"But you're not a woman," Adam asserted. "You're a big, hairy, foul-mouthed bullying biker who has just assaulted a harmless young lad and called my wife a bitch."

As Adam finished, he realised his opponent was changing before his eyes. With a pulsing of flesh and a creaking contortion of bones and cartilage, the biker was beginning to resemble the parking meter lady who had pestered them at the start of their journey. The open-face helmet morphed into a peaked cap; and the biker's leathers adopted the texture of the navy-blue cloth of the feared dispenser of parking tickets.

"Not you again!" exclaimed Adam.

"I'm sorry about the violence and the insults, but I'm only obeying orders," Grimrose – for it was indeed he, she or it – apologised.

"If you're going to be a woman, I suggest you dispense with the beard," Adam offered.

While Grimrose was completing the transformation, Adam noticed another biker, leaning against a chrome-adorned, highly polished cruiser which had been parked on its stand close to the back wall of one of the fuel station buildings. This new leather-clad rider stepped forward, out of the shadows. He removed his full-face helmet. He was tall, well-built, bronzed – and smiling.

"I have done what you asked," Grimrose, now fully feminised, whined. "Please let me go."

16

"You have done well," said the stranger, "for once," he added with a hint of amusement in his voice. "You may go."

The stranger beckoned to Adam who, after hesitating for a moment, approached. "It's really good to meet you at last," the stranger declared, extending a strong, sun-tanned hand and giving Adam a firm, warm, friendly shake. "I'm Nick, Nick Peters, and I've been wanting to meet you for some time."

Adam shook his head. Grimrose had disappeared. He might have slipped away when the stranger had approached or, for all Adam knew, he might have disappeared in a puff of smoke. Whatever. Grimrose, having effected a transformation from male thug to female traffic warden was gone and he, Adam, was shaking hands with a total stranger who was greeting him like an old friend. Except of course, both of them knew they had not previously met.

"Who or what is Grimrose?" Adam managed after a moment or two.

"Ah, Grimrose!" Nick Peters replied, leaning back to rest on the seat of his bike. "That's quite a tough question. He's a shapeshifter but I guess you know that."

"A shapeshifter," Adam repeated.

"Yes," Nick replied. "You must have met people who are not what they seem, who can, for example, appear to be pleasant, honest and friendly on one occasion and can then turn out to be mean, devious and hostile."

"Yes," Adam conceded, "but that's not the same as changing your entire appearance."

"Well," Nick persisted, "you must have met people, usually women, who can look very beautiful in the evening but are somehow transformed into creatures of only average or worse looks in the morning."

"Grimrose doesn't just change his appearance," Adam showed determination. "He changes his whole being. How is that possible?"

Nick laughed. "I'm not sure he has a being to change. He's a non-entity in the strictest sense of the term. You should think of him as a figment of his own and other people's imagination. For me, he's useful as a messenger, as an information gatherer, as a general, all-purpose menial assistant. He doesn't really have a mind, or for that matter, a body, of his own. But he does have his uses." Nick paused, studying Adam's face, apparently enjoying the mixture of expressions that flitted across it. "You take things far too seriously, my friend," he concluded. "Look, I needed to talk to you, in private."

"In private?" Adam repeated. "Why? What about? What can you have to say to me that can only be said in private?"

"I had to get you away from the Storyteller," Nick revealed. "I know what you are doing. I know all about the journey, the quest and the question. I just wanted to do you a favour and warn you."

"Warn me! Warn me of what?" Adam resented Nick's familiarity.

"Just that you are wasting your time."

"You set all this up, with Grimrose and the bikers and the young lad, just to tell me to cancel my trip?" Adam asked, with some anger and irritation.

"Not at all," Nick laughed that affable intimate laugh, "I'm not here to persuade you to turn back. If you want to go on, go on. I'm just warning you not to expect too much. Above all, don't expect any answers."

"There would be little point to a quest if the questors knew from the start they were going to fail."

Nick shrugged. "It's up to you. But, if it's truth you're after, I can give you all the truth you can take here and now, because here and now is the only truth there is. This is it. There's no secret, no hidden truth, no inner or outer meaning. Nothing makes sense in itself. Stuff happens – some good, some bad, most of it merely humdrum. You can make sense of it sometimes, but you have to do the making. There's no sense built in. And if you think there is, you're just kidding yourself. If you want to spend your time on a quest with the Storyteller, go ahead. But enjoy the journey because it's eating up your life – and you get only one of those, and this is it."

"You know the Storyteller?" Adam asked.

Again the laugh. "Oh, yes. I know the Storyteller all right. He and I go back a long way."

Adam waited for more information.

"He's not what he seems," Nick continued, picking his words carefully.

"What does that mean?"

"You think he can help you to find answers. He can't."

"How do you know what I want? How do you know he can't help?"

"I know what you want," Nick explained. "I know about Bella. I know what happened. And I know he can't help. Because there are no answers."

Adam turned away. He didn't know whether the stranger was right or wrong but his interference and his arrogant assumptions were intrusive and patronising.

"Let me show you," Nick called Adam back. "Will you let me show you what I mean?"

Nick pointed towards a large lorry coming out of the parking area for trucks. It was cruising towards the junction with the track that took cars from the fuel station back onto the M3.

Adam looked but didn't answer Nick's question.

"Now do you see that silver car, driving out of the fuel station?"

Adam nodded.

"Watch," Nick instructed.

The two vehicles headed towards the junction where the lorry had right of way. Both vehicles were doing around 25 miles an hour. As the silver car approached the junction, a large, red kite dropped out of the sky onto the bank to the left of the silver car. The driver of the car, Cedric Entwhistle, pharmaceutical rep, married, father of two, turned to look at the kite which was flapping on the verge like a large, landed bottom-feeding flat fish. It took no more than a couple of seconds before he turned his eyes back to the road.

While Cedric's attention had been caught by the kite, Sid Pervis, a truck-driver, with a clean licence and more than 20 years' experience, was adjusting the radio in his cab to his favourite station. He had a 200 mile journey ahead of him and, since he did not intend to stop again until he reached his destination, he needed a lively station to help keep him awake.

Cedric's car drove under the side of Sid's lorry, prising its way between the two front wheels and the second row of four wheels on the ten-wheeler. Sid hadn't seen him but he heard the noise. He braked immediately and, after the body of his vehicle had briefly risen a couple of feet and then sunk back to the ground, stopped. The grinding, squealing sound of metal being twisted and compressed hung in the air for a moment. What was left of both Cedric and his car was unrecognisable.

Adam gasped, exclaimed, "Oh my God!" and started to run towards the scene of carnage. There was nothing he could do. Cedric was dead, his wife widowed, his children fatherless. Sid was in a state of shock and, although he didn't know it at the time, his career as a truck-driver was over.

"You're not seeing the bigger picture," Nick suggested, now standing at Adam's side.

"We must get help," Adam ignored Nick's remark.

"I've already phoned for an ambulance and a fire engine," Nick soothed. "I just wanted you to understand that things just happen; accidents happen. There is no reason. There is no point. Most of the time, we avoid disaster. But sometimes, a few factors, entirely unrelated, come together and the results can be pretty bad. If Cedric hadn't decided to fill up here rather than at Winchester; if that kite had landed somewhere else, or ten seconds earlier or ten seconds later; if Sid here had stayed for that second mug of tea or taken a few seconds longer or been a few seconds quicker in the cafe to relieve his bladder, this wouldn't have happened. Cedric would be on his way to his next call; Sid would be a few miles down the road on his two-hundred mile journey. But, as it is, it's all changed. That's what happened to Bella. Just an accident. Now you want to make sense of it. But there isn't any. It's senseless. And if that old reprobate, the Storyteller, was honest, he would tell you so."

"You don't mean you engineered this appalling tragedy just to make a point?" Adam snapped. How had the stranger known what was going to happen? He had said: "Let me show you what I mean." He had known what was going to happen and was using it to illustrate his argument.

"Whoa!" Nick cried, affable as ever. "Of course I didn't engineer a thing like this. Being able to predict events doesn't mean I am responsible for them. And it was just a lucky guess, anyway. I can see you're upset," he added. "I must go, but we shall meet again." Nick walked back to his bike.

"What makes you think you know what I want?" Adam was angry. "Why do you think I can't accept that my daughter's death was an accident? Of course it was an accident."

Nick had swung his leg over his cruiser. "Not an act of God?", he enquired, as he pressed the starter button. The bike roared into life, vibrating as the two cylinders of the flat twin found their rhythm. He revved the engine. "Be seeing you," he shouted as he swung the bike round.

oooOooo

Adam walked slowly back to the car park in front of the shopping area. He didn't know what he felt, or rather he felt so many things that he couldn't sort them out into any kind of intelligible order or hierarchy. He had just seen a man die. That metallic grinding noise carried on in his head long after the sound had ceased. The biker he had thought he must fight had turned into a woman. Such a transformation was impossible in the real world but there they were, at Fleet services on the M3 – and that's as real as things get. And the tall, unnaturally bronzed biker, Nick Peters, a stranger who insinuated some kind of intimacy with him, had told him he was wasting his time, that things just happen, and to prove it had either used or engineered an horrific accident to illustrate or make his point.

20

Eve was leaning over Numpty. He was still lying on his back but his eyes were open and he seemed to be conscious. "If you are not badly hurt, you should try to get up," Eve cajoled. Both she and the older companion of Numpty had been trying to persuade the lad to rise for some time.

"I'm afraid," Numpty explained.

"Of what?" Eve asked.

"I'm afraid of falling into the sky," Numpty replied.

Eve looked at the older man, who removed his hat and started to fan young Numpty's face with it.

"No need to be afraid," the older man soothed. "Gravity will do its job; gravity will suffice. It always does."

"But the sky seems to be far below me and I'm looking down on it. I can't think of any reason why I'm not falling into it."

"Perhaps if you stood up, you would feel better. Then you would see the ground is below you and the sky above. You would then have to fear only falling down, not up."

Although not entirely convinced, Numpty sat up and rubbed the back of his legs. They were a bit sore but no real harm done. Eve helped him to his feet.

"There's been a terrible accident," Adam announced his return.

"Are you all right?" Eve had been relying on the Storyteller's assurances but she had still been concerned.

"I'm fine," Adam answered. "But a car just drove under a lorry. The car driver was crushed to death. He must have died instantaneously."

"Has someone called an ambulance?" Eve asked.

"Yes," said Adam. "Some fellow I met phoned for an ambulance."

"We haven't seen or heard any emergency vehicles approaching," observed the older man. He then added; "I am Rambler, and this is my nephew Numpty. I should have introduced myself and my nephew earlier but I was unable to identify an opportune moment."

"Not much use sending for an ambulance if the driver is dead," Numpty offered helpfully.

"Where did this accident happen?" the Storyteller asked.

"Just beyond the filling station, where the car slip road leads back onto the M3."

"Hmm!" The Storyteller was clearly unconvinced. "I think we would have heard something by now if there had been an accident."

Adam's brow furrowed. "What do you mean '*if* there had been an accident'? I was there. I saw the car crushed. I saw the man die."

"You say someone phoned for an ambulance," the Storyteller probed. "Was that your opponent in the fight?"

21

Adam had forgotten about Grimrose. "No," Adam answered. "There was no fight." He was about to explain but then thought better of it.

"Let's get back in the camper van and take a look," the Storyteller suggested.

Rambler coughed. "I would not for one moment wish to impose upon you, but could you possibly give us a lift? Young Numpty and I are heading down the M3 to Winchester and beyond. Sadly, I have failed to provide any means of transport other than that obtainable by the dextrous use of thumb or tongue."

The Storyteller looked at Adam and then Eve. "Of course we can give them a lift," Eve took the initiative. "Numpty is still a bit dazed – and we have room."

Adam nodded his agreement but added: "We won't get very far, not for a while. The lorry and the car are blocking the exit and I don't think we can drive round the accident."

The party, now of six, returned to the van. Rambler and Numpty sat in the back with the Storyteller. Adam and Eve sat up front with Gwoat who, sated with chocolate, for the first time seemed reasonably relaxed. Indeed, after settling into his seat, Gwoat was so relaxed he lent to one side and emitted a long, lugubrious fart.

The Storyteller, leaning forward, was quick to intervene. "I should have mentioned the flatulence issue before," he began. "I'm afraid, post chocolate, Gwoat's metabolism tends to adopt a more laissez faire modus operandi. I admit the sound is disconcerting until one becomes accustomed to it."

"It's not the sound," Eve gasped.

"That too, I'm afraid," the Storyteller apologised. "If we open all the windows, it will pass."

"So you mean our driver is either jerking about like a neurotic puppet or, if gorged on chocolate, releasing fumes so noxious that they constitute a serious health and safety threat. Are you sure he's the best person to be driving us? Is he really the right type of person to conduct us on the journey of a lifetime?"

"Either itching and twitching or starting and farting," Numpty giggled in the back.

Luke was sitting up, his nose held high in the air, assessing the odour in the manner of a professional wine-taster. The smell was indeed many-layered but essentially over-ripe and, although Luke took some pride in his catholic taste in smells, offensive to his hypersensitive, canine nostrils.

"I object to being talked of in the third person," Gwoat complained.

"Turd person, turd person," Numpty cried with delight.

"He's an excellent driver and a good friend," the Storyteller answered Eve's question. "Aren't you?" he added, segueing into the second person to address Gwoat and his objection directly.

"That I am, sir, to be sure, sir," Gwoat replied. "Don't you worry about that at all, at all," he added, turning to Eve. "If there's any worrying to be done, I'm your man. As for the flatulence, I can only apologise."

"I suspect it's a combination of the worry and the chocolate," Rambler offered helpfully. "The worry creates gases and the chocolate somehow facilitates their evacuation."

"Well perhaps if he ate less chocolate…," Eve responded tartly.

"I fear that might lead to hyperinflation in the lower bowel," Rambler mused.

"Then might he float up into the air, Uncle?" enquired Numpty, who remained fascinated by the idea of falling upwards into the sky.

Luke meanwhile had his nose pressed to the gap in the slightly opened rear window. "This is not going to be easy," he addressed the Storyteller. "My nose is extremely sensitive to odours. I trust Gwoat's flatulence is not a frequent occurrence."

"I think the dog is going to be sick," said Numpty, who was fond of dogs and, observing Luke's desperate need for fresh air, was concerned for his welfare.

"The sensitivity of canines to odours ensues from their highly developed sense of smell," Rambler explained. The average human is endowed with a mere five million scent receptors whereas dogs can boast two-hundred to three-hundred million. That would be up to sixty times more receptors. Furthermore, dogs devote forty times more of their brain to processing smells than we do."

Gwoat drove the van out of the parking area and along the curved service road towards the fuel station. Adam looked hard for the wrecked car and the lorry – but there was no sign of an accident. No one spoke. "There's the red kite," Adam shouted.

Sure enough, still flapping on the grass verge was the kite that had been at least partially responsible for the accident. Except that there was no accident.

"You been telling stories," Numpty goaded.

Adam was disconcerted and angry. "I've been doing nothing of the sort," he snapped. Then, turning to Rambler, he added: "It might be a good idea to tell your nephew to shut up."

"It's no good taking it out on the poor lad," Eve chided. "He's just had a bang on the head."

"Pity it didn't knock some sense into it," Adam muttered.

"Come now," the Storyteller intervened. "We are all in this together and it would be best if we all showed tolerance and understanding. We have a long and sometimes arduous journey ahead. While we are in each other's company, we should try to enjoy it or, if that proves impossible, at least put up with it."

There were several grunts of assent and perhaps one or two of resignation.

They were soon back on the M3. Gwoat accelerated to 78 miles per hour, set cruise control and settled into the centre lane.

They had travelled no more than five miles when Eve, who was sitting on the nearside front seat, noticed a biker undertaking and then keeping pace with the van in the inside lane. The rider seemed to be signalling. Eve nudged Adam and indicated the biker with her thumb. Adam leant across Eve and immediately recognised both bike and biker. "That's Nick Peters," he said.

"Who's Nick Peters?" Eve responded, "And why is he waving to us?"

"He's the chap I met when I went to fight Grimrose," Adam tried to explain.

"Grimrose!" Eve exclaimed. "That biker you picked a fight with wasn't Grimrose. Grimrose was that weird parking meter person who pestered us before we set out."

"I didn't pick a fight with anyone," Adam objected. "Grimrose picked a fight with me. And it *was* Grimrose. He's a shapeshifter. You saw how she changed when she was doing her clamping thing."

Eve was not convinced. "So who's Nick Peters?" Eve asked again. "The tooth fairy or the devil incarnate?"

"Titus Andronicus," Rambler murmured.

"Unlikely," Adam responded.

"No," Rambler hastened to correct the misunderstanding. "The first use of the expression 'devil incarnate' occurred in 'Titus Andronicus'. Shakespeare," he added. "Or was it 'incarnate devil'? Can't quite remember. Anyway, devil made flesh."

"Titus Andronicus; tight as a duck's arse," quipped Numpty.

"Ignore him," Rambler advised.

At this point, the Storyteller intervened. "Pull over into the inside lane," he instructed Gwoat.

"No, no," exclaimed Eve. "He's still there. If you pull over you'll hit him."

"Precisely," the Storyteller returned, and then repeated his instruction to Gwoat: "Pull over – and do it now."

Gwoat began to turn the wheel but, as he did so, the biker stopped waving, returned his left hand to the handlebars and, with his right hand, twisted the throttle sharply. The massive twin engine roared and Nick Peters, at one with his trusty silver steed, rocketed ahead of the van and clear of danger.

"You're crazy," Eve accused the Storyteller. "You could have killed him."

"Would it were so," the Storyteller replied wearily. "He's not that easy to despatch. In any case, there was no risk. He has exceedingly good reflexes and an extraordinarily powerful bike. We couldn't have hit him if we had tried."

"He said that you and he were old friends," Adam hazarded.

"Did he?" the Storyteller laughed. "Did he really? Well, it's fair to say we go back a long way. But friends! That's a bit of a stretch."

5 Yahweh

They continued for several miles. Adam was confused. Was his mind playing tricks on him, or was someone else? What was real? What had he imagined? And what was the difference? He'd seen a man die? Yet the Storyteller had doubted his account of the accident and, when they had left Fleet Services, there had been no sign of the crash. What on earth was Grimrose? Man or woman, aggressive or pathetic, a hairy biker or an overweight nagger? A shapeshifter! That's how Nick Peters had explained it. But that was no explanation. It was just a word to *describe* what Grimrose did or seemed to do; it didn't *explain* what he did. Or how what he did was possible.

"A bit like God," the Storyteller suggested.

"What is?" Adam asked, for evidently the Storyteller was addressing him.

"A being denoted but not explained by a word," the Storyteller replied.

"I thought God was the explanation for everything," Adam hazarded.

"For everything and nothing. God, as the First Cause, explains everything except himself and so, in a way, explains nothing."

"The Prime Mover, the First Cause, the cause of all change. Ah yes," mused Rambler. "Where would we be without Aristotle? 'πρoτον κιvον κίνητον'. Or indeed Akhenaton, a monotheistic precursor, if ever there was one."

"What is a monothickstick precruiser?" asked Numpty, who had been doing his best to follow the conversation while diligently picking his nose with the index finger of his left hand.

"I wish you wouldn't do that," Rambler responded.

"But you have always encouraged me to ask questions in the past. You said I had a curious mind."

"No doubt about the last point," Adam quipped, a little unkindly.

"It is not the asking of questions to which I object. Rather I was referring to the digital exploration of your nasal cavities. It is unpleasant, tasteless."

"It's not," Numpty answered grumpily. "It's salty."

"Enough," said the Storyteller. "We are turning off at the next exit. We will head for Hook, the first real part of our adventure, although 'real' might merit some careful scrutiny."

"And what will we find at Hook?" Eve asked.

The Storyteller smiled. This was always a memorable moment for venturers such as these. They would never forget this excursion from the M3.

"We will find God," the Storyteller answered Eve's question, and then waited for the import of this declaration to sink in.

"You mean we are really going to meet God?" Adam asked with manifest incredulity.

"Absolutely," the Storyteller replied. "He's such a ubiquitous being I thought we should get him out of the way at the beginning."

"So He's male," Eve said in a tone of disappointment and with a hint of defiance.

"'Fraid so," said the Storyteller.

Eve looked at Adam. Adam shook his head and spread his hands in a gesture which was intended to convey three clear messages, namely 'it's not my fault and obviously there's nothing I can do about it and I'm not in any way gloating'.

"Well," Eve opined, "I stopped believing in Him three years ago when Bella died, so I'm surprised He exists at all – but, given the way things are, I'm not surprised He's male."

The Storyteller seemed about to reprimand Eve but another, more subtle shake of Adam's head advised him to let the matter rest.

oooOooo

The camper van parked, the party, less Gwoat who was left to guard the van, walked across a sunlit meadow towards a very beautiful enclosure, with a profusion of daffodils at its entrance and roses of every colour bedecking the imposing gated archway.

"What is this?" Eve asked.

"This is the Garden. This is where God is," the Storyteller answered as though Eve should have worked that out for herself. "Of course, in a sense God is everywhere but, for the purposes of actually meeting Him, He has to be manifest in one place and, generally-speaking, when He's not out and about, here is where God is at."

"The Garden? *The* Garden? You mean the Garden of Eden?" Eve struggled.

"Of course, the Garden of Eden. After God had expelled your namesakes, He had the place to himself. Not that He stayed here all the time. No, He had a fair amount of thundering and smiting to do. But it was always a pleasant place to return to for rest and recuperation. Not that He needs rest and recuperation, of course."

"Are you seriously suggesting we are going to meet God?" Adam wanted to be sure he had understood.

27

"Goodness me!" the Storyteller exclaimed. "You're making very heavy weather of this. If every adventure is going to begin with a series of boringly repetitive questions, we are going to make disappointingly slow progress. Yes, we are going to walk along the pathways of this extraordinary garden and, when we reach its centre, we will meet God. It's arranged. He's pretty busy, in the sense that He has much to do, but He has plenty of time in that even after He's done everything, He still has a lot of spare capacity for doing more – Him being God."

"Always ask a busy person….," Luke mused.

"This is awesome," offered Numpty.

"Indeed," the Storyteller agreed. "Precisely. Awe was and is His speciality."

The party walked on in silence, through a garden seething with life, with all kinds of flora and fauna.

"How should we address Him?" Adam asked.

"*Lord* is favourite but *Creator* will do. *Father* is a bit too intimate on a first meeting. You could try *Yahweh*, although that's a bit ethnically narrow."

"Well this is a hell of a thing," Adam declared.

"It is pretty outstanding," the Storyteller conceded, ignoring Adam's solecistic turn of phrase. "We are pretty lucky to get an appointment. As you'd expect, there's quite a hierarchy and quite a bureaucracy under Him, so we we're lucky to get a slot at short notice. Someone must have cancelled. Anyway, you will have your chance to ask Him your question."

"I'll have one or two questions for Him myself," Eve said, with just with a hint of menace in her voice.

Adam looked at Eve and thought of asking what she had in mind. Then he thought better of it. Not even Eve would be rude to God.

"If He's the God of the Old Testament, we should really call him Yahweh," Rambler suggested. "Yahweh, the great name, the glorious and terrible name, or, in its more familiar but disputed form, Jehovah. The Hebrews had a problem with vowels. Modern scholars I believe favour a purely consonantal representation of the name – YHWH."

"As in 'You Have Weird Habits'," Luke suggested.

"That's not particularly funny," the Storyteller rebuked the dog.

"My uncle wasn't trying to be funny," said Numpty, assuming the Storyteller was rebuking Rambler. "Just telling us something really interesting. If you leave out the vowels," Numpty addressed his uncle, "how do you know how to pronounce the word?"

"The Hebrews knew how to pronounce the word, they just left the vowels out when they wrote the word down," Rambler explained.

28

"So they just slipped the vowels in when they read the word," Numpty said slowly. "And they always had enough?"

Rambler seemed slightly taken aback. Evidently Numpty had left the path of linear reason. "Oh, yes," said Rambler. "They had plenty of vowels. They had an inexhaustible supply of vowels up their sleeves."

"So they had very big sleeves?" Numpty persisted.

"Certainly. The religious leaders of the Hebrews had long flowing robes and capacious sleeves, up which they could accommodate more than sufficient vowels for a lifetime of talking."

"Like the eggs in a woman's body," Numpty declared. Despite his better judgement, Rambler always tried to explain how things were to his nephew – not always with the results he expected.

"Precisely," Rambler responded, knowing that the only way to silence his nephew in such situations was to agree.

"You mean 'prickly'," Numpty laughed.

Rambler was bemused.

"Prickly," Numpty repeated jubilantly. "Prickly. It's 'precisely' without the vowels."

Even though he knew he shouldn't, Rambler pointed out that Numpty had omitted the 's'. "Should that not be 'pricsly' which, though not a word, includes all the consonants of precisely?"

Numpty frowned, and then brightened. "The 's' is silent as in swimming," he declared triumphantly.

"It's a 'p' that is silent in swimming," Adam interrupted.

"That's silly," Numpty responded. "There is no 'p' in swimming."

Rambler shook his head to indicate to Adam that it would be best to let matters rest.

The party had reached the centre of the Garden, which was an open lawned area. The sun caressed the vibrant, neatly-cut green grass. "Come forward," said a deep, rich baritone voice. There, standing on a circular podium, overhung by the branches of a luminous, fruit-laden tree, was God.

'He's exactly what I might have imagined Him to be,' thought Adam.

'He's a dead ringer for Michael Angelo's portrait in the Sistine Chapel', thought Eve.

'He's a cross between Charlton Heston and Sean Connery,' thought Luke who, because of his master and mistress's predilection for feature films, was familiar with all major film stars.

God waited, apparently expecting formal introductions. The Storyteller obliged. "This is Adam and this is Eve," he began.

God frowned. "Is this a joke?" He asked, and there was a rumble of thunder in his voice.

"No, Lord," the Storyteller hastened to defuse the situation. "This is Adam and this is Eve. Not, of course, the original Adam and Eve. They are long dead. No, this is a twenty-first century couple, who happened to have been named Adam and Eve by their respective parents. It's just chance, chance that they met, chance that they married, chance they have set out on this journey…"

God waved him into silence. "I get it. It's just chance."

"And this is Rambler, and his nephew Numpty. We picked them up on the way here and they jumped at the opportunity to meet You. And this is the dog Luke."

Luke was sniffing around the base of the tree which overhung the podium. "Don't you dare," the Storyteller minded to Luke.

"You are welcome," said God. He too was keeping a wary eye on Luke. "Perhaps you would like to kneel," he added casually.

Only the Storyteller seemed to understand. He dropped to his knees and looked round anxiously at the others to check they were following his example. Rambler responded, removing his hat and kneeling immediately, closely followed by Numpty, dragged down by Rambler's pull on his sleeve. God smiled approvingly when Rambler removed his hat but then, momentarily, his brow furrowed.

Adam too knelt, although he felt awkward. It was of course entirely appropriate that they should kneel in the presence of the Creator but, for Adam, God had either been an illusion, hope triumphant over reason, or an evanescent, indefinable entity without form, a generalised spirit pervading but invisible to all. Yes, this tall, bearded, muscular, slightly overweight figure was exactly what God should look like if you thought we were made in God's image or, conversely, that God had been made flesh, but he just didn't seem plausible as the Creator of the entire universe and everything within it. Despite some misgivings, Adam knelt.

Eve, on the other hand, remained standing.

"Kneel," urged the Storyteller, with some urgency in his tone. Adam looked up into his wife's face, saw that immutable resolve in her eyes and realised she was about to initiate the mother of all scenes. "Please kneel," he whispered, but he knew it was useless.

"Kneel," said God. He said it rather cleverly, so that a listener could interpret the word either as a helpful reminder of his previous suggestion or as a command.

Eve didn't move. It was in fact a command.

"I see," said God. "Same problem I had with your namesake. Disobedience. Not an attractive quality. Will you women never learn?"

With that, the Almighty waved a hand and Eve found her legs swept from under her. She sat down on the ground with a bump. Luke growled.

"Now why have you come here?" God was not angry but there was now some irritation in his voice. It was the tone of a very busy person who has managed to allocate time to a relatively minor petitioner and now finds the petitioner cannot progress matters at a pace that will enable his benefactor to resolve the matter within the allotted slot.

"I have a question," Adam spoke hurriedly, partly because he sensed God's impatience and partly to prevent Eve speaking her mind and risking a more emphatic admonition from the Almighty.

"You have a question," God repeated.

The Storyteller nodded encouragement, so Adam persevered. "Yes, I have a question. Indeed I am here to ask **the** question, the question that is the very heart of this quest."

"I see," said God. "So you're on a quest? And if I help you, what benefit accrues to Me?"

Adam was stunned. "Well there isn't much, as a mere human being, that we can do for the Creator, the maker of heaven and earth, the ruler of the universe, et cetera," he said.

"Really!" God returned. "Well I don't think you're trying hard enough. You come to me, ill-prepared by all accounts, to ask a favour, indeed a great favour, indeed from your point of view perhaps the greatest of all favours. One of your party seems to find it difficult to extend to Me even the most elementary of courtesies. And, when I ask you what you will give Me in return for this great favour, you say 'nothing'. Nothing will come of nothing. Speak again."

"Isn't that King Lear?" Luke asked the Storyteller.

"Yes, it is. You're a remarkably well-read retriever."

"Not well-read. I just watch a lot of television," Luke replied modestly but secretly delighted at the Storyteller's compliment. "So God's not above a bit of plagiarism."

"He wouldn't see it like that. After all, He created Shakespeare."

"I'm sorry," Adam addressed God. "I really haven't got anything to offer."

"We could do a bit of praising." It was Numpty who, given his faltering grasp of most things, seemed happily unperturbed in the presence of God.

"Well done," God responded. "Well done," he repeated evidently delighted. "You see, Adam. Out of the mouths of the intellectually challenged…"

"Oh!" said Adam. "You would like us to praise You," he added rather lamely.

"It's not so much what I want. It is what you should want. You should feel an overwhelming urge to praise Me, to worship Me, to adore Me. I am, after all, the Creator of all. All the wondrous gifts of life flow from Me."

"And all the evils," Eve added.

"What did you say?" God asked. Once again, the tone exuded tolerance. He was giving the wayward woman a chance to recant and, if she took the opportunity, He would let it rest.

Adam's eyes pleaded with his wife. The Storyteller attempted to intervene. "Of course, we praise You, Creator of All," he offered. "Don't we?" he appealed to the others in general and Eve in particular.

"I said 'and all the evils'," Eve persisted.

Adam's eyes now looked upwards to the heavens with an expression on his face which, had they been praising God, might have been taken for unalloyed adoration. In fact, as the Storyteller realised, it was total resignation.

"And what do you mean by that?" God asked.

Adam felt the urge to tell God to leave it alone. He knew his wife and she was in no mood to compromise, much less retract.

Then he thought of the absurdity of the situation. Here they were in the presence of God, an extraordinary, if not a unique, privilege for 21st century humans. And his wife was about to give the ultimate deity the rough edge of her tongue. And he, with the experience of some years of marriage under his belt, was about to advise the Almighty, the same omnipotent deity, to back off.

Then, I'm afraid to say, Adam laughed. It was not a snigger, not even a short, reasonable, proportionate laugh. Adam gave vent to an hysterical, outrageous and entirely uncontrolled torrent of laughter.

"How dare you?" exclaimed the Almighty.

"Whoops!" muttered the Storyteller. Now they were going to see the notorious wrath of God. Thick, grey, menacing clouds gathered speedily above the great tree that overhung the podium of the Lord. "How dare you?" God repeated.

"I'm sorry," said Adam, desperately trying to control himself.

"Not you, her," God responded. "I who made the heavens and the earth and all the living things within it, I who gave form and breath to Man, I who gave Man dominion over the earth, am I to be berated by someone, an uninvited visitor, by a mere petitioner, by a woman?"

"Can't we get on with a bit of praising," suggested nephew Numpty. He didn't like the look in God's eyes, or the threatening storm that seemed to manifest itself in concert with the mood of the Lord.

For rather different reasons, Rambler agreed with his nephew. His knees were getting sore and he thought it would be perfectly acceptable, if he could initiate some adulation, to do the praising standing up. Furthermore, Rambler knew from his extensive study of such matters that praise was something craved by most deities and it seemed eminently reasonable that the ultimate deity, the one true god, should expect an extraordinarily high degree of praise.

"It's rather late for praising," snapped God.

"I was simply pointing out," Eve persisted, "that, if You are taking all the credit for what is good, You must also take the blame for what is bad. So, if You think we should be grateful to You for all the good things in life, it's only reasonable You should expect some stick for the bad."

"Expect some stick?" said God. "Expect some stick? What do you think I am – some kitchen maid who is to be chastised for some minor misdemeanour?"

"Why does He think we think He's a kitchen maid?" asked Numpty, genuinely puzzled.

"It's a metaphor," the Storyteller explained.

"And a tautology," Rambler added without thinking.

"What's a tautology?" Numpty asked.

"It's when you say the same thing twice." Rambler really didn't want to engage with his curious but dense nephew at what was clearly a critical juncture in their intercourse with the Creator.

"What, like Ha Ha?" Numpty looked puzzled.

"No, like minor misdemeanour. A misdemeanour is a minor offence. So a minor misdemeanour is like saying a minor minor offence."

"But it might be a minor, minor offence," Numpty wasn't to going to let it go. "It might not be a bad enough offence to be even a minor offence. So it might really be a minor minor offence."

"You're quite right," Rambler conceded.

"Are you criticising My use of language?" God asked. "Perhaps you have forgotten that I am, amongst many other things, the Word. I really don't need the help of an itinerant vagabond to communicate."

Rambler considered querying 'itinerant vagabond' on tautological grounds, and then thought better of it.

Adam spoke. "I think my wife is really preparing the ground for my question, the purpose of our meeting with You."

"I really don't need you to tell Him what I mean." Eve's voice exuded anger and determination. Adam shrugged. He had tried. Eve continued. "I'm not preparing the ground for anything. I'm simply pointing out that if You, God, are all powerful and omnipresent, if You care for each and every one of us like a father, and if You are essentially good, how could You possibly have let my Bella die at the age of seven?"

"Oh, I see," God responded. "So it's personal."

Eve looked at God, her eyes blazing. 'Oh dear,' thought the Storyteller. 'Now it's the wrath of Eve.' "Yes, it's personal," Eve exploded. "Isn't that the point about being human. People matter. Wasn't that the message that You sent Your son to deliver."

"I think you had better leave My son out of this. He's no son of Mine," God snapped.

"I'm not surprised," Eve returned. "You don't have a terribly good track record in looking after children, even Your own. Didn't You ask Abraham to sacrifice Isaac? And didn't You send Jesus on a fairly pointless exercise that ended with his crucifixion?"

"When you say he's no son of Yours," Rambler was intrigued, "do You mean he was not Your son, or that he was Your son but You disown him?"

"Your child," God said, addressing Eve, "was killed in an accident. Accidents happen. Get over it."

"What kind of a god are You?" Eve asked with contempt in her voice.

God raised a finger to the sky and the heavy, menacing rain clouds grew denser and began to swirl around ominously.

"Oh yes," said Eve unabashed. "I'm well aware You can summon up storms at a moment's notice. That, after all, is how You killed Bella."

"I didn't kill Bella. If I remember correctly, a lightning bolt struck a tree, a bough fell, it killed your daughter. I didn't summon that particular storm. It simply came out of a weather front. I didn't aim the thunderbolt at the tree. I didn't make you stand under that tree, a pretty stupid thing to do in a storm, if I may say so. And I certainly didn't kill your daughter. Believe it or not, I was not involved. Have you any idea how big the universe is and how many things are going on at any one time? You can't seriously think that I'm aware of everything that is going on everywhere all the time, much less responsible for it."

"Are not sparrows sold two for a penny? Yet it is impossible for one of them to fall to the ground without your heavenly Father's will; Matthew 10, Verse 29," Rambler offered helpfully.

"That's not one of mine," said God testily. "I think you'll find it was Jesus who said that. No one who has ever taken responsibility for running anything would make a claim like that. What did he know? 'Take no heed for the morrow', he said. Not exactly a sensible precept for running a baker's shop, let alone a universe," God scoffed.

"So Bella's death was nothing to do with you?" Eve said.

"She's got it. At last she's got it," God sneered.

"You're not a very sympathetic individual, are You?" Adam intervened. He loved Eve for her courage, for her indomitable spirit, and he was not at all impressed with God. "Do you think it clever to mock a mother's grief?"

"Do you think you could stop your dog from urinating on My tree. It is the Tree of Knowledge and deserves better." God ignored Adam's rebuke.

Luke was happily relieving himself. The Storyteller sent a mind message of mild disapproval. "I'm not urinating," Luke replied silently. "I'm expressing solidarity with my mistress, albeit in liquid form."

"So You're not all powerful, omnipresent, benign," Eve said as much to herself as to God. "So what are You? And why do You want us to kneel in your presence? And why are You so eager to be praised?"

"I'm not here to answer your questions," God declared with divine authority in his voice.

"That's a pity," Luke observed, "since that is why we came here - to ask Him to answer Adam's questions."

"Why did You ask Abraham to sacrifice his son?" Eve was still trying to set this strangely diminished Godhead into context.

"I thought we'd got past that," God answered. "I was testing Abraham; that is all. As you must know, assuming your generation is at all familiar with the source of the three monotheistic religions that venerate Me, I relented as soon as Abraham showed he loved Me before all others. I allowed him to substitute a lower, four-footed mammal as the sacrifice." God cast a menacing glance at Luke. "A goat, I think," he added, "on that occasion."

"But why did You want him to prove his love for You? And was willingness to kill his own son the best way to prove it?"

Eve was getting into her stride, and no one seemed inclined to stop her. Adam was uneasy about engaging in an argument with the Creator but, on balance, what Eve had said was right – and, if they were seeking the truth, then surely anyone or anything that claimed to represent or reveal the truth must be tested.

Rambler, who, with nephew Numpty, was a relatively new recruit to the questing party, did not feel it was his place to intervene. In any case, Eve's exchanges with God were proving extremely interesting to the ever-curious, erudite Rambler who was now taking notes in a pad which he carried with him at all times.

Numpty was happily playing with Luke who, by urinating in the presence of the Lord up against the Tree of Knowledge, had evidently earned Numpty's unstinting admiration.

The Storyteller remained strangely aloof.

"You know my generation, as You call it, would think anyone who asked a father to kill his son as a test of anything was a manipulative, self-obsessed, psychotic," Eve explained. "And anyone who felt the need to be praised all the time would probably be put down as an insecure, inadequate creature with very low self-esteem."

"You have no conception of respect, of gratitude, of obedience," God replied.

"Respect must be earned," Adam entered the fray. "Gratitude must be volunteered. As for obedience, we must all obey what is right. But we should not obey what is wrong. You were wrong to ask Abraham to sacrifice Isaac; he should not have obeyed You. As for our daughter, if You are not responsible, if indeed You don't really care, You should say so. You are supposed to be our divine Father but, as Eve has said, You seem primarily concerned with self-gratification. It's not what I expected. To be blunt, I'm disappointed. I'm having a real problem with You as God. I'm not a good man, not bad but not good – probably about average on the ethical spectrum. So I find it very difficult to accept as the Supreme Being an individual who falls below my own modest, moral standards."

"I've never tried to conceal My true nature," God answered. "If I fail to match up to your liberal views, spawned I might add by a delinquent and corrupt society, that is certainly your problem, not Mine."

"I think you're being a little unfair to the Supreme Being," Rambler addressed Adam. "He's never made any secret of his brand of divinity. We all know this is God who told his chosen people to show no mercy to their enemies but to annihilate them utterly. When He gave the Israelites a land where other peoples dwelt, he said 'When the Lord Thy God shall deliver them before thee.........'"

God intervened, evidently preferring to speak on His own behalf and, indeed, in His own words: "When the Lord Thy God shall deliver them before thee," his voice had dropped an octave and was now a sonorous bass, "thou shalt smite them and utterly destroy them; thou shalt make no covenant with them, nor shew mercy unto them."

"No peace and reconciliation here then," Adam observed.

"And what about this Chosen People thing?" Eve asked. "Why did You favour one people above another? And why did You give them land that belonged to other people?"

"Because," said God, with a smile of satisfaction, "because they

36

understood the meaning of the word obedience."

"I'm sure other tribes would have been at least as obedient, if You'd given them the chance," Eve returned. "And, in any case, although my recollection of the Old Testament is a bit sketchy, I don't think the Israelites were particularly obedient. Didn't You have to keep punishing them for disobedience?"

"Obedience has to be enforced with discipline from time to time," God explained in a lofty tone.

"Wasn't it more," suggested Rambler, "that the Israelites were not very successful in their battles with their neighbours or later, with the Romans, and, given they were the Chosen People and had You on their side, there had to be some explanation for failure − and disobedience filled the bill."

God appeared not to have heard him or, if he had, decided to ignore him.

"And since we're in the Garden of Eden, perhaps You could explain what happened here with our namesakes," Eve enquired, determined to expose the true nature of this God, who appeared to lack any sense of justice and seemed to be incapable even of human, let alone, divine, love. And she was angry and she was frustrated because, although it was three years since Bella had died, there was not a day when she did not replay the events that culminated in Bella's death and not a moment of the day when there was not a dull ache inside her which she knew would never go away. She had hoped to find an answer to her own question. Why? Why had her beautiful daughter, so full of life, of hope, of promise, why had she died? She could see this God, this pompous, vindictive, self-centred entity was not the one to understand her question, much less provide an answer.

"Same problem," said God. "We keep coming back to it. Disobedience."

"That's right," said Eve. "We were not allowed to eat the fruit of this tree, the Tree of Knowledge of Good and Evil."

"You, or your ancestor, were tempted. You ate. You persuaded Adam to eat. He ate."

"Yes, but why did You for forbid it?" Eve persisted.

"The thing about obedience, my dear girl," God said patronisingly, "is that you shouldn't question orders. Obviously you have a problem with the concept but, in essence, that is what obedience is. God commands; you obey. Is there any part of that you don't understand?"

"I think she understands," Rambler intervened, hoping to clarify the matter, "but she just wants to know why You didn't want humans to know the difference between right and wrong."

"When you think about it, it doesn't make any sense anyway." Adam's brow was furrowed, as though he had for the first time glimpsed an obvious truth and was worried he had not seen it before. "If You forbade them to eat of the fruit of the tree, You were in effect telling them it was wrong to eat of the fruit of the tree, so they already had some knowledge of good and evil. If you start from the position that the only good is obedience to You, there was an issue of good and evil from the moment You put us in the Garden, from the moment You created humankind."

"It's the same old story," Eve declared. "It was nothing to do with knowledge of good and evil; it was just a test of obedience. Just like with Abraham. You have a real problem with this authority thing. You're a father who is obsessed with controlling his children whereas we all know that the whole point of having children is to give them love and, when they are old enough, to allow them the freedom to be themselves."

"What a pity we shan't ever know whether, when it came to it, You would have been so magnanimous with Bella," said God.

It took a moment for the callous indifference and the awesome pettiness of that remark to sink in. "You're a fake," Eve said when she had recovered from the shock. "You're a fake. You could not have created the universe or anything else. You're an inadequate tribal deity, with all the flaws of such mythic beings. As Adam has said, You're not even as good as us – and we're far from perfect."

"You cannot speak to Me in that manner. I am the Lord thy God, I am the Word, I am, I am…"

As though by common consent, the party rose. All but Eve had been kneeling throughout this extraordinary exchange.

"How dare you! What makes you think you can insult Me, and then leave. Kneel. Prostrate yourselves before Me. Praise Me. I demand a sacrifice."

Luke growled.

"No thunderbolt, no rending of the heavens?" Eve observed.

"You came here to ask me your question," God reminded the party.

"The thing is," said the Storyteller to God, "the thing is, they don't believe in You and, as You know, Your power is precisely commensurate with their faith. No faith, no power. I know it's hard for You."

"Not hard enough," Eve blazed. "We can offer a fair portion of contempt instead of faith. How do You feel about that?"

"It's not as easy as you think to deny Me. I am revered by all three monotheistic religions. I am interwoven into the minds of billions. Do you really think you can walk away from Me with impunity?"

"Don't embarrass yourself," said Eve coldly. "You have nothing to offer us and we certainly want nothing to do with You."

"Enough," said the Storyteller. "We should go. We came here for answers, and clearly there are none for us here."

The party left the presence of God, retracing their steps through the beautiful Garden of Eden. There were clouds in the sky now but the meadows were still bright, illuminated by the vibrant yellow of the golden host of daffodils. Adam took Eve's hand and, with wandering steps and slow, they made their way towards the Garden's perimeter.

"What now?" Adam asked.

"Before we leave this particular adventure behind," the Storyteller said, "I think it would be useful to visit one of God's industrial estates."

6 God's R & D Department

"Hello," said a cheerful, ruddy-cheeked being, who stood almost seven feet tall. "I'm Rodney, and this is my colleague Derek – God's R & D department." He laughed.

Adam and Eve were stunned. Rambler whipped out his notebook. Numpty scratched his head. Luke cowered.

"Come on in," Rodney continued. "We don't get many visitors. Always delighted to explain what we do."

"The wings!" was all Adam could manage.

"They're angels," the Storyteller explained, "and angels have wings."

"Angels called Rodney and Derek?" Eve enquired, with just a trace of sarcasm.

"We're very much backroom boys," offered Derek. "That's probably why you haven't heard of us. Senior angels like Gabriel get all the publicity, and rightly so. They're in charge of communications."

"Ah, yes," Rambler nodded. "Gabriel foretold the coming of Jesus and, if I'm not mistaken, dictated the Holy Quran to the Prophet Muhammad."

"What would happen if you were mistaken?" Numpty asked.

"Isn't that interesting?" Rambler responded, mildly rebuking his nephew. "I've just mentioned an archangel, and the founders of two of the world's great religions, and what do you do, dear boy, but come up with a trivial and peculiarly irrelevant question? Focus, dear boy, focus."

"It's not trivial to be mistaken," Numpty mumbled, despondently. "You're always correcting me."

"No, you misunderstand," Rambler addressed his nephew consolingly. "When I say 'if I'm not mistaken', it's just a figure of speech. I don't mean I think there's a possibility I'm mistaken."

"Then why say it?" Numpty was not to be mollified.

"It's an idiom," Rambler answered wearily.

Numpty blinked. He thought he had better choose his words carefully. He didn't like the sound of the word 'idiom'. "An idiom," he said slowly.

"It's when what you say doesn't mean what you say but means something else which everyone will understand it to mean," Rambler explained.

"Well that doesn't make any sense," declared Numpty, "unless I'm mistaken," he added triumphantly.

40

"Perhaps we could move on," Adam intervened. He was beginning to understand the pattern of these exchanges between Rambler and his nephew. "What do you do here?" he asked, addressing the angel Rodney.

"What do we do?" Rodney almost squealed with delight. "What don't we do? We're the ones who make it happen."

"We're the ones who find solutions," added Derek, with equal enthusiasm. "We're the ones who make it work. To be honest," he confided, "some of them up there," he jerked a thumb in a generally upward direction, "don't really know which end is up."

"You shouldn't end a sentence with 'up'," Numpty declared. "You should say 'They don't really know up which end is'."

Derek looked at Numpty quizzically.

"It's all right," Rambler explained. "He has his little foibles."

Numpty responded, blushing and giggling uncontrollably, "They're not so little."

Derek glanced at Numpty. "I'm sorry," Rambler explained, "since reaching puberty, he's been fascinated by sexual innuendo."

"Sexual in your end o," Numpty squealed with delight.

Rambler's eyes appealed to Derek for understanding. Derek nodded. "A few feathers short of a fully functioning wing."

"Quite," said a relieved Rambler.

"It's not clever to mock the mentally challenged," Eve chided Derek.

"Wouldn't dream of it," Derek responded easily. "I thought he was just stupid."

Eve's hackles rose.

"Is he calling me stupid?" Numpty enquired of his uncle.

"Of course he isn't," Rambler attempted to pacify his nephew. He looked to Derek for some kind of concession.

"No way would I call you or any of your kind stupid," Derek offered helpfully. "After all, I'm partly responsible for the way you are."

"We pride ourselves," Rodney took charge, adopting a serious tone, bordering on the pompous. "We pride ourselves on making the impossible possible – and in making the manifestly impractical, practical."

"Perhaps you could give our friends an example," prompted the Storyteller.

"Well, there's the creation of Man," Derek suggested.

"Isn't that a rather large project to cite as an example?" the Storyteller queried.

"Not particularly," Rodney answered confidently, "and it does provide an excellent opportunity to illustrate the difficulties we face and our ingenuity in overcoming them."

"Difficulties!" Derek exploded. "I think it was the toughest job we ever undertook. Just about everything that could go wrong did."

"It wasn't that bad," Rodney resumed. "It worked out all right in the end – more or less. Anyway, let me explain. Please take a seat," he swept away a mass of documents from an L-shaped bench. "You might as well take the weight of your feet."

"How can you take the weight off your feet?" enquired Numpty.

"Shut up," Uncle Rambler replied. Numpty shrugged and turned away, patting Luke, who had just about recovered from the sight of these angelic, winged beings.

"Are we settled?" Rodney asked. "Then I'll begin."

"Some time ago – indeed as you will see, before time, before your time, began – we were sitting here, mulling over a series of minor tasks to do with the taxonomy of angels, when who should summon us but Gabriel himself."

"We don't get to see the senior management that often," Derek chimed in, "and we get to talk to them even less frequently. So a summons was something special."

"Off we go, and there he is. He's a big entity, Gabriel, and he sits on a big chair in a big room. We angels are pretty hierarchical and those at the top like to let you know just how important they are."

"Anyway he tells us he has a major project for us, a 'special'. That means it's an order direct from God. He tells us we have to create Man. So obviously, we ask him what is 'man'? 'Man' he says is to be made like God, only smaller and weaker. And he is to be mortal, that is to say he shouldn't live too long. And he should have moral issues, that is to say there should be some things he should do and some things he shouldn't do and he should be free to choose.

"Well, we ask a lot more questions."

"Too right," chimes in Derek. "In our line of work, it all depends on the brief and the specification. Give us a good brief and a precise and comprehensive specification and we're home free."

"Anyway," Rodney resumes, "all seemed pretty straightforward. Not easy, of course, but pretty straightforward. Physical appearance was a given – 'image of God'. Physical construction, a bit more problematical, because it had to make sense in the world the Man being was going to live in. We worked out some basic wiring and plumbing along the lines God put into us angels – but much more gross of course and with some significant additions, in keeping with Man's general physicality. It all seemed to work pretty well, so we made an appointment to see Gabriel. We didn't expect him to accept our initial efforts without some modifications, the odd tweak here and there, but we were pretty confident."

"Then he drops his first bombshell," Derek joins in. "He says don't forget to make a Woman as well."

Eve gave a wry smile. "Typical," she said with contempt. "Woman is an afterthought."

"Not according to Gabriel," Rodney soothed. Eve's rebuke of Derek when he had mocked Numpty had registered with him, and it seemed best to apply oil to troubled waters. "He told us that Woman had always been part of God's plan. So we went through the definition and specification process all over again."

"We were given a lot more latitude with Woman. We were able to apply a bit more aesthetic sense," Derek declared proudly, and then, remembering that pride comes before a fall, and all the inevitable associations of the word Fall amongst the Angelic Host, quickly added: "Not that there's anything unaesthetic about the image of God."

"But we thought a few curves and a little more softness would not go amiss," Rodney resumed, relieving Derek's unease.

"It was a labour of love," Derek said. "Not in any physical sense, of course," he added hastily.

"There's a bit of irony there," Rodney laughed. "You'll see what I mean in a minute. We go back to Gabriel and we present the two prototypes together. They looked pretty good, a handsome couple. I'll be honest with you, we thought we had done an outstanding job."

"What does that mean?" Numpty enquired of his uncle. Rambler appreciated that his nephew had remained quiet for some time and thought he should at least acknowledge Numpty's question.

"It means they thought they had produced a truly excellent piece of work, or rather two pieces of work."

"No," said Numpty, "not the 'outstanding job' bit, the 'I'll be honest with you' bit."

"Oh dear!" sighed Rambler, regretting his kindness, "it's just an expression."

"But does it mean that angel Rodney was not being honest before?" Numpty persisted.

"No, it means he's revealing something he feels very strongly, a very deep truth." Rambler was struggling.

"You mean some truths are shallow and some are deep. So which is best?"

Derek cast his eyes heavenwards and was about to tell Numpty to shut up but a withering look from Eve persuaded him to hold his immaterial tongue.

"It's just an expression," Eve explained, "People say a lot of things without really thinking what they're saying - or meaning what they say. It's hard but you have to understand, not everyone is as smart as you."

Derek grunted. Rambler smiled. Numpty grinned from ear to ear.

"That's when Gabriel delivered his second bombshell," Rodney continued. "He looked the Man and Woman up and down, said they seemed fine and then asked; 'How are they going to reproduce?'"

"Now I can tell you, we weren't too happy about this latest alteration to the spec," Derek confided. "It's such a waste of time if you don't think things through at the beginning."

"We took it up with Gabriel," Rodney resumed the narrative. "Gabriel was entirely unapologetic. They're an arrogant lot, the archangels, never admit they're wrong… something about loss of face. Anyway, he says it must have been obvious from the start that the Man and the Woman had to be able to reproduce because God planned to people an entire world with them and their offspring."

"This should have meant going back to the drawing board," Derek explained. "God doesn't reproduce, obviously, and we had, as instructed, designed Man in the image of God. And we angels are created by God, so no reproductive model there. So we had no template. It really called for some innovative thinking. But, we'd had enough."

"It wasn't just that we had lost patience," Rodney added. "We were up against a deadline. Why a divinity that has an infinite amount of time at his disposal should be so impatient is beyond me. But that's the way it is."

"So we looked for a quick fix," Derek admitted.

"A quick fix," Adam repeated.

It suddenly dawned on Rodney that his frank exposition of the creation of Man might just cause offence but Derek continued unabashed.

"We had to find a way for Man and Woman to interact in such a way that they could, jointly, produce offspring. We didn't want to start from scratch. As Rodney says, we were under pressure to produce a result, so we rearranged bits here and there inside the Woman to conceive and incubate an offspring and we modified the hips to allow for a birth. Not easy I might add, given the size of the baby Man head, but just about practical. Then we had to allow for the Man contribution. Not really a lot of choice there, given the basic design. There really was only one bit we could use."

Rodney interrupted. "I argued against it but, in the end, I had to accept there was no alternative."

"It wasn't an ideal solution," Derek ploughed on. "We had to package the Man's input to the reproductive process in a small space and, yes, use as the means of delivery, the pipe we originally designed for the excretion of waste liquid. And, of course, we had to find a way to make what was generally a limp appendage hard enough to do the business when called upon to penetrate the Woman and deposit his contribution. A bit of a botch but, with the use of basic hydraulics, just about practical."

"I said it wouldn't be acceptable," Rodney seemed eager to dissociate himself from the process, "that we would never persuade rational beings to do such a thing – both Man and Woman fiddling around in the least aesthetically-satisfactory area of the whole design in order to perform the wondrous act of procreation."

"But we worked on it together," Derek insisted, implicating Rodney. "Our first idea and part of the solution was to make it mandatory, a kind of fixed constant that all living things should be compelled to procreate. That was all right for most forms of life, but Man was different. He had to have free will and we were really worried that Man and Woman would find doing the business in the nether regions, so to speak, rather distasteful. There were further difficulties, as we shall see, when Gabriel informed us of his third requirement. Anyway we had to engage in some really creative thinking – and fast. The result was the pleasure principle. It was a unique, truly innovative concept. Let me explain. We angels go about our daily duties, we praise the Lord, deliver messages, create things. But we don't actually take pleasure. We invented pure pleasure, and that's what we used to make the quick fix work."

Adam was dumb-founded; Eve uncomprehending. Rambler was once again taking copious notes in his notebook. The angels' account of the creation of Man was bizarre but it did explain some of the oddities of the human design which in the past had troubled him. He was particularly intrigued by the angels' claim that they took no pleasure, given their obvious delight in recounting their expertise in fulfilling divine briefs. He made a note to consider how much value one should put on consistency in a search for the truth.

"I was far from confident," Rodney resumed the narrative. "It was fairly obvious we'd made the best of a bad job and I was afraid Gabriel would give us a hard time. But we took the design to him. He inspected the procreation mechanism, gave a brief laugh (which in itself was extraordinary because, as you probably know, God and the Angelic Host are not much given to laughter), and said just one word.

'Excellent'."

"And then he dropped his third and final bombshell," Derek declared.

"Yes," confirmed Rodney. "He hit us between the eyes with this one. He says the design is fine. There's only one problem. The whole thing has to happen by chance."

"I mean," says Derek, "That's a mega bomb-shell. It contradicts everything we stand for, it's totally against the way we operate. Like I said, we work to a brief and, given a brief, we then find a way of making it happen, making it happen as efficiently as possible..."

"What Derek is saying," Rodney interrupted his partner, preening his feathers just a little to assert his authority, "what Derek means is that the stipulation that we had to create Man by chance turned a challenging but eminently doable project into a creational nightmare."

"It sets us wondering whether there was some malicious purpose behind the whole idea," Derek contributed. "Maybe someone wanted to make us redundant by giving us a virtually impossible task and then dismissing us for failing to complete it. But Gabriel assured us this was not so. He said it was the most important project God had ever given out and we should be honoured."

"Let me get this straight," Rambler intervened. "This was before the universe existed, before time and space, before everything?"

"It was certainly before your universe and your time and space," Rodney confirmed. "Not, of course, before God and us and the heavenly empyrean and all the other creational projects we have undertaken, but surely before everything you know about."

"Before everything about which you know," muttered Numpty, neither expecting or receiving any acknowledgement for his helpful contribution.

"So what did you do?" Adam asked, eager for the angelic entities to get on with their story.

"We told Gabriel that, if it had to be purely by chance, it just wouldn't happen."

"Yes," added Derek supportively. "I mean, if you start with nothing and you just throw in chance, you'd be lucky to get anything at all. A piece of sand or a rock would be a miracle. The chances of getting an organism as complex as Man would be far south of zero. In any case, what was the point? Let's face it, God excels at creation himself. Why not just make it so, in the blink of an eye. Instead, he gives the job to us and makes a difficult task impossible."

"So...," Adam prompted.

"Gabriel said there would be one or two concessions," Rodney resumed. "We would be allowed to set certain values and parameters to get things moving but they had to be pretty obscure. It seemed the whole idea was to make sure Man wouldn't be certain about how he came into being."

"What sort of parameters?" Rambler asked. He had entirely worn out one pencil and was sharpening a new one.

"It's a bit technical," Rodney answered. "How much physics do you know?"

"I know a little," Rambler replied modestly. He had in fact studied cosmology for several years in a dilettante sort of way.

"Not my strong suit," Adam conceded, "but eager to learn."

"Well," Rodney resumed, "we were allowed to set one or two creational principles and some fundamental constants. I mean they had to let us do that or the whole project would have fallen somewhere between nothing and chaos."

"Creational principles, fundamental constants?" Adam queried.

"Yes. We first had to agree about time. We needed time for things to happen in a material world and, because we needed things to change in a comprehensible manner, we had to introduce cause and effect. And because cause had to precede effect, we had to make sure time flowed in only one direction." Rodney took a breath. "It's hard to explain."

"Isn't that obvious?" Adam asked. "If things happen, they have to happen in the present and when they're over, they're in the past. And anything that is going to happen, but hasn't happened yet, must be in the future."

"It may seem obvious to you but that is only because we made it so. You have to remember that when we started, there was no time. God and the entire heavenly host existed outside time and space. Time and space were really rather gross phenomena for us, very specific, crude, limited. The idea of being in one place, and only one place, at a time, and being carried along on the surface of a relentless river of time in one direction at a more or less constant speed, well, to us, it was all a bit contrived and constricting."

"It's interesting," Derek chipped in. "Adam says time is obvious. And to him it is. That was part of the trick. When Gabriel said we had to make it all happen by chance and that, if we had to resort to some underlying drivers, we should make them as obscure as possible, he was only half right. Some of the creational principles were best disguised by being so obvious that no one thought to query them. Take the fact that there is anything. If you start with nothing, why should you get anything? But, if when you're born, there is something, you don't realise that there being something rather than nothing is a bit odd. The same goes for time. If you build time into creation from the start, it appears obvious and inevitable. But it's only obvious and inevitable because that's the way we set it up."

"That's the way up which we set it," offered Numpty.

"Were there other creational principles?" Rambler asked. He was excited.

"Well, yes," Rodney responded. "We were allowed to make the rules governing things universal so, wherever you were, the rules of what you call physics would apply."

"We had some difficulty getting that one past Gabriel," Derek confided. "He said universality would be a give-away. Man would realise there was some kind of ordering design principle if everything obeyed certain precise laws. But we said there was no way we could engineer a universe that would enable life to develop without order, and in the end, after checking it out with God, he conceded."

"And he also conceded, and this was crucial," Rodney resumed, "that we could give the whole thing a sense of direction. We had to make the whole thing look as though it just happened but underneath we were allowed to insinuate ektropy."

"Ektropy?" Rambler queried. "That's a new one on me. I'm familiar with entropy but what is ektropy?"

"Well, if you think about it, it's obvious," Derek seemed pleased to be able to satisfy Rambler's curiosity. "If you just shake things up, they get more and more disordered, more and more random. Entropy, right? But we had to make things get more and more ordered, more and more complex. Shaking just wasn't going to do it. No sir! We could have shaken to the end of time and we wouldn't have had an amoeba to show for it."

"Hold on," Adam interrupted, "what about survival of the fittest? You try shaking things up until something comes along that's better equipped to survive, better suited to its environment, more complex, so it breeds more."

"Obviously you're not really thinking about it," Derek was dismissive. "We started off with hydrogen and helium. They didn't feel a need to become more complex, not until we gave it to them. There was no need for heavy elements, for sun, for planets, for energy, for life. We had to set all that up – and even then, entropy would have unravelled it quicker than chance could have ever put it together. Until we introduced ektropy. Ektropy is the drive we slipped in to your universe to prevent entropy from frustrating God's will. Ektropy gave the whole thing a sense of direction."

"Why?" Eve asked. She had been silent for some time and Rodney seemed slightly unnerved by her question.

"Why what?" Rodney asked tentatively.

"Why didn't God want us to know He was behind it all?" Eve explained.

"He wanted to see whether you chose good or evil," Rodney replied.

"Why?" Eve persisted. "I mean what was the point? Was it some kind of game, an entertainment?"

"Certainly not," Rodney replied. "God's not into fun."

"Then why?" Eve repeated. "If He's omniscient, He must have known how we would behave. And why would an all-powerful Being find satisfaction in creating rather pathetic, vulnerable mortal creatures simply so that, not knowing whether or not He existed, they might be tempted to disobey some moral code He had concocted?"

Rodney was taken aback. "You're a fiery one," he said. "If that last outburst was a question, all I can say in answer is that the ways of God are inscrutable."

"In other words, you don't know," said Eve dismissively. Adam wondered whether to suggest to Eve that she might consider being more polite but dismissed the idea. God had felt the edge of her tongue; what harm could the verbal battering of a couple of lowly angels do?

"What I do know," Rodney resumed, his feelings hurt and his pride pricked, "what I do know are those things which fall within my sphere of responsibility. Perhaps I might be permitted to continue my exposition of ektropy?"

Eve shrugged. Rambler nodded encouragement.

Rodney resumed: "Well, take the atom, a significant unit of the stuff of which you are composed."

Numpty nodded his approval. Rodney was puzzled.

"He's got a thing about prepositions," Rambler explained. "Doesn't like them at the end of sentences. You just tucked one away in the right place. Makes him happy."

"Jolly good," Rodney resumed, although still puzzled. "Anyway, the nuclei of atoms is held together by a strong force. That force had to be very precisely calibrated. If it had been even a bit weaker, the nuclei would have been unstable and disintegrated. One of the consequences would have been that your sun and most other stars would not have been able to sustain nuclear reactions, so they would have gone out. No sun, no life, no Man. If it had been even a bit stronger, almost all the hydrogen in the universe would have been converted into helium. No hydrogen – disaster! Again, no sun and no water, no life, no Man. We had to set the force just so."

"Were there other fixes to make it all happen?" Rambler asked. He was determined to have the complete picture.

"There were," Rodney answered, "but, after the initial act of creation, we kept the interventions to a minimum. That was the whole point. It all had to seem to happen by chance."

"What about the extra expansion we had to initiate, just after the initial act of creation?" Derek reminded his co-worker.

"Oh, yes," Rodney conceded, "I was forgetting that. We had a bit of a problem at the beginning. Someone hadn't done the maths."

"Hold on!" Derek exclaimed. "You can't put all the blame on me. You checked my figures."

"What was the problem with the maths?" Adam asked.

"Well, we knew from the start it would take a long time to get from nothing to Man. Even with the underlying principles, the fundamental constants and ektropy, it was going to be a long ride. But, shortly after the act of creation, what you call the Big Bang, we realised we had miscalculated. We had allowed six angelic days, or fifteen billion years in your time, to get to Man. I ran through the calculations again and realised we were out by a factor of ten at least. If we'd left things as they were, we wouldn't even have had any galaxies today, let alone a life-bearing planet. So we had to give it an extra boost. Speeded the expansion up and consequently enlarged the universe many times over."

"It was the 'It has to look as though it's happened by chance' problem again. To make it even remotely plausible that life and Man could emerge out of hydrogen and helium, we had to make the universe extend to ludicrous proportions. It was just about the most insanely wasteful use of resources you can possibly imagine. To shorten the time, we had to enlarge the space, just to make more random events happen more quickly. That was the only way to get back on schedule."

"Gabriel gave us a hard time over that," Derek grumbled. "It's not going to look like a random event if the first thing you do is intervene." Derek's mimicking of Gabriel was wasted on the travellers but it brought the hint of a smile to Rodney's angelic visage. Derek, encouraged, continued. "I let you set those parameters and the constants you said you needed to make it all happen – and almost immediately you break your own rules."

"Yes, it was a difficult moment," Rodney conceded. "But, once he'd calmed down, we explained the problem – and he had to agree that, if we hadn't intervened, then, just about now, there would have been an extremely grumpy deity asking why we hadn't made more progress in implementing His pet project."

"And you told him it wouldn't be the last time we might have to give things a nudge," Derek added.

"I did," Rodney agreed, with just a hint of pride. Clearly, it was not easy for an angelic engineer to tell an archangel what was what. It was not easy. Nor was it safe. But, on this occasion, Rodney had succeeded.

"And did you?" asked Numpty who had been concentrating hard on the words of the two winged entities.

"Yes, I certainly did," Rodney responded in a kindly tone.

"No, I mean did you nudge?" Numpty explained. "Were there other nudges?"

"Yes, there were. We've already mentioned the pleasure principle to get living things to procreate – that wasn't important lower down the chain of life but it was crucial for Man."

"Why was it so important for Man?" Rambler asked. His need to understand was insatiable. "I still don't see why you couldn't just make it a rule that living things had to procreate."

"Fair point," Derek stepped in. It was becoming obvious that Derek felt he had ownership of the genesis of the pleasure principle. "We probably wouldn't have needed it if we'd been told to build the sexual act into the design from the start. But, given the rather tacky solution we had to adopt, we needed to ensure that a self-conscious being capable of choice would go through with it."

"Gabriel was most clear on that point," Rodney added. "We could use creational techniques, fundamental constants, even ektropy, but we had to make it appear to Man that he had choice. Otherwise the whole exercise was pointless. So we had to make man and woman want to have sex."

"Yes," Derek confirmed, and then added, "And I mean *really* want to have sex."

Derek's eye twitched when he said the word 'really' and Adam thought for a moment that the angelic entity had winked at him.

"Of course it must seem obvious to you," Derek resumed, "obvious that if you wanted someone to do something and you couldn't force them to do it, then you had to make them want to do it. And the best way to make them want to do it would be to make doing it exceedingly enjoyable. But it wasn't obvious until we made it so. You see God doesn't take pleasure. He creates, or He gets us to create. He gets angry when things don't work out. He smites. But He doesn't take pleasure. And we angels don't take pleasure. We praise; we obey; we do God's bidding. But we don't have pleasure."

"So why do you praise and obey and do God's bidding?" Eve asked.

Derek seemed a little perplexed. "We do it because that's what we're for."

"Have you ever thought of not doing His bidding?" Eve persisted.

"No," Rodney stepped in, his wings all aquiver like the leaves of a silver-leafed poplar in a gentle breeze. "No, it's not in our nature."

"What about him?" Derek muttered darkly.

"We never speak of him. Merely mentioning his name is to invite the wrath of God."

"I didn't mention his name," Derek persisted. "I'm simply answering her question," he nodded towards Eve. "She asked whether any of us had ever contemplated disobedience."

Rodney cut him short. "Don't use that word. You know perfectly well it's not a permitted concept. We have enough on our plate without a visit from some officious seraphim."

"Do you like to eat?" asked a hungry Numpty. Everyone looked at him. It sounded as though he was offering food but none of the questors had brought any food and drink with them.

Rambler decided it would be best to bring the conversation back on track. "Are you saying there are things you can't say, words you can't use?"

"Yes," Rodney answered. "That's exactly what I'm saying. We know that some of you humans have this thing about freedom of speech but that's not the way things are here. It's very hierarchical. Well, given God is the Creator of all, it has to be."

"You said," Numpty was not to be put off, "you said you had enough on your plate. Does that mean you eat? I only ask because we have not had anything to eat or drink since we arrived."

"I ask only…," Rambler suggested.

"Sorry, Uncle," Numpty responded at once.

"That's a bit pedantic," Eve chided. "What difference does it make?"

"I was only offering a suggestion to improve his English," Rambler defended himself.

"Don't you mean you were offering a suggestion only to improve his English?" Eve came back tartly.

"Stop!" Adam intervened. "We're here on the most extraordinary journey ever undertaken and we're wasting our time on points of grammar!"

Rambler conceded.

"Were there any other interventions?" Adam took the lead, "other than the introduction of the pleasure principle."

"Yes," said Rodney. He was keen to continue his narrative. "You have no idea how this 'creation apparently without a creator' thing played out. Even with the early inflation (which, of course, wrought havoc with what we had hoped would be the universal laws of physics) the timescale was unutterably long. Yes, I know we are part of the heavenly empyrean and outside time. But that's not how it worked for this project. To make sure it all held together and pointed in the right direction we had to be inside time and space. Have you any conception of what four billion years is? We had to wait that long for a decent planet."

"There were times when we thought of giving up," Derek confided. "Of course, God is infinitely wise but, on occasions, we thought the whole humanity enterprise was infinitely stupid. We made all this ever-expanding space, and stretched out all this time, simply to create enough chances for some random chemical confluence to generate life. It was surely the most profligate waste of resources that anyone could ever imagine."

"We had regular meetings with Gabriel and we pointed all this out. We queried the budget. Not a problem. Whatever it took. We explained that even with our nudges and tweaks, creating Man, and Woman," Rodney acknowledged Eve, "even with ektropy and a sense of direction, the odds were still very much against us."

"'Keep at it.' That was what Gabriel said. 'Keep at it.' Aeons passed. 'Keep at it'."

"After all those aeons," Rodney resumed his narrative, "we had at least generated enough stars and planets to prepare for life. You have to understand that engineering all this space and time, energy and matter, had been a pretty draining, dispiriting exercise for us. You see, we ourselves are life; God is life. For us, existence is life. The idea of trying to create life from base materials went against the grain, to use a grossly material metaphor. We kept asking ourselves what was the point when God could have breathed life into our prototype humans in the twinkling of an eye."

Rambler interrupted. "When you say it was a dispiriting experience, is that just a turn of phrase, or do you mean you had to un-spirit yourself to create the essential dross of matter?"

Adam's brow furrowed. He was beginning to see whence Numpty, although not gifted with his uncle's intellect, had derived his obsession with some aspects of language.

"That's a very perspicacious question," Derek answered. "You are right. As angels, as part of the heavenly empyrean, we are used to a top-down creative process. God is perfect. God creates. Now He doesn't create anything better than Himself because, although God is all powerful, even He can't do better than perfect. So He created the archangels and the more senior angels who were really fine but not perfect. When I say 'not perfect', I don't mean any disrespect, of course. Compared to us ordinary angels, they are amazingly fine – and compared to humans, well, they are certainly as close to perfect as makes no difference. As I say, after the archangels and senior angels, you come to angels like us, who are pretty good but not in the same league. And it's left to us to design Man. You can see a trend there. Creation from above, a sliding scale. You know, a traditional hierarchy.

"Well this project turned everything upside down. We had to start with a couple of elements and a lot of energy and build things from the bottom up. To us, it was a really perverse way of doing things. It was a bit like setting out to write a poem and, instead of appointing a poet, simply tossing the letters of the alphabet into the air over and over again in the hope that a master sonnet would emerge."

"We did try to explain all this to Gabriel," Rodney stepped in. "Maths is not his strong suit. Archangels tend to argue that maths is too crude a discipline for them." His tone implied there might simply be a lack of archangelic comprehension. "I gave Gabriel a simple example. I said if you toss a perfectly balanced coin, with heads on one side and tails on the other, what are the odds it will fall on the heads side? I suggested it was one in two."

"Unless it balanced on its edge," offered Numpty.

"Gabriel agreed," Rodney continued, ignoring Numpty. "I then asked, 'what are the odds of it coming down heads twice in a row?' After a bit of discussion we agreed the odds were one in four. I then asked what would be the odds of the coin coming down heads one million times in a row? I managed to persuade Gabriel that the number was bigger than all the atoms in the universe."

"What did Gabriel say to that?" Rambler asked, pen in hand.

Rodney sighed: "He said, in effect, 'so what!' He didn't understand. So I said, 'Look, there are some things in a universe of time and space that are not going to happen however often you toss the coin or shuffle the pack'. I told him the odds against generating human beings out of hydrogen and helium were much higher than tossing a coin and getting heads a million time in a row. He just wouldn't have it. He kept saying 'Keep at it'."

"So we fixed it," Derek spoke.

The look from Rodney, which bespoke a mixture of anger and fear, indicated that Derek had spoken out of turn. "We didn't fix it," Rodney contradicted his winged companion. "We simply made full use of ektropy and the sense of direction thing."

Derek grunted. "That's one way of putting it," he conceded without conviction.

"It's the only way to put it," Rodney returned with emphasis, "unless you want serious repercussions." He glanced skyward. "It happened by chance; it had to happen by chance."

"I don't understand," said Numpty. "Every time you toss a coin it's fifty fifty. So if it's heads the first time, it's fifty fifty it will be heads the second time. And if it's heads twice in a row, it's still fifty fifty the next toss will be heads."

"We must talk about this later," Rambler responded. "It's an interesting subject. If, for example, you worked out the odds for getting ten heads in a row before you started tossing, they might be over a thousand to one, but if you tossed a coin for long enough, the chances *against* getting ten heads in a row would gradually decrease until the odds became very much in favour of getting ten heads in a row."

"Whatever," said Adam who was becoming keen to reach the end of the angelic tale. Of course, he was on a quest for the truth but you had to be alive to seek the truth and Numpty had been right about one thing, they hadn't eaten since they had arrived in the Garden of Eden.

"And so life began," Rodney had sensed a hint of impatience in Adam's voice.

"By chance?" Rambler was determined to have a clear answer.

"Yes," said Rodney and "No," said Derek, in unison.

"Does it really matter?" Eve asked. She too was hungry and could see that, with Rodney and Derek arguing with each other and Rambler and Numpty providing endless prompts and interventions, they might well be stuck in Eden's industrial estate for hours.

"Does it really matter?" the Storyteller queried Eve's indifference, some teasing mixed with the rebuke. "I thought you sought the truth."

"We have the truth," Adam responded. "Whether life was created or happened by chance, these entities have made it clear the creation of life was divinely willed."

"Now do you see," Rodney exploded, his anger directed at Derek. "If this gets back to Gabriel, it is beyond doubt the superfluous ethereal essence will really hit the eternally whirling circle of light."

"It's no use," Derek was unbowed and uncowed. "When you get to the actual creation of Man, you'll be stretching even the human propensity for credulity beyond breaking point."

"Ignore him," Rodney instructed the audience. "Life began and, given its determination to replicate and its propensity to evolve, all we had to do was wait. After a billion years or so, we had some promising self-replicating molecules. From then on, although it all seemed chaotic, indeed was chaotic, we made progress. Of course, we took a few wrong turnings, or rather chance did. The dinosaurs were a case in

55

point. They really got completely out of hand. Went for size and/or aggression. They were king-pins for about sixty million years. Constituted a real block on diversification."

"Be honest," Derek persisted. "We had to intervene."

"What, another nudge?" asked Numpty for whom both the word 'nudge' and its meaning held a peculiar but inexplicable fascination.

"Bit more than a nudge," Derek replied happily. "We had to get rid of them. Otherwise, the world would still be ruled by dinosaurs – and your ancestors, if they survived at all, would be little shrew-like mammals, scrabbling around in the undergrowth. And that wasn't the plan."

"So how did you 'nudge' the dinosaurs out of existence?" Rambler asked, throwing away the pen he had been using for his copious note-taking and pulling a fresh pencil from his breast pocket.

"I favoured simply removing them," Derek replied. "It could have been done in a blink of an eye. But no, we had to make it look like a random act of chance. So we pulled in an asteroid, big enough to create a dust cloud that would block out the sun but not big enough to damage the planet beyond repair. Put a bit of a dent in Mexico. In fact, we overdid it a bit. Killed off most of the plant and animal life as well as the dinosaurs. But that's what happens if you have to conceal your real purpose. It's what you call collateral damage. If we could have just taken out the dinosaurs, it would have been much neater, much less harm to the environment and a much quicker route to human beings. But that wasn't allowed."

"You mean you devastated the planet just to keep up the pretence that everything was happening by chance," Eve accused.

"It wasn't a pretence," Rodney rejoined the debate. "Everything did happen by chance. Let's face it, it had to be chance. You can't possibly imagine anyone would plan anything in this way. Assuming planning is all about the best use of resources to achieve an end, this would have been the worst example of planning ever. We were responsible for the almost unimaginable squandering of resources, of time, of space, of energy and matter to achieve our goal. But the profligacy was essential if you humans were not to know for sure how it all came about."

"If all this secrecy was so important, why are you telling us now?" Adam asked.

"You have a dispensation," Rodney replied. "Anyone brought here by the Storyteller has a dispensation."

"What does that mean?" Adam persisted.

"It means we are permitted to tell you the truth," Rodney answered and, as he said the word truth, a halo formed around his angelic head, spinning gently in a clockwise direction.

"It seems a bit odd that, after billions of years of divinely ordained secrecy, you should feel able to tell us the truth now," Eve pointed out.

"Ah but, although we have told you the truth, there is no necessity for you to believe us," Derek explained. "We ourselves are not fully conversant with God's ultimate plan but I think we can share with you our understanding of the divine purpose as far as it goes. The real goal is doubt."

"Doubt is the real goal of God's plan?" Adam was unable to disguise his dissatisfaction and disappointment.

"'Fraid so," said Derek soothingly. "You see we had to conceal God's involvement in all this…"

"It's a bit more than involvement," the Storyteller interrupted. "According to you he was the initiator, the Creator."

"We had to conceal his involvement," Derek continued, "but only to make you doubt. Given the existence of a universe, any rational, conscious being would be inclined to assume there was a creator. Our job was to obscure the divine hand, to raise doubts."

"None of this makes sense," Eve declared, more as a final judgement than a comment.

"Well I'm sorry you feel that," Rodney responded. "As Derek said, if you don't like the truth, you don't have to accept it. Although," he added with a hint of rebuke while plumping out his angelic wings, "I thought that's what you came here for."

"We came looking for truth and all you offer is doubt," Eve retorted.

"It's not for us, and it's certainly not for you, to question the divine Will," Rodney warned. "I say this off the record. God can be a tad vengeful. Best not to upset Him."

The Storyteller, who was more familiar with God's vindictive side than his companions, intervened: "I think we should take our leave. You have given us much to consider and we thank you for your time."

Luke gave a small growl which tapered off into a whimper. He felt something he didn't like.

They said their farewells, some with more grace than others, and departed.

Rambler alone was sorry to leave. He had so many questions but, as is often the case in life, the thirst for refreshment took precedence over the hunger for knowledge.

As they made their way through the Garden and back through the flower-bedecked meadow, Numpty could not suppress his excitement. "That was wonderful," he exclaimed.

"Do you feel you have learned a lesson of value?" his uncle asked, as a schoolmaster might enquire of a bright pupil.

"The wings," said Numpty, "and the light around Angel Rodney's head. It was wonderful."

"Well, I for one am not so impressed," Eve declared. "The angelic duo in God's R&D department seemed to be misapplying their talents. And as for God, well I think He needs therapy." With that, Eve strode on ahead of the group. She was not in the mood for any further discussion.

She reached the gate of the Garden of Eden and, with some relief, stepped out. As she did so, there was a sliding noise behind her, similar in sonic quality to the noise of an electrically-powered window closing in a luxury car. Eve turned.

The Garden had disappeared.

7 Banished

Eve looked around. There was no sign of the entrance to the Garden. There was no sign of the Garden itself. There was no camper van and no Gwoat. Eve felt a mixture of confusion and panic. Where were the others? How had they become separated? Where was she?

"Hi," said a friendly voice. "You look a bit lost."

Eve took in the lean handsome man sitting astride a gleaming, chrome-accoutred motor-bike but did not answer him at once.

"You're a bit off the beaten track," the biker continued. "There's no public transport around here."

"Where am I?" Eve asked.

"Well, the nearest main road is the A30," the biker replied. "We're somewhere between Nately Scures and Hook."

Eve considered asking the stranger if he knew the whereabouts of the Garden of Eden but thought better of it. "You're not the motorcyclist we nearly drove off the road on the M3?" she asked. He had the same helmet and the bike looked similar.

The biker laughed again. "That's me," he conceded, "but before you conclude I'm stalking you or seeking revenge on your lunatic driver, I should tell you that I live nearby and I'm just on my way home. Incidentally," he added, "where is your van?"

"I wish I knew," Eve sighed. "We left the van here when we set off. We were all together, in a country park," she added uncertainly. "I must have wandered off. We became separated."

"Well, they can't be far," the biker consoled. "I know the area. I should do, I've lived here long enough. I'll give you a hand looking for them, if you like. By the way," he added, "I'm Nick, Nick Peters."

Eve shook the outstretched hand briefly. "I'm Eve, Eve Smith, Mrs Eve Smith."

She felt really foolish. He had told her his name so she had felt obliged to reciprocate. It would have seemed rude not to. So she had said: 'Eve'. She had added Smith because he had told her his surname and she had responded in kind. But she had also told him her surname because it was her married, not her maiden, name and, for some inexplicable reason, she had thought it important to let him know she was married. But of course, he couldn't know whether Smith was her maiden name or her husband's, so she had added the 'Mrs'. And as a result, she felt awkward and embarrassed.

Nick Peters just smiled. "Where did you last see your friends?" he asked.

What could she say? 'About twenty yards behind where I am now standing,' would sound ridiculous. "Back there," she indicated the landscape behind her which, she could see, was now simply a forest of fir trees.

"You all went wandering in the woods?" Nick queried. "Were you looking for mushrooms or some exotic lizard?"

'No, we just popped into the Garden of Eden to have a chat with the Creator,' Eve thought but did not say. "Isn't there a country park near here?" Eve avoided Nick's question.

"There's a country house hotel not far from here," Nick answered, "and it's set in its own grounds. That's about the closest we can get to a country park."

"How far?" Eve was hopeful.

"It's about a mile from here."

"That can't be it," Eve muttered, as much to herself as Nick. "They were only a few yards away."

"And some minutes ago," Nick added enigmatically.

"Some minutes ago," Eve repeated. "What has that to do with it?"

"I'm just pointing out that you have become separated from your husband by time as well as space. It's time more than space that measures how far apart we are."

"Have we met before?" Eve suddenly felt the biker was somehow vaguely familiar.

"I hope you're not trying to pick me up," Nick laughed that warm, confidant, unthreatening laugh.

"Of course not," Eve replied, flustered. "No, it's just that...I don't know," she faltered. "It's just that you don't seem like a perfect stranger."

"Oh, I'm far from perfect," again the intimate chuckle. "But, if I seem familiar, it's probably because we are alike...maybe?"

"How alike?" Eve asked, and then wished she hadn't. He kept leading her into co-operating with him in developing their nascent relationship. "No," she said firmly, "you have no idea what I'm like. I just thought we might have met before but obviously I'm wrong. I need to find my friends."

"I can help you," Nick adopted an earnest tone, "but not immediately. We have to do a bit of deconstruction first." Before Eve could ask what on earth he meant, he continued. "I know what you've been doing. You're travelling with that mad bugger, Tel, Terrence Torrance, the Storyteller to you. Now I don't know where he's said he's taking you. But I can put you straight on that. He's leading you up the garden path."

60

"You know the Storyteller?" Eve accused. "Do you know where he is? Do you know where my husband is?"

"Not exactly," Nick replied cautiously, "but we can work it out, you and I together. And when we have, you'll be back with Adam in no time."

"You know Adam?" Eve blurted out.

"This is becoming a bit repetitive," Nick responded, gently chiding. "Let's get it over with. I know you and Adam and the Storyteller, and, for that matter, the odd couple you picked up at Fleet, Rambler and Numpty, and of course Luke. I also know of Gwoat, the homicidal, chocoholic van driver."

"So you have been following us?" Eve accused.

"Yes, I have – but only to save you time and a great deal of disappointment. And I wasn't lying. I do live nearby."

Eve felt utterly confused, frightened and close to tears.

"It's all Tel's – sorry, the Storyteller's – fault. And yours a bit," he added, "for being so gullible. You had all those questions. He encouraged you to think you could find the answers. But there are no answers. I tried to tell Adam that back at Fleet but he wouldn't listen. I know you will be more reasonable."

"You don't know me. You don't know what I want. And you certainly don't know what I think," Eve rebuked Nick for his presumptions.

"I know you want to get back with Adam. I can help. In fact, only I can help."

8 Trapped

"What the hell!" exclaimed Adam, as he walked into an invisible barrier which bounced him backwards.

"Damn!" said the Storyteller.

"Extraordinary," offered Rambler as he gingerly felt in front of him until his fingertips touched something that prevented further probing.

"It's a force field," the Storyteller explained. "It's what stops people from wandering into the Garden. And, in our case, it's stopping us from getting out."

"We have to find a way," Adam snapped. "Eve is outside."

"We had better find out why we have been locked in," the Storyteller responded. "Eve is safe. As you say, she is outside. We, on the other hand, are trapped inside."

"It could be worse," Rambler offered. "I mean," he hastened to explain, "being trapped in the Garden of Eden is not so bad."

If Rambler's intervention had been intended to calm Adam, it failed. "I'm not going to be trapped anywhere," Adam retorted. "Least of all in a place governed by a psychotic God and a hierarchy of nerdish but manipulative angels. So how do we get out of here?" Adam addressed the Storyteller.

"Whooa!" the Storyteller exclaimed. "This is your quest. It's not up to me to solve all the problems. I mean, I'm happy to help but you can't rely on me for all the answers."

"We haven't had any answers at all so far," Adam returned. "Not from you, and not from that pathetic excuse for God."

"I think perhaps you should watch what you say," Rambler intervened. "I don't know why we have been detained but it would seem reasonable to assume it is with the approval, and possibly at the command, of the afore-mentioned deity."

"I suggest we retrace our steps to the industrial estate and see if Rodney or Derek can enlighten us," the Storyteller suggested.

Adam had one more try at forcing his way through the invisible barrier but the unseen hindrance became firmer, the harder he pressed. "Very well," he conceded, turning and setting off back along the path they had followed.

"Come along," Rambler spoke to his nephew. Numpty was giggling at the sight of Luke urinating against an invisible wall. The urine cascaded out in a parabola only to splatter inexplicably in mid-air and then trickle vertically to the ground. The limpid light of the garden illuminated the yellow liquid so it sparkled like a waterfall of gold. "It's pretty," Numpty explained.

"So it is," Rambler conceded. "But we must move on. Perhaps," he added, addressing Adam and the Storyteller, "we can find somewhere to take a little refreshment. It seems like an age since we ate or drank anything at all."

They made their way though the meadow, full of daffodils, buttercups and daisies, until they reached the industrial estate. They had walked briskly, with Rambler regularly urging Numpty to keep up, while Luke ran ahead and then behind the group, ensuring they all kept together.

When they reached the offices of the R & D department, they found Rodney outside, clearly in some distress.

He greeted them with "Oh dear!" which he repeated several times. "You are in serious trouble," he elucidated. "We are in serious trouble. Derek, in particular, is in serious trouble."

"Where is Derek?" the Storyteller asked.

"He's been detained, or worse," Rodney answered. "They came, Seraphiel and Metatron. I couldn't see what happened. They emit so much light, it is unbearable. But I heard their voices. They said: 'We are the Seraphim of the Lord and we have come to do His bidding. The Lord is greatly angered for you have betrayed His trust. You have spoken to His creatures, creatures out of favour with the Lord, and told them that which they should not know.' Then there was a kind of rumbling noise and a whirlwind of light and, when the light had diminished sufficiently for me to be able to see, Derek was gone."

"You mean Derek's being punished for talking to us?" Adam felt some anger.

"Yes, that's exactly what I mean and," Rodney added, "I'm likely to face the same when they've finished with Derek. He said too much and was not respectful. As for you, you are being 'sought'. All angels have been told to look out for you and, if we see you, to report immediately to the nearest archangel."

"We just want to leave the Garden," Adam said, "but our way out was blocked somehow. So we've come back to ask how we can get back to our world."

Rodney looked puzzled. "I'm not sure I know what you mean. This is your world. It is more your world than any other. As for leaving, that is up to God. He lets entities in, and he lets them out. Those who seek to enter but who are not welcomed by God, cannot enter. Those who wish to leave but whom God wishes to stay, cannot leave. There is nothing I can do to help you and, even if I could, I wouldn't dare. At the least, I'm likely to have my wings clipped, both metaphorically and literally."

Adam turned to the Storyteller. The Storyteller widened his eyes, furrowed his brow and puckered his chin in an expression which clearly indicated he had no idea what to do.

"While we mull over the situation," Rambler hazarded, "would it be possible for you to provide us with some light refreshment?"

Rodney's wings ruffled. "This is scarcely the time to be thinking of food," Rodney responded. "You don't seem to understand. Derek is being interrogated. Have you any idea what that means?"

Adam and the Storyteller looked blank. Numpty seized the opportunity to contribute. "Is it something to do with terror and gates?"

"No, no," Rambler soothed. "It just means he is being asked questions."

Numpty persisted. "We can't get out through the gate, and we're frightened. Are you sure that isn't what it means? Like we're gated in terror."

"It means," Rodney almost choked on the words, "it means Derek's very being will be challenged; it means he will suffer; and then, when they have finished challenging and hurting him, he may well be ended. If there is one thing God and his seraphim can't stand, it's disrespect and I am afraid they will judge some of Derek's remarks as disrespectful. Oh, God!" he ended.

Suddenly, a light of unbelievable intensity suffused the travellers and the distraught angel. All of them shut their eyes and covered them with their hands.

"I am Metatron," said a voice. "And you are nicked".

9 The trial

The light gradually diminished in intensity. As the eyes of the travellers adjusted, they could see they were surrounded by shadows, although it soon became apparent that the shadows were themselves exceedingly bright, just not as amazingly bright as the seraph Metatron. These were lesser angels, grander than Rodney but far less bright than the seraphim. Each displayed four wings, compared with Rodney's more modest two.

"I have always been industrious and faithful to the Lord," Rodney babbled. He was clearly terrified. The light of Metatron had been so intense that some of Rodney's feathers had been singed. A slightly acrid smell hung in the air.

"You will all come with us," said one of the arresting angels, ignoring Rodney's whimpering.

"I should like to construe that as a prediction or an invitation but I fear it is a command," Rambler observed.

Adam looked around. There were nine angels, excluding Rodney. All were about the same height as Rodney, approximately seven feet tall. Their luminous white robes would have done credit to a detergent commercial, Adam thought.

"You can see through them," Numpty exclaimed. "Look!"

Numpty was right. The angels were existent entities but, rather like some species of exotic fish, it was possible to see through them if you looked closely.

"They are the Potestates, the Powers," Rodney whispered. "They are God's enforcers. Believe me, they are not to be argued with."

"Don't!" Rambler addressed his nephew, whom he could see was unsuccessfully wrestling with a way of eliminating the sentence-ending preposition.

"We're nicked?" Adam queried. "Surely that's an odd turn of phrase for a seraph?"

"Not at all," Rodney explained. He had regained some composure now his feathers had ceased to smoulder, but he still whispered. "It refers to the Fallen One, known colloquially in Eden and, I believe, on earth, as Old Nick. Following his fall, anyone who succumbs to the temptations of evil is described as 'nicked', that is associated with the Fallen One. Metatron was simply explaining why we were being arrested; he was telling us we have been contaminated by evil."

"Is he the same person as the Nick of Time?" asked Numpty who was doing his best to follow Rodney's exegesis.

"Out of the mouths of babes...," the Storyteller observed,

enigmatically.

"Move along now," said the spokesman of the Powers. And move they did but not as they expected. The nine angelic Potestates formed a ring around Rodney and the questors. Then they linked their angelic arms and swept themselves and their detainees up into the lucid, cloudless, blue sky.

Seen from a height, the vast proportions of the Garden were revealed. Adam spotted two rivers in the distance, joined together far away before each forked off on its own meandering way. The M3 was nowhere to be seen. The flight was exhilarating rather than frightening. It ended when the Potestates descended and landed before the entrance of a fine three storey building. Marble steps led up to the entrance which was furnished with a fine oak door, strengthened by iron supports.

"This is the Hall of Justice," Rodney explained. "This is where God passes judgement."

"Why have they brought us here?" Adam asked.

"Where's Luke?" Numpty interrupted. They all looked around. Luke was nowhere to be seen.

"He must have been left behind when the Potestates took off," the Storyteller surmised.

"We must go back," Numpty insisted. He had become very fond of the dog in their short time together. The thought of the dog wandering aimlessly and alone around a strange, albeit heavenly, industrial estate upset him deeply.

"This is not the right time." Rambler attempted to calm his distraught nephew.

"You are to be judged shortly," said the leader of the Potestates, confirming, with the deep sonorous tone of his angelic kind, Rambler's assessment of the gravity of the situation.

"It is the right time," Numpty contradicted his uncle. "Luke is all alone and we should go back before he wanders off and gets lost."

"We are about to face God's doom," Rodney intervened. "I fear our predicament is rather more terrifying than Luke's."

"Well I'm not terrified," Numpty responded. "I haven't done anything wrong. I just want to go and find Luke."

"We cannot transport dogs," said the leading Potestate.

The travellers were rather stunned by this seemingly banal pronouncement.

"And why is that?" Rambler asked, reaching for his notebook. After all, even if they were to face the judgement of God, the quest for knowledge must continue and it sounded as though he was about to learn something of the nature of the Potestates.

"We don't do dogs, or any animals for that matter – except for humans, that is," the Potestate explained. "We can transport humans because they have a small divine component but even humans are a bit like hard work. Animals are too material, too gross."

"Two hundred and eighty eight," Numpty proclaimed. "That's just one short of the square of seventeen." Numpty's eclectic bank of knowledge was ill-organised but, thanks to his uncle, extensive. Numbers, as well as grammar, held a peculiar fascination for the boy.

"The lad's certainly one short of something," Adam snapped. "Could someone answer my question," Adam addressed the leading Potestate. "Why have you brought us here?"

"You have angered God. You must therefore face His justice."

"On what charge?" Rambler enquired, closing his notebook and slipping it into this coat pocket.

The Potestate looked puzzled. "As I have said, the charge is that you have angered God."

"That's not really a charge," Adam picked up Rambler's line of thought. "Making someone angry is not a charge, not a real charge. What exactly have we done wrong?"

"There is scarcely a more serious offence than angering the Creator of All."

"No," Adam persisted. "Just making someone angry is not a chargeable offence."

"Excuse me," the Potestate returned, "but you're in the Garden of Eden and we have our own rules here. What's more, our rules are *the* rules, by which I mean, they are God's rules, eternal, immutable, absolute. We are well aware of the kind of rules you favour outside the Garden, a totally confusing muddle of pragmatic relativism and psychobabble. But they are irrelevant here and, to be frank, not much use in your world either. Except, of course, for lawyers."

"That's my point, really," Adam countered. "If we are charged with some offence, presumably we have legal counsel to defend us. They will need to know the charge," he explained. "To defend us properly," he added rather lamely.

Rodney took Adam's forearm and gave it a warning squeeze. "Wait until you see how things work," he advised.

The group of travellers and Potestates entered the Hall of Justice. Numpty was still bemoaning Luke's fate but his uncle, with more hope than confidence, assured him they would give the matter a high priority as soon as circumstances permitted. The Hall was a fine building. In the foyer was a great statue of God, with His foot firmly planted on the neck of a fallen angel, presumably Satan. "Yes," Rodney answered Rambler's unasked question. "He bears a grudge for an infinitely long time."

Once across the foyer, having circumnavigated the massive statue, they entered, through open double doors, the Judgement room. On a raised stage in a rather grand chair, burnished with brass knobs, sat God. On either side sat two archangels, identified by Rodney as Uriel and Gabriel.

"They've got more wings," observed Numpty. The archangels did indeed sport six wings apiece. "Shhh!" warned his uncle, who nevertheless made a mental note to record the number of arch-angelic appendages when the opportunity arose.

The travellers were ushered forward by the Potestates who, their duty done, lined up behind the defendants. Adam stared up at God and then whispered to the Storyteller who was standing next to him: "I thought we'd finished with Him. I thought He didn't have any power if we didn't believe in Him."

"Silence!" Uriel commanded.

Adam studied the panel seated in judgement. God looked a good deal more impressive now than He had when they had left His presence at the end of their previous audience with Him. Perhaps it was the elevated position afforded by the raised podium, or perhaps it was the throne-like chair on which He sat or perhaps it was the obvious solemnity of the occasion – but God definitely seemed to have reacquired some of his majesty. God's words at the end of their previous encounter came back into Adam's mind: 'It's not as easy as you think to deny Me.....Do you really think you can walk away from Me with impunity?'

"Where is the woman?" God thundered.

There was an uneasy shuffling noise from behind the line of defendants and a nervous fluffing and shivering of feathers. The Potestates' spokesman began; "Lord of this and all other Universes, Creator of all things animate and inanimate, not to mention any and all other existent entities, the Source of all order and Conqueror of chaos..." The Potestate would have continued along these lines for several minutes, had not Uriel shot him a warning glare. The Potestate decided it would be best to address the question. "We quickly located these four offenders and trapped them before they could leave the Garden. These we have brought swiftly before you."

All eyes were on God. "Where is the woman?" He asked again, this time in even more thunderous tones than before. The atmosphere within the hall became darker and suddenly distinctly oppressive.

"We acted as soon as the archangel Gabriel told us of Your will," the Potestate resumed with a shaky voice. "None could have acted more swiftly than we."

"I ask you one more time, and for the last time," God returned.

There was now a clammy, leaden silence in the hall. Although less familiar with God's ways than the Angelic Host, even the defendants could feel the onset of God's wrath.

The awful silence was broken by Numpty who gave vent to a sneeze of inexcusably loud and moisture laden proportions. Rambler frowned at his nephew and briefly shook his head to indicate that Numpty should make every effort to take control of his nasal passages. "It's the feathers, Uncle", Numpty explained, "I think I'm allergic to the feathers of the angels."

"Will you or will you not tell me where the woman is?" God resumed.

Numpty sneezed again; "Sorry Uncle, but I can't help it."

Just as Numpty sneezed for the second time, Rambler reached for his notebook and pencil inside the pocket of this coat. At once, the Potestates closed in on him. "Hold back," Rambler shook himself free, "it's only a pad and a pencil." There was confusion amongst the Potestates.

"And why, when you stand before God in mortal peril of your lives, would you feel the need for a pad and pencil?" demanded Uriel, instructing the Potestates to stand down with a wave of his hand.

"Well," Rambler responded with a confidence that surprised Adam, "I wished to make a few notes. Whatever our fate, while we live, it is our duty to understand, and, in order to understand, we need to take notes - or I do, at least. I wished to record that the archangels have six wings, compared with the Potestates' four and Rodney's more modest quota of two. I assume the number of wings corresponds to the level of seniority in the angelic hierarchy."

"I noticed that too," Numpty interjected in between sniffs and suppressed sneezes.

Adam looked towards the Storyteller. Uriel's question seemed a good deal saner to Adam than Rambler's answer. The Storyteller just widened his eyes and shook his head. Evidently he had no better idea than Adam what was driving Rambler.

"Then there is the possibility that my nephew is allergic to angelic feathers. This would be particularly interesting because the angels seem to us to be spiritual beings whereas allergies are peculiarly material, being the result of particles irritating the membrane of the human respiratory system. I should really like to examine the composition and structure of an angelic feather should the opportunity present itself."

Uriel was about to speak but Rambler had not finished.

"But more important," Rambler went on, "I wished to note that although, as I understand it, God is omniscient, He currently seems desperate to know the whereabouts of the woman. Now if God knows where Eve is, the question is pointless, unless He simply wishes to humiliate this poor Poestate. On the other hand, if He doesn't know where Eve is, evidently He's not omniscient."

'What was it with his team of travellers?' Adam asked himself. Last time it had been Eve who had harangued God over His callous treatment of His creatures; now Rambler seemed equally intent on picking a fight with the Creator.

"It is not for you to question the Lord of this and all other universes," Gabriel spoke for the first time. "Your minds cannot comprehend Him."

"With all respect," Rambler rejoined, "I was not trying to comprehend Him. I was merely pointing out that, unless God is beyond reason, He cannot, at one and the same time, be all knowing and yet not know all. What's more, I noticed that God said He was asking about the woman for the last time and then, bless my soul, within less than a minute he asked again."

"You won't put one over on my uncle," Numpty proclaimed proudly. "He doesn't know everything but he knows an awful lot."

"Tell your nephew to keep his mouth shut," Gabriel addressed Rambler, "And, while you're at it, advise him that if he sneezes once more, I shall personally fuse his nostrils together to ensure it is the last sneeze he ever emits."

Rodney whispered urgently in Rambler's ear: "Do as he says. Gabriel's very fussy about personal habits. It was one of his criticisms of our work on Man. He complained you were too gross. All that eating and excreting, coughing and sneezing, sweating and smelling. Anyway, don't doubt he'll make good his threat."

"A sneeze is an involuntary, or at least semi-autonomous, act," Rambler responded rather haughtily. "I will certainly advise my nephew to suppress future sneezes as best he can but, should he fail, I shall take a very dim view of any punishment imposed on him, especially if, as threatened, any punishment is entirely disproportionate."

Throughout this exchange, it was evident God's patience had become exhausted. The dark clouds outside the hall were now so heavy and leaden that only the light from the assembled angelic entities

70

illuminated the proceedings. "What is your purpose?" God addressed the leader of the Potestates.

"It is to do your bidding, immediately, without questions," the Potestate replied, with a quiet resignation in his voice.

"Then where is the woman?" God asked.

"By the time we reached the boundary of the Garden, she had slipped through the gate and was out of reach," the Potestate replied.

"It was the woman, above all, whom I wished to punish, for her audacity, her ill-manners and her lack of faith," God mused aloud. "Now I shall have to destroy one of you, her fellow-travellers, in her place. I shall allow you to choose amongst yourselves who it should be, who," and at this point God seemed to smirk and sneer at the same time, "who amongst you should, how do you say it – 'take a hit for the team'."

To demonstrate His serious intent, God turned His gaze upon the hapless leader of the Potestates: "As for you, you have admitted that you have failed to fulfil your purpose. Those without purpose have no reason to exist." As God spoke these words, the Potestate began to shake and then shimmer. This magnificent seven foot tall being, who had lifted and transported the travellers across the land of Eden, who emitted a radiance that could dazzle mortal eyes, was coming apart and fading. The Potestate reached out to his angelic team, who responded by taking his hands in a gesture of compassion and solidarity but they could do nothing. Their leader was being deconstructed, uncreated, entirely destroyed by the will of God.

Numpty sneezed.

"If he does that one more time," said Gabriel to Rambler, "I tell you now you will have one less to choose from when you pick who of your number must die."

10 A ray of light

Luke was very unhappy. He was not a demanding sort of dog. He liked two good meals a day, a crackling log fire on cold days and a chance to savour the rich tapestry of odours which suffused every corner of the earth. These were his pleasures and, it seemed to him, they were very reasonable. In return, he gave total loyalty and great affection. Not a bad deal for humankind.

There was one other factor which Luke required for complete satisfaction. Indeed it was really a *sine qua non*. He needed the company of his master and mistress.

When Eve had slipped out of the Garden and the invisible barrier had separated Adam from his wife and the dog from his mistress, Luke had felt a tremor of panic. His emotions when the Potestates gathered up Adam and his companions and departed with them into the sky is difficult to describe. He certainly felt utterly abandoned – but it was worse than that. He felt inconsequential, of no significance, a non-being. The Potestates had not counted him as a member of the group they were abducting, and worse, no one in the group seemed to notice he had been left behind. No one had looked back when they rose into the air and swept skywards.

Luke crouched down with his belly pressed to the ground. Truth to tell, he was terrified. After a few moments of uncontrolled panic, he took a grip on himself. There was only one thing he could do. He must set off to the north, in the direction which the air-borne, angelic entourage had taken. It seemed a hopeless venture but Luke had to do something and anything which might bring him closer to his master gave him some comfort.

He had not loped along for more than a mile when it began to rain. It had been threatening rain for some time. Grey clouds had gathered overhead and the air had felt dank. For some reason, Luke had assumed it would not rain in Eden. He had thought of Eden as an habitually sunny place, an assumption strengthened by the glorious weather they had enjoyed on their entry to the Garden.

He was wrong. The sky became leaden and then the heavens opened. Misery now joined fear in the heart of Luke's troubled being. Rain fell in long, languid drops, which splashed when they hit the ground. His long-haired coat soon became soaked and, although it was not particularly cold, Luke began to shiver. This was the worst time he had ever experienced, so bad he thought it could not get worse.

He was wrong again. Luke had not looked up since he had decided to pursue the Potestates. Although there was no scent to follow, since the Potestates had taken an aerial route, it was in his nature to keep his nose close to the ground when following a track. He had not therefore noticed two creatures, with wings of flame and bodies, seemingly, of smouldering fire, flying some thirty feet above and just behind him. The rain that fell on these terrifying creatures sizzled and evaporated in small eruptions of steam.

"Yours or mine?" Hemah asked.

"Surely we can share," returned his brother Af, "but let us not rush things. We can take a little time. Let us scare the bedraggled, golden-haired, four-footed creature first; then I would propose a little singeing; only when the dank hair has been burned from his body and we smell the odour of burning canine flesh should we together dispatch it."

That said, Af launched a shaft of fire at the ground in front of Luke. Luke swerved, fell and rolled on the slippery grass. As he turned on his back, he saw, hovering above him, his tormentors.

"Leave me alone," he screamed. He was frightened out of his wits, but he was also angry. Why would anyone wish to harm him when he was already at his lowest ebb? "Bugger off!" he snapped.

Hemah and Af, angels of wrath and slayers of domestic animals, looked at each other in astonishment, their flaming eyes, with burning coals for pupils, enlarged by surprise. It was not the colloquial invitation to depart which had taken them by surprise. It was that a creature even lower than Man was capable of speech.

"It's a freak of nature," opined Af.

"I'm a freak of nature?" Luke returned, having scrabbled to his feet. "If I'm a freak of nature, what the hell are you?"

"We are God's enforcers and we are here to clean up a loose end," Hemah spoke.

"Oh, I see," Luke responded, trying to maintain his dignity in exceedingly difficult circumstances, "so I'm a loose end to be tormented and destroyed by a couple of demonic firelighters."

"We are not demonic; we're angelic. And as for describing us as firelighters…" Hemah began.

Af intervened. "Hemah, can you hear yourself? You're arguing with a talking dog. We, the feared instruments of the Creator, are engaged in a heated exchange with a canine anomaly." Without waiting for Hemah to acknowledge the idiocy of his behaviour, Af delivered a sliver of flame on to the top of Luke's rain-soaked head. The hair steamed, smouldered and then burned. Luke yelped. "That's the only kind of heated exchange that this impudent abomination will get from me," Af declared.

Hemah shook his wings to indicate that, following his brother's admonition, he was himself once more. He spewed out a stretch of fire from his mouth and carefully moulded it into a pulsing ball. He prepared to hurl it at Luke, aiming for the base of Luke's spine, just before the tail. If well-delivered, the missile would disable Luke, render him helpless, cause him intense pain but would not kill him.

"Leave the dog alone," said a voice.

Luke looked around. Ahead of him, half-hidden by the heavy rain, was the figure of a man, leaning on a stick. "Come to me," the man said, addressing Luke.

Luke did not know what to do. He liked the sound of the man's voice. And he really liked the idea of going to be with a human who sounded kindly. On the other hand, the angels of wrath were not to be trifled with and there must be a question about whether they would take the slightest notice of an ordinary man. And his head hurt. It hurt really badly.

"Come," the man repeated.

Luke looked up at the angels of wrath. It was difficult to read their expressions. It seemed to Luke they might be exchanging knowing glances, or perhaps expressions of some uncertainty, or possibly even fear. Whatever, they seemed disinclined to oppose the man. Hemah in particular seemed disconcerted. He was tossing the pulsing ball from one hand to the other as though he had no idea what to do with it. Luke made up his mind and trotted over to his saviour.

"Can you hear me?" Luke asked tentatively.

"Yes, I can hear you," the man smiled.

The rain was stopping. Luke looked back up into the sky. Hemah and Af were nowhere to be seen. The clouds were breaking up and shafts of sunlight were turning the grey land to green once again.

"I can hear you but, sadly," the man added, "I can't see you." He patted Luke on the head and, as he did so, the simmering pain inflicted by Af's sliver of fire, dwindled and ceased.

"That's amazing !" Luke exclaimed.

"Not really," the man replied, equally surprised. "I was born blind, so I'm quite used to it. I have never been able to see, so I don't miss it."

"No," Luke interrupted, "I mean why did the pain go away when you patted me on the head?"

The man laughed: "It's probably just your imagination. We all like to be patted on the head. It's comforting. I expect it just took your mind off the pain."

Luke wasn't entirely satisfied. Af's shaft of fire had burnt the hair on his head and the flesh underneath. The pain had been intense at first and had not reduced so much after the initial burst. Luke knew the injury, although not life-threatening, was serious and would take time to heal. "Well," said Luke, "whatever it was, I'm grateful."

"No need," said the man.

"So, if you're blind," Luke had more questions, "how do you get around? And why would you take on those demonic firebrands? And what are you doing here anyway? You're a man and this is God's domain?"

The man laughed. "So many questions! I get around by moving slowly and carefully, using my stick to check out any unfamiliar ground; and I have pretty good hearing, which helps. I took on your demonic firebrands probably because I couldn't see them. If I had seen them, I'm sure I would have been as terrified as you. But I heard them teasing and taunting you, and that was wrong. So I intervened. What am I doing here? Well that's a rum question from a dog. What on earth are you doing here?"

"That's a long story too," Luke answered.

"Well, I think we may have time enough to tell each other any number of long stories," the man chuckled. "I think we should team up. You obviously need protection; and I could surely benefit from a good pair of eyes."

"I'd like that," said Luke. The last few hours had been the worst in Luke's life, even worse than when Bella had been killed. The death of Adam and Eve's daughter had been dreadful but it had been an accident. Here the problems he had faced in this strange place were not accidents. They were caused by a malign spirit. His master and mistress had been seized by soldiers of God; he had been pursued by malicious, spiteful, sadistic entities. Yes, teaming up with a kindly, brave man whose pat on the head had a remarkable analgesic effect seemed to Luke an excellent idea.

"So what's your name?" the man asked.

"I'm Luke," the dog replied, wagging his tail. "And what should I call you?" He referred to Adam as 'master' so that would be inappropriate.

"I'm Kit," said the man. "Just call me Kit. 'Though, since there's only the two of us, names are not so important. You need names more when you are talking about people than when you are talking to them. Anyway Kit will do. Now, tell me, where were you heading?"

"I have to find my people," Luke began to explain. "My master and mistress came here on a quest. They were seized and flown away by some angelic enforcers. I don't know why. And I don't know where they have been taken. But I have to find them."

"Wait, wait," said the man. "I can't keep up. You came here on a quest. What quest?"

Luke felt a little embarrassed. "My master wanted to seek the truth," he hazarded.

"The truth," Kit repeated. "The truth about what?"

"I don't really know," Luke confessed. "I don't think it was the truth about something in particular. I think he wanted the Truth. You know. With a big T."

"I see," said the man, although the way he said it suggested he didn't really understand. "And what do you mean, they were seized and flown away?"

Luke was on firmer ground. "It means what I said. A bunch of Potestates, that's a rank of angels, arrived, arrested everyone in our group, except me, and flew them off. I think they are going to be put on trial or punished because they have offended God."

"Do you mean they actually flew?" Kit asked.

"Well, yes," Luke answered.

"But people can't fly," said Kit. "Can they?" he added uncertainly.

"Well, no, they didn't fly under their own steam," Luke explained. "The Potestates picked them up."

Kit was clearly puzzled. "I'm sorry, I don't like to appear thick but are you telling me there are beings that can fly and that they can pick up a man or a woman and fly away with them?"

"Er, yes," said Luke, "that's exactly what I'm telling you."

"Well, I never," said the man. "I've heard a fair amount of whooshing and flapping since I've been here – and I wondered. But obviously I haven't been able to see what has been going on. That's amazing."

"It's not just amazing," Luke suggested with some urgency. "It's terrifying. The Potestates just took them away for some kind of trial and I got the impression that it was a trial that wouldn't involve much justice."

"Well, in that case," said Kit, "we had best make haste to the place of the trial and see what we can do."

"It's not that easy," said Luke. "I'm not really sure where the Potestates took them. It was in a general northerly direction but I have no idea exactly where they were going."

"Well, if it's a trial they had in mind, they were almost certainly heading for the Hall of Justice. Bit of a misnomer, if you ask me. I know where that is. I've had some personal experience of the judicial process in the Hall of Justice."

Luke didn't ask the man what he meant; he wanted to rejoin his master as soon a possible. "How far is it?" was his only question.

"It's about half a mile from here," the man answered.

They set off at once with Luke trotting along beside the man, ready to warn him of any dangers, if need be. The man was surprisingly sure-footed. In half an hour they came to a stream that bubbled and gurgled happily over a stony bed.

"This stream forks into two a bit lower down. We can cross there without getting wet," said the man.

When they stepped over the second stream, Luke could see a rather imposing three storey building. "Is that it?" Luke asked his blind companion.

"I guess so," Kit answered, with another of his chuckles, "unless they've moved it since I was last here."

11 Betrayal

When Eve awoke, she felt exhilaration – and an appalling, limitless sense of shame. It had been an extraordinary night.

Nick Peters had booked her into a local inn which provided rooms for one or two guests. After she had settled in her room, he had called her and said he was sending a friend over to pick her up. He told her they needed to plan how to reach Adam.

The friend turned out to be an attractive young girl called Rose. Eve took Rose, with blonde hair, buxom figure and ringless fingers, to be Nick's girlfriend. They drove in Rose's Smart Car to Nick's cottage which was less than half a mile from the inn.

Nick was all charm when she arrived, charming but also business like. He had a large sheet of paper laid out on the dining table in the capacious kitchen. "Here is the plan," he said proudly.

The plan was a map of southern England, with a large number of symbols inscribed at different places.

"We are here," he pointed on the map to Hook, lying off the M3, a little to the north. "We won't be able to reach Adam and the others here. It's just not possible. But, with a bit of luck, if we go to Stoney Cross tomorrow, we should be able to catch them there before they set off again. In fact, if we can catch them at Stoney Cross, perhaps I can talk some sense into Adam and persuade him to stop the quest altogether."

Eve didn't know what to say. Nick seemed so confident, and so knowledgeable, and yet nothing made any sense. But then, the Garden of Eden, the interview with God, the explanations of creation offered by Rodney and Derek, none of it made any sense.

"How do you know all this?" Eve eventually asked lamely.

"Get us some drinks, Rosy," Nick instructed Rose. "Open a bottle of my best Merlot."

Rose happily did as she was told, humming softly as she poured the drinks and then moved over to the Aga, evidently to prepare a meal.

"And don't hum," Nick added, "we need to concentrate".

Rose stopped humming but did not seem upset by Nick's abrupt manner.

Eve took a sip of the Merlot. It was rich and deep, and provided a lingering, seductive aftertaste.

"I've been through this many times before," Nick confided in Eve. "It's that bloody Tel - sorry the Storyteller. He really ought to get a proper job. He spends all his time trying to persuade naive folks like

Adam, sorry I don't mean to be rude, to set out on entirely pointless adventures in search of something that doesn't exist. As a result, I spend a lot of my time trying to prevent all this questing or, if I fail to prevent it, sorting out the mess afterwards."

Nick paused but, since Eve didn't speak, he continued. Eve took another, longer sip of the Merlot.

"I mean, let's examine your own case. You set off on this fool's errand at Tel's behest. And the first thing that happens is that you and Adam get separated. You end up alone and lost in deepest Hampshire. Adam disappears altogether."

"Do you know where we have been?" Eve asked tentatively. "I mean do you know where we were before we became separated?" If he knew so much, perhaps he knew that they had been in the Garden of Eden, perhaps he knew they had stood before God.

"Well, you told me you had been in the woodland where I found you. You said you had only just got separated."

So he didn't know or, if he did, he certainly wasn't going to admit it.

"Hey, Rosy," he called to his curvaceous housemate, "don't hog the wine. Eve's glass is empty."

Rose returned smiling from the Aga and refilled Eve's glass. Eve felt inexplicably relaxed. She heard a voice in her head telling her that she should be panicking, that the world, or at least her world, was dissolving into chaos, that nothing was certain. There now seemed to her to be only two realities: the Storyteller's and Nick's. And both were totally alien. Both had some kind of internal logic but it was a logic that had nothing to do with the real world, or, at least, nothing to do with her real world.

And yet she felt relaxed.

"I expect you would like to see Bella again," Nick said in a casual tone.

Eve tried to pull herself together. "For a moment that sounded like an offer," she managed.

"It was," Nick Peters replied. "Oh yes, it was an offer, and a generous one."

"How could I see Bella again?" Eve asked. "You shouldn't joke about such a thing," she added, but her voice didn't convey the anger she should have felt. More strangely, she didn't even feel the anger she felt she should feel.

Nick did not reply at once. He leant forward, took her hand and looked into her eyes for what seemed to Eve an inappropriately long time. Then he said simply: "Come with me."

It had been an extremely busy day. Arranging Bella's birthday parties was always a pretty demanding operation. The invitations had to be sent out, number of acceptances checked, entertainers booked, catering planned, gift boxes organised. Normal domestic routines were thrown into chaos. It really was a nightmare but, as with so many aspects of their lives, it was what was expected of them by their peers and not least by their daughter – and therefore there was no choice.

Adam did his best to help. Indeed, Eve knew he was convinced his help was invaluable. In fact, it was easier if she managed things on her own. Instead of just doing what she wanted, he was forever suggesting 'better ways'. "It would be a lot quicker if we put all the presents in a big box and let the kids take their chances. You know, a lucky dip. It doesn't really matter which kid gets which present." By the time she had explained that Miriam probably wouldn't want a model car and Josh would obviously be embarrassed by a pink hair grip, she could have packed two more of the goody boxes and got on with something else. Still, he meant well.

Eve stood back and reviewed her handiwork. A trestle table had been set up in the games room. Places had been laid for the twelve guests. Adam had queried whether a marauding band of seven years olds would appreciate a beautifully laid table and he was of course right. But Eve wasn't doing it for the kids.

"How's it going?" It was Nick's voice. She turned. It had been Nick's voice but it was Adam who stood before her.

She should have said something. She should have said: "Who are you?" or "What the hell is going on?" or "Am I going mad?" How could Adam speak with Nick's voice? And, in any case, she hadn't yet met Nick Peters, not back when Bella was alive. So, without resort to time travel and possession, what possible explanation could there be? But Eve didn't ask any of these questions. Instead, she said; "Everything is ready, I think."

"Well, in that case, we have time to take Bella and Luke to the park," Adam replied with Nick's voice. "Bella's been pestering all morning. She wants to see what the puppy thinks of a wide open space."

"He'll probably think it's a good place to run off and get lost in," Eve suggested, and then added: "I should really stay here and make sure everything is ready."

"It is ready," Adam cajoled. "You just said so. It's hours before the kids arrive. And it's a really lovely day. Come on."

"I thought they said it was going to rain," Eve countered.

"When did we ever believe a word they said? Politicians and weather forecasters – always telling us what to do and what is going to happen; and almost always getting it wrong." That was just what Adam would have said, Eve thought. Perhaps she was imagining the voice thing.

"Yes, Mummy," Bella ran into the room. "Please let's take Luke to the park."

There she was. The prettiest little girl in the world. Full of life, full of joy, full of hope! Eve grabbed the child and cuddled her. "Can we go," Bella persisted, "please, Mummy."

"Oh well," Eve conceded. "It won't do any harm, so long as we're back here by three."

Bella took her mother's hand and Nick's hand. "Come on then, let's go. If we've only got an hour, we should run."

"Whoa!" said Nick, "I have to put Luke on a lead, at least till we are in the park."

Bella did not seem to have noticed that her father's voice was not his own.

The walk in the park was just as Eve remembered it. There was the old man, feeding the birds by the pond. There were the two joggers, a man and a woman, perhaps husband and wife, running along the path that skirted the boundary of the park. There was the young mother pushing a pram and chatting soothingly to the baby within.

Bella and Luke were enjoying a romp. "He's really taken a shine to Bella," Adam laughed. "They're soul-mates. Both young, with all their lives before them."

Why had he said they had all their life before them? There had been no hint of irony in the remark. She studied Adam's face for a moment. All she saw was an almost imperceptible nod which seemed to say 'Don't worry'.

"It looks as though it is going to rain," Adam observed. "Well, even weather forecasters can't be wrong all the time."

He was right about the rain. Clouds were gathering quite quickly – thick, dark, rain-laden clouds.

Eve suggested they return. She wasn't sorry the walk was being cut short. Although she had prepared for the party as thoroughly as she could, she knew she would feel happier at home, just to keep an eye on things.

"Oh please, can't we stay out a bit longer?" Bella pleaded. "Luke's having a great time."

"Come on Bella," Eve was firm. "You'll get soaked and then you'll catch your death of cold."

"Your mother's right," Adam added.

They turned round and began to retrace their steps. Half way back, the heavens opened.

There was the tree. It was a fine oak tree, with a rich canopy and wide-spreading boughs. No one knew hold old it was but it was certainly older than any living human. It stood there, proud and full, surely ready to take anything the elements threw at it.

Bella headed for the tree. Eve suddenly felt paralysed. Why couldn't she speak? Why couldn't she move? Was she going to have to live through that appalling tragedy all over again?

"Bella, stop!" Adam barked in Nick's voice.

Bella stopped. It was not like Bella to obey so promptly but the tone of the command was compelling. For a moment, it seemed to Eve that everything had stopped. Even the heavy drops of rain seemed suspended in mid air.

"Come here," Adam commanded. Bella trotted back, with Luke by her side. "Where is the very last place we go in a thunder storm?" As he spoke, there was a distant rumble of thunder. Eve didn't remember any thunder. Eve was sure there had been no warning when they had sheltered under the tree – just a flash of lightning, the bough struck, and Bella dead.

"Well?" Adam prompted Bella.

"Under a tree," Bella replied.

"And why is that?" Adam persisted.

Before Bella could answer, the lightning struck. It was an amazing spectacle. The bolt came out of the sky like an enormous, shining, crooked stick, hurtling into the tree where the main boughs forked and then sending rivulets of light and fire down the trunk and along the branches. Flames began to lick along the twigs, forcing the damp leaves to curl up before consuming them. Eve suddenly felt sorry for the tree. This mighty, proud, ancient oak had sustained a blow from which it would not recover. The tree groaned and the bough that had killed Bella fell to the ground. This time it harmed no one. Eve failed to register that this time the thunder had come before the lightning.

Bella's party was a great success. There was a good deal of screaming and squealing and, at the end, half-eaten sandwiches, fragments of cake and sticky plastic mugs everywhere.

"That went pretty well," Adam observed, "if you can measure such occasions by the amount of detritus they leave behind."

They cleared up together. Eve felt completely happy. Bella was alive. The freak event that had taken her life had been avoided, neutralised. Bella was alive and could live her life. She would study, have a career, marry, have children, fly to the moon, do whatever she wanted to do with her time, her talents, her life. Eve began to cry.

"Hey," said Adam, "what's the matter?"

"Nothing," Eve replied. "Nothing at all. It's just that I'm so happy."

That night, when they went to bed, she knew the moment that he touched her, she knew it wasn't Adam.

12 Who shall die?

Adam, Rambler, Numpty and the Storyteller were escorted from the court to a small adjoining room. God had given them one hour to decide who should die.

Numpty sneezed. Not waiting for a rebuke, he explained that it was the dust from the furniture which now assailed and provoked his nasal passages. The room was furnished, if that is not too grand a term, with some very old, musty armchairs and a ragged, dilapidated sofa.

"Is there anything else you're allergic to?" Adam asked. "Feathers, dust! How do you feel about imminent death?"

"Don't take it out on the boy?" Rambler intervened. "It's not his fault we're in this predicament."

Adam felt ashamed. Rambler was right. It wasn't Numpty's fault. If there was any blame it must rest either with Eve for alienating God or with himself for embarking on a quest he had been warned would be hazardous.

"What are we going to do?" he asked, with little hope of a reply. He then added: "Thank God Eve escaped" before realising the idiocy of the remark.

After an embarrassed silence, Rambler suggested they should analyse the situation.

"That's pretty simple," Adam snapped. "We've just been sentenced to death by a psychopathic deity for crimes as yet undefined."

"Perhaps we could explore the possibility of an appeal," Rambler mused.

"I don't think they have any provision for appeals," the Storyteller advised. "You see God sees himself as absolute, so there is no room for appeal."

"Like the Pope," offered Numpty. "There's no arguing with the Pope. He's unfillable."

"I think you mean infallible," Adam corrected before suggesting: "Is there any way we could escape? Maybe one of us could cause a diversion while the rest of us make a run for it."

"I don't think we would have much chance of making good our escape," the Storyteller opined. "We have seen what the Potestates are capable of. You cannot think we could outrun them."

"In any case," Rambler argued, "whoever caused the diversion would surely be caught and killed. Since God only wants to kill one of us, we would be no better off."

The Storyteller seemed to brighten up. "You might have something there."

Both Adam and Rambler looked at him, awaiting an explanation. Since none was offered, Adam probed. "How so?"

"You said God only wants to kill one of us," the Storyteller hinted.

"Oh, I see," said Rambler. "Quite right. I stand corrected."

"What are you two talking about?" Adam was angry and fearful.

"I should have said, 'God wants to kill only one of us'," said Rambler.

"No you shouldn't," the Storyteller insisted. "You were right the first time. I have been here before. We can't always have everything we want, not even God, not if He loses your faith in Him. Pursue that line and all is not lost. Courage, my friends!"

"Well all may not be lost – but I certainly am," said Adam.

"There, you see," said Numpty triumphantly, "my uncle is nobody's fool." With that he struck the arm of the sofa triumphantly, precipitating a cloud of dust.

"Oh dear," said Rambler.

At that moment a two-winged angel entered and asked: "Have you decided who shall die?"

Numpty's sneeze exceeded even Rambler's expectations and, since Numpty had been facing the door when the two-wing entered, the celestial being bore the brunt of Numpty's nasal ejaculation. Some forty thousand particles, some bearing bacteria and viruses, splattered into the angel at around 65 miles an hour. The effect was not dissimilar to God's deconstruction of the hapless Potestate who had failed to detain Eve. The mucus-mired angel shimmered and then, while expressing some disgust at the grossness of Numpty's emissions, began to dissolve.

"My God," Adam exclaimed. "You've killed him."

"Whoops, sorry", offered Numpty, recovering himself and apologising to the fast-dwindling angel.

"'Twould appear my nephew's nose constitutes a lethal celestial weapon, although I fear its employment on this occasion may not elicit divine approbation."

"It's not my fault I sneezed. It's God's fault," Numpty had no intention of taking the blame. "He gave me my nose and loaded it with anti-angel stuff. And He put us in here with all this dust which is His dust. And He gave me my allergies. My allergies are His allergies."

"He didn't seem too keen on taking responsibility for things when we first met Him," said Adam, cutting off Numpty's defence, "and I'm pretty sure He won't take kindly to you decimating the Angelic Host with nasal mucus."

The angel was by now almost entirely gone, having both evaporated and fragmented.

The Storyteller could see this conversation was unlikely to be productive. "Of course the other thing we could do is decide who it is that should die," he suggested. "As plan B," he added hastily. "If all else fails."

"Excuse me," said Adam. "But what's plan A? I must have missed it."

"I'm just suggesting that we had better decide who is going to die, if it turns out there is no alternative."

"No," said Adam emphatically. "No, that would be playing His game, accepting His rules. We should just refuse to co-operate."

"Interesting strategy," the Storyteller mused, noncommittally.

"I agree with Adam," Rambler said. "He is presenting us with an intolerable and unacceptable moral conundrum. We have been condemned without a charge, a trial, a defence or right of appeal, and he is now trying to drag us down to his own level of moral depravity by agreeing amongst ourselves which of us should be slaughtered on the altar of his megalomania."

"Well said." The Storyteller gave a couple of claps.

"You tell Him, Uncle, you tell Him," Numpty urged, starting to perform a war dance. "We don't have to accept this crap from anyone."

"Language, nephew, language!" Rambler chided. To discourage his nephew, when a young child, from using the more offensive swear words, Rambler had deceived his young charge into thinking the mildest of colloquial expressions were in fact absolutely taboo. He had told the young Numpty that even the most incorrigible swearer, the most hardened blasphemer, would be taken aback by words such as 'bum' or 'crap' or 'damn'. Despite his machinations, young Numpty had, from time to time, fallen into bad company and picked up some rather bad habits. Amongst these was the use of truly foul language. The ever-vigilant and conscientious guardian, Rambler had taken Numpty aside on one occasion when he had heard his nephew tell a friend to 'go away and fuck himself' and had told him that, if he really wished to shock, he should tell his friend to 'give his bum a damn good crap'. Numpty had been somewhat confused, querying why he should urge his friend to evacuate his bowels, when his intention had been simply to express irritation and a wish to be left alone. "Why was 'go away and fuck yourself' any more apposite?" his uncle had countered. "At least," he had added, "fucking yourself is impractical, whereas expelling a poo is within everyone's competence, except of course the profoundly and chronically constipated."

"We don't have to take this crap from anyone?" Adam repeated, with more than a hint of sarcasm. "We may not have to take it from anyone, but we may indeed have to take it from God Almighty."

"I'd back my uncle against Almighty God any day," said Numpty, entirely undeterred.

It was while Numpty was eulogising his uncle that the door of the holding chamber opened and another angel of the two-winged variety entered. "Where is Beryss?" the new angel asked.

"Ah," said Rambler, rising to take control of proceedings, "we need to explain. My nephew here," he patted Numpty affectionately on his head, "my nephew Numpty is sadly afflicted by allergies. Particles, which to most of us are innocuous enough, can wreak havoc in my nephew's nasal passages. As a result, he is subject to involuntary ejaculations of bacteria and virus laden moisture, or sneezes. I assume that members of the angelic fraternity are not subject to allergies, nor indeed sneezes, being of a predominantly non-corporeal composition, assuming that is not a contradiction in terms. In mankind, however, allergic reactions are common, and indeed, have become commoner. There is a theory that it is the modern obsession with cleanliness that has intensified the problem. It is possible that I myself may have aggravated, if not caused, the condition in young Numpty through pursuit of an over-protective policy in his early years."

"What has this to do with the whereabouts of Beryss?" The angel seemed impatient and nervous. "You should be back in court. You are keeping everyone waiting."

"I'm afraid we have killed Beryss," Adam said. "It was an accident." Best to be straight and get to the point, he thought. "Numpty sneezed and..." here he hesitated because, having seen the funny side of what he was about to say, thought it best not to say it – but then decided to go ahead anyway. "Numpty sneezed and blew your colleague away."

"You blew Beryss away?" the angel repeated. "How could that be?"

"One of his nasal ejaculations," Adam adopted Rambler's terminology, "inadvertently smacked into your colleague in a full frontal manner when he opened the door. The grossness of the sneeze was evidently too much for his refined essence. I fear this young man, harmless though he may seem to the casual observer, can be lethal." Adam was feeling slightly light-headed and disorientated. He was unsure whether to laugh or cry; his fear made him reckless.

"You have killed Beryss?" The angel seemed unable to comprehend what had happened. "You have killed an angel?"

"Yes," Rambler confirmed, "but it was an accident. It was not intended, nor indeed was there any way we could have foreseen the tragic consequences of Numpty's puissant nasal effusions."

"You must come with me," said the angel. "Now," he added emphatically.

The four companions gathered themselves together for the coming ordeal. "We haven't decided who has to die," Rambler whispered to Adam.

"No, we haven't", said Adam loud enough for the others and the angel to hear. "And we're not going to."

Escorted by the angel, the four made their way back into the court. Rambler put his arm around Numpty's shoulder in a gesture of protection and solidarity. For all his bravado, Numpty was terrified and his uncle knew it.

Adam was surprised at the size of the courtroom. It seemed larger than when they had first stood before God. "It's bigger," he exclaimed.

"Silence," commanded the angel.

"It just seems bigger," the Storyteller addressed Adam, "because God is making us feel smaller. Nothing can be bigger on the inside than it is on the outside and the walls of the building have not moved."

Having lined the defendants up before the dais on which God sat in his burnished throne, the escorting angel hurried over to a senior Potestate and whispered in his ear. There was a brief inaudible exchange between the two angels in which the superior Potestate's face expressed first incredulity and then shock and anger. He then waved his angelic, albeit, lower ranking, colleague back to his station beside the defendants and strode over to Uriel.

Uriel listened to the Potestate. His brow furrowed. Then he spoke.

"Forgive me, Lord of all, for breaching court etiquette, but it seems there are new charges to bring against the defendants."

"Really," God responded, with some sarcasm. "I can't imagine you can bring any more serious charge against the defendants than offending Me. And, since I'm going to execute at least one, if not all, of them, I can't see the point of adding further offences to the charge sheet."

"Murder," Uriel declared, undeterred by God's discouragement and obvious lack of interest. "Murder of a member of the Angelic Host. Beryss, a devoted and faithful enforcer of God's will, Your will," he directed the last two words to God directly, "is no more."

Uriel now had everyone's attention. "Excuse me?" said God.

Uriel spoke slowly, partly to ensure everyone in the assembled throng heard the news and partly to irritate God by implying he was not as sharp as he used to be. Uriel was totally loyal to God but he couldn't stand sarcasm, even if its source was the Almighty. "Beryss was sent by me to bring the defendants back into this court to face their punishment. Unprovoked one of these delinquent mortals struck Beryss without warning, without provocation, and destroyed him."

"A mortal cannot kill an angel." God gave expression to the thought in every angel's mind. "It is against the natural, and supernatural, order of things."

"Nevertheless, Beryss, as I have already said, is no more," Uriel responded.

"Which of you?" God asked with the now familiar rumbling of thunder in his voice, "which of you perpetrated this outrage?" God's eyes were on Adam. Rambler was too old and too discursive to commit murder. The Storyteller had never seemed eager to participate in the proceedings in any way and made a most improbable murder suspect. As for the stripling known as Numpty, he was clearly one of the weaker brethren even by the disgracefully low standards of fallen humanity. God's suspicion focused on Adam.

Before anyone could answer, Rambler intervened: "Dear God, if I may address You so, it is true that the angel Beryss is no more, for which I, on behalf of my companions, express the deepest regret, but there has been no crime. What happened was an accident, an entirely unforeseeable turn of events, almost, one might term it, an act of God."

A murmur of confusion rippled around the Angelic Host.

"Sorry," Rambler tried to explain, "but when something really bad happens in our world, when there's an earthquake or a tsunami and thousands, tens of thousands, of people die, we call it an act of God."

"So that's it, is it?" God was very angry. "You are trying to blame me for Beryss's death. You are accusing Me of killing My own angel. What is the matter with you people? First the woman Eve accuses Me of killing her daughter; now you are accusing Me of killing one of My own."

"No," Uriel whispered in God's ear, "they're not accusing You. It's just an expression. They use 'act of God' to describe any natural, unexplained disaster."

"Well, that in itself is insulting," snapped God, entirely unmollified. "Who killed Beryss?" he returned to the matter in hand. He really felt the need to do some heavy-weight industrial punishing.

"I did, Sir," quaked a very nervous, but very brave Numpty. He knew his uncle wished to protect him but, in the end, the truth would come out, and it would be best if he confessed willingly and quickly.

"Really!" said God, somewhat taken aback. "You don't look up to it. Not that any human is up to it. A mortal killing an angel is profoundly unnatural. But, if I had to pick one of you as the despatcher of a member of the Angelic Host, you would have been bottom of My list of suspects."

"Well that just shows how much You know," Numpty returned, goaded by the Almighty's rather dismissive sentiment.

"Show some respect," his uncle hissed in Numpty's ear. "We stand here in peril of our lives."

"No need to chide the lad," God soothed. "He can be as rude as he likes." He then added, by way of explanation: "Because he is going to die in the most excruciating agony anyway and, obviously, if it's the most excruciating agony already, I can't make it any more excruciating."

"But, my Lord," Rambler stepped forward, "I must protest. It was an accident. It was no more than a sneeze. How could we know that an angel could be annihilated by something as common as an involuntary expulsion of moisture through this lad's nasal passages?"

"Oh, I see, now it's an accident," sneered God. "What a pity the woman Eve isn't here! When it's her daughter, it's my fault. I aimed the lightning that struck the tree that broke the bough that killed Bella. But when this delinquent wilfully spray's some noxious effusion into the face of an angel, I'm supposed to say 'Ah well, these things happen' and forget about it."

"Eve blamed You for Bella's death because You are God," Adam spoke. "Are You seriously asking us to apply the same rules to Numpty as we apply to You?"

Uriel rose. "It is not for you to apply rules of any kind to God Almighty."

"You're missing the point," Adam replied, undeterred and uncowed by the risen Uriel.

"Good for you," murmured the Storyteller. "The hero speaks."

"We are not drawing any parallel, we didn't start this; God did," said Adam.

"Enough!" God thundered at maximum volume. "Numpty must die for killing Beryss. You," and here he indicated Adam, "must die for taking My name in vain. And you," he turned to Rambler, "must die for showing reluctance to allow your nephew to be sacrificed when you should be embracing his death as a way of showing your obedience to Me. And there's something else. That hat you wear is a porkpie hat. I can only assume you chose such headgear on purpose to insult me, knowing, as I'm sure you do, that I have a thing about pork."

There was a quiet hum of excitement in the Angelic Host, a traditional precursor to one of God's spectacular acts of vengeance.

"That just leaves you," God said, addressing the Storyteller. "And you must die as the only one left to stand in for Eve."

13 The place of execution

It took some time to prepare the Hall of Justice for a ceremonial execution.

There was the gallows to erect, and the positioning of the granite slab on which the disembowelling had to take place, and the sharpening of knives to ensure precise butchery.

The defendants were kept in the Hall while the arrangements were made. Uriel took it upon himself to explain, in the most matter-of-fact but profoundly sadistic manner, the process of execution.

"It's not as simple and straightforward as it looks," he confided to the terrified mortals. "First there's the hanging. We have to take into account the subject's weight. It's quite critical. The last thing we want to do when we hang you is to kill you. No, no, no, that wouldn't do at all. There are quite serious penalties for any official who makes that mistake. You have to be alive when we take you down from the gallows and, ideally, conscious. The last bit's not absolutely critical, of course. If you're a bit unconscious we can always wake you up with a bucket of cold water."

Adam managed to interrupt. "This can't be happening. This is God," he indicated the impressive, white-haired, grey-bearded figure on the throne. "God wouldn't do this. This is barbaric. It's what the worst of mankind did at the worst of times in our history."

"You don't know your God, then," Uriel rebuked Adam gently. "Do you not recall that God urged his chosen people to exterminate all those who dwelt in the Land of Canaan – men, women and children. What were his words?...

'When the Lord your God brings you into the land that you are about to enter and occupy, and he clears away many nations before you – the Hittites, the Girgashites, the Amorites, the Canaanites, the Perizzites, the Hivites, and the Jebusites, seven nations mightier and more numerous than you – and when the Lord your God gives them over to you and you defeat them, then you must utterly destroy them.'

"He's not a soft touch, our God, oh no, not by a long chalk. And then there's all those natural disasters. Of course, He doesn't cause them; but He doesn't stop them either. Truth to tell, they give us some welcome light entertainment. You might not think it but sometimes," Uriel added in a confiding, almost conspiratorial, tone, "it can be a tad boring here, and, in any case, such cataclysmic events tend to rekindle worship of God amongst humanity. It's ironic that. Anyway, where was I?"

"You were explaining to us how we are to die," offered the Storyteller. He seemed somewhat less terrified by the prospect of an excruciating death than the others.

"Right," said Uriel, resuming his account with renewed enthusiasm. "When we have you down off the scaffold, we lay you on the sacrificial granite slab. Then one of the archangels, you might even get Michael, takes one of the Lord's ceremonial carving knives, slits you open and removes your intestines. This, if it's well done, doesn't actually kill you, at least not immediately. You will probably lose consciousness because of the extreme pain but we will do everything we can and, given we are superhuman that's quite a lot, everything we can to revive you. The next bit is considered by some simply an abrupt end to a rather messy business but it need not be so. Of course if the beheading is done with a single blow, it is indeed abrupt and bloody, but, if it is done with finesse, it is possible to cut around much of the neck without actually severing an artery. In that way, you can be kept aware of what is happening to you up to the very last moment when we snap off your head and impale it on a spike. The quartering of your body is much appreciated but, at that stage, only by the audience."

None of the defendants spoke. Numpty had wet himself and was clinging to his uncle. Rambler was deathly pale, no longer the avid note-taker, the keen observer; now he was, however reluctantly, at the centre of the action.

"We'll be doing you one at a time," Uriel continued. "So the last of you will have seen your three companions despatched. Difficult to know whether it's best to be first or last. Anyway, not to worry. God decides."

"No," said Adam.

"No?" queried Uriel. "What exactly does 'no' mean?

"Which bit don't you understand?" Adam snapped back. He was turning fear into anger and he felt better for it. "You are a disgrace to your kind. You and your God are evil beyond belief. We will not be butchered by you."

"Really," sneered Uriel. "And what exactly do you intend to do?"

At this moment, purely by chance, Numpty, who had been quietly sobbing, sneezed. His nose had been running for some time and the frenetic activity of the angels in preparing for the executions had no doubt increased the level of angelic feather dust. The combination of agitated mucus membrane through sobbing combined with a higher concentration of dust led inevitably to the sneeze.

On this occasion, the expelled virus-laden moisture diffused harmlessly into the air but Uriel took a step back. Evidence of archangelic fear did not pass unnoticed.

"Perhaps you should bear in the mind the fate of Beryss," said Adam, assuming as menacing a tone as he could muster.

God, who had been following the exchange between Adam and Uriel barked to Uriel: "Get a grip on yourself. He's a mortal about to be executed. No need to engage in conversation with him. Just get on with it. Youngest first."

Uriel nodded to two of the Potestates who had been guarding the defendants. They moved forward to seize young Numpty but they advanced warily, fearful of another nasal effusion. Rambler tried to hold onto to his nephew who was now almost delirious with fear. Adam too stepped forward to protect the young lad but both were swept aside. Rambler's hat was knocked from his head and immediately blasted into non-existence by an over nervous Potestate, hopeful of ingratiating himself with the Almighty by destroying the headgear which, through its porcine associations, had so offended the Creator. Numpty was taken.

The two Potestates rose from the ground, holding Numpty between them and floated over to the scaffold. God shuffled in His seat, turning slightly to get a better view. The Angelic Host generated a persistent hum of excitement.

"Are you ready?" Uriel enquired of the figure that stood by the disembowelling slab of granite. The figure threw back the white hood that had covered his head and concealed his face. The crowd roared its approval. It was the archangel Michael. Michael acknowledged the applause from the Angelic Host and nodded to Uriel.

"Then with the authority vested in me by the Almighty, whose power exceeds even archangelic comprehension…"

"Do get on with it!" God urged.

Uriel knew the likely consequences of his Master's impatience, so he cut to the chase: "I order the hanging, the drawing and the quartering of one Numpty for a crime both evil and unnatural, the destruction of Beryss."

As one of the Potestates placed the rope around Numpty's neck, there was a knocking on the great oak door of the Hall of Justice.

14 We are such stuff

Eve lay in the warm bed, struggling to make sense of the last few hours.

What had she done? She had spent the night with a man who had the physical appearance of her husband but had neither his voice nor his touch. The voice was that of the man who had befriended her when she had become separated from her party, the man who had claimed he alone could reunite her with her husband, the man who had promised to let her see her daughter once again. Yes, it was his voice and, she felt certain it was his touch.

And he had kept his word about letting her see her daughter once again. More than that, he had somehow recut the fabric of reality so that Bella had survived the storm. He had warned Bella not to stand under the tree. He had done what Adam could have done, should have done. He had protected their only child. Bella had not died. She had lived, was still alive.

The telephone rang. No one answered it. She ignored the persistent ringing. It was not her place to answer the phone in Nick Peters' cottage. It might be anyone. It might be his wife, if he had one, for all she knew; or it might even be Adam if he had managed to escape the Garden of Eden and somehow tracked her down. What on earth could she say to Adam if he found her in another man's bed within hours of their enforced separation? How could she explain it? How could she explain it to herself?

And what a night it had been! Her bedfellow had shown the passion of a new lover combined with the awareness and sensitivity of an experienced partner. She had spent the night in an ocean of sensual pleasure with wave after wave licking at every part of her body until she felt she was floating on some higher plane of exquisite physical delight.

The telephone was still ringing. Then it stopped. Eve felt relieved.

There was a knocking on the door. "Are you all right?" enquired an uncertain female voice. "Is it all right for me to do your room? Oh! and there's someone downstairs asking for you."

Eve was confused. She sat up and looked around. This wasn't Nick Peters' cottage; this was the room in the inn. How had she ended up back in the inn? She leapt out of bed and threw on some clothes.

"Coming," she said as she slipped her jeans on. She opened the door. The chambermaid smiled nervously and apologised for disturbing her. "I expect you were very tired. You missed dinner last night and, if you don't hurry, you'll miss breakfast too".

"I'm not hungry," Eve said.

The telephone rang again. "I expect that'll be the gentleman," said the chambermaid. "He's been waiting for you for a good half hour."

Eve answered the phone. It was Nick. "Hi," he said casually, "I hope you had a good night's sleep." There was not a trace of irony in his voice. "I thought we should make some plans," he continued. "After you've had some breakfast, of course."

Eve went downstairs in a daze. The reception area of the inn was just as it had been yesterday.

"Are you OK?" Nick asked. "You look a bit out of it."

Eve studied Nick's face. Not a hint. "I'm fine," she said. She needed time. None of it made any sense.

"Well, if you're sure, let's get some coffee and make plans."

They sat down in a corner of the inn's bar and Nick brought the coffee over.

"We need to decide where to try to intercept your friends, your husband and the others," said Nick. "I know Tel, the Storyteller as you call him. He will want to move on. That's his way. The problem is that there are several options. They could take the B3349, up through Mattingley, take a left to get on to the A33, and then head for Reading. Or they could turn off before Reading on to the M4 and make for Bristol. Or they could go back on to the M3 and head west, or even go back to London."

"I thought we were going to Stoney Cross," Eve said. Her conversation with Nick at his cottage the night before was perfectly clear in her head. He had said that, with a bit of luck, they should be able to catch up with them at Stoney Cross tomorrow. That's what he had said.

"Down the M3," said Nick. "OK. If that's what you think."

"It's not what I think," said Eve sharply. She was tempted to add it was what Nick had told her they should do on the previous evening. But Nick gave no sign they had talked at all about how they should proceed, much less exactly where they should go. "I thought you knew what we had to do," was all she added.

"To be honest," said Nick, "we need to work as a team. I can help but you are really the one who has to choose. It's just the way it is. You won't get back to Adam and the others without me. On the other hand, I can't make it happen unless you take most of the decisions."

15 My son, my son

For a second time, Kit knocked with his stick on the great oak door of the Hall of Justice. At his side was a rather nervous Luke.

"They don't seem very keen to let us in," said Luke. He wanted to be re-united with his master and mistress more than anything but he was intimidated by the impressive building and the great oak door that remained stubbornly closed.

"They will probably be even less keen when they know who it is," Kit chuckled.

Luke felt fear begin to gnaw away at his stomach. "Have you been in trouble here before?"

"I've certainly been here before," Kit answered. "And I suppose it's fair to say I have been in the middle of some trouble. Some would say I was the cause of the trouble. But I wouldn't say I had really been in trouble."

"Perhaps I could find another way in," suggested Luke, "a side entrance or even an open window." His concern was growing and Kit's remarks were doing nothing to set his mind at ease.

Kit struck the door a third time. The stick connected with one of the iron supports and a long reverberating clanging ensued. "That should do the trick," said Kit.

In the Hall of Justice only God had heard the first knock. He had waved a divine hand and silence had followed. Numpty was standing on a stool on tip-toes trying to relieve the tightness of the rope around his neck. He wanted to live. At the same time, he wanted to die before they took him down and cut him open. Adam was struggling with two Potestates. They had gagged his mouth to silence the raging diatribe, liberally peppered with expletives, with which he was expressing his contempt for the Creator. Rambler too had struggled to protect his nephew but, with his fear greater than his anger, it took only one Potestate restrain him.

"It is him," said God. "It is him."

"How can You know?" asked Uriel.

"I know," said God emphatically. "It is him. Perhaps, at last, he will acknowledge me."

"Let us at least complete the execution of the callow youth, the murderer of Beryss, he of the aimless mind but puissant, noxious, lethal nose," Uriel urged.

There was a second knock. All the assembled host heard the sound this time, and all could see from the lined, strained face of God that this was no ordinary visitor.

Since God had not actually forbidden it, Uriel nodded to one of the Potestates on the scaffold to kick the stool away from Numpty's feet. The archangel was determined to see the one who had defied nature by killing an angel, albeit one of lower rank, destroyed in the prescribed manner. The execution would restore order. The Potestate approached Numpty to obey Uriel's command.

It was not a sneeze this time, more an effusion of tears, nasal congestion and some mucus, ejaculated from Numpty's mouth, in a frothy mixture, as he tried to appeal for mercy. The Potestate first reaction was disgust, quickly followed by the realisation that the deeply offensive spray which had splattered on to his face could not simply be wiped away. "Sorry," said Numpty. It was an involuntary apology. "Oh my God," said the Potestate. "I am defiled." The feathers of his wings began to turn brown and droop.

"He's done it again!" exclaimed Uriel with a mixture of anger and horror. There was a gasp from the assembled host as those nearby saw the damage Numpty had wrought on one of their own and those further away learned of it by word of mouth.

"Quite extraordinary," Rambler remarked. "I wonder if any of us could do it, or whether it is a gift peculiar to Numpty."

Adam said nothing, for his mouth was gagged, but the same thought had crossed Adam's mind. If they all had Numpty's 'gift', then maybe they weren't as powerless and vulnerable as they had thought.

There was a third knock. This time the sound resonated through the entire Hall and continued to reverberate for almost a minute.

"Go," commanded God. "Disperse the host of angels. This court is no longer sitting. I must speak with him. Do it."

Uriel knew further resistance would be pointless. "You heard what God said," he barked.

The host of angels departed. "Am I to leave you with these felons?" Uriel asked.

"Just leave," God answered. "And let him in."

When Kit entered the Hall, with Luke at his side, there was a squeal of delight from the scaffold, followed by a choking noise. In his excitement at seeing Luke, Numpty had toppled off the stool and was now choking at the end of the rope. Adam and Rambler, no longer restrained by Potestates, rushed to the scaffold and, while Adam lifted Numpty's body, Rambler loosened and removed the noose.

"My dear boy!" said Rambler, "are you all right?"

"Well enough, Uncle," Numpty answered, "although my neck aches and my throat is sore."

"Silence," God demanded. "You have returned," he addressed Kit.

"It would seem so," Kit replied.

"It is good to see you once again." There was a strange tone in God's voice. There was a warmth and a sadness. It was almost as though God was asking, perhaps even begging, for something.

"I'm sorry I can't say the same," said Kit. It was unclear whether Kit was rejecting God's overtures or whether he was simply referring light-heartedly to his blindness.

"Have you considered what I said at our last meeting?" God asked.

"What can I say?" Kit replied.

"You could say 'Yes'," God suggested.

"Very well," said Kit. "Yes, I have considered what you said, and what I said, and I'm afraid, as a result, I have concluded there is little more to be said."

"Then why have you come here, why have you come back?" God asked with the hard edge returning to his voice.

"I have come here," said Kit, "mainly because of this rather handsome dog. I was out for one of my walks when I heard a couple of thugs tormenting this poor creature. I intervened. I learned the dog had been abandoned when another bunch of thugs, though I understand this lot were official thugs, seized this dog's master and his companions and dragged them off to this so-called Hall of Justice. Well, I couldn't let that happen, now could I?"

"You seem to be in an intervening phase of your life," God observed. "And now you are here, what do you propose to do?"

"That's easy," said Kit. "I'm going to take these good people and set them on their way. I'm reliably informed they have done nothing wrong and, even if they had, I'm sure You could find it in Your heart to forgive them."

God scowled. "And if I chose not to let them go. If I decide to continue with the judgement against them. If I have them hanged, disembowelled and dismembered, what will you do?"

Kit smiled. "I think You know the answer," he said.

There was an audible choking in the divine voice when God said, "My son, my son, why has thou forsaken me?"

16 Things paternal

Kit walked with them from the Hall of Justice through God's land all the way to the Gate of the Garden of Eden and as they walked they talked.

"How did you do this?" Adam voiced the question in everyone's mind. How had a blind man with a walking stick tamed the all powerful Creator of the entire universe?

"Well," said Kit with a chuckle and, had he not been blind, a gleam in his eye, "it's a strange story."

"Then why don't we rest by this stream, take some food and refreshment, and listen to your tale?" said the Storyteller. "We are not far from the Gate but there is no need to hurry. No one will try to stop us leaving. So let's sit here and listen to your story. After all, you have saved our lives and we are all curious to know how you managed it."

"Well, if you boil it down to its bare bones, it's all based on a misunderstanding," Kit said, as he sat himself down on a boulder covered in dry moss.

"Go on," said the Storyteller, as he and the others settled at Kit's feet.

"What was that about food and refreshment?" queried Rambler. He had been hungry since their meeting with the angels Rodney and Derek.

"I have some bread, enough for all of us," said Kit, opening the knapsack he carried with him. "But I have no meat or cheese."

"I can catch some fish in the stream," offered Numpty. "Luke and I will catch them."

Luke got up and wagged his tale. He had little confidence in Numpty's fishing expertise but, it was worth a try and he had grown fond of the lad.

"It's a strange tale," Kit resumed. "I was staying at a nearby inn. I travel a good deal and I know the best places to stay. There's a very nice hostelry not that far from here. Anyway, I went out for a walk."

"When was this?" Rambler asked. Kit couldn't see but Rambler had produced his notebook and was keen to catch the timeline of Kit's tale.

"Well, there you have me," Kit replied. I've been wandering around here or hereabouts, for some time, but for exactly how long, I'm just not sure."

"Does it matter?" Adam threw at Rambler. He was impatient for Kit to continue with his story.

"It's odd," said Kit. "Obviously, this place was strange, and yet I felt very much at home as soon as I wandered into it. I found my way around, and food and shelter, without any real effort. It was almost as though I was being looked after by some unseen beings." Then he laughed. "They'd have to be unseen, wouldn't they?"

The others smiled at Kit's light-hearted reference to his blindness.

"All was going rather well, when I was visited by a fellow who claimed he worked for the Lord. He said that the Lord wished to see me and that I should go with him."

"We've caught one," screamed Numpty. "We've caught a fish." Truth to tell, it was Luke who had caught the fish but he was more than happy to share the triumph with his new friend.

"Well done," Rambler called over to his nephew, and then added "Sorry", addressed to Kit.

"So I went with him. My time is very much my own and I thought, 'Why not?' I hoped I hadn't been trespassing or anything like that, anything that might have offended the Lord. Of course, I assumed the Lord in question was the Lord of the Estate or Lord of the Manor, or some such Lord.

"My companion or escort took me into the heart of the Garden, the Garden of Eden he called it, a bit of hyperbole from an over proud gardener I guessed. There I met...," here Kit paused.

"God," prompted Rambler.

"Yes, God," Kit agreed. "At least that's who He said He was."

"I can understand your reservations," Adam spoke. "We found it difficult to accept."

"Yes," Kit continued, "but that wasn't the half of it. He said He was God and He also said I was His son. Indeed, He was pretty emphatic about the paternity."

"You were His son," Rambler said slowly.

"Yes, that's what He said," Kit confirmed.

"But why would He think you were His son?" Adam queried.

"There are two answers to that," Kit responded. "There's a series of coincidences and there's some history, especially of the psychological kind. I'll start with the coincidences because they are easy to explain, and easy to explain away.

"My name is Christopher, Kit for short. My father was Joe Turner and my mother was Mary. They're both dead now. God was convinced that, because my name had Christ in it, and my father was Joe (he assumed it was short for Joseph) and my mother was Mary, I must be the original Jesus. I thought He was joking to start with. I told Him my father had been christened Joe; it wasn't short for Joseph or anything else. And I told Him Mary was one of the commonest girl's names. He said 'What about 'Turner'?' That proved I must have come from a family of wood-workers because carpenters 'turned' wood to make chair and table legs. I told Him my dad was a welder and that Turner was a pretty common surname. I asked Him if His son had been born blind. He said 'Yes, metaphorically', whatever that meant. I just couldn't get through to Him. So I tried a different tack. I asked Him to tell me about His son.

"He said, since I was His son, there was nothing He could tell me that I didn't already know, but He agreed to humour me. He said He had sent me down to earth as a mortal to knock some sense into you, the human race. He said He had tried to sort you out through prophets and natural disasters but it just wasn't working. He said He had realised that what the human race needed was leadership, not revelation."

"We've caught another one," shouted Numpty. This time his claim was fully justified. He had managed to spear a fish with a sharpened wooden stick and was now waving the still squirming, impaled prey above his head, like an animated flag.

"Very good," said Rambler, "but there's no need to tell us every time you catch one. See if you can catch one for each of us and then bring them here for us to cook them. You are doing very well, you and the dog," he added to ensure he had not discouraged his enthusiastic charge.

"So He sent you to be the leader," Adam prompted Kit.

"He arranged for me to be born which He said was difficult, even for God. Putting the divine essence through a womb is no mean trick apparently. My mission, which I had to accept whether I liked it or not, was to take over, punish anyone who opposed God's will and get things back on track."

"Take over?" Rambler queried.

"Yes," Kit said, "take over, take over everything. God told me I could work with the Romans. He said the Romans hadn't got the message about obedience to God but they certainly knew how to impose discipline. He liked that. He suggested I should replace the Roman Emperor and use my position as the leader of Imperial Rome to kick some devotion into the masses. He said He would support the Roman legions with natural disasters, as and when required, but that it was up to me to explain to humanity in the clearest of terms 'what they were for' which, according to God, they had either forgotten or never understood. Above all, I should make it clear that the consequences of disobedience would be unimaginably unpleasant."

"But that's not what Jesus did," Adam interrupted.

"No. Quite. And that's the psychological history bit. Jesus didn't do what his Father wanted."

"The classic father/son conflict," mused Rambler. "The son asserts his individuality and independence and the father feels diminished. He loses control over the being he has created."

Kit shrugged. "I guess so, though I never had a falling out with my own father, my real father. Anyway, the long and the short of it is 'they lost touch'. That's how God put it, though if He was really God and Jesus was His son, 'losing touch' doesn't really do justice to a separation measured in millennia."

"It's possible," Rambler suggested, "that two millennia is not that long for God who is, after all, eternal."

"No, but it's a hell of a long time for anyone born of a woman's womb," Adam countered. "So God has been pining for the son He rejected two thousand years ago and you happen along. On the flimsiest of excuses, He decides you're His long lost son. It all seems totally bizarre. What does He want from you? Forgiveness?"

"No," Kit laughed. "No, the Old Bugger is set in his ways. He wants me to apologise, to admit I was wrong and that I failed Him. Most of all, He wants me to acknowledge Him."

"When you refer to Him as 'the Old Bugger', am I to take it that you do not believe He is God?" Rambler asked.

"I've no idea," said Kit happily, "and I don't really care. I just know for certain He is not my father and I am not His son."

"Why is it so important to Him that you acknowledge Him as your father?" asked Adam.

"I'm not sure. I think it's to do with obedience. He's got this thing about people doing what He wants. He seems to think we owe it to Him. He sees Himself as the Great Father and humanity as a rather large family of children. If I am His son, not just in the sense that we are all God's children, but literally His son, whatever that might mean, I more than anyone must owe Him obedience and my disobedience is therefore all the more reprehensible and His disappointment and resentment all the more justifiable. So He's desperate for me to accept that He's my Father. But I'm not and I won't."

"That's all a bit convoluted," said Rambler who had made several attempts to record Kit's analysis of God's psyche only to cross each effort out to start again.

"The funny thing is," Kit mused, "my refusal to acknowledge Him seems to give me some power over Him. He won't cross me. That's how I knew I could rescue you. At my first meeting with Him, He threw this wobbly about how He would smite all those who sinned, and that meant He wouldn't mind smiting all humankind because you were all sinners. Just as a joke, I said, 'Let him who is without sin cast the first stone'. He exploded with rage. He said 'That proves it'. He said I could no longer deny my provenance since I was still spouting the same drivel I had spewed forth when I was born in Palestine. He was really angry but I knew it was the anger of weakness, not strength. So I said it certainly wasn't drivel. I tried a few more quotes from the New Testament. Each one seemed to cut Him and weaken Him. His anger lessened. By the time I finished I could tell from His voice He was close to tears, so I showed a bit of mercy – and that seemed to upset Him even more."

"Well whatever your power over Him, it certainly worked. One minute He was preparing to disembowel us; the next, after your intervention, we were free to leave." Rambler put his pencil away and shook Kit's hand. "It's nothing less than a miracle."

"Seems to me we have a bit of a paradox here," Adam mused. "The original Jesus claimed to be the Son of God but at the end, his father forsook him. Now we have God desperate to assert His paternity and a son who denies Him."

"I'm not His son," Kit corrected. "He may think I'm His son, just as Jesus thought God was His father. But I have no doubts. I know who I am. I'm a Turner through and through."

Numpty rejoined the group. "How many have you caught?" his uncle asked.

"Just the two," Numpty replied. "They worked out what we were doing after the first two and kept out of reach."

"Not to worry," said Kit. "They'll be enough for all of us if we share the bread." He was right, though it has to be said more by luck than judgement since he couldn't see that the fish were indeed of a good size.

17 The odd couple

Just before Adam and Eve and the others had entered the Garden of Eden, Nick Peters and Grimrose had observed them from an excellent position in the trees that surrounded the grounds of the country house hotel.

"They will leave Gwoat behind. He's no use to them in the Garden. They will expect him to wait for them and guard the van," Nick mused. "Ideally, we need to get rid of him and the van. That way we can put an end to the quest before they go any further."

"What do you want me to do?" asked Grimrose. He was currently in the form of a middle-aged, respectable middle-class gentleman, of medium height and medium weight, obviously with a middling income. When not on a job, he felt most comfortable in this guise. It was certainly a relief to have abandoned the form of Rose, partly because of the gender conflict and partly because it had cast him in an uncomfortable implicit relationship with Peters. "Would you like me to discombobulate Gwoat and his van?"

"Discombobulate!" Nick repeated. "You really are a prat."

"What now?" asked Grimrose defensively.

"If you don't know what a word means, don't use it," Nick snapped back. "I don't want you to 'discombobulate' him. I want him gone, blanked out, no longer extant, destroyed, annihilated. Not merely discombobulated. Discombobulation is for pussies."

"Right, right," said Grimrose. Evidently Peters was in one of his carping moods. "Fine. So what do you want me to do?"

Nick paused. "Well I want him dead but it's no use just slitting his throat here. That would cause a fuss. We would have the police all over the place. If the questors manage to get out of the Garden, they might think someone was prepared to do anything to put them off their quest and, given human nature, that would probably make them more determined than ever to pursue it."

"I could simply knock him out and set fire to the van," Grimrose suggested.

"How exactly does that help?" asked Nick with ill-concealed contempt. "We would still have the police. And we would have the added element of mystery. 'Irish van driver spontaneously combusts in Hampshire lay-by'."

"He could have had an accident with the calor gas," mumbled Grimrose. He knew it was pointless. Even if he came up with a brilliant, fool-proof plan, Nick would dismiss it with contempt.

"No," said Nick, "we need to persuade him to drive the van far away. We can then dispose of him and the van in such a way that no one knows who he is. And the questors will think he got bored, fed up with waiting and drove off somewhere."

"And how do we persuade him to drive off?" Grimrose hit back. He could pick nits with the best of them. "He would be disobeying the Storyteller's explicit instructions and the Storyteller is his employer. In any case, he seems to be a pretty loyal sort of person."

"You're absolutely right," said Nick. "That's why I want you to become a fairy."

"What?" exclaimed Grimrose. "What did you say?"

"You heard me," Nick returned. "He's Irish, right? Ireland is the land of the fairies, right? If you come to him in the form of a fairy, it will stir up all that atavistic nonsense about elves and pixies. We know he's not all there to start with – all that fidgeting and jumping about and flatulence. Anyway, he'll think you've come from the Garden. Tell him you have orders direct from the Storyteller that he should make his way down the M3 and then on to the A31. Tell him the questors will meet him at, say, Stoney Cross. He'll believe you because obviously you'll present the appearance of a good fairy, white tutu, etc."

"He's not the only one who's not all there," Grimrose responded with uncharacteristic vehemence. "There are limits you know, even to my grovelling obsequiousness. You cannot be serious."

"Never more so," Nick responded entirely unperturbed. "You are to wait until the Storyteller and his companions have entered Eden. Then, it's into the tutu, and off to sprinkle fairy dust all over Gwoat."

"Do you not understand", Grimrose explained, "that, although I can shift shape, I cannot reduce my body mass beyond a certain point? I cannot adopt fairylike proportions. It just can't be done."

"Do your best," Nick said, evidently tiring of the exchange. "OK, so you'll be a slightly large fairy. You can say you're the Queen of the Fairies, or that you're a giant among fairies, or that your fay parents weaned you on growth hormone. It doesn't matter, so long as he thinks you're magical, and an honest messenger from the Storyteller. You can skip the tutu, if you like. We don't want you looking at all grotesque, now do we? Just get him to drive away. Go with him to Stoney Cross. Find a quiet spot. Then you can slit his throat and burn the van. How's that?"

"I can try," Grimrose yielded, "because I have no choice in the matter but I wish to register my reservations."

"Noted," said Nick. "Isn't that where all those Indians who didn't do what they were told ended up? Ah look," he added, "They've entered

106

Eden, so why don't you get on with it?"

With that, Nick Peters walked back to his motorbike, swung a long leg over the machine, hit the starter button and was off.

To the casual observer, Grimrose's contortions as he tried to form and reduce himself into a shape that could be mistaken for a fairy would have seemed much like a large globule of jelly being pulverised by powerful, merciless, unseen hands. There was much squeaking and squelching, and grunting and sighing. By the time he had finished, Grimrose had reduced his height by half but his girth had increased substantially. He had compacted his mass as much as possible but, as he had told Nick, there were limits. He, or rather she, for a fairy must be female, was now certainly the fattest fairy ever to emigrate from Ireland. She was also almost certainly the ugliest because, however hard she tried, she could not reduce the florid complexion that such compression of Grimrose's entire mass inevitably entailed. "Well," she said to herself, "If I can't charm him or magic him, I'm pretty sure I can frighten him into driving away."

Grimrose, now in fairy guise or as close to it as she could get, waddled over to Gwoat, who had his head under the bonnet of the van, checking the oil, while humming nervously.

"I come from the Garden of Eden, flying on gossamer wings, to bring you a message of gravest import from him whom you call the Storyteller," Grimrose tried. She waited for a reply. None came. She repeated her message more loudly.

"I'm just a little bit busy at the moment," Gwoat answered from beneath the bonnet. He was worried that the van was using too much oil and in any case, although Grimrose had repeated her message twice, Gwoat had missed most of it, being preoccupied with things mechanical. It was also the case that Grimrose, in diminishing his stature and changing his sex, had inadvertently raised the pitch and lowered the normal volume of his voice.

Desperate to attract Gwoat's attention, Grimrose thwacked Gwoat across the back of his knees with a twig which she was using as a makeshift wand.

"Ouch!" said Gwoat, followed by another "ouch!" when he hit his head on the raised bonnet of the van, followed by an almost hysterical "Be Jazuuus!"

"I come from the Garden of Eden...," Grimrose began for the third time.

"Mother of Christ!" screamed Gwoat, backing away and then hopping from one foot to the other. "What, what, what... are you?" he managed to get out at last.

107

Grimrose seized the opportunity: "I come from the Garden of Eden to bring you a message of gravest import from him whom you call the Storyteller." She dropped the 'gossamer wings' bit since she didn't have any and, given her gross weight, would not have been able to get off the ground without the aid of engines from a Harrier jump jet.

"No," said Gwoat. "I mean what are you?"

That kind of question was always a problem for a shapeshifter. When you can adopt almost any organic form, it's quite hard to define what you are in physical terms. This existential problem was aggravated on this occasion by Grimrose's far from successful attempt to pass herself off as a fairy. "I am of fairy stock," was the best she could do.

"You're not like any fairy I've seen," observed Gwoat, desperately trying to compose himself and to drive the fear from the pit of his rumbling stomach.

"And how many fairies would that be?" Grimrose asked, clearly hurt.

"I meant you're not like any of the pictures of fairies that I've seen," Gwoat explained. "Are you sure you're not a gnome?"

This was all Nick's fault. He had warned Nick that a fairy was out of his range. And a gnome would have done just as well. Gnomes had magic, not in the fairy class, but magic nonetheless. A gnome could have carried the message just as well as a fairy. In fact a gnome would have had more gravitas. "Bugger," she thought and then, inspired, added, "My mother was indeed a gnome. 'Twas my father who was the fairy."

"Fairies can't cross-breed with gnomes," said Gwoat dismissively. "And wouldn't want to," he added as an afterthought. "In any case, fairies are female, aren't they?"

Grimrose pushed his tongue to the back of his front teeth, just touching the roof of his mouth and then withdrew it abruptly to make that noise that indicates mild contempt for another's ignorance or stupidity. "If all fairies were female, they would soon die out, now wouldn't they?"

"I thought fairies were born when the sun shone on the morning dew on Christmas Day. I had no idea they engaged in rumpsy dumpsy. And, if they did, I can't believe they'd do it with gnomes," Gwoat returned.

'Now we're an expert on fay folk interbreeding, are we?' thought Grimrose. She puffed out her chest: "My parents fell in love and received a special dispensation from the local wizard," she explained. "It was indeed an odd match but," and at this point her voice took on a distant, dreamlike tone, "as it turned out, a deeply, happy, fulfilling and enduring one." What, Grimrose asked herself, what on earth was she doing, expounding fake fairy lore to a camper van driver, albeit an Irish one?

"Well, if you really are the offspring of a fairy and a gnome, I'm guessing you took after your mother." Gwoat had calmed down a little and had ceased hopping from one foot to the other.

"You really shouldn't impose your human aesthetic on beings of another kind," Grimrose chided. "To a gnome, a gnome can be beautiful." As a shapeshifter, Grimrose genuinely understood the relativity of beauty. "Somewhere in this world, there will be someone who finds even a creature such as yourself," her face adopted and bestowed a kindly smile on Gwoat, "if not attractive, at least tolerable."

"That's very kind of you," said Gwoat, "But I'll have you know I do all right in the lady stakes. In fact, I do better than all right." His claim to success with the fairer sex was unfairly suborned by the involuntary emission of a resounding, reverberating and lingering fart. All that fidgeting, combined with the shock of seeing Grimrose in his contorted fairy-gnome guise, had conspired to engender a considerable volume of gas in the Irishman's lower bowel which, in the end, he had no alternative but to expel.

"And is that one of your subtler attractions for the ladies?" asked Grimrose, pulling away from Gwoat as the noxious fumes spread like a pyroclastic cloud from the Irishman's nether regions.

"If you weren't very small, already extremely ugly and, here I'm guessing, of the female gender, I'd be sorely tempted to effect an introduction between my boot and your face." Gwoat's flatulence caused him much embarrassment, which he tended to hide behind forced anger.

"If such an introduction rendered me unconscious," said Grimrose, holding her nose, "I should be eternally grateful."

"You could always just go away," suggested Gwoat, eager to be rid of this freakish interlocutor.

"Sadly, I cannot leave until I have delivered my message and am sure you will obey," said Grimrose in a conciliatory tone. "Your master, the Storyteller, bids you to depart down the M3, on to the M27 and thence on to the A31, seeking out the place known as Stoney Cross. There he and his party will meet you as soon as they have left the Garden."

"And how are they supposed to get to Stoney Cross if I'm not here to drive them, tell me that?" Gwoat asked.

"Ah," said Grimrose, desperately trying to think of a plausible answer. "When they leave the Garden they will depart, not as they entered, but through a portal which, as it happens, opens onto a deserted area at Stoney Cross."

Gwoat, who had travelled far and wide with the Storyteller, was familiar with the portal phenomenon. They had made much use of it in the past, not just to shorten journeys but also to leap back and forth in time. "Why Stoney Cross?" he asked.

"Because the Storyteller knows that the next part of the quest begins at Stoney Cross." Grimrose was winging it but he knew Gwoat was programmed to follow the Storyteller's instructions. So long as Gwoat believed the message came from his master, he would obey. Grimrose continued: "Adam and Eve are keen to pursue their quest, and Rambler and his nephew Numpty are happy to proceed to Stoney Cross as it is on the way to their destination in the West Country."

Gwoat nodded. Evidently, the fairy-gnome knew the identity of all those in the Storyteller's party and what they were planning to do. And why would the fairy-gnome lie? It was of course all very worrying but it did make sense in a way. Gwoat nodded again. "In that case, I'll just top up the engine oil and I'll be on my way."

"*We'll* be on *our* way," Grimrose corrected. "The Storyteller was most explicit on this point. I should accompany you to Stoney Cross for it is not impossible I may be of further service when we all meet there."

"That's up to you," said Gwoat. "I can put up with your company if you can put up with the odd fart."

When Gwoat was satisfied the camper van could survive the next leg of the journey, he started the engine. Having invented a fairy-gnome interbreeding provenance, Grimrose took the opportunity to expand a little to make herself more comfortable for the journey. She morphed gnomewards, adding an inch or two to her height and making a similar adjustment to her girth. She thought to herself that Gwoat probably wouldn't notice such enlargements and, if he did, well, what the hell, it was all just magic.

They quickly found their way back onto the M3. For the first few miles, Gwoat said nothing and Grimrose was content to remain silent. After all, she had to slit the man's throat, so any unnecessary intercourse between them could only complicate matters.

As they approached Basingstoke, Gwoat pulled out two bars of chocolate, offering one to Grimrose, who declined it. Gwoat chomped his way through his bar and then consumed the one he had offered to Grimrose. It was in Gwoat's nature to worry and he was beginning to feel distinctly uneasy. Although Grimrose has been peculiarly well-informed, it still seemed odd that so soon after entering the Garden, the Storyteller had determined they should meet at a distant place, especially as, before he entered the Garden, he had been so emphatic that Gwoat should wait for them at the entrance.

Gwoat began to quiz his companion about the world of magic that must have been her home. It was, after all, a unique opportunity for Gwoat, as a thoroughbred Irishman, to brush up on his fairy lore but his real purpose was to gauge Grimrose's integrity.

"Is it coming from a large family that you are?" he asked, exaggerating his Irishness to justify his curiosity.

"No," Grimrose answered, "I am an only child."

Gwoat was prepared to accept that any sane couple whose mating had produced a Grimrose, would probably call it a day procreationally.

"Do you have any magic?" Gwoat persisted.

Grimrose was wary. She could surely shapeshift which, to a non shapeshifter, would seem like magic but she certainly didn't wish to reveal that particular talent. It would only serve to raise more doubts in Gwoat's troubled mind, especially as shapeshifters tended to have a reputation, not entirely undeserved, for dissembling. "I can do a few tricks," Grimrose replied cagily, "but my ability has been somewhat repressed by the gnomic side of things."

"Like what?" Gwoat was not to be fobbed off.

"Oh, just this and that," Grimrose replied. She was out of her depth. She knew that the more Gwoat asked, the less coherent and convincing would be the answers. "I can make a flower wilt," she hazarded.

"That's an odd use of magic, to be sure," Gwoat opined. "I thought fairies were fond of flowers." None of this rang true in the Irishman's ears. In fact the only things ringing in Gwoat's ears were warning bells. "What else?"

Grimrose thought of saying: 'I could turn into a very large gorilla and rip you limb from limb' but decided against it. "That's about all," was her lame response.

"Well, I don't mean to be rude but that's a tad disappointing. Are you telling me that a being such as you, with two magic bloodlines running through your veins, can do nothing more than make flowers wilt? And that's not a particularly nice thing to do anyway."

"Well, I guess that's the gnome coming out in me. Gnomes are not well-versed in the magical arts, not compared to fairies, and I'll have you know flower-wilting is a gnomic speciality and competence in wilting is highly regarded in gnomic circles," Grimrose responded rather petulantly.

"So you don't grant three wishes, or turn mice into horses, or leave silver for teeth?" Gwoat probed. "The gnome blood must have been so strong in your mother it utterly overwhelmed your father – who was, after all, to be sure, just a big fairy."

Gwoat realised his last remark could be construed as provocative. Still unsure of Grimrose's authenticity and even less sure of his own ground, the Irishman suddenly felt the gases building up in his bowels. Rather than cause further offence to his strange travelling companion, he decided to take the slip road off to Winchester services which, fortuitously, they had just reached. He pulled in to the service station and parked to right on the side allocated for those who wished to use the shop without buying fuel.

"I just need to stretch my legs", Gwoat explained, as he climbed out of the van, walked a few paces and let rip. "My God!," muttered Grimrose to herself, "that's a stretch that could rend a bloody great hole in the fabric of time."

"Feeling better?" she enquired when Gwoat returned.

Gwoat was a little embarrassed. He had been hoping for a gentle, controlled and above all silent easing, but the build-up of gases had been too long constrained and, on release, a little like thunder, the relief of his lower bowel had been accompanied by a profoundly audible sonic boom.

"Have you ever thought that it might be your predilection for chocolate that wreaks havoc with your gastric juices?" Grimrose enquired solicitously, eager to divert the conversation away from her notional magical abilities.

"It's nothing to do with chocolate," Gwoat responded indignantly. "It's a condition engendered by a genetic disorder aggravated by worry and it's worrying about my genetic disorder which aggravates my condition. If anything, chocolate alleviates my condition by distracting my attention from my genetic disorder, thereby reducing my capacity for worry."

Gwoat was standing by the van on the passenger side in this exchange with Grimrose, who had remained seated and was conversing through the open window. A young girl, dark-haired, with white, translucent skin, no more than twenty and probably younger, walked up to Gwoat, smiled and asked him if he was heading towards Bournemouth.

"I think we are," he replied, "heading towards but not actually going there."

"Well, could you take us as far as you are going?" the girl asked.

"Us?" Gwoat queried.

A young man, as pleasant-looking as the girl, came over to the van. He had light brown hair and gentle blue eyes. "Sorry about Maizy," he said. "She just asks anyone. No shame. I'm Sandy, by the way. Now

112

we've introduced ourselves," he said with an easy smile, "is there any chance of a lift?"

"No," said Grimrose from inside the camper van. "Sorry but we're in a hurry." She realised it was a pretty stupid excuse as soon as she had said it.

The young man was even quicker. "No problem. We're ready to leave as soon as you are." He peered briefly into the van to see more clearly who had spoken. It was a very small person because the eyes of the owner were not much above the bottom of the car window.

"Hold on," said Gwoat. "It's my van and I'm the driver. This," and here he hesitated, "she is just a passenger. I decide who rides in my van."

"Please," said Maizy. "We won't be any trouble."

Gwoat mused and frowned and hopped a little, and then, mainly because Grimrose had said no, he said yes.

"You're a sweety," cooed Maizy. "We'll just grab our bags and be back in a jiffy."

Sandy and Maizy trotted back to where they had left their rucksacks, laughing and joking.

"Nice van," said Sandy. "Looks really well equipped."

"It's perfect," Maizy replied. "Just make sure you don't get any blood on the furnishings."

18 Talk around the fire

Kit was right; there was more than enough fish for everyone and, although it was cooked crudely on a makeshift barbecue, it tasted as good as any meal any of them had ever eaten.

By the time they had finished and cleared up as best they could, the sun was setting. "We will sleep here tonight," said the Storyteller. "Tomorrow, we leave the Garden."

"What about Eve?" Adam said. "I want to find her as soon as possible, to let her know we are safe."

"Don't worry about Eve," the Storyteller responded. "She is safe and well and you will be together again soon enough."

Adam was not really satisfied but before he could pursue the matter, the Storyteller looked him in the eye and asked: "Well?"

"Well what?" Adam responded.

"You have just been through an extraordinary experience. You have stood in the presence of God. You have consorted with angels. You have been judged and condemned. You have come close to death, and a peculiarly unpleasant death at that. So I say again 'Well?' – by which I mean what do you make of it all?"

"Well, if you mean do I think I am any closer to finding the truth, the answer is a resounding no," Adam replied. "The God we met was grotesque, a psychological cripple, mean, spiteful, vindictive, corrupted by power. I'd be better off asking Numpty here for answers to my questions."

"What is he saying, Uncle?" Numpty enquired, unsure whether Adam's reference to him was a compliment or an insult.

"He's saying you are smarter than God," said Rambler, patting his nephew on the arm.

"Isn't that blasphemy?" Numpty asked, apparently mildly shocked but secretly pleased.

"Don't be despondent," advised the Storyteller, addressing Adam. "When all that is false is eliminated, what is left will be the truth."

Adam was unconvinced. "That could be a rather long and, if our recent experience is a reliable guide, dangerous way of proceeding. And it presupposes there is a truth."

"You're right, absolutely right," replied the Storyteller. "But we are at least able to set God, that particular God, to one side. Is there anything at all positive that you have been able to take out of this adventure?"

Adam pondered. "Not really," he said eventually. "It's been a terrifying experience. I have felt fear; and I have felt anger. And I have wondered if any of it was real. I guess I realised we were stronger if we stuck together but, even sticking together wouldn't have done any good if Kit here hadn't intervened. No, I don't think I've learnt anything, other than perhaps next time to check out with you more thoroughly where we are going before we go there."

"I learned a number of things," offered Rambler. "I saw for myself that power corrupts. I discovered that my nephew is even braver than I thought. I observed that the best antidote to fear is anger. I very much enjoyed our chat with Rodney and Derek. I have taken copious notes which I shall study and revise at my leisure. And I deduced that the status of angels is determined by the number of their wings. Or that the number of an angel's wings is determined by their status. I'm not sure which. While I have the greatest respect for statistics, I find them to be rather tricky, sometimes devious."

Rambler was preparing to expand on the intractability and waywardness of statistics, when Numpty interrupted. "I learned not to give up hope. Even when they put the rope around my neck, I still hoped for a miracle. And one came along."

Kit smiled. "I've been called many things in my life but never before have I been described as a miracle. I tell you what I learned," he went on, "I learned that a blind man often sees more than the sighted."

19 Many happy returns

Maizy and Sandy dumped their rucksacks in the back of the camper van and settled into the rear seats.

"This is lovely," said Maizy appreciatively. "When you're hitching around, you end up in some very odd vehicles, with some very odd and uncomfortable seats. This is great."

"Glad you like it," said Gwoat, as he started the engine.

Grimrose, who had taken the opportunity to expand upwards another couple of inches, simply grunted. Gwoat hadn't noticed the first inflation and probably wouldn't register the second. Grimrose still felt uncomfortable, her essence unnaturally compressed, but the second adjustment certainly relieved some of the discomfort.

Maizy peered over at Grimrose. "You're not quite as small as I thought," she mused.

"What are you?" Sandy joined in. "Are you," and he hesitated a moment, "are you a dwarf?" Maizy giggled.

"You're very rude," Grimrose snapped back. "How dare you?"

"Sorry, I was only asking," Sandy apologised, but with a laugh.

They drove on in silence for several miles. "You take the left fork here onto the M27," Grimrose advised Gwoat.

"Are you two an item?" Maizy suddenly asked.

"What does that mean?" asked Gwoat, unfamiliar with the term.

"Are you two a couple, you know, in a relationship?" Maizy elucidated.

Gwoat bridled but was unsure how to respond. He could hardly say that the small figure next to him was a crossbred fairy-gnome sent by his master, the Storyteller, to direct him to a portal where he was to collect a group of questors in search of the truth. No, that might be the way it was but it just didn't sound right, no, not at all.

In the end, it was Grimrose who replied, or rather didn't. "It is none of your business," she said tartly in a tone that made it clear further questions would be unacceptable. When he next saw Nick, Grimrose determined to give his master a very large piece of his mind. And he was going to set some ground rules. In future, no shapes smaller than four foot and none larger than seven foot. Furthermore, once the broad outlines of the required form had been established, Grimrose would insist the precise shape should be left for him to determine to ensure maximum comfort consistent with the brief. He had shifted shape for Nick many times, changing his shape and gender according to the brief, but this was the most ridiculous assignment and the most embarrassing predicament into which Nick had ever thrust him.

"Soo-rrry," said Maizy with affected contrition. "I was only asking."

The van moved smoothly down the M27 onto the A31. Sandy and Maizy chatted quietly in the back. There was a fair amount of giggling and chuckling.

"We're almost there," said Grimrose.

"Almost where?" asked Maizy.

"We're heading for Stoney Cross. Do you want us to drop you on the A31?"

"No, we'll go with you to Stoney Cross," said Sandy quickly.

"You'd probably find it easier to pick up another lift on the A31," Grimrose suggested.

"No," said Sandy. "It's fine. Stoney Cross is fine. We don't have a fixed schedule."

Gwoat certainly didn't want the young hitch-hikers to hang around at Stoney Cross. Those unfamiliar with travel via portals could be quite unsettled by the sudden emergence of figures from a fissure in the space-time continuum or, as it would seem, out of nowhere. Nevertheless, he let the matter rest.

"I really think we should drop them off now," said Grimrose. She wasn't looking forward to eliminating Gwoat. He seemed a nice enough fellow if you disregarded the flatulence. No, it was not going to be a pleasant task but, pleasant or not, it was surely one best accomplished without witnesses.

Gwoat pulled into a lay-by. "She's right, you know. We have a few things to do and you'll get another lift much quicker here on the A31."

Sandy was about to argue but Maizy pre-empted him: "I've always wanted to visit Stoney Cross. It's near Rufus Stone where William the Conqueror's son was killed, isn't it? It would be really kind if you took us there. We won't stay – just have a quick look around. I'm sure there will be other visitors and we will take a lift with them."

Gwoat relented. She was a pretty girl with rather winning ways. With her dark hair and green eyes, she could well have been Irish. Gwoat pulled out of the lay-by. Sandy relaxed.

And Grimrose thought to herself 'this has got all the makings of a truly gargantuan fiasco'. "Very well," she said, "we'll drop you at Rufus Stone and then drive on to where we need to be." She hoped Gwoat would appreciate the need to part company with the youngsters, albeit for different reasons.

"You're very tetchy," was all Gwoat said, but he turned off the A31 to head for the nearby Rufus Stone.

"Thanks ever so much," said Maizy.

"You know that William Rufus probably wasn't killed at the Stone at all," Gwoat confided. "It was more likely near Beaulieu. It's an interesting tale," he went on. "By all accounts, Rufus, or William II, to give him his regal title, was a total turd, hated by Normans and Saxons alike. The chap who killed him, by accident or accidentally on purpose, was a bit worried about how people might react to his apparently inadvertent act of regicide and buggered off, post haste, to France. But he needn't have bothered. No one gave a toss, not at all."

They pulled into a parking area near the iron-clad stone.

Grimrose was amazed. That was the most Gwoat had said since they had met. She was about to congratulate Gwoat on his unexpected erudition when she felt a piercing pain in her back. Sandy had driven a long stiletto though the back of Grimrose's seat into her body. Grimrose responded swiftly, moving vital organs out of the way of the knife.

"You little toe-rag," she expostulated.

"What's the matter now?" Gwoat asked.

"Only that the little bastard has just impaled me on a knife," snapped Grimrose.

"Well finish her," suggested Maizy to Sandy with a hint of urgency. "Spike the midget!"

"She's got six inches of steel through her back," returned Sandy. "That should be enough." He pulled the knife out, thinking the open wound would bleed more freely.

"Well it's not enough," said Maizy, "because the little abomination isn't dead, doesn't even seem to be dying. And I told you not to get blood on the upholstery."

"Really," Sandy was not happy. "How am I supposed to kill them without a bit of blood. It's what happens when you stab someone."

"What the hell are you doing?" screamed Gwoat. He was hearing this matter of fact exchange between two of his passengers while they calmly discussed the murder of the third. And, it seemed, him too.

"Well," said Sandy, "this is really a simple act of vehicle acquisition. We want your van."

As Sandy spoke, Maizy threw a cord over the back of the driver's seat and Gwoat's head, retaining the two ends. She planned to pull the cord tight around Gwoat's neck and by placing her knees in the back of his seat and pulling hard, strangle him, thus demonstrating to her partner an effective method of bloodless killing. Unfortunately for Maizy, Gwoat had turned to rebuke Sandy, so the cord, when tightened, simply pulled the side of Gwoat's head into the head rest of the driver's seat.

"Be Jasus, you ungrateful little shites," Gwoat screamed as he extricated himself from Maizy's ineffective garrotting manoeuvre and leapt from the van.

Sandy stepped out of the van and moved towards Gwoat, the stiletto in his left hand. Gwoat was hopping from one foot to the other, not so much as a means of avoiding any attack and certainly not, as Sandy thought it might be, an eccentric version of Irish dancing but simply out of nervousness. "Sorry about this," said Sandy, "but needs must."

"Needs must! What does that mean?" Gwoat asked, not really hoping to initiate a conversation.

"Well it means, if you could just stop jerking around for a minute, all your troubles will be over."

Meanwhile in the camper van, Grimrose was morphing into a shape more competent to perform defence and retribution. Maizy was mesmerised. The fairy-gnome was growing before her eyes. The figure of Grimrose now filled the front passenger seat which, with its high back, had previously towered over the highly compressed shapeshifter like the mountains of the Scottish highlands. Indeed the seat could no longer fully accommodate Grimrose with his enlarged, heavily muscled proportions, now clearly of the male gender.

"You've been stabbed," Maizy offered rather pathetically.

"Yes, and you, if I remember correctly," said a deep, menacing male voice emanating from the erstwhile fairy-gnome, "you urged your friend to 'spike the midget'. That was it, wasn't it? 'Spike the midget'."

Maizy decided that the conversation could only go from bad to worse. She attempted to jump from the van but the newly enlarged and clearly enraged Grimrose was too quick for her. An arm shot out. The fist at the end of the arm rendered Maizy unconscious.

There was a creaking noise from behind Sandy. He stopped and turned. The camper van was slightly lop-sided. A very large, heavy and emphatically male entity was emerging from the front passenger seat. Under his arm was Maizy's head, sadly for her no longer attached to her body.

"What the devil!" exclaimed Sandy and Gwoat in unison. Grimrose had adopted the form of an all in wrestler, with powerful psychotic drives. Now very male, with an excess of testosterone coursing through his shapeshifter veins, he said nothing but emitted a snarl. Gwoat, for his part, not surprisingly and, on this occasion, excusably, emitted a heady mix of noxious vapours occasioned by what he thought might be an imminent threat to his life.

And so it was that Sandy's last sensory experience before Grimrose, using Maizy's cranium as a club, cracked his skull like the shell of a hard-boiled egg, was the heady odour of a pernicious concoction of methane and other gases engendered by Gwoat's unstable gastric juices. Sandy sank to the ground with splinters of Maizy's skull embedded in his own, and with the grey matter of her brain seeping down the sides of his head over his light brown hair, like ash-covered lava from a dying volcanic eruption.

Gwoat made a bolt for it. Running around the now monstrous Grimrose, he made it to the camper van, jumped in, turned the ignition key and was off. He was heading back to Hook as quickly as the van would take him. Obviously, the fairy-gnome had been an imposter, no more a fairy or a gnome than Gwoat himself. Why Grimrose had adopted such a guise was unclear but that the imposter had meant him no good was obvious. And the message Grimrose had claimed to have come from the Storyteller was equally obviously false. So best go back to Hook and wait for the questors as he had been instructed.

Grimrose made no effort to stop Gwoat. Truth to tell, he was relieved the nervous Irishman had made his escape. Discouraging people from questing was fine. Even killing people was fine, on condition you didn't know them. But slitting the throat of someone who had given you a lift, with whom you had shared a journey, who had offered you a bar of chocolate, that was something else.

The shapeshifter adjusted himself into the form in which he felt most comfortable, with the simple addition of a council worker's high visibility orange jacket. While he set about clearing up the carnage, he mused how his next conversation with Nick might go. There would be recriminations on both sides. Nick would complain that he had failed to eliminate Gwoat. Grimrose would explain how events had intervened and how his manifestation as a highly improbable fairy-gnome had been a major impediment to the success of the mission, if only because it made him feel uncomfortable and embarrassed. In the end, Nick would have the last word but not before Grimrose had set some ground rules for future assignments.

Gwoat on the other hand was in a highly nervous state and, had he not been driving which, oddly, calmed him, would almost certainly have gone into convulsions. He tried very hard to relax himself and to prepare for his next ordeal – explaining to the Storyteller how he had been duped by a false and highly improbable fay entity. The Storyteller would ask him why he had not waited for the questors to return as he had been instructed.

Gwoat did not know it, but the questors themselves were more concerned about the missing Eve. It was therefore quite a coincidence that, while these thoughts occupied Gwoat's troubled mind, Eve, in the company of Nick Peters, shot past on the other side of the M3, travelling west.

Nick, with Eve beside him, was moving at pace in his small red sports car towards the New Forest and the destination Eve had stipulated. Stoney Cross.

20 Moving on

Kit accompanied the questors to the gate of the Garden of Eden.

"Why don't you come with us?" suggested Adam. Adam had taken a liking to the blind man. Kit had saved all their lives and of course they all felt grateful. But there was something else. He seemed entirely at ease with himself. There was no pretence, no angle, no edge. He was at the centre of himself. And he was good company.

"Thanks for asking but I'm going to stay here for a while," he replied. "I feel at home here and, in any case, I'm pretty sure there is some unfinished business. That grumpy old delinquent is certainly not my father but he thinks he is. And that imposes a moral responsibility on me. I know it shouldn't, but it does. So I'm going to try to disabuse him, sort him out, put him on the right path. If only to stop him perpetrating GBH on visitors," he added with a laugh.

The questors said farewell to Kit and the Garden. As they passed through the gate, the weather changed. The bright sunlight of Eden was replaced by a grey, tedious sky.

It was the Storyteller who noticed first. "O dear! No Gwoat."

There was no Gwoat and no camper van. Adam had assumed that, while they had been trapped in the Garden, Eve had been with Gwoat, waiting in the camper van for the others to return. This was all wrong. No Gwoat, no van and no Eve.

"They have probably just gone for some food or fuel," Rambler suggested.

"Do you know where they are?" Adam turned to the Storyteller.

"No idea," the Storyteller replied.

"You don't seem very concerned." Adam could feel the anger growing inside . "You have some responsibility in all this."

"I have a responsibility to escort you on your journey. You and Eve must decide where we go and what you make of it. I warned you there would be dangers. If you had wanted a life without risk, you should have stayed at home. At home, there were no risks, only the certainty of growing old, enduring the waning of your powers, and death. I thought you understood."

"I understood we would have a chance of finding some answers. And I assumed you could help us to find them. Instead, you seem to have decided to be a passive observer."

"That's not really fair," the Storyteller replied, seemingly hurt by Adam's criticism. "I stood with you in the presence of God; I too was condemned in the court of His judgement; I shared, and will share, your journey, however it turns out. And I may even help you to find the answers you seek – but not by answering your questions."

Adam was about to challenge the paradoxical aspect of the Storyteller's last remark when the camper van, with Gwoat at the wheel, skidded and slithered into a parking position beside the questors.

"Gwoat," said the Storyteller, "how nice to see you!"

Gwoat stepped out of the van and began to perform a neurotic jig.

"Good heavens, man!" said Adam. "What on earth is the matter with you – and where is Eve?"

"'Good heavens', 'what on earth'?" Numpty enquired of his uncle.

"It's not important," his uncle soothed. "The important part was asking the whereabouts of his wife."

Gwoat looked blank. "I thought she was with you."

"She left the Garden before us," the Storyteller explained. "You must have seen her come through the gate."

Gwoat now looked embarrassed, and was hopping about like a puppet manipulated by a palsied puppeteer.

"For God's sake, stand still," Adam snapped.

"If you shout at him, he will get worse," the Storyteller intervened. "His hopping is a symptom of acute nervousness. If you shout at him, obviously you will make him more nervous." He turned to Gwoat; "Now calm down and tell us what happened."

It took some minutes before Gwoat could compose himself sufficiently to begin his account of events. He knew it would not be an easy story to tell, especially if he was not to appear a complete fool.

"Shortly after you left," he said eventually, addressing the Storyteller, "I received a message I thought came from you. I was instructed to drive down the M3 and the M27 onto the A31 and to rendezvous with you at Stoney Cross."

"And how were we to meet you at Stoney Cross?" Adam asked.

Gwoat started hopping again. This was the difficult part. He had known they would ask him questions and he knew the answers would make him look ridiculous. 'Oh well,' he thought.

"The messenger claimed to be a fairy, sent by you to tell me to go to Stoney Cross," he blurted out. "I was to go to Stoney Cross because that is where you were to leave the Garden, using one of those portholes."

"Portals," the Storyteller corrected absentmindedly. "You say 'claimed to be a fairy'. Was the messenger not a fairy?"

"Have you both gone mad?" Adam exploded. "What is all this about fairies? Fairies don't exist. Obviously, anyone claiming to be a fairy couldn't actually be a fairy."

"Every time someone says fairies don't exist, a fairy dies," Numpty rebuked Adam's scepticism.

"Perhaps you could explain to your mentally challenged charge that, in common with elves, gnomes, imps and pots of gold at the end of the rainbow, fairies are simply figments of the febrile imagination of ignorant people."

"You will need to open your mind a tad if your quest is to have any chance of success," the Storyteller chided. "Don't forget you recently stood before God whom many would say is also a figment of the febrile imagination of ignorant people."

"He was not really a fairy," Gwoat answered the Storyteller's earlier question. "He was something else."

Gwoat then recounted how they had picked up a couple of hitch-hikers at Winchester and how the hitch-hikers had turned out to be murdering hooligans who wanted to kill both him and the fraudulent fairy in order to steal the camper van.

"And how did you survive the murderous intent of your fellow travellers and escape with the van?" There was just a hint in the Storyteller's voice that he suspected he knew the answer.

"Well," Gwoat paused, because he would now have to relive the trauma of recent events. "Well, the fairy-gnome turned itself into a big, hairy homicidal thing. He ripped off Maizy's head and used her skull to club Sandy to death. He was somewhat pissed off because Sandy had tried to kill him, had in fact stabbed him, or so the big hairy fairy claimed, although I must say he didn't seem any the worse for the stabbing."

"That was almost certainly Grimrose," the Storyteller said, as much to himself as anyone else. "This is the work of Nick Peters."

"Hairy fairy," Numpty repeated with a laugh.

"It's not funny," rasped Adam. "Where the hell is Eve?"

"He seems very religious," observed Numpty to his uncle, bridling at Adam's reprimand. "There's always a bit of heaven, earth, hell or God's sake in what he says."

"If I'm right," said the Storyteller, "either Eve will be with Nick Peters or he will certainly know where she is."

"So how do we find Nick Peters?" Adam asked with some urgency. He was not happy with the thought that his wife was in the company of the enigmatic biker, especially as the Storyteller seemed to blame Peters for Gwoat's misadventure.

"Well, we have to ask ourselves why did Peters, if I'm right, send Grimrose to persuade Gwoat to drive to Stoney Cross. He told Gwoat that we would meet him there. But clearly that wasn't going to happen.

If Gwoat hadn't made it back here, we wouldn't have known Peters knew about Stoney Cross, and the idea that we would leave the Garden through a portal and arrive at Stoney Cross was pure nonsense. I suspect Gwoat was supposed to die at Stoney Cross. Nick Peters thought without Gwoat and without the van, we would have to abandon the quest. Ironically, Gwoat was saved by the homicidal hitch-hikers. Their attempt to murder Grimrose and Gwoat actually saved Gwoat. There must be some reason why Peters picked Stoney Cross, so I think we should head there."

"That's a bit thin," said a worried Adam. "Just because he sent Grimrose and Gwoat to Stoney Cross, that's no reason to suppose he would take Eve there, or even go there himself, especially if he thought it was a crime scene. More likely, he'd stay away from the place."

"There's another reason," said the Storyteller. "Stoney Cross was our next stopping place. I mean, if we had all been together, we would have set out for Stoney Cross as soon as we had left the Garden."

"How could Peters know where we were going?" Adam asked. "We didn't know. I didn't know. You hadn't told us. We knew we were heading southwest but we didn't know where we were stopping."

"I need to explain something to you," said the Storyteller. His voice seemed strained, shot through with an undertone of pain. "You should think of Nick Peters as our adversary. I'm not saying he is evil or that he will do you or Eve any harm. But he will do all in his power to frustrate your quest. And he is an adversary to be respected. He has at his disposal some powerful weapons. He can play tricks with your mind; sometimes he can play tricks with reality. He will mislead, deceive, seduce, use any stratagem to achieve his end, which is simply to persuade you to return home and cease your seeking of the truth."

Adam really didn't like the sound of any of this. He particularly didn't like the sound of the word 'seduce' in connection with a man who might well have spent the recent past alone with Eve.

"Stoney Cross it is then," was all he said.

21 The little red sports car

When they had decided to go to Stoney Cross, Eve had been concerned Nick would expect her to ride pillion on his monstrous, chrome-gleaming motorbike. In the car park of the inn, it was some relief for Eve when he opened the door of a small red sports car.

"Do you like it?" he asked.

Eve nodded. She had always hankered after a small, red sports car, but she had not been able to afford such a car when a student before she and Adam married. Then, when Bella came along, it was completely impractical. And when Bella had died, it seemed unimportant, almost frivolous. "I was rather afraid you were planning to use your bike," she confessed.

He laughed. "Not today. Truth to tell, I prefer to ride my bike alone."

'Truth to tell'. That was an odd expression to come from Nick the biker. Perhaps she would have to readjust her perception of him, especially in the context of a rather fetching small, red sports car.

"Get in," Nick said. "It's quite comfortable – for a sports car. "It's a Porsche. A 911, Turbo S Cabriolet," he added. He was not boasting. He was just informing her, as though he was saying, if you ever get round to buying the car you've always wanted, this is it, this is what you should ask for.

Once settled in the car, Nick drove off smoothly and headed for the M3.

After a few miles, Eve began to feel hungry. She was sorry now she had skipped breakfast.

"You must be a bit peckish," said Nick as though he had read her thoughts. "Coffee helps to wake you up but it's not much of a breakfast. We can stop at Winchester services if you like."

"No, I'm all right. Really," Eve answered.

"I haven't got any food in the car," Nick ignored her protestations. "I think there might be some apples somewhere on those ridiculous back seats. Take a look."

Eve turned, found the opened bag of apples and gratefully took one.

"I need to explain something to you," said Nick, as Eve chomped her way though the Golden Delicious. "It's about the Storyteller." He paused to make sure he had Eve's full attention. "The clue's in the name," he continued. "He tells stories, tall ones, short ones, all kinds of stories. Some are amusing; others exciting; many of them really entertaining. And there's no harm in them. So long as you don't take them seriously. The problem is he really wants you to take them seriously. He wants you to think his stories lead somewhere, mean something, that they conceal some kind of underlying truth. And that is a big mistake. Those who fall for it can waste their money, their time and their lives. I don't want you and Adam to be his most recent victims."

Eve popped the core of the apple out the car and wiped her mouth. "Why does it concern you?" she asked. "What does it matter to you? You don't know Adam; you don't know me." She stopped. She was not too sure about that last bit, not after yesterday evening.

"You might just as well ask why the Storyteller picked on you," Nick countered. "Have you ever asked why he befriended you, why he spent so much time with you and Adam, why he talked you into going on your quest?"

Eve had no answer.

"I'll tell you why," Nick resumed. "He picked you because of Bella's death. He could see you and Adam were vulnerable, ready to clutch at any straw to make sense of it all. They are the ones he seeks out; those are the ones he goes for. Victims. Victims of life, of luck, of fate, whatever. Victims are vulnerable and, like a jackal, he smells out the weak and pulls them down."

Eve was a little shaken by Nick's vehemence. "You obviously feel strongly about this," she said, knowing her response was inadequate even as she said it.

"You asked me why I have taken up your case," Nick continued. "Tel, the Storyteller as you call him, has been at work for years, for as long as I can remember. He has picked on some of those closest to me and taken them off on these pointless quests. Some end in disaster. In other cases, the questors return but they are never the same. I've been fighting him from the start. It's what I do. I track him; I watch him; and when I see him closing in, I decide."

"Decide?" Eve queried.

"Yes, I decide. I decide whether or not the victims are worth saving."

Eve was silent. She had been party to the decision to go on the quest. The Storyteller had not forced her or Adam to set out; indeed he had gone out of his way to explain the risks. Nick seemed to think that the Storyteller had some ulterior motive but he had never asked for anything. As for the quest, he himself had provided the means of transport, albeit merely a modest camper van, and a driver, albeit a weird and worried one.

There was something else. Eve had been into the Garden of Eden.

She had stood before God. She had put her case to the Almighty. And she had found Him wanting. The experience hadn't resolved anything; it hadn't given her answers; but it had given her some satisfaction; it had been cathartic. Nick didn't seem to know anything about the Garden or, if he did, he wasn't revealing what he knew. Yet he claimed to be able to reunite her with Adam and the others.

"You know dreams can seem as real as life; and, if you're not careful, you can dream your life away," Nick said.

Eve wondered where that comment had come from. She was about to say that she hadn't been dreaming but then she remembered the previous night, the night when, as far as she could tell, she had dreamt that Bella was alive and that a man with Adam's appearance but Nick's voice and touch had made love to her.

They drove on for a few miles in silence. Then Eve asked: "You say you decide who is worth saving; how do you decide?"

Nick laughed; "That's easy," he said. "I always go for the pretty women."

22 On the road

Adam, Rambler, young Numpty and the Storyteller piled into the camper van. Gwoat turned the key and the still warm engine grunted into life.

"You'll soon know this route like the back of your hand," said Rambler to Gwoat. He could see the driver had been traumatised by his recent experience and thought a little gentle, aimless conversation might help to calm his mind.

"Why, is this road like the back of his hand?" asked Numpty.

"No," said the ever patient Rambler. "It just means he will know this road as well as he knows the back of his hand."

"Does he know the back of his hand especially well?" Numpty pressed.

"It's just a part of him that it's easy for him to study," Rambler replied, hoping that would be an end of it.

"When you said 'like he knows the back of his hand', was that a smile?"

"Smile?" queried Rambler.

"You know, when you say something is like something else," Numpty explained.

"Oh! A simile," Rambler laughed. "Well, yes, I suppose, in a way, although I wasn't saying the road was like the back of his hand, I was just saying he will soon know the road as well as he knows the back of his hand."

"God! You've got the patience of a saint," said Adam to Rambler. "I think I'd have given him the back of my hand by now."

"Would that be for me to study?" enquired Numpty cheerfully. "Then I could say, I know the back of your hand like I know the back of my hand."

The Storyteller offered Adam some help. "You could always bribe him to be quiet. A backhander!" he quipped.

"Is a backhander someone who studies the back of people's hands? I thought that was a psalmist." Numpty, ever eager to extend his grasp of things, enquired.

His uncle laughed. "You're thinking of a palmist, not a psalmist. And no, that is not what 'backhander' means." He could see that the only way to silence Numpty was to change the subject. "I have a question to ask," he announced. The others listened. "I was wondering if it would be possible, be acceptable for my nephew and me, myself, to remain with you on your epic adventure?"

There was a stunned silence which Rambler felt obliged to break by explaining the reason for his request. "My nephew and I were on a journey to Winchester first, and then beyond. Just a break from the routines of life. We had no particular purpose, other than for me to satisfy my curiosity and for young Numpty here to extend his sometimes tenuous grasp on the nature of things. That adventure in the Garden has made a difference. I learned so much. And young Numpty showed qualities heretofore unrevealed. I just feel our journey would be so much more fruitful if conducted in your company. And it's just possible, if I may say so without seeming impertinent or arrogant, that we might have something to contribute to the quest."

"Well, it's really up to Adam," said the Storyteller, "and Eve," he added.

Adam had mixed feelings. He had no objection to Rambler, although he found the older man's obsession with detail and his uncritical curiosity slightly irritating. No, the problem was Numpty, who clearly had the capacity to rile Job. "I don't know," he said, by which he meant 'No'.

"Let's wait until we have rejoined Eve," the Storyteller suggested diplomatically.

"But that means you will miss Winchester," Adam pointed out.

"Not at all a problem," Rambler responded. "Winchester was just a place on the map. I'm happy to go further west. That was our intention after Winchester in any case."

Adam gave way. He wanted to get to Stoney Cross as quickly as possible, and a detour to Winchester to drop off the odd couple would inevitably involve some delay.

The Storyteller addressed Adam. "Well at least one of our companions learned something from our excursion into the Garden."

"Oh, I learned something," Adam responded to the goad. "But I didn't learn much about the truth. I discovered that God, at least the God we met, was inadequate. That He was either an evil tyrant or a psychological cripple. He threatened our lives. Yet, with Kit, He was pathetic, claiming paternity without any justification. I assume He was driven by guilt which, in a way, would make sense. After all, if we are to believe Him, He sent His son on a mission which ended in His son's death, a death almost as cruel and barbaric as the one He proposed for us and which we must assume He could have foreseen. He was desperate for obedience but entirely unworthy of it. So, in short, He eliminated Himself from the quest. He had nothing to offer."

"Well that's quite a step forward. You've just eliminated one of the big Truths, a truth that hundreds of millions of people have accepted as

THE truth," mused the Storyteller. "Quite a step!"

"I have to say," Rambler interjected, "that I was not in the least surprised. The God of the Old Testament was essentially a device employed by the Israelite priests to give their people identity and hope. The Old Testament was written hundreds of years after the supposed historical events it described, many of which were simply rehashed versions of even older stories of other peoples. A bit of embroidery here; a bit of embellishment there. Rather like the Arthurian legends. The biggest problem the priests had to solve was reconciling the Jews as the Chosen People with the undoubted historical fact that they were far from the most successful peoples of the time. Indeed almost everyone seemed to do better until, in the end, the Romans, losing patience with one of their most problematic provinces, razed Jerusalem to the ground and then dispersed the Jews, driving them out of Palestine. It must have seemed to the Israelites that being chosen was a bit of a handicap."

"What does being 'the Chosen People' mean?" asked Numpty. Being chosen sounded rather attractive to the young lad but then he thought that being chosen by a tyrannical despot probably had its down side.

"The Jews believed, and some still believe," said Rambler, "that they were chosen by God out of all the peoples of the world for special treatment. They were the ones he spoke to and told them what to do."

"So does that make God a racist?" asked Numpty, rather pleased with himself. His uncle had told him many times not to generalise about races. He had been reprimanded even when he had said good things about other races.

"Well, I suppose in a way it does," conceded Rambler, "although he had to choose someone to impart his wisdom and instructions to."

"To whom," said Numpty cheerfully. He was on a roll.

"To the Jews," answered his uncle.

"No," said Numpty triumphantly. "You meant he had to choose someone to whom to impart his wisdom."

"Thank you," Rambler responded with just a hint of irritation in his voice.

"And if the Jews were so unsuccessful, why did they still believe they were the Chosen People?" Numpty persisted.

"Well," said Rambler, "the priests came up with a rather clever ruse. They said that being chosen meant the Israelites had to be particularly obedient to God's will and meet his exacting standards. Every time the Jews had a setback, the priests were able to blame the people. They were not good enough; they had failed God in some way."

131

"So were the Jews a particularly bad lot?" Numpty asked, determined to understand how 'being chosen' worked. "I mean, if other people kept doing better than the Jews, was that because they met God's standards or were more obedient?"

"No," said Rambler slowly. He could see Numpty was going to ask more questions and he had had enough. "As I said, it was just a story, made up by priests to hold their people together at a difficult time."

"How can you say that, Uncle?" asked a genuinely perplexed Numpty. "We've just been in the Garden of Eden. We stood before God. He judged us. That was very real. Not just a made-up story. I still have the rope marks around my neck."

Adam intervened. "Whatever it was, it was not a very productive experience, that's for sure, and it didn't reveal anything of value. Eve tried to find out why Bella died. God had no answers; he prevaricated; he said he was too busy; that he wasn't responsible, that he couldn't be blamed. He sounded like a bungling and incompetent bureaucrat, desperately trying to excuse the latest fiasco. Then he revealed another even less pleasant side to his nature, the unhinged tyrant, bent on terrorising and destroying anyone who offended him. Finally, we had the rather pathetic delusional old man, desperately asserting a false paternity. The only good thing to come out of the whole episode was Kit, and it seems he had wandered into the Garden as a stranger just like us."

"He was extraordinary," Rambler agreed. "He was totally blind and yet he walked strange and unfamiliar paths with the confidence of a sighted person."

"Why was he blind?" asked Numpty.

"You really are one for questions," muttered Adam.

"As indeed are you," the Storyteller rebuked.

"I think he told us he was born blind," Rambler answered his nephew. "It must have been some defect at birth." Rambler paused and then added: "It is a miracle that any of us can see. It's such a complex mechanism. We are very lucky we have eyes. Indeed, I had meant to ask the angel Rodney about the eye. It has troubled many that so complex a faculty should have developed purely by chance."

"No doubt Rodney or Derek would have told us that, given time, you could make anything evolve," Adam suggested, "and, if not, they would have explained it as another tweak they had to slip through to make things the way that Gabriel wanted them."

"It may not be necessary to invoke any tweaking by Rodney and Derek," said Rambler. "There are those who have devised a plausible process whereby a light sensitive patch in a single-celled creature might have become slightly recessed for protection, and then progressively more recessed in ensuing generations over millions of years till this light sensitive patch found itself encased in a protective cup. The mouth of the cup narrowed, facilitating the focusing of light. It would only need a chance mutation to provide a transparent film across the eye to point future generations of the creature in the direction of a lens."

"That's a bit of a stretch," commented Adam.

"Well I probably haven't done justice to the theory."

"You told me we see everything upside down," said Numpty.

"Certainly seems true in your case," suggested Adam.

"No, no, dear boy," Rambler explained. "It is indeed the case that the images we receive though our eyes are upside down, but the brain reverses the images instantly so we see the world the right way up."

"Isn't that odd?" said Numpty with wonder.

"The development of the eye is one of the oddest of all human features," mused Rambler. "The eyes are the one part of the brain exposed to the world. Is it not strange that an exposed extrusion of an internal and, let's be honest, not very attractive internal organ could be a thing of beauty, a window to the soul?"

"Mirror," said Adam. "I think it's the eyes are the mirror of the soul."

"That, too," conceded Rambler. "Oculus animi index."

"How can the eyes be a window and a mirror?" enquired Numpty. "A mirror only shows you what is on your side of the glass; but, through a window, you can see what is on the other side of the glass."

"Quite right," Adam agreed. "Windows and mirrors are not the same thing at all. And, if we're going to be picky, who said we have a soul?"

"Would you prefer mind? 'The eyes are the window of the mind'," Rambler offered. "Animus could mean mind or, indeed, courage or spirit, as well as soul."

"We do have a soul, don't we, Uncle?" asked a bemused Numpty.

"I certainly believe so," consoled Rambler.

"That's a bit of an oxymoron," said Adam. "If it's a matter of belief, you can't believe with certainty."

"No," responded Rambler, "but I can be certain that I believe, which is all I was saying."

"What is an oxymoron?" enquired Numpty.

"A stupid creature of bovine appearance," offered Adam.

"Don't confuse the lad," chided Rambler. "An oxymoron is a figure of speech, a form of words which seem to contradict each other. Adam was querying my juxtapositioning of 'certainly' and 'belief'. As I explained, however, the certainty referred only to the fact of my faith about which I can certainly be certain, not to the certainty of the thing in which I believed, which must remain a matter of faith."

Numpty said nothing. He preferred Adam's definition.

"I need some chocolate," Gwoat mumbled in the Storyteller's ear. "Do you mind if I pull over at Winchester services? They're coming up in one and a half miles."

Adam had overheard Gwoat's request. "No, we can't stop. If we think Eve is at Stoney Cross we need to get there as soon as possible. She doesn't know we are coming. And if Nick Peters decides to persuade her to go somewhere else, we will have no idea where. In any case, what's happened to all the chocolate you bought at Fleet?"

"I finished that yesterday," said a disgruntled and twitchy Gwoat. "I've had a very stressful time," he added.

"That is certainly true," the Storyteller agreed, "but Adam is right. We really do need to reach Stoney Cross without delay."

Gwoat resigned himself to chocolate deprivation. He consoled himself with the one bar he kept for such emergencies. He chewed it slowly as they shot by the turn-off to Winchester services.

Had they acceded to Gwoat's request, they would almost certainly have come across Eve and Nick Peters seated in the eating area, demolishing an all day breakfast.

23 Unanswered questions

Taken as a whole, the quality of the Winchester services all day breakfast was no better than mediocre. Only the egg was freshly cooked. Most of the bacon, lying in its steel trough under the heat-radiating light, was undercooked. You could request well-done bacon (or properly cooked as Adam always insisted on saying) but even then you were quite likely to be assigned a rasher crisp at one end and palely flaccid at the other. The sausages were average, not an entirely unacceptable combination of sawdust and meat products about which the less said the better but certainly not a well-packed skinful of coarsely minced succulent pork, sensitively seasoned with herbs and spices. The black pudding was over-cooked and dry; and the hash browns, noxious interlopers from the United States, were both over-cooked and soggy. All in all, mediocre but, if hungry, as both Nick and Eve were, deeply satisfying.

"I had a dream last night," Eve hazarded. She felt the need to find out whether Nick had any idea what had happened to her.

"Oh, yes," he said, "I hope it was a pleasant one."

He didn't even ask what the dream was about. Obviously she wanted to tell him but he gave her no encouragement. Was he just not interested? Or was he playing with her?

"It was really strange," Eve prompted. Still no invitation from Nick to explain. "I was back in London," she added lamely.

"That's not so strange," Nick responded, wiping his lips with the paper napkin. "That's where you live, isn't it?"

"I dreamt of the day Bella died, but this time she didn't die. This time, Adam warned her to stay away from the tree. This time the lightning struck, the bough fell but no one was harmed."

"A good dream then," said Nick, with a smile.

"Except it was only a dream," said Eve sadly.

"You know some people think dreams are a glimpse into a parallel universe. Maybe there is another world where Bella is a lovely young girl, ten years old, quite an accomplished pianist, just starting to take an interest in boys."

Eve laughed, but the laugh was empty. "In that case, I'd rather be in that world," she said, "because in this world Bella is dead and I'm trapped here in grief that has no end."

"This is going to sound harsh," said Nick, his voice both serious and concerned. "You are going to have to get past Bella's death. You are going to have to give up your grief. Your grief will last only while you

135

hang on to it."

"You seem to be rather keen on giving up on things," Eve returned. "As I understand it, you want us to give up our quest, and you want me to stop grieving for Bella. Is there anything else you think I should abandon?"

"Whooa!" said Nick, backing off. "I'm only trying to help. Your grief does no good for Bella and I reckon it's doing you a fair amount of harm. You should really ask yourself what it's for. If it's driven by guilt, you should try to understand, it wasn't your fault. If you want to feel guilty, you'd be better employed worrying about the motorcyclist who crashed when the apple core you threw out of the window was caught by a gust of wind and splattered on his visor. Now, in that case, you have some justification for feeling guilty, although of course there was no malice, no intention to cause harm." Nick took a sip of his coffee.

"What did you just say?" Eve was stunned. Nick's voice had been so calm, so reasonable but his words were devastating.

"The apple core," Nick answered seemingly surprised she needed further explanation. "The one you threw out of the window. I don't blame you. There's nowhere in a Porsche to put an apple core."

"You said it hit a motorcyclist and he crashed?" said Eve.

"Yep," Nick replied. "Just one of those things. The wind took it, we were doing eighty, and it hit the biker's visor. At that speed, even a pip can have a bit of an impact. Anyway the core splattered and spread. I guess the rider was surprised and blinded. He wobbled and skidded, the bike hit the deck, and he and the bike skidded onto the hard shoulder. That's the last I saw. We were a good quarter of a mile away by then."

"You saw this and you didn't think to mention it?" Eve asked incredulously.

"What was the point?" asked Nick. "There was nothing we could do. We couldn't get back to the biker without risking another accident. We couldn't help him. If we had stopped and you had admitted you had caused the accident, the police would have charged you. You would certainly have been delayed for hours. You'd be facing prosecution and, if the poor bugger is seriously injured or dead, you'd have had another bundle of guilt to carry around with you for years to come. Instead, I drove on. If you think about it, that was the only sensible thing to do."

"So why tell me about it now?" asked Eve, now angry as well as contrite.

"Just making the point that you weren't responsible for Bella's death. There are degrees of responsibility. You were a bit responsible

136

for the biker coming off his bike, I'll grant you that. But you were entirely innocent of Bella's death. I'm just trying to cheer you up."

"Well you've a funny way of going about it, that's all I can say," said Eve. "We will have to go back. We will have to find out what happened."

"I thought you were in a hurry to get to Stoney Cross," Nick hazarded.

"Yes, I want to get to Stoney Cross. I need to talk to Adam, to be with him. But, if I've injured someone, perhaps even worse than injured, I can't just walk away."

"Interesting," mused Nick, as though calibrating his assessment of Eve. Then he continued: "Right, well now I can cheer you up. I was lying about the biker. No apple core splatter; no biker wobble, no crash. I just wanted you to know when you should feel guilty and when you shouldn't. Apple core, splatter, wobble, crash – responsible, at least partly. Thunder, lightning, cracking bough, Bella dead – not responsible."

Eve didn't know whether to laugh with relief or throw her coffee into Nick's happily smiling face. She settled for verbal abuse. "You're a total shit," she said.

"Yes, ma'am," he said with mock deference. "Total shit, but I kept my word. You did see Bella again, didn't you? If only in a dream."

It was several moments before Eve realised that the only time Nick had made such a promise was on the evening she had spent at his cottage – except spending the evening at his cottage had been part of the dream. Or so she had thought.

Their meal finished, they left the Winchester services, back on the M3 heading west. Traffic was slow on the other side but, going west, the road was surprisingly clear.

24 Reunions

The camper van performed well on the last stretch of road to Stoney Cross, taking the M3 and the A31 in its stride. It clearly preferred long runs.

"It's preparing itself for the next stage of our journey," the Storyteller confided to Adam. "Over the hills and far away."

"What does that mean?" asked a wary Adam. He really didn't fancy any more of the Storyteller's surprises.

"Exactly what it says," said the Storyteller, "over the hills and then far away. If you seek the truth, or indeed, any truth, you cannot expect to find it staring you in the face. It wouldn't be much of a challenge if it was that easy."

"I'm not looking for a challenge," Adam snapped. He found the Storyteller's playful reticence intensely irritating. "I'm just looking for answers. You seem to think this is some kind of a game. Well, it isn't."

Luke pricked up his ears. "He's not usually this grumpy," Luke minded to the Storyteller in defence of his master. "He's uneasy about his separation from Eve and you didn't help with your description of Nick Peters."

The Storyteller acknowledged the dog's attempt at mitigation. He addressed Adam soothingly: "I realise you're a bit tetchy after your recent experience...".

"Excuse me," Adam interrupted. "Whipping us into the Garden of Eden and the presence of God was bad enough..."

"It is quite an honour to have an audience with God," the Storyteller interpolated.

"But being judged, condemned and threatened with an horrific death," Adam continued, "well I think we can do a tad better than describe it as 'an experience'. A little neutral, don't you agree, considering we were about to be ripped apart? And while we're on the subject of words, I'd like to suggest that 'a little bit tetchy' does what I am feeling at the moment a grave injustice."

"An injustice that could have put us in the grave," quipped Numpty proudly, looking to his uncle for praise.

"Well done, my boy," Rambler responded. "A fine pun, Numpty. Well done."

"The lowest form of wit," said Adam dismissively.

"That, I believe, is sarcasm," Rambler corrected Adam amiably. "It is of course true that many have a low regard for wordplay. Was it not Dr Johnson who described the pun as the fatal Cleopatra for which

Shakespeare lost the world and was content to lose it? On the other hand, many wordsmiths find satisfaction in play on words and, should it come to a battle between Dr Johnson and the Bard, much as I respect the eminent lexicographer, I should prefer to stand beside the greatest master of the English language this country has yet produced."

Numpty preened himself a little at his uncle's eloquent defence of the pun.

Adam considered continuing the argument. After all, even if you went along with puns, they were supposed to be relevant to the subject under discussion but, happily, before he could respond, they arrived at Stoney Cross.

"A good argument always makes time pass more quickly," the Storyteller remarked as he opened the camper van door and disembarked.

"You can't leave that van here," said a ruddy-faced man in a smart green blazer, white trousers and knee high black boots. "I'm an Agister," he added, as though that settled the matter.

"Bugger off," was the Storyteller's unexpectedly emphatic response.

"I am an Agister, an instrument of the Verderers, who are masters of the Forest. I have the authority to impound your vehicle and exact a fine of gargantuan proportions."

"No you're not, and no you can't," the Storyteller responded and then, turning away from the purported Agister, addressed the occupants of the van. "Everyone out."

The outraged official prepared to launch a verbal tirade: "You cannot ignore my authority…"

"Grimrose," said the Storyteller, with obvious exasperation, "you are not an Agister, you are a pillock. Do you really think, after all the many times our paths have crossed, I cannot see through your always obvious and generally pathetic disguises? And what is this with parking? Every time we meet, you seem obsessed with matters relating to parking."

By now Adam, Rambler and Numpty had disembarked. Luke, relieved to be free after the long journey, was happily sniffing around and paying particular attention to some newly laid turf beside a pile of earth.

Grimrose who had just altered form from humble 'hi vis' jacketed council worker to smartly turned out officer of the New Forest was not prepared to concede so quickly. "These are not disguises. I am a highly professional shapeshifter."

"So you admit you're not an Agister?" said Numpty with impeccable logic. And then asked his uncle; "What is an Agister?"

"Oh, no!" exclaimed Adam, hoping to abort Rambler's answer. But to no avail.

"An Agister is one of five employees of the venerable profession of Verderers."

"What's a Verderer?" was Numpty's inevitable follow-up.

"The Verderers date back to the thirteenth century. They were the forest court enforcing the king's authority over the rather extensive royal hunting ground, the New Forest. They were able to impose fines for minor offences and, no doubt, had there been problems with parking in those days, parking offences are precisely the type of offences with which the Verderer's court would have dealt."

"Fascinating," Adam interrupted, "but, since we've established this person is not an Agister and not therefore in the employ of Verderers, not entirely pertinent."

Luke by now was digging the ground with some determination. "Get that dog under control and stop it from digging!" shouted an alarmed Grimrose. He had spent several hours clearing up after the final confrontation with Maizy and Sandy. He had meticulously gathered the body parts, sliced off a mat of turf, dug a shallow trench, deposited the flesh and bone in the trench and re-laid the turf. The surplus earth from the trench lay in a pile beside the grave. Grimrose had been about to remove the tell-tale mound when the camper van had arrived.

Adam called Luke to him and the dog reluctantly obeyed. "There are bodies under the turf," Luke confided to the Storyteller, "human bodies."

"That would be the errant hitch-hikers," observed the Storyteller out loud.

"Would that be errant in the sense of wandering or errant in the sense of doing wrong?" enquired Rambler. "If the former, I would suggest the expression 'errant hitch-hikers' is somewhat tautological."

"My uncle taught me to be logical," claimed Numpty with pride.

Rambler was about to explain tautology to Numpty once again when a red Porsche swept round the bend and came to a dramatic screeching halt behind the yellow camper van.

"Eve," exclaimed Adam when he realised the passenger was indeed his wife.

"There you are," said Nick to Eve, "another promise kept."

Adam frowned. "Are you all right?" he asked Eve. He embraced her.

"I'm fine," Eve responded, "and I'm really glad to have found you all."

Adam turned his attention to Nick. "How come you're here? Did you follow us from Fleet?"

"It's a long story," Nick replied easily.

"That's all right. I'm prepared to listen," Adam responded with ill-concealed hostility.

"Adam," Eve chided. "It's all right. Nick helped me to find you." She didn't know whether that was true or not. That evening at his cottage, he had said they should go to Stoney Cross. But she was pretty sure that evening had been simply part of her dream, so really it had been she who had decided on Stoney Cross. Whatever. Nick had at least driven her to the reunion.

"No," Adam persisted, "it's really not all right. The last time I saw Nick, he showed me a very nasty accident in which the driver of a car died. But when we left Fleet, there was no sign of an accident. So I think Nick here can play tricks with your mind – which means he's not to be trusted."

"You never said a truer word," said the Storyteller. On arrival, Nick and the Storyteller had acknowledged each other with a slight nod but neither spoke to the other.

"So I think you had better explain to me," Adam continued in the same aggressive tone, "how you found Eve and what the hell you've been doing with her."

"Adam," Eve intervened, "for goodness' sake, what's the matter with you?"

Eve's apparent defence of Nick did nothing to mollify Adam.

"No," said Nick with a smile to Eve, "he's surely within his rights to show concern. If you were my wife, I'm sure I'd feel the same."

This last remark threw Adam off balance; he was unsure whether to be reassured or even more angry.

"Let me explain," Nick continued. "I don't know why you and your party went to Hook, but the reason I went there is simple enough. I live there. I'm on my way back from my local pub to my cottage when who should I see but Eve, standing near the road looking totally lost, entirely out of it. So I offer to help, that's all. She seemed confused, said she had been with you all and that suddenly you weren't there. I give her a lift. I find her a room at the local inn where she stayed yesterday evening. I picked her up this morning and brought her here."

"Why here?" Adam asked more calmly.

"You had better ask Eve. She told me to drive here. She thought this was where you would be."

Adam looked at Eve for an explanation. Eve was perplexed. "I don't know. Just intuition. Anyway, it worked." Then she added: "But why did you come here?"

"According to him," Adam indicated the Storyteller, "Stoney Cross was the next place on our itinerary."

Nick snorted: "An itinerary to nowhere!"

"Excuse me," Adam snapped back. "What does that mean? What the hell has it got to do with you? What has any of this got to do with you?"

"I told you at Fleet," Nick replied calmly. "You're on a wild goose chase, except there are no geese, wild or otherwise. I'm just trying to save you from some bitter disappointment."

"Well, I suggest you mind you own business," Adam responded, sharply.

"Adam, what's the matter with you?" Eve asked. "Nick's done nothing but help me. He's behaved like a perfect gentleman throughout. I don't know what's got into you."

"Almost everything worth having seems like a wild goose chase or a fool's errand at the beginning," offered the Storyteller. "There are no guarantees. But nothing ventured, nothing gained."

Rambler had whipped out his notebook and was busily scribbling away. "What are you writing?" enquired Numpty.

"It seems the Storyteller and this driver of the red sports car favour proverbial exchanges," said Rambler. "And, nephew, as you know, I am an aficionado in such matters. I like to check the origins of such expressions as 'a wild goose chase'."

"Will you be looking it up in Fowler or Partridge?" Numpty asked, unaware of the puns.

"Either would seem eminently appropriate," replied Rambler with a smile.

"It is time we were moving on," said the Storyteller.

"Well," said Nick, "I've warned both of you. You're wasting your time. Tel isn't being honest with you. The next part of your journey will be just as pointless as the first but even more dangerous, and I don't just mean life-threatening. But, as always, it's entirely up to you."

"Gwoat," the Storyteller summoned his driver. It was getting dark and the Storyteller was eager for them to be on their way. Gwoat had been chatting to Grimrose who, in the shape and uniform of an Agister, seemed paradoxically somehow a much less threatening figure to Gwoat than a small, densely-packed fairy. Grimrose had apologised for the traumatic conclusion to their earlier trip to Stoney Cross and had assured Gwoat that, whatever his orders, he would never have murdered a travelling companion, unless, of course, like Maizy and Sandy, they had tried to murder him first. "I'm not a bad person," he said to Gwoat.

"You're not really a person at all," said Nick, as he started back to his red Porsche.

"Any chance of a lift?" enquired Grimrose, as Nick settled into the driver's seat.

"Absolutely," Nick replied, starting the engine, "but not with me," he added, as he sped off. Given Grimrose's failure to obey orders and fulfil his mission, Peters felt the need to indicate his displeasure.

"Are we ready?" asked the Storyteller. "Is everyone on board?"

Adam and Eve sat behind Gwoat and the Storyteller, with Rambler and Numpty behind them. Luke curled up on the floor between Adam and Eve.

"The next part of our journey is going to be a little choppy," said the Storyteller. "I suggest you hold tight. Some of you may find it easier to close your eyes."

"Where are we going?" Adam asked. He had been determined to question the Storyteller before embarking on another adventure but, in his eagerness to make clear his rejection of Nick's advice, he had been the first to take his seat when the Storyteller had called them.

"You'll find out soon enough," said the Storyteller. Gwoat released the handbrake and pressed the accelerator to the floor.

25 Up to speed

The van shook violently for about a minute and the noise was deafening. Eve looked at Adam; Adam looked at the Storyteller, who seemed entirely unperturbed. So Adam shrugged and squeezed Eve's arm to reassure her.

Rambler was clearly concentrating hard as though whatever was happening could only be resolved satisfactorily if somehow he could comprehend it. Numpty nudged his uncle and asked: "Why is the van shaking?"

Now obviously Rambler had no idea why the van was shaking but he recognised the need to calm his nephew's fears. "Do you remember, Numpty, when we first flew on an aeroplane and I noticed that, at take-off, you were clutching the arms of your seat so fiercely your knuckles turned white?"

"I do," answered Numpty at once. "It was because I could not understand how a heavy container, with chairs and luggage and trolleys, could lift us up and fly though the air, and I thought that maybe I could help to keep it in the air by the power of my thinking."

"Well," said Rambler, "I don't really know what is happening, but I feel now as you felt then. If I concentrate really hard, whatever the van is doing, it will turn out all right."

"But I clutched my seat because I was terrified," confessed Numpty. "Are you terrified, Uncle?"

Rambler realised that summoning the memory of Numpty's first flight was unlikely to allay his nephew's present fears. It was simply an honest answer to his nephew's original question. He was concentrating because he felt the van was likely to fall apart if he didn't use his mind and will to hold it together. "The point is," he explained, "it did turn out all right, didn't it?"

Just as he finished speaking, the shaking stopped and the deafening noise settled down to a quiet, comforting hum.

Adam rubbed the window beside him and looked out. It was dark, very dark. He peered intensely into the blackness. There was movement. He knew the van was in motion because the darkness was not entirely smooth and uniform but he couldn't judge the speed. There were tiny irregularities but these shot past him so quickly that he couldn't be sure what he had seen or indeed whether he had seen anything at all.

"What's happening?" Adam asked.

"We are on our way to our next appointment," the Storyteller replied. "It will take some time," he added with a smile.

"Our next appointment?" Adam queried.

"Yes," said the Storyteller, "and I hope you find our next host more congenial than the last."

"Well, since the last host set about disembowelling us, that shouldn't be too hard," Adam replied. "So who is it?"

"Disembowelling!" exclaimed Eve. "What on earth are you talking about?"

"There's a lot to tell you," said Adam.

"Well start now. Disembowelling! Who wanted to disembowel you?"

"After you went off on your own...," Adam began.

"I didn't go off on my own," Eve corrected. "I was cut off from you somehow."

"You wouldn't have been cut off if you had been walking with us," said Adam.

"I was walking with you," said Eve determined to make her point. "If we were separated, it was because you weren't walking with me."

"Just like old times," said Luke to the Storyteller. "It's their way of relating."

The Storyteller laughed; "Well, arguing or relating is fine. We have some time to kill."

"Whether you wandered off or the rest of us failed to keep up doesn't matter," Adam continued. "God decided He hadn't finished with us. He shut the gate on us. You slipped out. We were trapped."

"What more did he want?" asked Eve.

"Basically, He wanted to punish you. Your abuse must have festered in His divine mind. His anger finally erupted and He decided you needed to be taught a lesson."

"To be precise," interrupted Rambler, "it was really us to whom he wished to teach a lesson, because the lesson in question was your execution for taking His name in vain. There would be little you personally could take out of the lesson if you were dead. I think in your case, it was simply punishment."

"He wanted to execute me because He felt I had been rude to Him?" said Eve incredulously.

"It does seem a trifle excessive," Rambler offered, "but I have noted in my studies of politics that power corrupts and, as I believe Lord Acton wrote in a letter to Bishop Mendel Creighton in 1887, absolute power corrupts absolutely. In the case of the Creator, if you'll excuse the use of a comparative with a superlative," he nodded an acknowledgment towards Numpty to forestall any possibility of an interruption from his nephew, who had recently been chided for using such expressions as 'more complete' and 'very excellent', "you can't get much more absolute than God. Even those with no claim to absolute power are seduced into abusing their position. Indeed, I sometimes conclude that the only point in having power is to abuse it. Why else would one want it?"

Rambler would have been more than happy (assuming happy is not itself an absolute) to have expanded on his theme of corruption burgeoning as one ascends the levels of a hierarchy, but Adam cut him off. "And when He found you had slipped though His divine fingers, He decided to take it out on the rest of us."

"There was the little incident of the sneeze," Rambler reminded Adam. He was not in any way defending God but he thought it only fair that Eve should be apprised of all the facts.

"Yes," Numpty chimed in, unable to conceal his pride, "I destroyed the Angel Beryss with a sneeze."

"Are you telling me," Eve asked, "that the angelic servants of the Creator are susceptible to the common cold?"

"It was rather more dramatic than that," Rambler explained. "Young Numpty here did not infect Beryss with the coryza virus. No, no. He merely sneezed and, in effect, blew the angel away."

"As a result," Adam continued, "God decided to execute all of us. His chosen method, it seems, was hanging, drawing and quartering."

"My God!" said Eve.

"And He would have done it," said Adam. "Numpty here was on the scaffold and the archangel Michael was sharpening the sacrificial knife in readiness for the disembowelling."

"What happened? How did you escape?" asked a stunned Eve.

Luke's tail wagged with excitement. This was the bit where he had come to the rescue.

"A stranger arrived. A blind man. He talked with God and he told God He must let us go," said Rambler simply.

"A blind man told God what to do!"

"That's exactly what happened," Adam confirmed to his wife. "Kit, that was the man's name, told God He had no right to detain us, much less execute us. God seemed to think Kit was His son which, according to Kit, was total bollocks, but bollocks or not, we owe our lives to Kit."

"What about me?" queried a deeply disappointed Luke.

"And Luke helped," the Storyteller added, for the benefit of all those who could not hear Luke.

"It was a bit more than help," Luke complained. "I found Kit; I told him of your plight; I led him to the place where you were being held.

146

Dammit, short of kicking God's butt myself, I was the one who rescued you. 'Luke helped.' Is that it? Come on!"

Eve hadn't heard Luke's heart-felt appeal for recognition. "So who was this Kit?" she asked.

"He was a pretty extraordinary fellow," said Adam. "First of all, he was blind but it didn't seem to handicap him in the least. He said he had wandered into the Garden, like us; and had stayed for a while, really just because it suited him. He told us he was a traveller who went where his fancy took him. He seemed very relaxed and entirely unintimidated by God. If anything, God seemed intimidated by Kit. In an odd kind of way, and I know this sounds stupid, he seemed more secure in himself than the Creator. I liked him. Quite apart from the fact that he saved our lives, I liked him."

The van gave a shudder before resuming its comforting background hum.

"What was that?" Adam asked. He hadn't had an answer to his original question. The Storyteller had yet to tell him about their 'next appointment'.

"Relax," responded the Storyteller. "Just passing a major temporal node. We are well on our way. It won't be too long now."

"Major temporal node?" enquired Adam. "Is that another word for a speed hump?"

The Storyteller laughed. "No, it's a key point in human history, a significant development in the story."

Adam peered out of the window again. It was still pitch black, with almost imperceptible specks of light flashing past. "We're not on a road, are we?" he hazarded. "This isn't the M27 or the A31. In fact we're not in Hampshire at all, are we?"

"No," answered the Storyteller. "Not Hampshire or Dorset or England or indeed now. For your next appointment we are travelling through space and time. You underestimated our humble camper van and its intrepid driver. As I said, over the hills and far away. And I should have added long ago, long, long ago."

Rambler's ears pricked up. "Time travel," he announced. "Convinced it was impossible on the grounds of reason and common sense, two sound principles I had always rather depended on, although both have taken a bit of a knocking with all this quantum stuff. Even so, when we look at the sun and see it as it was eight minutes ago, that doesn't mean that what it was eight minutes ago is still there, it just means the picture of the sun, as it was eight minutes ago, took eight minutes to reach us. I understand that if I was observing a planet a thousand light years away, I should be seeing it as it was a thousand years ago, but, if I could be instantly transported to that distant planet, it would be as it is today, not as it was a thousand years before."

"I think we get the picture," Adam interrupted, fearful that Rambler was going to cite longer and longer time-spans to make exactly the same point.

"Well, if that is what you believe," said the Storyteller to Rambler, "I suggest you prepare yourself for a shock. And, while you're at it, prepare yourself for some bitterly cold weather. If you look in the trunk at the back of the van, under the bench seat, you will find some rather fine, albeit second or third hand, winter clothing; coats, scarves, gloves. There should be enough for all of us.

"And for you Gwoat, there is an emergency chocolate supply. We failed to stock up before leaving Stoney Cross and I've no doubt you are already experiencing withdrawal symptoms."

Gwoat, who seemed to be concentrating hard on driving the van into an endless stretch of night, nodded an acknowledgement but kept his eyes on the way ahead. "Hold tight," he instructed his passengers, "the last part of the journey is going to be a bit rough. We have some climbing to do."

26 The Caucasus

The questors were badly shaken by the last leg of the journey. On arrival, Gwoat was a jabbering wreck and, had it not been for the copious supplies of chocolate bars, would almost certainly have succumbed to a complete mental breakdown. Even the Storyteller's nerves had been stretched.

When the van finally bumped to a halt, Adam looked out of the side window. The blackness had been replaced by a light misty grey, with cold winds churning the air but not clearing the clouds sufficiently for Adam to get his bearings. Eve, now wrapped in a brown fur coat which she was certain had been stripped from a large brown bear, was nevertheless shivering.

"Where the hell are we?" asked Adam. "Not the end of the world, I hope."

"No, not at all," the Storyteller replied. "We're where one world meets another, where Europe meets Asia. We're in the Caucasus, on top of one of the Caucasian mountains."

"Why on earth would we come here?" asked Adam. "There's nothing here – and it's so cold."

"You're right about the cold," said the Storyteller. "Come on, we have to walk, or rather climb, the last part."

No one was eager to leave the protection of the van. The bitterly cold wind was blowing around the van and those inside could feel the icy fingers probing through any crack or crevice. "Come on, we have to make a move," insisted the Storyteller. "I promise you it will be worth it. And I promise that you will be more comfortable where we're going than we are here."

It was the second promise that persuaded the passengers to disembark.

As they stepped from the van, they felt the full force of a biting gale, so cold it took their breath away. Adam, gasping, managed to shout his concerns to the Storyteller. "We have to find shelter. It's too cold."

Luke suffered most. He had no coat to protect him against the raging elements. Never had he experienced such icy conditions. Indeed, as he minded to the Storyteller, he had never imagined such an inhospitable place could exist.

"Well at least we won't have any problems parking," the Storyteller shouted to Adam, and then, since he could see neither Adam nor Eve was in the mood for joking, added; "Follow me and we can be out of this wind in a few minutes."

Adam looked around. It was difficult to see how they could escape the dreadful weather. They were on a flat rock, a granite platform. Above the platform a sheer, dark mountain face louered over them. Adam looked back down the mountain and noticed there was no track leading to the granite platform on which Gwoat had parked the van. However they had reached that desolate place, it was not by driving up a mountain path.

"Follow me," the Storyteller shouted and the questors fell into line, with Adam at the front and Gwoat at the rear. As was his habit, Gwoat had taken some time to secure the van, but the Storyteller had urged Gwoat to leave the van unlocked. "The lock will ice up," he had shouted above the piercing wind. "And who is going to steal a van up here anyway, with nowhere to drive it?" So, despite some misgivings, Gwoat had returned to the van and unlocked it.

The Storyteller was as good as his word. The questors made their way around the granite platform, with the higher reaches of the mountain towering over them. Within minutes, they were sheltered by the wall of the mountain. "That's better," said the Storyteller to himself and the others. "At least we can hear each other without screaming at the top of our voices."

"Are you all right?" Adam asked Eve.

Eve nodded. She was shivering; it was too much effort to speak.

The Storyteller waited for everyone to catch up. "I think it best I prepare you a little for your next encounter."

Adam put his arm around Eve, and Luke rubbed against Eve's legs, both welcomed by Eve most of all for the warmth they imparted.

"We are here to meet a Titan," the Storyteller continued. "We are here to meet the greatest Titan of them all. We are here to meet Prometheus."

Adam and Eve had been more than a little surprised when the Storyteller had arranged a meeting with God, but an interview with a Titan, a mythic being from the folklore of ancient Greece, this was utterly bizarre. Adam and Eve looked at each other, and then back to the Storyteller, hoping for more information.

"Prometheus!" exclaimed Rambler, "Wonderful!"

"What's a Titan?" asked Numpty.

"The Titans were a race of gods," Rambler explained, "the offspring of Uranus, the sky, and Gaia, the earth. Most of the Titans fought the gods of Olympus for supremacy, I believe. Prometheus, the son of Iapetus, sided with the Olympians and, when the Olympians were victorious, was rewarded by Zeus, king of the Olympian gods."

"You are well-versed in the tales of ancient Greece," observed the

Storyteller approvingly.

"But they're just myths," Numpty blurted out. "They're not true, Uncle, are they?"

"I had not thought so," Rambler conceded, "but, if we are to meet Prometheus, I may have to revise my opinion and subdue my scepticism."

"I guess Titans are no less likely than God," Adam suggested.

"Are we to learn anything useful from this Titan?" Eve asked.

"That is why we are here," the Storyteller replied. "There are no guarantees but Prometheus is well worth a visit. He was the most intelligent of the Titans, smarter than Zeus himself. His name means forethought. He was indeed a deity with vision."

"Didn't he end up having his liver consumed by an eagle?" hazarded Adam, who was scrabbling around the corners of his memory for the few snippets of Greek mythology he could recall from his childhood. "If he's the one I'm thinking of, he didn't plan his own fate that well."

"You assume that someone capable of planning ahead would use that facility simply for their own benefit," Rambler intervened. "As I recall, his punishment was for helping mankind. He no doubt understood the consequences of his philanthropy, but went ahead anyway. For a greater good."

Adam grunted.

Rambler turned to the Storyteller: "Is he still undergoing punishment?" An interview with a deity chained to a rock, suffering exquisite pain inflicted by a ravening eagle feasting on titanic liver seemed an inauspicious setting for an hospitable welcome, let alone a possible moment of enlightenment.

"No," replied the Storyteller, "don't worry. Heracles released him from his torment some time ago. He's in pretty good shape now. The odd twinge but generally fit and, if not full of enthusiasm, content and benign. Anyway, let's meet him."

They walked on for a few more minutes, stumbling occasionally on the rocks or slipping on the ice. "We're lucky we have arrived in the summer. There's still snow on the peaks, always is snow here, all year round, but it's really not too bad at this level." No one responded. It was quite cold enough, even in summer, and the wind, from which they were now at least partially sheltered, was still managing to reach them with some cruel gusts.

"Which mountain is this?" enquired Rambler, determined to have an accurate chronicle of the adventure.

"This is Elbrus, known in ancient times as Strobilos. It's the tallest mountain in Europe."

151

"Strobilos means twisted object, if my memory of ancient Greek serves me well," mused Rambler. "The name must refer to its peculiar formation. From the type of stones and rocks, I guess the mountain is of volcanic origin."

Just as the party navigated their way round a rocky outcrop, a flaming missile whistled past, a large burning arrow soared out into the sky, battering its way through the wind and clouds.

"What was that?" said Eve. Of the four questors, or five if you include Luke, Eve was suffering most from the cold. She felt miserable and threatened. Unlike the others, she had not been arraigned before God and sentenced to death, so she felt the hardships of the Caucasian mountains particularly acutely. Adam, Rambler and Numpty were just happy to be alive and, rather like anyone who has survived a particularly challenging or dangerous ordeal, they felt increased self-confidence.

"That," the Storyteller replied, "that was Prometheus practising his archery."

"What was he aiming at?" asked Adam. "The sky is a pretty easy target."

"He was sending a message," said the Storyteller.

"To the gods," suggested Rambler.

"Yes," the Storyteller laughed. "And to any large birds that might be circling the mountains looking for a tasty morsel to gorge on."

As the Storyteller spoke, they reached a vast round opening in the side of the mountain. No doubt it had been the mouth of a cave originally but it had been enlarged and carved into a perfect circular form by an intelligent being with not inconsiderable building skills.

"Who visits the dwelling of the Titan Prometheus, son of Iapetus?" boomed a voice from within the cave.

"It's me," responded the Storyteller, a response which seemed wholly inadequate to the questors. Not only did it fail to match in tone the dignity and authority in the voice of the questioner; it failed even to identify the speaker.

"Aha!" said the booming voice, "'tis indeed you, unless my ears deceive me."

There was the sound of heavy footfall and then, at the mouth of the cave, stood a mighty figure, at least seven feet tall, as tall as any of the angels but considerably more substantial. "It's good to see you once again," said Prometheus, extending a very large hand towards the Storyteller, who, rather than risk a single hand, embraced the offered hand with both of his own. "And whom have you brought with you?"

The Titan seemed to be, in human terms, in his fifties, a little past his prime but still generally in good physical shape. His face was heavily lined, the marks of experience and of pain etched deep, but his blue eyes were clear and still sparkled with humour and intelligence. The grey hair at his temples signalled wisdom rather than age or decline.

"But wait," said Prometheus, "this is no way to greet those who make the arduous journey to this place. Formal introductions can wait. First, enter the home of the Fire-bringer." With that invitation, Prometheus stood to one side and, with the sweep of his arm, invited the questors to enter his domain.

This was no ordinary cave. All the questors gasped in astonishment. They had entered an enclosed space as large as a small town, with its own landscape. In the distance, waterfalls cascaded down the cave walls. In the ceiling was a bright light which illuminated the entire interior like a miniature sun. The floor of the cave was level, much of it paved with marble. Widely spaced were large buildings that would not have looked out of place in some of the ancient world's greatest cities.

"I see you've been busy since my last visit," said the Storyteller. "I like the marble, although, if the floor is ever to endure much wear, I would have recommended granite."

Prometheus smiled. "What do you think of the new lighting?" he asked. "A gift from Apollo. He says it will outlast me and, since I am immortal, that's a damn good guarantee."

"It's great," said the Storyteller, "but does it ever go off? It's a bit bright if it shines all the time."

"That's the really clever bit," said Prometheus. "It's synchronised with the real sun. It comes on at dawn and fades away when evening falls."

Rambler was by now writing frenetically in his notepad.

"I see you've brought a scribe with you," observed the Titan.

"I'm so sorry," said the Storyteller. "Allow me to introduce Adam and Eve, who are the principal questors, and Rambler, the scribe, and his nephew Numpty, the latter two travellers whom we picked up on our way here. And my driver, Gwoat, whom you have met before. Oh! and not forgetting Luke, the dog of Adam and Eve."

Luke wagged his tail, but as much with irritation as pleasure. Why did humans so often preface his introduction with 'not forgetting'? It seemed to suggest that forgetting him was almost to be expected and certainly, if it happened, forgivable. So Luke got up, shook himself emphatically and trotted towards the Titan.

Prometheus seemed a little perplexed as Luke approached. "I'm pleased to see he's imbued with only one head," he said, which the

Storyteller and Rambler both took to be a light-hearted reference to Cerberos, the three-headed dog that guarded the entrance to Hades.

"He's a pet," explained the Storyteller. "Humans today often share their homes with dogs and cats. This one is a particularly intelligent golden retriever."

Luke, preening a little at the Storyteller's compliment, expected a welcome from the host but, since the Titan made no move to pat him, he adopted a dignified sitting position at the Titan's feet.

Adam spoke. "I'm Adam," he began, unnecessarily confirming the Storyteller's comprehensive introduction of all members of the party. "I'm just not sure why we are here," he ended lamely.

"I guess you are here for the same reason those who have come here before came. You have questions."

Adam looked to the Storyteller for help. Prometheus seemed a decent enough chap, albeit a very large one, but a possibly mythical god from ancient Greece was really not the most likely provider of answers to questions from the 21st century.

"You have your doubts," the Titan laughed. "Well, come with me to my home; eat, drink, make yourselves comfortable; and I will tell you how this world, which raises so many questions in your mind, how this world came into being, how mankind was created and where you and your quest will end."

27 Group dynamics

Prometheus was as good as his word on the hospitality front. He made his guests comfortable in every way. They were given rooms to rest in; baths supplied with water from springs heated by the magma far below; food and drink to please the gods, let alone questing mortals.

He also gave them time to settle in to their new and strange surroundings and to talk to each other. He knew that their journey to Mount Strobilos had been stressful and that they would benefit from an opportunity to discuss their different experiences and take stock of their quest to date.

"We shall dine together later," he had told them before sending them off to their rooms.

As soon as Adam and Eve were alone together, Adam asked her about events after she had been shut out of the Garden. He tried to strike a neutral tone.

Eve's response was not what he expected or wanted. Both of them had been itching to ask each other questions. Rather than answer Adam, she demanded "What on earth got into you? Why were you so rude to Nick?"

"You seem very keen to defend Nick Peters," Adam responded sharply. "I haven't attacked him yet."

"But it's obvious you're going to," Eve returned. "You were so hostile when we met at Stoney Cross. You were snapping at him before you said you were pleased to see me. In fact, I don't think you said you were pleased to see me."

"Don't be ridiculous. I was worried sick about you!"

"It's not me who's ridiculous," Eve returned. "I wasn't trapped in an alien world with a psychopath determined to disembowel me. I'm sure you spent most of your time understandably worried sick about yourself."

Luke, who had followed his master and mistress to their room, decided he had heard enough and went off to look for more congenial company.

"I was worried about you because of what the Storyteller told me about Nick," said Adam. "He said we had to view him as our enemy. He said Nick would do anything to persuade us to abandon our search."

"Well I can only speak as I find," Eve replied carefully. It was true Nick had tried to persuade her that their quest was pointless but he had done so without any sign of malicious intent. "He helped me when I found myself alone outside the Garden. And he drove me down to

Stoney Cross to meet you. He behaved like a perfect gentleman throughout." She didn't know why she had added the last remark. It didn't quite ring true. There was the dream. There was the dream in which Adam had adopted or been possessed by Nick's voice. There was the dream in which she had slept with a man in Adam's form but whose touch was that of a stranger who spoke as Nick spoke. "As for what the Storyteller said about him," she added hurriedly, "that Nick is our enemy, I think it might be the other way round. If you remember, the Storyteller told Gwoat to force Nick's motorbike off the road when we were driving down the M3." Eve stopped talking.

Adam looked at her. After a moment, he said: "So what happened? Something happened?"

Eve thought of denying it. She could say nothing happened, and that would not be untrue. A dream is a dream, not an event in the real world. But then, she asked herself, what is the real world? Were they in the real world when they had sat watching television before the Storyteller knocked on their door? Were they in the real world in the Garden of Eden where God and his host of angels created, judged and annihilated? Were they now in a real world, thousands of years ago and thousands of miles away in the cavernous home of a Titan? That dream had seemed more real to her than any of these other worlds. Bella had been alive. Bella had survived. In that dream, everything that had been wrong was put right. In a way, the quest had been fulfilled.

"I had a dream," she said.

"You had a dream?" Adam prompted.

"I saw Bella," said Eve

"You saw Bella?" Adam was worried now.

"Please don't repeat everything I say." She felt awkward enough trying to explain without Adam echoing her words with the addition of a questioning inflection.

"What do you mean you saw Bella? You mean you had a dream about Bella," Adam offered a rational formulation.

"It was more than that," Eve replied. "It was as though I relived that day, as though we had a second chance, and this time you told Bella not to shelter under the tree. The storm came and the lightning struck and the bough fell but this time no one was hurt."

"But it was just a dream?" Adam wanted her to confirm she understood.

"It was an alternative," Eve replied enigmatically.

"What does that mean?" demanded Adam with a mixture of frustration and fear. "I think he's been messing with your mind. You're not making any sense. Bella's dead. You had a dream. I've had dreams

156

too. I've also been through that day a thousand times in my head. I've thought 'what if' and 'if only' and 'why her?', 'why us?' and I'll tell you what. At the end of it, I haven't known whether to scream or cry because it doesn't make any difference. What happened, happened. That's it."

"It was more real than this," Eve insisted, indicating with a sweep of her hand the luxuriously appointed room where they were talking. "It was more real than anything else. Nick said I could be with Bella again. And I was. And we put things right."

"What do you mean 'Nick said'?" There was a tremor in Adam's voice. "What has Nick Peters got to do with Bella? What has Nick Peters got to do with us? He's putting ideas into your head. You just had a dream. It wasn't chance he picked you up at the gates of the Garden. And why did you say this time I told Bella not to stand under the tree. Why me? It wasn't just me. You could have told her. Can't you see what he's doing? He's trying to come between us and it seems he's succeeding."

"It's all right," said Eve soothingly. "It's all right. Of course he's not coming between us. I know it was only a dream." Eve felt she had said more than enough. Even so, she couldn't help adding: "But it was just so real."

oooOooo

After leaving his master and mistress, Luke made his way to the chamber assigned to Rambler and Numpty. As he slipped into the room, he heard Numpty ask his uncle a question: "Why does Adam keep picking on me?"

Numpty's uncle prevaricated. "It's just his way. He's not picking on you. He's joshing you. He thinks it is amusing."

Numpty was not to be fobbed off. After a minute of silence, Numpty asked: "Is it because he thinks I'm stupid? Is it because I am stupid?"

"Rambler took his nephew by the shoulders and looked into his eyes. "You are not stupid, my boy. You must never say that, or indeed think it."

Luke could see the lad was upset. He made his way over to Numpty and rubbed against his legs in a gesture of manly solidarity. Luke knew well enough what it was to be underestimated.

"Why do you try so hard to teach me?" Numpty pressed his uncle. There was a tone of resignation and an undertone of despair in his voice. "Why do you bother? Why do you bother at all?"

"Listen to me," his uncle spoke firmly. "You are an apt pupil. You

157

are always ready to listen and to learn. You have made tremendous progress and I truly believe you have a gift for language and a love of ideas. Don't ever think I begrudge you a moment of my time. And there is something else, my boy. You have shown great courage. You stood up to those bullying bikers at Fleet; and you were a hero in the Hall of Justice when you stood before that travesty of a God. I am truly proud of you. As for Adam, I think he is unhappy and insecure. Those who are feeling vulnerable themselves often seek relief in denigrating others."

oooOooo

While Adam and Eve were catching up and Rambler was doing his best to restore his nephew's self-confidence, the Storyteller was debriefing Gwoat.

The Storyteller summarised Gwoat's tentative explanation of his abrupt departure from the gate of the Garden: "So you took the word of a grotesque fairy-gnome type person and, without so much as a second thought, disobeyed my explicit instruction to stay where you were, that is to wait for us to return from the Garden, and instead you shot off down the M3, M27 and A31 to Stoney Cross."

"No, no, no!" Gwoat objected. "Of course I gave it a second thought but the fairy seemed so well informed. She knew who was in the party, who was leading it, where you were going. And she said you had been most insistent that she should come with me. If it had been a ploy to get me drive away, why would she have wanted to come with me? In any case, where I come from fairies are, generally speaking, reliable. 'Giorraíonn beirt bothar', she said to me. 'Two people make the road shorter'."

"Oh well, now I understand," the Storyteller was cutting. "A few words of Gaelic and off you go. Didn't you think it just a little suspicious that I should have changed my mind so soon after entering the Garden? You say you left almost as soon as we had passed through the gate. What do you think could have happened so quickly that I should completely contradict myself? After all the years we have been conducting these expeditions, did it not cross your mind that this fairy-gnome person might be Nick Peters' side-kick, the ubiquitous shapeshifter Grimrose? You said she seemed a tad on the fat side and a little uncomfortable. I'm not bloody surprised. Squeezing Grimrose's essence into the form of a fairy, even a grossly fat one, must have taxed his shape-shifting capacity to the limit."

"To be sure, I did have my suspicions," Gwoat, now with beads of sweat trickling down his forehead, conceded, "but I thought, if you were really going to materialise at Stoney Cross and I failed to meet you there, you would have been even more upset than you are now."

The Storyteller hadn't finished. "And on the way, you picked up a couple of young travellers! Did their arrival on the scene not strengthen your suspicions?"

"That was strange," Grimrose conceded, "but, to be honest, I was quite pleased to have more company. The fairy-gnome was making me feel nervous."

"And the two travellers turned out to be homicidal maniacs intent on eliminating you and Grimrose?"

"Well they made a mistake there all right." Gwoat, still sweating, shivered as he recalled the final act of his journey with Grimrose. "The fairy-gnome became a killing machine. I doubt if Maizy and Sandy knew what hit them. Well, I'm pretty sure Maizy didn't. Sandy might just have recognised Maizy's head as Grimrose swung it down to crush his skull."

"Had you not by then realised the whole purpose of persuading you to drive to Stoney Cross was to get you and the van far away from me and the questors? Grimrose had been given orders to eliminate you but Peters was worried his acolyte might weaken. Grimrose still has some threads of decency woven through his shape-shifting fabric. So Peters devised a plan B. Maizy and Sandy. He was confident they wouldn't fail him because he knew they really enjoyed killing people. After all, that very morning, they had murdered Maizy's parents. Indeed they were so enthusiastic about 'offing' people that they decided to 'off' Grimrose as well as you. I doubt if Peters ordered Grimrose's death but I guess he didn't much care either way."

"So there's some irony there," observed Gwoat, now sweating, shivering and hopping from one foot to the other. "If Peters hadn't sent Maizy and Sandy, Grimrose might have done the deed, I would have been dead and you would have been undone." Then he added: "I'm feeling the need to use the facilities." With that, he trotted off to the marble clad bathroom to perform the necessary ablutions, to relieve his overstretched bladder and to evacuate his by now tumultuously gaseous bowels.

28 Background

A gong struck to advise that dinner was ready. The questors gathered in the reception area. Prometheus was nowhere to be seen.

"What an extraordinary place." Rambler broke the silence. "Who built this place and what is it for?"

"I'll tell you what I know," the Storyteller offered. "But you will have to address many of your questions to Prometheus. He himself has built this place – not entirely on his own, he has had help from some of the gods – but certainly most of it is his own work. You must remember he is a god as well as a Titan. It was simply a large cave when he found it. After Heracles released him from his torment, he could have gone anywhere but he chose to make this cave his home. And what a home!"

"But what is it all for?" Adam probed. "The place seems empty. Does anyone else live here? What are all the buildings for?"

The Storyteller grimaced. "So many questions!" He gathered his thoughts: "All I know is that Prometheus was scarred by the punishment Zeus inflicted on him. I don't mean physically scarred, although the dreadful daily punishment has indeed done some permanent physical damage. I mean mental scars. I think we would call it post-traumatic stress syndrome. Zeus can't harm him now but the damage he did to a Titan he considered to be a traitor, the damage was appalling. Every day, Prometheus makes giant arrows almost two metres in length. He dips their heads in tar. Every few hours, he takes his mighty bow, lights the tip of an arrow and fires it into the heavens. It is obsessive-compulsive behaviour. He is driven partly by anger and partly by fear, anger at Zeus for the pain he suffered, fear of the eagle that Zeus sent to carry out its gory task. It's also fear that has driven Prometheus to build this fortress inside the mountain. As for the buildings, I just don't know. He once told me he had in mind the setting up of a rival seat of power to compete with Olympus but I don't think he was serious. It is more likely, in my opinion, that it is another symptom of his Obsessive Compulsive Disorder. He built the first house to live in and, when it was finished, he built another, and then another. After all, if you're immortal, you must find something to fill your time."

"So how is a neurotic god, exhibiting extreme forms of OCD, going to help us in our quest?" asked Adam. "Our meeting with God was negative in many ways but it had one constructive outcome. It eliminated that avenue as a path to the possibility of finding answers. I really can't see how this Titan can help us. We would never have considered him as a likely source of enlightenment, so eliminating him doesn't move us forward at all."

"Even though he created mankind, or at least made us what we are," the Storyteller interrupted.

"Another creator of mankind with psychological problems," observed Eve.

"Yes, but I think you'll find Prometheus rather more benign, despite his neuroses, than the God of the Old Testament," soothed the Storyteller.

"So this Titan claims to have been mankind's progenitor," Adam mused. "I knew he was supposed to have given us fire. I didn't know he also gave us life."

"Oh yes!" Rambler joined in enthusiastically. "After Zeus had prevailed, with the help of Prometheus, in his battle with his father, Cronus, Zeus rewarded his Titan allies (Prometheus and his brother Epimetheus). He allowed them to fill the world with living things, including Man."

"My word!" said the Storyteller to Rambler, "I can see you are going to be a real asset. I'm beginning to feel redundant."

"My uncle is a classy something or other," asserted Numpty proudly. "He studied Greek at Oxford. He knows all about the gods and the heroes. Homer is all Greek to him."

"Funnily enough, if I'm not mistaken, Prometheus was not mentioned at all in Homer's works," said Rambler, confirming his erudition and his propensity for digression.

"Could I say things like that?" asked Numpty.

"Of course you could," encouraged his uncle. "As you acquire more knowledge it is perfectly acceptable, if not obligatory, to share your treasure trove of information with others."

"No," said Numpty. "I mean could I say 'if I'm not mistaken'? Could I say 'I'm the cleverest person in the entire world, if I'm not mistaken'? Could I say 'I never make mistakes, if I'm not mistaken'? Could I say, 'There's no such thing as truth, if I'm not mistaken'?"

"You could say all those things," Adam interrupted, "but most of us would think the engine was revving but the car was firmly stuck in neutral, if I'm not mistaken."

"You are too hard on the lad," said Rambler, stepping in to protect his nephew. He had made a mental note to defend his nephew robustly against any future jibes from Adam. "He has a point. By introducing the notion of error, the expression 'if I'm not mistaken' raises the possibility that the statement is false, and yet it is generally taken to confirm the proposition and the authority of its proponent. It is an instance of false 'false modesty'. You are quite right, lad. It is a confusing and misleading idiom."

Adam ignored Rambler. "But if Prometheus was a Titan, why did he side with Zeus against Cronus, who was the Titan leader?"

"It's not an easy question," said the Storyteller. "Of course, Prometheus could see which way the wind was blowing. His name, associated with forethought, indicates his ability to think things through. He foresaw that Zeus would be victorious. So that's one reason why he abandoned his fellow Titans to support Zeus. But I'm pretty sure there was more to it than that. I think he had plans, plans to create the human race and plans to make it the master of the gods of Olympus."

"He's beginning to sound like a pretty tricky character," said Eve. "First he betrayed his own kind, the Titans, then he helped mankind against his new master Zeus and his Olympians".

"Obviously loyalty isn't his strong suit," observed Adam.

"I wonder what he has in mind for us?" Eve mused.

"Whatever it is, I guess it must already have happened," the Storyteller pointed out. "We have travelled back in time thousands of years. If Prometheus has had a hand in our future, we have only to look at the world we left behind to see the results."

"So are you saying we owe our world to this Titan?" Adam asked.

"That's for you to judge," the Storyteller answered. "But, for sure, the gods of Olympus are no more and Man rules the earth and all that is in it. Whether we are fulfilling Prometheus' vision, I have no idea. Perhaps you would like to ask him."

On cue, Prometheus strode into the reception area of his grand house and suggested they should join him in the banqueting hall.

29 Talking with a Titan

After a sumptuous feast, prepared and served by a bevy of rather fetching Oreads, or mountain nymphs, Prometheus took the floor.

"You have no idea how pleased I am to receive you all," he boomed. "I don't have too many visitors."

Not really surprising, the questors thought, given that the location of Prometheus' cavernous home appeared to be entirely inaccessible, except to birds and, evidently, the Storyteller's camper van.

"Now what can I do for you?" The Titan paused.

'That's a better start,' thought Eve, 'better than God and his "Get down on your knees and worship me or I'll rip you open".'

"We have come," the Storyteller spoke on behalf of the group, "in search of the truth."

Prometheus laughed. "So it's no trivial matter that has brought you to my domain. If you want the truth," he continued, "I am going to have to give you a history lesson. It's a lesson with some frustrating gaps but it is true as far as I know and, from it, you may be able to grasp as much of the truth as you want or need."

Both Adam and Eve had many questions to ask, and Rambler was almost incontinent with curiosity, but they all settled back, well satisfied by the rest, the baths and above all the excellent dinner. Prometheus was offering to teach, and they were prepared to be taught.

"As you may know, I helped Zeus to overthrow Cronus, despite the fact that most of my fellow Titans sided with Cronus. Why did I do that? I did it because Cronus' rule was based on a lie. It is a lie that all the gods have promulgated. I challenged Cronus. I urged him to tell the truth but he would have none of it. 'What do you want?' he said to me. 'Do you want chaos? Do you want anarchy? Do you want to destroy us all?' I told him the lie would destroy us far more certainly than trying to maintain it. He called me a fool."

They were all itching to ask Prometheus what the lie was but they didn't feel sufficiently comfortable in the presence of a Titan to interrupt.

"You probably know the story that the world began with Chaos," Prometheus continued. "And that out of Chaos came Gaia, the Earth goddess, and one or two other primeval divinities, including Eros, the god of love. Gaia spontaneously gave birth to Uranus, the god of the sky. Eros was eager to instigate a mating. Given the limited number of options at the time and unsympathetic to or possibly unaware of taboos on incest, Eros made Gaia and Uranus fall in love. Out of their union came a panoply of Titans including Cronus and Rhea, and indeed my own father, Iapetus. Cronus and Rhea, brother and sister, mated and gave birth to all the gods of Olympus, including of course Zeus."

Rambler coughed and Prometheus paused. "I should have mentioned before I began," Prometheus said, "if you have any questions, please ask them. It is quite a long lesson and it will be easier for you and for me if you break it up with questions."

Rambler spoke. "Was there not something before Chaos? It is a long time since I read the Greek myths," he hesitated, fearful that referring to Prometheus as a myth might be construed as offensive but Prometheus waved him to continue, "but I seem to recall that Chronus and Ananke preceded Chaos."

"You are absolutely right," said Prometheus enthusiastically. "Time and Necessity, without them there would have been nothing or so we Titans were told to believe. Who really knows what happened before we were born? Who knows what happened when the universe was born?"

Adam spoke. "You mentioned that you fell out with Cronus because of a lie. What exactly was the lie?"

"I'll come to that in a moment," Prometheus replied, "but first I need to explain why, in the end, I fell out with Zeus. For ten years, Zeus battled with his father Cronus and for ten years I and my brother Epimetheus helped him. I fought Cronus because of the lie, and because of a promise that Zeus gave me. The promise was simple, that I should be allowed to help mankind fulfil their destiny; the lie made it complicated."

"The lie being...," Adam persisted.

"The lie that the gods created Man or, to be more precise, that I created Man," Prometheus replied.

"So you didn't create mankind," Eve summarised.

"That was the lie?" said Adam, a little disappointed.

"The lie was that the gods existed before Man. We didn't. And none of us created mankind. I helped mankind. I gave you fire. But all that stuff about creating you out of clay, total nonsense."

"So what are you saying?" Adam probed. "Are you saying we created the gods? Because if that is what you are saying, it won't cause the earth to move. Most people have thought that was the case for ages."

"No, I'm not saying that either," Prometheus returned without any resentment. "No, you didn't create me. But you did have the power to create. That's what I saw in you, a limitless power for creativity. I tried to explain this to Cronus. I told him you were the future, not because you were more powerful than the Titans or the gods of Olympus, but because there were no limits to your thinking, your understanding and what you could imagine and create.

"When I sided with Zeus, he said he understood that mankind was unique. He certainly took a profound interest in at least some members of the female sex. Poor Io!"

For a moment, the Titan's mind seemed to wander but he quickly snapped back to the point. "To be fair, once Zeus had dealt with Cronus, he did allow me to nurture mankind but it soon became clear he had no real interest in mortals. He never took my ideas seriously. He was as myopic and self-centred as his father and, as it turned out, as sadistic. Matters reached breaking point when I gave Man the gift of fire, or rather restored it after Zeus had withdrawn it."

"You mean Man had fire before you gave it to him?" Rambler interrupted.

"Yes, of course," Prometheus confirmed. "The gift of fire story was all part of the lie. Men had fire long before I restored it to them. Zeus took fire away from mankind simply because humans decided that, when they sacrificed an animal in honour of the gods, they would eat the meat themselves and leave the bones for Zeus. Now this was a perfectly sensible decision. After all, the sacrifice was purely symbolic. Given the riches of Olympus, the king of the gods had no need for meat from mortals. If Zeus hadn't been so egotistical, he would have accepted the arrangement. But, no. He took it as a slight. There's a story, put about by the Olympians, that I tricked Zeus into choosing the bones rather than the meat, that I gave him the choice between the meat hidden inside an unappealing bull's stomach and the bones concealed in appetising fat. Total nonsense. Never happened. It was Man's decision to take the meat and offer the bones to the gods, and it was Zeus who considered the offering of bones an insult and decided to punish Man by withdrawing fire.

"I couldn't let that happen. I knew the future was yours, or at least could and should be yours. So I gave fire back to mankind. You see I knew that fire was the key. It enabled Man to keep warm when the icy wind blew; it gave him power over the wild beasts because he alone could control the licking, ravening flames; it allowed him to extract and work the metals buried in the rocks so he could make weapons and devise engines. It opened up all the possibilities that Zeus wished to deny mankind, possibilities that went far beyond the imagination of the immortals.

"So Zeus was angry, although 'angry' doesn't do it justice."

Numpty, who had remained silent and attentive throughout the

Titan's narrative but had nonetheless fallen a little behind, suddenly interrupted: "Who is Io?" Rambler hushed him, preferring that Prometheus should continue with his history, but Prometheus, good to his word, took the question.

"Io was a princess who had the misfortune to attract the attentions of Zeus. Her father, Inachus, was powerless to protect her from the ardour of the king of the gods. The oracle at Loxias warned him that, if he tried to frustrate Zeus, punishment would be swift and cataclysmic. With heavy heart, Inachus drove his daughter out of his home into the countryside where she would be accessible to Zeus. Whether Zeus loved her or simply lusted after her, I do not know. What is certain is this. Zeus came upon her in the form of a cloud and possessed her and then, because of a goddess's jealousy, Io suffered unimaginable humiliation and appalling pain.

"One day, when Zeus had been disporting himself with Io in an earthly bower, Hera, his sister and wife, located him and shot down from Olympus. Understandably fearful of Hera's notorious temper which was certain to be unleashed if she found her husband entwined in the embrace of a beautiful, naked, mortal maiden, Zeus turned his lover into a heifer, albeit an attractive one, claiming that the animal had somehow suddenly sprung forth from the earth. Hera had many attributes but stupidity was not amongst them. 'That's a really beautiful heifer, my lord,' she said. Whenever she addressed him as 'my lord', he knew trouble lay ahead. 'Indeed that heifer is so beautiful', she said, in dulcet tones, 'I should like you to give it to me.' Zeus, understandably, was not very keen but there was nothing he could say. According to him, the animal had only just appeared, so there had been no time for him to have developed an affection for the animal. With much regret, he agreed. Thus the king of the gods delivered his mistress into the hands of her implacable enemy, the goddess of marriage."

Numpty had more questions but Rambler intervened: "Anyway, you gave fire back to Man."

"Yes," said Prometheus, returning to the main thread of his narrative, "I gave fire back to Man and, as I said, Zeus was enraged. He summoned the blacksmith Hephaistos, the god of fire, his son with Hera, and commanded him to chain me to a craggy rock on this same mountain. Hephaistos, as my kin and my erstwhile companion, was reluctant to do his father's bidding but far too fearful of his father's anger to disobey. So I was bound by adamantine chains to this cold unforgiving mountain – by the will of Zeus, my cousin, and the hand of Hephaistos, my nephew.

"Then Zeus sent the eagle to torment me. By day the cruel, beaked avenger tore at my liver; by night, my liver rejuvenated. Each succeeding day I had to face the eagle and the agony, for years, decades and centuries."

"Was your crime so heinous in the eyes of Zeus?" asked Rambler.

"I had foreseen the death of the immortals, the demise of the gods," Prometheus answered. "I knew that Zeus' rule was threatened, not by gods or giants but by mankind. I knew that this was so because I knew that the gods' dominion over the world was based on a lie. Zeus wanted my help to subvert the future. He wanted me to save the gods. He wanted me to endorse the lie. I knew I couldn't."

"So how did you escape?" asked Adam. Both he and Eve could not yet see how Prometheus' story could answer any of their questions but the tale was dramatic enough for even Adam to subdue his impatience.

"I owe my freedom to Heracles," Prometheus answered. "Yes, that's right, I was freed by a son of Zeus, a hero produced by a union between the king of the gods and the beautiful Alcmene, daughter of Electryon, granddaughter of Perseus and yes, therefore, great granddaughter of Zeus himself. No doubt at all that the blood of Zeus coursed strongly through Heracles' veins!

"Heracles came to this barren, wind-scraped mountain. He saw my plight. He took his bow and, with an arrow tipped with poison, he shot that cursed eagle. Then, with his bare hands, he ripped apart the chains which Hephaistos had forged to last forever. Heracles did not fear his father's anger; Heracles did not accept that adamantine chains could not be broken. There are those who say that Heracles performed great feats because he was half god; I say to you his feats were great because he was half mortal."

Prometheus was clearly moved by his memories and the retelling of them. Breaking from his narrative, he took up the mighty bow and quiver that he had kept by his side throughout his account of past deeds and suffering. Without another word he strode from the banqueting hall, through the reception area, out of his house to the mouth of the mighty cave. There, he dipped an arrow into a brazier in which the flames ducked and dived, tossed by the gusting wind. The arrow head took the fire; Prometheus slotted the arrow into the bow and then, with a howl which drew its depth and strength from centuries of pain, he shot the arrow into the sky, flaming and high, in the direction of Mount Olympus.

At his side was Luke, who had listened intently to Prometheus' tale and had followed him out of the banqueting hall. Luke had stood by him as Prometheus fired his arrow deep into the sky and had felt the hurt and the anger in the Titan. More than that, he had seen a decent soul, an honest and courageous soul, within the Titan's giant frame. After the cry that had sounded above the wind, Luke sat close to Prometheus, leaning against his legs, looking up into the Titan's face, where he saw tears in the Titan's eyes.

30 Precedence

With Prometheus' abrupt departure, the questors were left in the banqueting hall to ponder the Titan's words.

"He seems to think that we humans have some kind of a destiny," Adam mused. "But it was all very confusing. I couldn't work out whether the gods, or rather Prometheus himself, created Man, or the other way round. I think he said neither, which implies both Man and the gods exist, or at least existed."

"He certainly told us we had fire long before he gave it to us," said Eve. "He said he simply restored it to us after Zeus took it away because of some problem about animal sacrifices."

"Yes, that's right," said Rambler. "Zeus sounds a bit like God in the Garden of Eden – self-centred, despotic and obsessed with sacrifices."

"So where should we see Prometheus in all this?" Adam asked. "In a sense, he is our saviour. He stands up for us against Zeus and, for his efforts on our behalf, he is chained to a rock and tortured by an eagle. He himself is a god, immortal, but he is Man's defender, Man's helper, a god who sees Man as the future, as the vanquisher of the immortals. He saves us from Zeus' anger; is condemned to a dreadful, eternal fate; but is somehow released from it. It's all bit paradoxical and some of it sounds rather familiar. Then there's the lie, the lie that the gods existed before us and created us. He seemed to think it was really important to expose the lie. I'm not sure whether he was saying it was the lie or exposing the lie that destroyed the gods – or will destroy the gods, since they still seem to be around at this time."

"What interests me is the destiny thing," said Rambler. "Prometheus not only saw potential in Man, he foresaw our dominance. How can anyone predict the future so far ahead? We all know the problems that beset weather forecasters – the butterfly effect. A tiny variation in initial conditions can lead to enormous and unforeseeable differences in outcomes. Hence the dubious record of meteorologists. The weather may be complex but nowhere near as complex as predicting the future of a species thousands of years in the future."

The Storyteller spoke quietly. "Unless of course you know the outcome before you make the prediction."

"It's not a prediction if you know the outcome," Adam was dismissive, "and, since the outcome lies in the future, long after you make the prediction, you can't know the outcome when you make the prediction."

Neither Eve nor Rambler was prepared to dispute Adam's

reasoning, but both of them refrained from comment. The Storyteller had so far contributed little to their debates about the purpose and progress of the quest. Eve, in particular, wondered why he had offered this particular intervention at this particular time. It did cross her mind that, since they had travelled back in time, they had not only brought their own present into the past; they had also brought Prometheus' future into his present. The thought prompted a question. In the telling of a story, obviously time was important but, in a way, it was illusory for the storyteller. After all, the teller of stories always knew the end before he even began to tell his tale.

Luke padded back into the banqueting hall. His coat was wet from the cold, moist air that swirled around the mouth of the cave. He was shivering. Two Oreads attended him at once and gently dried him with warm towels. He thanked them and, although they could not hear him, they understood his appreciation. Luke addressed the Storyteller: "He is a good man, I mean god," he said. "I stood with him as he looked out across the valley. I saw him light an arrow and fire it into the sky. I felt his pain and his sorrow but it was not for himself that he cried out. It was for us, for our mortality, and against the cruelty of the immortal gods who had condemned all men, and dogs, for that matter, indeed all living things, to die."

"I don't see how any of this provides answers for our questions," said Eve, pursuing her own line of thought. "Prometheus talks about our destiny and our victory over the gods, but it's all so impersonal and irrelevant. Why did Bella die? Why do the things that change our lives happen? Why do they happen to us? Why don't other things happen? These are questions this Titan wouldn't understand, let alone answer. They are real questions about the real lives of real people."

Adam put his arm round Eve's shoulder. She was frustrated and upset. "I know it's hard," he said, "but we won't give up, will we?"

31 Flight and fight

At the foot of Mount Strobilos, where the mountain slopes gently into grassland plain, two figures were to be seen, one busily preparing a meal of rabbit, consisting of two carcasses cooking on a makeshift spit; the other relaxing on a pile of sheepskins. "I like my rabbit well done," said Nick Peters, "and put some salt on it while it's cooking. It brings out the flavour."

Grimrose, for the other figure was indeed Nick Peters' shapeshifter, said nothing but obediently sprinkled salt on the now browning rabbit. The wood fire under the spit burned well in the breeze. Grimrose, who had adopted the form of a Caucasian peasant of middle years, turned the meat carefully to ensure the rabbit was evenly cooked, adding more salt as he thought fit.

When Nick Peters had abandoned him at Stoney Cross, Grimrose had assumed he should expect some form of punishment, or at least, a severe reprimand for his failure to terminate Gwoat. Not so. Shortly after the questors had piled into their camper van and departed, Nick had returned to Stoney Cross.

Instead of delivering a diatribe about Grimrose's bungling incompetence, Nick had simply asked: "Have you got the co-ordinates?" Grimrose was taken aback. He had prepared a robust defence of his conduct, based on the idiocy of forcing him to compress himself into the form of a fairy and on his master's duplicity in initiating a plan B without any consultation, a plan B which could have entailed his own termination. But defence was unnecessary. On this occasion, Nick seemed intent on moving on.

"Yes," Grimrose answered Nick Peter's question. "I have the time co-ordinates precisely; as for the space co-ordinates, I have them within an acceptable margin of error, probably about half a mile."

"Excellent," said Nick. "We shall get something to eat and then make our move."

So it was that, after a splendid lunch of steak and kidney pudding, followed by a generous slice of black forest gateau, Nick and Grimrose had set off in pursuit of the questors. "Bloody good meal!" Nick had remarked, as he locked on to the shapeshifter's mind and started to tap into the meta-energy they would need to transport themselves across a few thousand miles and back a few thousand years. "It may be the last really good meal we have for some time," he had added, just before he locked on to the co-ordinates and hit the lobe that effected the spatial and temporal leap to place them where they now found themselves, at the foot of Mount Strobilos.

"Smells good!" said Nick, sniffing the aroma of the thoroughly cooked rabbits wafting to him on the clean highland air. They should have been sated by the high calorific value of their lunch but travel can be exhausting, especially when it involves traversing such large extents of space and time. They both tucked in to the meat with considerable enthusiasm.

Grimrose's eating habits were rather unrefined. He had, after all, assumed the persona of a Caucasian peasant of several millennia ago. With mouth open most of the time, he chewed the smaller rabbit bones and then either swallowed them or spat them out if they were still too large or hard. In normal circumstances, such behaviour would have elicited a stern rebuke from Nick Peters, who valued good table manners, but, on this occasion, he let it pass.

After eating, the pair settled back to digest the meal. "You have done well," said Nick.

Grimrose, unused to praise even when he had done well, was doubly surprised by this unexpected compliment. And nervous. The only occasions on which Nick had expressed appreciation of his servant's redoubtable efforts in the past had been precursors to even greater demands for service in the future. It was to be so again.

"You have done well," Nick repeated. "Now all we have to do is to reach the cave where Prometheus lives and currently entertains the questors." They both turned to look at the mighty mountain that reared up behind them. By chance, at the same moment, Prometheus unleashed one of his flaming arrows deep into the grey sky.

"What on earth is that?" exclaimed Grimrose. "It looks like a flaming spear."

"That," said Nick with satisfaction, "is one of the Titan's arrows and, more importantly, its starting point is an exact marker of the entrance to his cave. Every couple of hours, Prometheus lets fly one of his flame-tipped arrows. It's a meaningless gesture but, apparently, it relieves the tension in him. He bears this grudge against Zeus and he thinks firing off an arrow in the direction of Mount Olympus is an appropriate way of expressing his feelings. Fairly obvious he needs therapy."

"So how do we get up there?" Grimrose asked, while using a makeshift toothpick to remove a piece of meat caught in a food trap between two of his Caucasian peasant's teeth. "I guess there's a mountain path, a track of some sort."

"It's funny you should mention that," Nick responded. "Bit of a problem there. Sure, there's a track which will take you some of the way up but, unfortunately, the track doesn't reach the cave, not by a long chalk."

"So we're going to have to climb," suggested Grimrose. 'Climbing would probably be more of a problem for Nick than for me,' thought Grimrose. 'I can adopt the form of an experienced mountaineer. I don't think Nick has done any rock-climbing.'

"Ah," said Nick, ignoring the irritating sucking noise Grimrose made in his continuing efforts to extricate the recalcitrant gristle still lodged in his dental food trap, "'fraid it's not quite as simple as that. You see the platform which supports the mouth of Prometheus' cave is a massive horizontal granite overhang. There's no way you can reach it by climbing." Nick paused and waited for Grimrose to speak.

After a moment, Grimrose said: "Well if it can't be reached by climbing, I guess that's it."

Still Nick said nothing.

Grimrose was puzzled. "So it's impossible – unless we sprout wings."

No sooner were the words out of his mouth than he felt a sickening, sinking feeling in his stomach. "Absolutely not," he said.

Nick smiled. "I think we have to discuss it," he said gently. "We've come all this way. We can't give up now."

"Maybe you can't," Grimrose responded, "but if you're thinking what I think you're thinking, I can. You're on your own on this one."

"Why are you so hostile?" Nick responded. "Why don't you see it as a challenge? Why don't you see it as an adventure into a new world?" Then his tone changed. Nick spoke quietly but the subtext of his words reeked of menace: "Why don't you see it as something you have to do because it's so much better than the alternative?"

"It wouldn't work," said Grimrose. "Have you any idea how big I would have to be. I would need a wing span of at least thirty feet. In any case, I have never shape-shifted into an animal."

"That's why it's an adventure," said Nick tartly. "And do stop the tooth-sucking thing." Even in these circumstances, there was a limit to Nick Peters' tolerance.

Grimrose ignored the rebuke. "Even if I could shapeshift into a giant bird, and even if I could lift and land you on the platform, I'm far from sure I could shapeshift back into human form. I need a human brain to will the shape. What would happen if I ended up with a bird brain?"

"You seem to have managed well enough so far," Nick quipped.

"This is scarcely the time for levity," snapped Grimrose. "Not if you want my help."

"Funnily enough, levity is exactly what we want," Nick replied.

"I've really given this some thought. Of course, there are problems – and risks. But, if we pick the right time, and we get a really good updraft, it's possible."

Grimrose changed tack. "Why do you want to go up there anyway? What can you do there that you can't do more effectively when they leave?"

"I need to disrupt whatever is going on up there. Prometheus is nobody's fool. He outwitted Zeus for a start."

"And ended up chained to a rock for millennia with an eagle pecking away at his liver. Not that smart, I'd say."

"Zeus had power which he used and abused but he made a serious error in underestimating Prometheus. I don't intend to make the same mistake. Punishing the Titan may have assuaged Zeus' anger but it didn't change anything. Prometheus was right about the future, and that's what worries me. The sooner I can get in amongst whatever is happening up there, the sooner I can put a stop to it."

"You sound worried, almost frightened," Grimrose hazarded.

"Every day Adam and Eve pursue their quest, the harder it becomes to scupper it. The more time and energy they devote to the Storyteller's idiotic venture, the less inclined they will be to write it off as a fool's errand. That's why I need to intervene now. And that's why you have to put me on that granite platform."

Grimrose realised his master's mind was made up. He reverted to his concerns about practicalities. "I'm not even sure I can do it. It's theoretically possible but there's something almost perverted about a shapeshifter adopting an animal form – at least that's how it's seen in shapeshifter circles."

"Well I won't tell anyone if you don't," offered Nick. "It'll be our little secret."

Nick's flippancy irritated Grimrose. "Have you any idea what is involved in shape-shifting into another species? It requires extreme mental and physical exertion, and will power, a concentration of mental energy that is beyond the comprehension of other life forms. I would have to configure every atom of my material existence to conform to the essential nature and physical composition of a bird, and then scale it up to a size that has never existed. You say your plan involves some risk. The first risk and, to me, the most disconcerting, is that I might well disintegrate while undergoing the process of shape-shifting."

"All right, all right, enough," said Nick. "It's a tough call. It will take a lot out of you. It may even kill you. But, shucks, let's give it a try anyway. I suggest you spend the rest of today experimenting and, when you've transformed and tried a few practice flights, you can take me up

174

over the foothills to see whether the big trip up the mountain is practical."

32 Prometheus and Numpty

After Prometheus' history lesson and the brief discussion of its meaning and significance, the questors decided to withdraw to their rooms.

Rambler and Numpty were the last to leave the banqueting hall. As they were leaving, Prometheus returned.

"Excuse me, sir," said Numpty, "but I have some questions which I did not ask. Would it be possible for me to ask them now?"

Rambler immediately intervened to rein in his nephew. "I'm sure our host has many things to do and we have already no doubt occupied more of his time than we deserve."

"Not at all," responded the affable Titan, who had taken a liking to young Numpty. "I will enjoy your company. Fire away and I'll do my best to answer you."

Rambler was as delighted as his nephew for he too had many questions.

"What happened to Io?" asked Numpty. "You left her at the mercy of Hera, who didn't sound a very merciful goddess."

"Quite right, lad," Prometheus laughed, "and that's putting it mildly. You don't mess with Hera. To answer your question about Io, I need to explain a bit more about the gods in general. As you know, I have the gift of foresight so, to some extent at least, I can explain the gods to you in terms you will understand. You should begin by taking on board that the family of the gods (of which I am a member) is profoundly dysfunctional.

"What do I mean by that? Well, the family begins with psychotic violence and incest. From the start, there is bickering, conniving, treachery and compulsive sexual promiscuity. Gaia mated with her own son, Uranus. From that incestuous union came, amongst others, the Titans of which Iapetus, my father, was one. Cronus rose up against his father and castrated him. Interesting that – cutting off the source of his own creation, a peculiarly intimate way of offing his father! Cronus then mated with his own sister Rhea, who gave birth to Hestia, Hades, Poseidon, Demeter, Hera and Zeus. Cronus swallowed the first five, fearful that one of them would kill him, so we should add infanticide and cannibalism to the list of deviant familial behaviour. Zeus avoided the swallowing thing through the good offices of his mother Rhea, who, I guess, was fed up with birthing only to see her offspring consumed by her husband. She wrapped a stone in swaddling clothes and Cronus, happily not given to chewing his offspring, gulped the stone down in one, thinking it to be his latest son. Zeus, on reaching maturity, rose up against his own father and overthrew him. Obviously patricide runs in the family, a little joke I used to have with Iapetus, my father."

Rambler had been scribbling furiously, not to record the history with which, through his classical education and subsequent study, he was already familiar, but to list the many questions which had always troubled him and which till now had remained unanswered.

Before Numpty could remind Prometheus of his interest in Io, Rambler leapt in.

"Forgive me for interrupting," he began, "but, in our own time, we tend to interpret the history of the gods as myths with symbolic rather than literal meaning. For example, we see Uranus as the sky and Gaia as the Earth."

"That's entirely up to you," Prometheus replied. "Something you might like to take up with the Storyteller."

"Tell me what happened to Io." Numpty pleaded. "What happened to the poor cow?"

"As I told you, Hera, sister and wife of Zeus, was not stupid. She knew that if Zeus hankered after a girl, it would take some ingenuity to frustrate his lust. She tied Io, now locked in the form of a heifer, to a sacred olive tree and assigned the giant, never-sleeping hundred-eyed Argus Panoptes to guard her. Zeus, my cousin, was also no slouch on the craftiness front. He sent Hermes to beguile the monster with some rather nifty flute-playing which was designed to induce a soporific state. As soon as Argus nodded off, Hermes offed his noddle, so to speak. Io was now free from her bonds but not free from Hera's persecution. Hera sent a gadfly to sting her unrelentingly, to drive her to distraction and far away from home. Poor Io wandered far and wide pursued by Hera's gadfly until she eventually reached the Caucasus, this very mountain to which I at the time was chained, my liver daily sustenance for Zeus' eagle. I did my best to comfort the poor girl."

"That was very good of you," said Numpty with unalloyed admiration. "You must have been in dreadful pain, yet you felt pity for the girl."

"I felt for her," Prometheus explained. "We were both victims of the same dreadful couple, I tortured by Zeus, she tormented by Hera. I was honest with Io. I told her the journey ahead for her was long but that, in the end, she would regain human form and bear Zeus a son. That son was to be the forebear of Heracles, the greatest of all Greek heroes, the demigod who would set me free. So she and I were bound together by our suffering and our final fulfilment. Io set off once again; she swam across the Bosphorus, which means the crossing of the cow, and the

177

Ionian sea that, to this day and yours, still bears her name. So it is as I foresaw, that in your time, thousands of years from now, Io will be more remembered than her relentless persecutor."

"If her father had protected her in the first place, she would not have had to suffer so much," observed Numpty.

"Inachus had no choice," Prometheus explained. "If he had tried to deny Zeus, retribution would have been swift and overwhelming. Zeus would have laid waste Argos, Inachus' domain, and destroyed all living things within it, including Io. It is one of the ironies of life that the parents' irresistible drive to protect their children from the vicissitudes of life is invariably frustrated, if not by Zeus, by life and age and, finally, death. It is Pandora's gift, her gift and her curse, but that's another story."

33 On the wings of a bird

Grimrose was not in the best of moods. Shape-shifting was always demanding but some shifts were far more demanding than others. If the overall size remained the same, the shapeshifter could concentrate on the specifics of molecular arrangement. That could be challenging but simple in comparison with shifts involving compression or expansion. Compacting his original mass into the form of a fairy had been extremely demanding and, indeed, uncomfortable. It was also extremely tiring since a much smaller frame still had to maintain an organism with the same weight as an uncompressed alternative.

He had often tried to explain the nature and complexities of shape-shifting to Nick Peters but Nick had remained loftily uninterested. "It's what you do, isn't it?" he had said on several occasions, "so why do you make such a fuss about it?" When Grimrose had persisted in a vain attempt to persuade his master to be less demanding, to limit his requirements to shifts of an easier, more readily attainable form, Nick had responded with idiotically simplistic analogies. "It's a bit like me complaining how difficult it is to ride a motorbike. Of course, if you can't do it, it might seem a tad intimidating, but once you've got the hang of it, you just do it. You don't burble on about how demanding and challenging it is." Oh yes, Nick knew how to irritate people.

Shape-shifting across species was extremely uncommon and generally frowned upon by the shape-shifting community. In recent times, there had been some liberalisation. A hundred years ago, gender changes had been considered perverse but nowadays most shapeshifters thought nothing of flipping from male to female and back again. There was indeed now even some kudos attached to size-shifts from normal humans to giants or elves and fairies. Such morphing was seen as demanding but not outside the bounds of propriety. Cross-species shape-shifting, on the other hand, was still viewed with suspicion by most and distaste by some. The term heterophobia had been coined by the few shapeshifters who engaged in cross-species shifts in an attempt to suggest that aversion to the practice was irrational and bigoted.

Grimrose's reservations about adopting the form of a giant bird were not, however, based on a consideration of the social values and behavioural norms of his fellow shapeshifters. They were much more to do with the practical difficulties of morphing into a bird capable not only of maintaining flight but also of lifting a full-grown adult up a mountainside and depositing same on a granite platform some 4,000 metres above sea level. That in itself was a serious concern but there was another issue that took precedence even over the practicality of flight; the issue of reversion.

To the casual observer, the process of shape-shifting seems to be a predominantly physical process but behind the rearrangement of molecules is a mental phenomenon of extraordinary concentration. The target form has to be delineated in the mind of the shapeshifter and then 'projected' onto the material that constitutes the shapeshifter's physical essence. Nick Peters would say dismissively: 'That's just what shapeshifters do!' But what happens if the shapeshifter morphs so far away from the original form that the ability to muster that extraordinary mental concentration is lost or only partially attainable? How does the morphed creature restore itself to its original form?

Grimrose had decided to proceed in stages. First he had elongated an arm and hollowed out the humerus and ulna to make the limb lighter; then he had restored the limb to its erstwhile natural form. There was no problem but he realised that this was not merely inconclusive; it was almost certainly completely irrelevant. Not until he morphed his head would he know whether restoration was possible and then, if he found it wasn't, it would be too late.

"How's it going?" enquired a cheery Nick Peters, who had been resting in their makeshift shelter. "I was hoping to see you at least flapping energetically, if not majestically wheeling around the sky."

Grimrose did not reply.

"Not sulking, I hope," Nick goaded.

"I'm not sulking," Grimrose responded controlling his anger with difficulty. "I'm concentrating. This particular shape-shift is pushing me to the limits, and possibly beyond."

"You really are a big girl's blouse," Nick replied, with a mocking but hard-edged tone in his voice. "Just bite the bullet. You know what we need. Go for it. Let's face it, I'm taking just as much risk as you are. I'll be dangling from your talons as we ride the thermals up Mount Strobilos. And then, if we make it, I've got to communicate with a traumatised and unstable Titan in whose ear, I've no doubt, Tel is whispering a shed-load of lies, or even worse, the truth. But am I whimpering on about the dangers? No, I'm bloody well not."

Grimrose had to admit Nick Peters had a point. Nick was taking as big a risk. Indeed, in terms of the actual flight, Nick was probably taking the bigger risk. After all, if Grimrose, in giant eagle form, had a problem, he could probably glide back down to the base of the mountain but if, heaven forbid, Grimrose lost his grip on Nick when they were, say, 3,500 metres up the mountain, poor old Nick would drop like a stone before splattering on the tundra below.

"Come on, my little soldier," Nick prompted. "Give it your best shot."

Grimrose decided it would be better to make the shape-shift rather than listen to any more of Nick's banter. Without another word, Grimrose disrobed and projected the eagle form onto the mirror of his mind to begin the process of transformation. Nick observed with some curiosity. 'You look as though you're about to do a mammoth dump', Nick thought to himself, but he said nothing for fear that any break in Grimrose's concentration, whether through anger or laughter, might produce a monstrosity with one enormous wing and a face with a large eagle beak at its centre.

It took Grimrose more than half an hour to complete the transformation and another 30 minutes to fine-tune his avian form for flight. He had seriously underestimated the power he would need to control the wings, so he had to transfer more of his substance into muscle, which in turn depleted his fat and energy reserves.

Nick could see what had happened and threw a couple of dead rabbits in front of Grimrose who, without hesitation, used his beak to tear at the flesh.

"Well, you could frighten the life out of me," said Nick, "so Christ knows what you'll do to Prometheus. Understandably, he's got some reservations about huge birds with big beaks."

Nick was right. Grimrose looked totally intimidating and, given Prometheus' unhappy relationship with Zeus' eagle, could not have chosen a better shape to induce in Prometheus a Titanic panic attack. "You'd better do a couple of circuits to get the hang of it. Then try a couple of lifts carrying this sheepskin sack, weighted with stones. Whenever you're ready, we'll give it a go."

"Shouldn't we wait until after Prometheus has fired his next flaming arrow?" Grimrose asked. He could still speak but, because of the anatomy of the eagle, his words sounded as though they were the product of simulated speech.

"Absolutely right," Nick agreed. "Excellent thinking. He's not due for another shot for at least an hour, so you've got time to practise. When he fires his next arrow, we'll wait for half an hour and then, off we go."

Grimrose's first attempts at flight oscillated between the comic and the grotesque. Fully stretched, he had a wing span of some 30 feet. It was hard to stop the wing tips from brushing the ground as he stumbled over the rocky terrain, desperately flapping to achieve lift.

"Oh dear!" observed Nick, when Grimrose returned after yet another abortive run. "Not a total success. Might I suggest you run into the wind and try to glide a little before flapping? I think the flapping might be part of the problem. The wings are causing more turbulence than lift."

To Grimrose's intense irritation, Nick proved to be right. Running into the wind with wings outstretched, Grimrose felt his entire body rising from the ground. By adjusting the wing feathers, he could achieve even better results. On the third attempt, when he had risen from the ground a few feet, he slowly raised and lowered his wings almost gently and found he was truly flying. The size of the wings which had proved an encumbrance on the ground now enabled Grimrose to catch and exploit acres of wind. "Just like riding a bicycle!" he heard Nick shout from below.

It was nothing like riding a bike. Grimrose began to feel the exhilaration of an earth-bound mammal that has found a way to reach and conquer the skies. He was free from the flat, two dimensional world of length and breadth, left and right. These mundane bearings were now immeasurably enhanced by up and down. The sky offered 10,000 layers of length and breadth and he, with the wings of a great eagle, was truly master of that vast bowl of air that accommodated not only the rolling plains but massive mountains as though they were no more than modest blemishes on the surface of the earth. He would not tell Nick Peters but this had turned out to be the most exciting and uplifting, literally and metaphorically, shape-shift he had ever undertaken. Indeed, at the next shapeshifter convention, Grimrose determined to deliver a paper on the possible benefits of inter-species transformation. He was now convinced that the virtual prohibition on adopting the form of other species must go the way of previous prejudices against gender-flipping and size-modification. This could be the beginning of an entirely new chapter in the evolution of the shapeshifters.

"Pretty good," Nick conceded, when Grimrose returned after completing a mile long flight in a wide circle some 100 feet above the ground.

"You've no idea," murmured Grimrose.

"There," said Nick, dumping the sheepskin sack of stones in front of Grimrose. "Let's see what you can do with that."

After such a promising start, the introduction of a burden proved problematical. "How exactly do you think I can become airborne", Grimrose enquired, "if I am carrying a sack of stones? I need to take a run at it to get off the ground. I can't use my talons to hold the sack while using my legs to run for take-off."

Nick seemed momentarily flummoxed. Then he offered a

suggestion. "All right, get yourself airborne and then do a low swoop and grab the sack. I'll stand it up to make it as much like a man as possible."

Grimrose seemed doubtful but Nick insisted. Grimrose took a run into the wind and rose majestically into the air. He flew in a large arc, keeping his extraordinarily sharp eyesight on Peters far below who was plumping up his makeshift substitute for a man. Down Grimrose swept, modulating his course with an intuitively delicate control of his main flight feathers. He felt at one with his adopted form and with his new element, the billowing air.

Grimrose came in at the perfect height. On his final approach, he slowed as much as he dared. When he reached the target, he leant back a tad, and, with outstretched talons, grabbed the top of the sack. At the same time, he swung forward, driving hard with his wings and flapping strongly. The weight of the sack pulled him down but he beat the wind with as much power as he could muster and, with the sack dangling back at an angle from his talons, he eventually managed to gain height and catch some lift. As he flew higher, Grimrose took advantage of some light thermals and it became easier. His talons were surprisingly strong and were able to retain their hold on the neck of the sack without too much difficulty. After a few minutes proving the practicality of Nick's scheme, Grimrose returned to earth.

"Well, it works," he announced. "It's not easy, but it can be done."

Nick looked less than convinced. "I don't wish to appear negative but I'm slightly concerned about the pick-up. Had that been me, rather than a sack of stones, that would have been my head you grabbed. You would surely have killed me. We could ponder whether my neck would have snapped before those rather impressive talons succeeded in gouging their way into my head. Or perhaps the initial grab would simply have torn my head from my spinal column. Severe brain damage or the entire removal of my head would certainly impede my efforts to dissuade Adam and Eve from pursuing their quest, although I suppose dumping a zombie or a decapitated head on Prometheus' granite landing stage might frighten them sufficiently to bring them to their senses."

That was the problem with Nick, Grimrose thought. All right, he has a valid point, but he can't just make the point and leave it at that. No, he has to make a meal of it and then thrust it down your throat. Images of birds feeding their young came to mind. "Oh well," said Grimrose. "I guess we had better call the whole thing off."

"Oh no you don't," Nick laughed. "I'm afraid it's not that easy."

"It never is," Grimrose answered.

"We'll have to find another way," said Nick. "I think I may have the answer."

34 Taking stock

When Adam and Eve returned to the rooms allocated to them by Prometheus, Eve announced she was going to have a bath. It was in fact a second bath because she had bathed as soon as they had arrived. Adam did not comment.

"He seems like a decent enough god, Prometheus, don't you think?" Adam called to Eve, who was leaning back in the large hollowed-out block of black granite that occupied the centre of the oversized bathroom. Two Oreads had prepared the bath by pouring jugs of water from taps fed by hot springs from deep under Mount Strobilos. To the water they had added flower petals that exuded a delicate fragrance which at once sharpened the senses and relaxed the body. When the Oreads' work was completed, Eve dismissed them and, as they left the apartment, Adam could not help noticing that both these Oreads and indeed all the others they had seen were exquisitely lovely. Prometheus might not have many visitors but evidently he was not short of some delightful female companionship.

"Did you hear what I said?" Adam asked, since Eve had not answered him. Still there was no response. Adam walked into the bathroom. "Hey, are you all right?" Adam looked at his wife. She was lying back, totally relaxed, with the warm, fragrant water caressing her body. Her eyes were closed, her lips slightly parted and it crossed Adam's mind, in that pose, she made an excellent model for a study of both spiritual and physical ecstasy. It was an odd thought. He and Eve had been married for thirteen years. The original passion in their relationship was long gone. It had been replaced by a tender love which, although obviously less intense than the lunacy of irresistible physical desire, promised to be rather more enduring and was, in many ways, more satisfying. Yet here he stood, looking down on the body of his wife and seeing her afresh. He felt the stirring of a desire to possess her.

"Sorry," said Eve, suddenly opening her eyes. "I was miles away."

"I was just saying that Prometheus seems a decent enough fellow, chap, being, god, whatever," Adam explained. His mind was no longer on the Titan.

"Yes, he seems decent and honest and, if what he says is true, mankind owes him a great deal," Eve conceded, "but I can't see how he can help us, or me anyway."

"Would you like a towel?" Adam asked.

"Yes, all right," Eve replied somewhat hesitantly. She had been planning to spend more time in the bath.

The Oreads had made sure the bathroom was supplied with everything the guests might need. In addition to the baskets of flower petals, there were scented candles in gold candle-holders, glass jars of perfumed oils and an abundance of white towels and cloths. Adam picked a large towel from the pile, opened it in front of him and invited Eve to step into it. Eve rose from the bath. The water trickled down her body. Adam watched the droplets trace the contours of her breasts. Eve looked refreshed, her white skin slightly flushed by the heat of the water, her nipples raised. Adam wrapped the towel around her and pressed it to her gently, to dry her and to feel her body. "There are some interesting oils in these jars," said Adam. "Let me rub some on you."

Eve did not object. Since they had left Harrow she had not been able to follow her normal routine of skin protection. She had not brought any make-up at all, no lipstick even and certainly none of the various washes and creams she used to clean and protect her skin from the ravages of life in a city and the passage of time. She lay face down on the bed, while Adam uncorked several of the oil jars, sniffing each in turn. "This one smells good," he said on the third sniff. "Smells a bit like Chanel Number Five. What do you think?" He put a little oil on his hand and invited Eve to assess it.

"I'm sure it's fine," said Eve.

Adam pulled back the towel from Eve's shoulders and poured a small stream of oil into a serpentine shape on to her back. He noticed, as though for the first time, how well-proportioned Eve's shoulders were.

"That feels good," said Eve appreciatively. Sure enough, like the water in the bath, the oil seemed to confer heightened awareness and relaxation simultaneously.

"I haven't started rubbing it in," Adam laughed. "If it feels good now, you'll be in a state of orgasmic bliss by the time I've finished." He began to massage his wife's shoulders. The oil seemed to guide his hands. He knew he was performing like a professional masseur, and so did Eve. "My God, you're good," said Eve.

"Only because I'm inspired," Adam replied gallantly. The closest Adam had ever come to applying the skills of a masseur was slapping some suntan oil on Eve when they had been on holiday in Greece. Eve wriggled slightly as Adam repeatedly applied exactly the right pressure in the right place on her shoulders and between her shoulder blades. He pulled the towel away exposing the length of Eve's body. In suddenly struck him that she, his wife, was an extraordinarily beautiful woman.

He poured a trickle of oil down his wife's back. The aroma of the oil which was sweet without cloying now enveloped both of them. He smoothed the oil into her silky smooth skin. He massaged the oil around her waist and, as he did so, she shifted her legs, rubbing them gently against each other. He placed his hands upon her buttocks and, with sensual circular motions caressed her, rousing both himself and her. He slid his oil covered hand down and up the back of her legs and then between her white inviting thighs. With a sigh she turned onto her back, eyes now smouldering with desire. Adam was on her. It was only as he entered her that he realised she was not his wife. She was another woman, similar in looks and form to Eve, but not Eve. He should not do what he was doing. But it was far too late to stop.

When they had both finished enjoying each other, the woman said easily and without any embarrassment: "Hello. I am Pandora".

oooOooo

In a separate but nearby suite of rooms, Rambler and Numpty had settled onto the generously cushioned couches and were picking at some succulent black grapes provided by the Oreads.

"This is a wonderful place," observed Numpty. "And yet it has seen terrible suffering."

"We are privileged to meet Prometheus," Rambler replied thoughtfully. "How someone who has suffered so much can be so kindly and benevolent is truly awe-inspiring. More than that, he has been mankind's champion. He helped us against his own kind."

"I still don't really understand why he did that," said Numpty.

"He saw we could be better than the gods. He understood that, contrary to Zeus' assertions, we did not need the gods as much as they needed us. He understood the lie."

"But if we are better than the gods, and we don't need the gods, does that mean there are no gods?" Numpty wrestled with these strange ideas. "We also met that evil creature in the Garden of Eden. He was worse than Zeus. He was full of rage and spite. And he proved powerless in the end when Kit arrived."

"I know it's difficult," Rambler nodded. "I wonder what Adam and Eve are making of it all. They are seeking the truth, a clear and simple truth. It doesn't look as though they will find it, not a clear and simple truth. You're quite right. The gods whom Prometheus despised and stood against were, in the end, weak, incapable of hindering us mortals and, on any ethical scale, not even equal to mankind's flawed moral integrity. As for the God of the Garden, well, He had serious psychological problems and, for all His bluster, was humbled by a blind

187

traveller."

Luke came padding in and settled at the foot of Numpty's couch. He had thought it best to leave his master and mistress alone for a while and had been exploring Prometheus' domain. He now felt the need for some human company.

"I liked Kit," Luke said, picking up on Rambler's last remark. "He stood up for me against a couple of fiery angels and he rescued all of us from the clutches of God, so obviously I feel grateful. But there was something else about him. I liked being in his company. I mean obviously God was entirely off His trolley but I can see why He was so desperate to stake a claim over Kit. He wanted Kit's company too."

And, although Rambler had not heard what Luke said, his own thoughts mirrored those of the dog. "And there's something else," he added. "Although he was blind, I suspect he saw more than any of us."

35 Going up

It had taken Nick Peters and Grimrose, now returned to human form, several hours to reach their destination about a thousand metres up Mount Strobilos.

Nick's solution to the flying 'pick-up' problem involved climbing part of the way up the mountain. "We climb part of the way up, find a ledge and you then, with me tied to you by a couple of shoulder straps, jump off. If you spread your wings as you jump, you will pick up enough speed and lift to come out of the fall before you hit the ground. You can then circle around till you find some thermals."

It all sounded straightforward. There was only one problem. Nick's suggestion was without any evidential support.

"You worry too much," Nick had said. "It all makes sense. What could possibly go wrong?"

"Well, what happens if I don't come out of the fall, if your weight is too great?" Grimrose had asked.

"I'd be really upset," Nick had replied. "And you know what I'm like when I'm upset," he added menacingly.

'You'd be more dead than upset', Grimrose thought to himself. 'And, unless I let go, I'd probably be dead too.' For a moment, Grimrose held on to that last thought. If he jumped off the ledge and then, because he was plummeting to the ground, he were to let go of Nick, Nick would be no more. After all, he would argue, there would be no point in them both ending up splattered on the rocks at the foot of the mountain, if one of them could be saved. And, of course, he wouldn't have to argue anything at all because the only other person involved, the only witness, would definitely be out of the picture.

"So the way this is going to work is as follows," said Nick, as though he had read Grimrose's thoughts. "I am going to tie my shoulder straps securely to your legs. The release knot will be here," he said patting the middle of his chest. "I will do the releasing when we are safely on Prometheus' entrance platform. After you have dropped me off, you will keep the straps tied to your legs so that, when I wish to leave, you can simply fly back up. I will then be able to grab the dangling straps and you can glide safely down to the foot of the mountain".

Grimrose knew there was no point in arguing with Nick and, in any case, he had no alternative to suggest. If Nick was to pay Prometheus a visit, this was the only possible way of getting him up there.

"This will do," said Nick, when they reached a ledge that provided a good dropping off position. "We're about due for one of Prometheus' arrows."

As he spoke, they saw a great flaming arrow shoot out from the mouth of Prometheus' cave some 3,000 metres above them. The missile disappeared into the clouds without falling away. "That must be a powerful bow," Grimrose observed.

"And a powerful archer," added Nick. "One day, one of those arrows will bring down Mount Olympus."

Nick settled himself on a moss-covered boulder. "You'd best get shape-shifting," he suggested.

It was cold on the ledge and Grimrose had to undress before adopting the form of a great eagle. "No need to be embarrassed," said Nick with a laugh, when Grimrose hesitated.

"Why should I be embarrassed?" snapped Grimrose. "You really don't understand shapeshifters at all. I can be any shape I like. If you were wondering about the effect of the cold on my procreational apparatus, just remember I can make it any size, as well as any shape, I like."

"What is the matter with you?" Nick responded, snorting with laughter. "I was just telling you not to feel embarrassed about stripping off on a mountainside. Where do you get these weird ideas from?"

"It's not me that's weird," Grimrose retorted.

"'Course not," was Nick's sarcastic closer.

The transformation took only five minutes. Once a shapeshifter has performed a transformation, he retains a template of the necessary stages so that subsequent adoption of the form is relatively straightforward, although still physically demanding.

When Grimrose had completed the process, Nick knelt down in front of the great eagle and tied leather thongs of cowhide to each of Grimrose's feet. He then looped the ends around his shoulders and tied the two ends together across his chest.

"I think we've waited long enough," he said. "Let's do it."

The great eagle moved to the edge of the ledge, with Nick close beside him. Then Grimrose opened his wings and stepped into space.

For both bird and passenger, the first few seconds were terrifying. Nick's weight and the slightly thinner air at 1,000 metres above the base of the mountain combined to make a successful flight even more difficult than Grimrose had feared. He spread his eagle's wings and attempted a glide but he found he was moving forward too slowly and dropping down too quickly. He considered flapping his wings but he knew that flapping would preclude any chance of achieving a glide. He leant forward, to generate more speed. It was a gamble. The only way he could achieve more speed was to accelerate his descent. He knew that he might not have enough height left but it was his only option. He was no more than 30 feet from the ground when his wings got lift. He levelled out immediately and then gently gained height.

Immediate catastrophe had been avoided but there was still a serious risk the flight would have to be aborted in an ignominious crash landing in the tundra at the foot of the mountain.

"You have to gain height," screamed Nick, dangling below Grimrose.

Grimrose was concentrating on the flight so he said nothing but he did think that, if there was some kind of higher qualification in the blindingly obvious, Nick would be a first class candidate.

"Try flapping, you pillock!" Nick shouted. Grimrose's failure to acknowledge or respond to his advice galled him.

If it had been within his power, Grimrose would have dropped his master. The fall might not have killed Nick and, had he survived, Grimrose knew Nick's vengeance would have been terrible. Nevertheless, the risk would have been worth it. Sadly from Grimrose's point of view, it was not in his power to abandon his passenger. Only Nick could loosen the knot that bound them together.

It was while Grimrose was pondering the cruel vicissitudes of life and while Nick was preparing further and fouler abuse for his avian companion that Grimrose caught a thermal. He adjusted his wings to take full advantage of the lift and gained several hundred feet before he slid off to find a more powerful updraft. Closer to Mount Strobilos he found exactly what he needed. A powerful current of swirling wind took hold of the great eagle and his dangling human appendage and swept the pair of them up and up until they were circling well above the mouth to Prometheus' cave.

Grimrose circled twice at an altitude almost level with the peak of the mountain to ensure he had a feel for the atmosphere and the strength of the icy wind. He took some pleasure from knowing that the silence from Nick probably indicated his erstwhile abuser was too cold and too short of breath to talk. Then Grimrose began a gradual descent, losing height carefully to ensure he could make a smooth slow sweep across the platform at the mouth of the cave.

It was a perfect delivery. Nick's plan had seemed hair-brained and almost certainly doomed to failure. In addition to compelling Grimrose to undertake an uncertain and hazardous shape-shift, the scheme involved risk of death or serious injury to both of them. There had been so many imponderables that, given a choice (which, of course, he wasn't) Grimrose would have refused to co-operate. The trial run with the sack of stones had been inconclusive, since they had not been able to check Nick's weight against the sack. The assumption that Grimrose would be able to achieve a glide before hitting the ground was at best a guess. The possibility of finding sufficiently powerful thermals to lift them at least 4,000 metres had seemed to fall somewhere on a scale from highly unlikely to entirely impossible. And yet, the plan had worked. After circling level with the peak, Grimrose had glided into a head wind over the cave's platform, had slowed as much as he dared without stalling and had seen Nick perform an almost perfect landing, releasing the knot as his feet touched the ground.

Nick found himself alone at the entrance to the cave. He turned to see Grimrose wheeling away from the mountain out over the plain, now unburdened and evidently enjoying mastery of his new element. 'All that complaining,' Nick thought to himself, 'and it turns out to be the experience of a lifetime.' The view had much to recommend it. From where Nick stood he could see many miles across the Caucasus. Far below was the foot of Mount Strobilos, skirted by rock-strewn tundra. Further away, the tawny grass that dotted the grey ground became more luxuriant, the rich green colour of a fertile plain where wild horses and game had room to roam.

Nick was wary of wandering into the cave unannounced and obviously unexpected. He was pondering his best approach when two Oreads emerged from a concealed path, carrying baskets of fruit. The Oreads were taken aback. For many years no strangers had found their way to Prometheus' cave.

"Don't be afraid," said Nick, who could see the mountain nymphs were a little apprehensive. "I mean you no harm. Indeed," he added, adopting his mildly flirtatious manner, "Given your extraordinary grace and beauty, I could have nothing but the warmest sentiment and greatest admiration for both of you."

The Oreads giggled, partly at his unsubtle flattery and partly because he spoke in terms that, even at that time, were considered rather old-fashioned and contrived. Nick made a note to calibrate his language more carefully. These tussles with the Storyteller were always tricky. For everyone's convenience, all those whom the questors visited spoke English but that did not mean that there weren't differences in vocabulary and style that survived the translation process and which, as a matter of courtesy, visitors should at least try to observe.

"I believe some friends of mine are now guests of your master," Nick continued.

"How did you reach us here?" asked one of the Oreads.

"I flew," Nick answered. "Economy," he added unnecessarily.

"Are you a lesser god?" enquired the other nymph.

"Well, I suppose if I flew economy, I can't be a major deity," he answered with a smile.

"What's 'economy'?" asked the first Oread.

"You should know the answer to that, my sweet," Nick replied in a paternalistic tone. "It's a bloody Greek word, isn't it?" He really didn't want to have to explain about aeroplanes and the different fare classes, especially as it was irrelevant in that he had arrived by eagle.

"Would it be possible for you to let Prometheus know that I am here?" Nick cut to the chase. "Just tell him Nick is back."

"Is he expecting you?" asked one of the nymphs.

"Well, let's put it this way," Nick replied with a grin, "it shouldn't come as a total surprise."

The two Oreads entered the cave. Nick waited outside. After a few minutes, the large figure of Prometheus approached, his bow slung across his back.

"Who is it who comes to the cave of Prometheus uninvited?" Prometheus asked.

"It's Nick," said Nick. "Don't tell me your eyes are failing? After all you've been through I'd have laid money your liver would have packed up long before your eyes. And what's with the 'uninvited'? If the only visitors who you had were invited, you'd lead the life of a hermit, except of course for those fetching mountain nymphs. But perhaps you'd rather keep them to yourself anyway."

Nick waited for a response but Prometheus said nothing. "Come on," said Nick, with a hint of irritation. "It's me. N. Peters, regular if not frequent visitor. How about a 'Hi, Nick, come on in. Must have been a helluva journey! Put your feet up. Have a drink. Have a meal. Have an Oread'. At least say something."

Only then did Nick notice that Prometheus was not looking at him but squinting over his shoulder. Hurriedly, the Titan slipped the bow from his shoulder and took an arrow from the copper quiver that stood at the entrance of the cave.

"Whoa!" said Nick. "I don't know if it's me or something else but put the arrow down."

Prometheus ignored him, notched the arrow into the bow string, stepped forward, effectively brushing Nick aside, and took aim at what Nick thought was the empty sky. Prometheus pulled the string back until it seemed the bow might break and then unleashed the arrow. The string twanged and the arrow, launched with unimaginable power, sang as it cut through the air.

"Missed," was all Prometheus said a few moments later, as he

193

rearmed his bow.

Nick peered in the direction the arrow had taken. In the far distance he could see a black shape wheeling in the sky. Then it dawned on him. The target was Grimrose. The Titan was trying to off his shapeshifter. Prometheus was already taking aim for a second time.

Nick leapt forward and nudged the Titan's arm. "You can't shoot him. He's my transport out of here."

"He's an eagle," roared Prometheus. "Don't you understand? He's an eagle."

"Ah come on," soothed Nick. "Get over it. He may be an eagle, but he's not *the* eagle. Heracles killed that eagle. You remember. It's not fair to tar all eagles with the same brush, so to speak, although of course it is true that birds of a feather… never mind. You should move on, get past it. In any case, this one's not an eagle. He's a shapeshifter called Grimrose. And he works for me."

"You talk in riddles," said Prometheus, stringing a third arrow. "I would prefer you not to talk at all. And do not jog my arm again." He began to take aim once more but then lowered his bow. The eagle had gone.

It was obvious the Titan was distraught. "I missed," he choked on the words. "The eagle came back. I must kill it. I cannot face that pain again."

"Excuse me, but why don't we go inside?" said Nick, hoping to bring Prometheus back to normality. "The bird's gone. It wasn't really an eagle, believe me, and it certainly doesn't mean you any harm. Let's go inside and have a drink for old times' sake."

"Who in Hades are you?" Prometheus asked, looking at Nick closely for the first time.

"You're kidding, right?" said Nick.

"No, I'm not kidding," snapped Prometheus. "Who are you and how did you get here?"

"Nick Peters," Nick replied unabashed. "If you want to pretend you don't remember me, that's fine, though why, I can't imagine. But whether you know me or not, it's fairly obvious I've made an effort to get here, so a soupçon of the famous Greek hospitality wouldn't come amiss."

"This isn't Greece; this is the Caucasus," said Prometheus, a little ungraciously. He didn't like his visitor. There was something about him, about his casual manner and his glib dismissal of the Titan's fears, that grated.

"So Greek hospitality doesn't extend beyond the borders of Greece?" Nick queried. "I assumed it travelled with the Greek people."

Prometheus relented. "You may enter," he said.

Before leaving the granite platform, the Titan surveyed the sky once more. He looked hard for any sign of the great black bird. When he was satisfied the sky was empty, he turned on his heel and led his not entirely welcome visitor into the cave.

36 An odd gathering

Nick's attempts at light-hearted conversation with the Titan were not even partially successful. As they walked through the massive cave towards Prometheus' impressive mansion, comments such as: 'Nice place you have here!' and 'I like the lighting; I always think lighting is so important' left the Titan unmoved and unresponsive. "I must say your taste in nymphs is impeccable," said Nick as they passed a bevy of Oreads, lightly clad in diaphanous tunics.

"No you mustn't," was Prometheus reply. "All my Oreads must be treated with respect. My attendants are chosen for their efficiency in serving me and their limitless willingness to do so, not for their appearance."

"Well some Titans have all the luck", Nick returned. He was determined not to allow Prometheus to put him down. "So it's just a happy coincidence that they're all extremely pretty, lithe and lissom limbed."

When they reached the antechamber of Prometheus' mansion, they met Rambler and Numpty who, after their conversation with Prometheus, had retired to their rooms, rested and had now returned refreshed. They waited for Prometheus to introduce his uninvited guest.

"I'm Nick," said Nick, since Prometheus remained silent. "Nick Peters. You at least remember me. I dropped Eve off at Stoney Cross. Porsche. Any bells?"

"I remember you," said Numpty. "You look different without the little red sports car. And I don't remember any bells."

Rambler too acknowledged Nick. "How exactly did you get here?" asked Rambler.

"That's a long story, involving some luck, a good deal of determination and a pretty heroic flight of fancy," Nick replied, intentionally leaving his audience none the wiser.

"How did you climb the mountain?" Prometheus probed. Mount Strobilos was Prometheus' domain and his cave inaccessible, except to the Oreads, who knew every mountain path, each cave and tunnel and every possible climb.

Good question! How had Nick climbed the mountain? Nick really didn't want to associate himself in any way with the eagle. He had seen the Titan's hysterical over-reaction to the possible presence of such a bird. "I am here with a message for Adam and Eve," he said. "I am a messenger from the future."

"Do you understand what he is saying?" Numpty enquired of his uncle. "Has he really been on an heroic flight? And who is Fancy? His answers don't make much sense to me."

"Nor to me," offered Prometheus. "Are you a messenger of the gods? Do you come from Mount Olympus? Do you bring me word from Zeus? The only message I want to hear from Zeus is an apology for the terrible wrongs he has done me and others."

Nick laughed. "No, I'm not a messenger from Zeus. Where I come from, Zeus is long dead. If it's any consolation, Prometheus, in my world we all agree you were right. You backed a winner when you restored fire to Man. No, I am not here as a messenger of Zeus or any other fabled deity. I'm here to try once more to dissuade Adam and Eve from their futile quest."

"And what is their quest?" Prometheus asked. His guests had yet to make clear to him the purpose of their visit.

"They seek the truth?" said Nick in a tone that suggested such a purpose was so absurd that it stretched the limits of credulity some way beyond breaking point.

"And why are you so keen to dissuade us from seeking an answer," Adam asked. He and Eve had joined the group in the antechamber. "Why does it matter so much? And what has any of this it got to do with you?" After his lovemaking, Adam had fallen asleep. When he awoke, Eve was dressed, fully refreshed after a long, languorous bath. Pandora was gone.

"Before I answer that question," said Nick, "if I may, I should like to take advantage of Prometheus' legendary kindness to all men and soak my travel weary body in a warm bath. After a bath, a little light refreshment would certainly not come amiss." Then he added: "Hello, Eve, how are you?" as though he had just noticed her and asking how she was, after a journey across thousands of miles and back through thousands of years, was a perfectly normal pleasantry.

"I'm fine," Eve replied. "But how did you get here?"

"Why does everyone want to know how I got here?" Nick laughed again. "This time I did follow you, you and Adam. I admit it. My work with you is unfinished but," and here he turned to Prometheus, "any further explanation can surely wait until I have had a chance to freshen up?"

"Very well," Prometheus summoned an Oread. "You may have your bath, and my nymphs will serve you food in your room. You will treat them with respect. We have already eaten. Tomorrow, we shall all meet in the banqueting hall. There we shall feast and, when we are all replete, we will talk. I have some questions for you and you have many questions for me and, evidently, for each other. Tomorrow shall be a day of feasting and answers."

With that, Prometheus turned on his heel and strode back to the mouth of the cave. There, he spent some time scanning the sky. The sun had set and the grey sky was becoming darker by the minute but still the Titan peered out across the plateau. When the last light had faded, Prometheus dipped an arrow head into the brazier which the Oreads fed with wood both day and night. The arrow head ignited and flame spurted back along the shaft. The Titan slotted the string of his mighty bow into the nock, pulled the string back with a strength that Ulysses would have envied and fired the flaming missile high into the darkling sky.

 oooOooo

Far below and some distance away from the foot of the mountain, Grimrose, now in human form, was sitting on a crudely crafted stool just outside the makeshift shelter that he and Nick had put together. A small fire was crackling and spitting, burning well enough to take the edge off the late evening chill.

Grimrose caught sight of the arrow as it soared through the night sky and, despite the fire, he shivered. The arrow Prometheus had aimed at him earlier had missed, but it had come close enough for Grimrose to realise that, had the missile struck him, he would not have had time to reconstitute his vital organs before hitting the ground. Impaled on a blazing shaft of fire some five feet long, he would have plummeted from the sky and crashed into the boulder-strewn plateau. With vital organs almost certainly damaged and quite possibly slowly roasting around the glowing shaft of the arrow, with his bones broken in a dozen places and with his head suffering serious trauma, he would have been in pretty bad shape for a shapeshifter. Because of their extraordinary regenerative powers, shapeshifters have the potential to live forever, but it is a potential, not a guarantee and, as the saying goes in shapeshifter circles: 'We're always only one concussion away from oblivion'.

While Grimrose sat on his stool, warming his hands at the fire, and giving thanks he had survived a fairly close shave with death, he began to ponder the way his life had turned out. The black, velvet sky was full of brilliant stars and the evident immensity of creation seemed to demand he should make some effort to set his own existence in context. It has to be said shapeshifters are not much given to introspection. It is hard enough to know oneself when there is only one self to know. For shapeshifters, who can adopt any form they choose, the search for self-knowledge is further complicated by the question of identity. Of course,

Grimrose was always Grimrose, whatever form he adopted, but, when he took on the guise of a parking meter attendant, or a hairy biker bully, or a rotund gnomic fairy, some of the character of each of these entities inevitably asserted itself and left traces on the core of his being. The older, longest-lived shapeshifters, those who had performed the largest number of transformations, inevitably found that the accumulation of traces gradually eroded, or at least diluted, their core identity.

Of course, to some extent, humans themselves are shapeshifters, Grimrose mused. They adopt different personae for different occasions. The ruthless dictator who thinks nothing of ordering the elimination of his enemies is and is not the same man as the loving father of his children and the dutiful son to his mother. The pontificating, puritanical cleric might well claim he is not himself when he hangs around public toilets hoping to pick up a rent boy. The politician who talks of public service and integrity surely shifts the shape of his conscience at least when he accepts bribes to change policy. Grimrose had often pondered this phenomenon and, although he did not wholly accept the explanation offered by his fellow shapeshifters, namely that humans were simply a less evolved form of the superior shapeshifter species, i.e. less gifted in the transformational department, he did recognise that the question of identity was not unique to his own kind.

Of even more concern to Grimrose than the issue of identity was the nature of his relationship with Nick Peters. His secondment to Peters had been a great honour and an opportunity for an exciting, challenging, rewarding career. Few shapeshifters were ever given the chance to work for a Breaker, fewer still for one with Nick's reputation for outstanding success.

The early years had been full of excitement. They had travelled throughout Nick's territory (Hampshire and Dorset), spotting likely targets for the Storyteller and, as often as not, closing them down before Tel even reached them. Nick had a way with him, so relaxed, affable, plausible. Women in particular seemed susceptible to his charm. Men tended to be more difficult, mainly because they were, generally speaking, more quest-orientated but, if they were tempted to embark on such a venture, Nick generally found a way of diverting their energies into their careers, sport (whether as a player or spectator) or extramarital affairs. Very few took matters as far as Adam and Eve.

In one sense, the cards were stacked in Nick's favour. It took a particular kind of person to embark on a quest. Most didn't see the need or point. Even those who were troubled enough to consider such a venture generally needed some traumatic event to nudge them into action. It was Grimrose's task, under Nick's supervision, to head off such nascent questors before they set out. In most cases, he succeeded. A life of routine, inertia, laziness, fear of the unknown were all useful aids in deterring venturers. When, as in Adam and Eve's case, he had failed to deter his marks, it was invariably because the Storyteller had got his teeth into them. On such occasions, Grimrose's role had brought him into contact with the Storyteller, usually, from Grimrose's point of view, with humiliating consequences. He was no match for Tel. That was when Nick became directly involved and would bring to bear the guile and techniques of persuasion which made the Breakers such a potent force. Nick and the Storyteller were old adversaries.

Of course, Grimrose had only his master's version of events but, according to Nick, most of the time the Storyteller was defeated. Questors would give up, either because of Nick's eloquence and manipulation, or because they found the quest too demanding. Since Grimrose had been working for Nick, however, the outcomes had suggested that his master and the Storyteller were more or less evenly matched, because they were level-pegging in terms of success.

The air was becoming colder and the fire was faltering. Wisely, the shapeshifter had gathered a good supply of wood on his return from delivering Nick to Prometheus' cave and he now added some larger logs to the dwindling fire. He knelt down and blew on the embers until the new wood took. Soon there was a goodly blaze.

'The real problem,' said Grimrose to himself, as he settled on his stool, 'is Nick. I'm really fed up with him. In fact, if I'm honest, I think I dislike him. He asks for more and more, and thanks me less and less. Half the time I think he gives me assignments, not because they are necessary for the success of our work but simply to see how far he can push me. He seems to take some perverse delight in requiring me to adopt the most difficult and incongruous forms.'

Grimrose leant back, away from the fire, which was now blazing heartily, to look at the night sky. There was no back to his stool so he suddenly found himself lying on the ground looking up at the myriad of stars. Although there was no one to witness his fall, he felt mildly embarrassed and, rather than leaping up immediately thereby confirming his tumble as an instance of untypical slapstickery, he decided to lie where he fell as though his toppling from the stool had been intentional.

As he scanned the sky, he picked out some of the constellations that all shapeshifter youngsters were taught to recognise before they reached puberty. Astronomy was a key subject in the shapeshifter syllabus. Grimrose knew there were 100 billion stars in our own galaxy, the Milky Way, and at least 100 billion galaxies. He knew these figures but they were so large that, other than indicating that the universe was exceedingly big, they were incomprehensible.

The constellations on the other hand gave some structure to the night sky. They made patterns out of the myriad of lights. They imposed order on chaos. Of course Grimrose knew that the patterns were not based on any real spatial relationship between the objects, other than how they appeared to the human eye as seen from earth. And yet the constellations gave some structure, some meaning, to the seemingly random distribution of stellar objects.

And it was then that a blasphemous thought crossed Grimrose's mind. Why shouldn't humans seek the truth? Why was it so important to frustrate their quests? Even if the search was futile, what harm was there in it?

He looked again deep into the black night sky and he had a second thought, which took him back to his earliest astronomy classes. "It may seem chaotic," the teacher had said when presenting pictures of the Milky Way, "it may seem too vast and too anarchic to grasp. But it isn't. It is all governed and organised according to some very simple and universal rules which your maths and physics teachers will be only too happy to elucidate for you."

oooOooo

While Grimrose was indulging in some profound introspection, Gwoat was enjoying an equally unfamiliar experience. He was feeling totally relaxed, content and unworried. Even the craving for chocolate had disappeared and his condition of perpetual flatulence had waned to the level of a scarcely perceptible occasional tummy rumble.

The cause of his benign condition was the Oreads. Prometheus, who seemed finely tuned to human emotional states, had assigned no fewer than three Oreads to administer to Gwoat. On his arrival in his apartment, the Oreads had prepared a perfumed bath and provided him with refreshment in the form of nectar.

Now Gwoat, in common with many of his countrymen, took a particular interest in beverages of all types. Indeed, in the village in Connemara where he had spent his youth, he had been considered an aficionado of the sometimes sadly lethal potcheen and other cereal-based whiskies with which he and his friends frequently entirely obliterated whole evenings, and sometimes the following day as well. When offered a goblet of nectar by Chione, a particularly fetching Oread, he had sniffed the liquid before drinking. This was no affectation since Gwoat's nose was renowned throughout Connemara

201

for its ability to distinguish between dozens of different brews from different regions and of different ages. He was particularly adept in assessing the alcohol content of such concoctions and had proved in blind tests he could assess the levels of ethanol in any production run to within plus or minus two per cent.

Gwoat was therefore somewhat taken aback when his nose informed him that this extraordinarily beautiful substance had no alcohol content at all. He sniffed again, and then asked himself a seemingly odd question. Why had he immediately described the nectar as beautiful? That was not a word he used when assessing potcheen. He used words such as smooth, powerful, rough; he would use metaphors such as 'the kick of an Irish mule' or similes such as 'as sharp as a tinker's tack', but he would not use a word such as beautiful for alcoholic beverages, however good they might be. Such a word he would normally have reserved for someone like the nymph Chione.

And yet the drink in the goblet could only be described as beautiful. He took a deep draft and, as the wondrous substance ran down his throat, he felt his whole body suffused with a feeling of well-being. His mind was flooded with all the best memories of his childhood, of the mellow, sweet, green air of his home in the rolling landscape of his native Ireland, of the endless games he had played with his friends in and around his village, of the distant sound of a barking dog when his mother tucked him and his brothers into one great bed and then, as always, sat down beside them to read them to sleep with stories of Irish heroes whose shadows fought their battles once again in the flickering light of the old brass oil lamp.

When Gwoat lay in the perfumed bath, Chione stayed with him. She washed his shoulders and his neck. She added hot water when the bath cooled. She refilled the goblet when Gwoat emptied it. He had never felt so good. Gone were the worries which habitually plagued him. He felt deeply refreshed, revived, renewed. Without a word, Chione slipped off her tunic and stood before him. She was indeed truly beautiful, her young breasts full yet taut, her limbs so graceful, her slender waist smoothly eliding into shapely hips. She stood before him, entirely natural and unashamed. She undid her black hair so it cascaded down over her snow-white shoulders. She smiled at Gwoat and then, lifting one long leg and then the other, she joined him in the bath.

An hour later, when Gwoat lay on the bed feeling, as indeed he was, a very lucky man and at ease in every way, his thoughts turned to his adventure with Grimrose. It had been the oddest experience of his life. He had come across shapeshifters before – it was inevitable you met the oddest creatures if you worked for the Storyteller – but the trip with the fairy-gnome from Hook to Stoney Cross had been something else. Funnily enough, he felt no hostility to Grimrose. Indeed he felt something like gratitude and admiration for the way the shapeshifter had disposed of the homicidal youngsters. Gwoat recalled Grimrose's assertion that he would not have obeyed his master and killed Gwoat, not after sharing a journey with him. "I'm not a bad person," Grimrose had said, and Gwoat believed him. It must have taken some courage to stand up to Nick Peters. For all his charm and affability, Peters was not someone to be crossed. After all, if the Storyteller was right, and he usually was, Peters had casually ordered Grimrose to kill Gwoat and then, apparently as a back-up plan, just in case things went awry, had arranged for Sandy and Maizy to kill them both.

oooOooo

And so it was that while Grimrose, the shapeshifter, lay on his back in the tundra at the foot of Mount Strobilos, staring up at the stars and pondering his life and his place in the universe, Gwoat, his erstwhile target for assassination, was also considering Grimrose's nature and substance and, perhaps because Gwoat was feeling peculiarly benign, reaching rather generous and positive conclusions.

37 Speculation

After a light breakfast, the questors spent most of the next day discussing their new situation and the questions they would ask. The cave of Prometheus, for all its size and artificial light, was a far cry from the Garden of Eden. Although massive, it was nevertheless an enclosed space, with only the gaping mouth of the cave to provide a view of the outside world. Given the nature of the place, encased as it was in a mountainside with millions of tons of rock and snow on top, it might have seemed oppressive but all agreed that the warmth of Prometheus' personality and hospitality and the ever-present ministrations of the delightful Oreads more than compensated for any residual feelings of claustrophobia.

"I'd certainly rather be here than in the Garden," said Numpty, voicing all the questors' thoughts. "Everyone is so kind here, not at all like God and His angels."

"The lad's right enough," said Adam. "I've no idea why we are here or how being here will help us in our quest but certainly the company is far more congenial than the Old Testament psychotics in the Garden of Eden."

Numpty could not help but preen himself a little at Adam's support, and Rambler smiled, pleased to see Adam showing some respect for his nephew.

"That's all very well," Eve spoke, "but we are here to find answers, not to enjoy our host's company, and I can't for the life of me see how a Titan out of ancient Greek mythology is likely to be able to help us."

"What do you mean by 'out of ancient Greek mythology'?" the Storyteller enquired gently. "This is not a dream or some elaborate trick. This is the most real experience of your lives. You are here, now. Prometheus, the wisest and most prescient of the Titans, is also here, now. It would be disappointing if you were unable to learn anything of use from him."

"That's a tautology, isn't it?" enquired Numpty. Having elicited some praise from Adam, young Numpty thought he might have hit a winning streak. Everyone looked at him quizzically. "Most real!'" explained Numpty triumphantly. "You can't be more real than real, can you?" He looked to his uncle for support.

"I wish you'd stop doing that," Adam interrupted. "It's really irritating and, believe me, when I say really irritating that's not a tautology, because there's irritating and then there's what you are, which is really irritating."

"You're absolutely right," said Rambler, frowning at Adam and springing to his nephew's defence. "The 'most' in 'most real' is, strictly speaking, redundant, since something is either real or it isn't."

"Well, if we are going to spend our time being picky," Adam retaliated, "surely something is either right or it isn't, so when you say your nephew is absolutely right, I think we have an 'absolutely' hanging about with absolutely nothing to do."

"For goodness' sake," Eve exploded. "This is ridiculous. Adam, leave Numpty alone. He means no harm." Luke, who had been sitting at Adam's side, rose, moved and lay down on Numpty's feet, thereby silently rebuking his master and comforting Numpty.

"He might actually be doing some good," the Storyteller interceded. "If you want precise answers to your questions, you need to make sure your questions are precise. Numpty's concern with the trickiness of words is well-placed and may in future serve us well."

"You mean, when the going gets really rough, we may find ourselves in dire need of an ingénue pedant," muttered Adam grumpily.

Eve's look advised Adam to shut up. She addressed the Storyteller: "What do you mean we should be able to learn 'something of use' from Prometheus?"

"Prometheus is unique amongst the gods," the Storyteller explained. "He favoured Man over his own kind and, as a consequence, he suffered a dreadful fate. But there is more. There was a difference between the gods and Man. Man is mortal."

"Man that is born of woman hath but a short time to live, and is full of misery. He cometh up, and is cut down, like a flower," Rambler intoned.

"So?" Adam prompted.

"So Prometheus realised Man needed something more, something not merely to cope with the realisation of mortality but to transcend it."

"Well, whatever it is he gave us, it hasn't really worked," said Eve. "A sense of mortality hangs over us, however hard we try to ignore it, and, when you lose someone you love, you feel bitter, battered, betrayed."

"'In the midst of life, we are in death', Book of Common Prayer, I think," Rambler offered.

Eve began to sympathise with Adam. Rambler and Numpty were a good pair. Adam gave her a 'told you so' look.

"So what is it he gave us?" Adam asked the Storyteller.

"Hope, dear boy," suggested Rambler. "Hope, which, I think I am right in saying, 'springs eternal in the human breast'."

"It's like having a permanent link to an online dictionary of quotations," observed Adam.

"Although," Rambler mused, "I was unaware hope was a Promethean gift. I thought it was the one thing left in the bottom of Pandora's box."

Adam started at the mention of Pandora's name. Eve looked at him, puzzled.

"You had best keep your questions for Prometheus," said the Storyteller. "It's not a straightforward story and it will make more sense if Prometheus tells it in his own way."

The evening feast, served to the questors in Prometheus' absence, was, if anything, more splendid than the one they had enjoyed the previous evening. "Where does all the food and drink come from?" Numpty enquired of his uncle.

"I have no idea," was Rambler's unexpected reply. "The cave is inaccessible and, even if there are secret mountain paths, I cannot explain how our host can offer us a feast which includes food from the four corners of the world."

"You forget that Prometheus is a god," said the Storyteller, "and one whom even Zeus himself fears."

On cue, Prometheus strode into the banqueting hall. There were two men with him. On his left was Nick Peters, rested, relaxed and evidently rather pleased with himself. On Prometheus' right was a blind man carrying a stick.

"My God!" exclaimed Adam. "How did you get here?"

"Allow me to introduce my guest of honour," Prometheus intervened. "This is Kit Turner, an old friend of mine, a man I would trust with my life. From your exclamation, Adam, I guess you have met Kit before."

"Yes," Adam replied uncertainly. He looked to the Storyteller for some explanation. Of course the whole quest was outside everyday experience but, even so, there had to be some internal logic. How had a blind man wandering around the Garden of Eden, located somewhere off the M3 between Hook and Mesopotamia, travelled to Prometheus' cave up a mountain in the Caucasus?

"Good to see you all again, or at least hear you," Kit laughed.

"But how did you get here?" Adam repeated.

"Kit is my guest," Prometheus explained. "He has been my guest before, not often enough I might add, and I hope shall be my guest again."

"Why does everyone seem obsessed with how we got here?" queried Nick. He turned to Kit. "I had the same problem when I arrived."

"Enough," said Prometheus. "However any of you reached my cave, you are welcome and we are all well met. I understand you have come here to ask me some questions. I will do my best to give you answers but I must warn you I have no monopoly on wisdom."

There was silence. It was such a blunt and abrupt invitation. Eventually, Eve spoke.

"I had a daughter...," she began.

"We had a daughter," Adam corrected.

"We had a daughter," Eve resumed, "who died."

"Here we go again," Nick interrupted. "Look, I really don't wish to appear rude or callous, but this absurd desire to explain an accident suggests you don't understand the word accident."

"Something that happens by chance," offered Numpty.

"Well done," Nick approved. "You see, even this mentally challenged young man can grasp the concept."

"Do not interrupt again," Prometheus warned. "This woman has scarcely spoken a sentence. Allow her to explain herself and, if she so wishes, ask her question."

Nick seemed for a moment inclined to argue but thought better of it.

"My daughter, our daughter, Bella, was seven years old. She died when a lightning bolt struck a tree where she was sheltering. A bough fell. She was crushed."

"She must have done something to offend Zeus," Nick suggested mockingly. "He's always been profligate with his thunderbolts. Oh, yes, obviously poor little Bella pissed off Zeus."

"I told you not to interrupt." Prometheus' voice now carried a threat. "Do not do so again."

"OK, OK," Nick seemed to comply, but then added, "but before I shut up just let me explain. Eve's life was shattered by Bella's death. Before Bella died, Eve's life made sense or, at least, she thought it did. She was happily married. She had a daughter. She had a good life. Of course, she knew she was going to die. She knew Adam was going to die. She even knew Bella was going to die. But she put all that dying out of her mind. That's what humans do. Anyway, when the accident happened, she couldn't put Bella's death out of her mind any longer. So she started to ask a question that had been there all the time. Why do humans have to die? And then she asked the real question, the question she has come here to ask, the question I keep telling everyone has no answer. She wants to ask: 'What is the point?'."

"You must allow Eve to speak for herself," said Kit quietly. Nick acquiesced.

Eve spoke. "I know that bad things happen. I'm not an idiot. I know every day, through acts of Man or acts of God, people die. I know that diseases are indiscriminate; babies miscarry; children are born with defects or incurable diseases. I know that accidents happen. Cars crash, planes crash, people die."

"Did you know that you are far more likely to die of an infection acquired during a stay in hospital than you are in a car accident?" Rambler interjected.

Eve ignored Rambler's contribution.

"So I know these things happen. I just need to know why."

"Well, the hospital-acquired infections result quite simply from lack of basic hygiene," offered Rambler. "There are many countries where the incidence of such fatalities is either very low or entirely eliminated. Adherence to strict rules of hygiene and the rigorous application of these rules is the key. As for road accidents, given the numerous improvements in the design of cars to improve safety, most accidents are attributable to driver error, through drink, drugs, tiredness or carelessness."

"I think Eve is asking a rather more profound question," the Storyteller gently chided the well-meaning Rambler.

"No, she's not." Nick could no longer remain silent. "She asked why accidents happen and Rambler here answered her. There are causes for accidents. Natural disasters, stupid or irresponsible people, whatever. That's it. There is no answer to the question why Bella died other than that she happened to stand under a tree that was hit by lightning. Look, I'm as patient as the next man, and as sympathetic. But we all know Eve's account of Bella's death. I've heard it more than once. Of course it's sad. Like deaths caused by earthquakes, tsunamis, volcanic eruptions. Yes, all very sad. But then we have to move on, get past it, make a fresh start. After all, humans only have one life."

Adam could see Eve was close to tears. "What is your problem?" he snapped at Nick. "Why do you feel the need to interfere? None of this has anything to do with you. It's personal."

"I'm just trying to help Eve and you," Nick replied. "I don't like to see people being conned. Eve's question is not a real question. There is no answer. You are being tricked."

"When someone is conned," Adam replied angrily, "the conman has something to gain. He tricks his mark out of money. That's the point of the con. Perhaps you can tell me who is doing the conning and what they are getting out of it?"

"Tel's the conman," said Nick without hesitation. "And it's your time he's stealing from you and, if you're not careful, your life."

"And what do you gain from your interference?" enquired Kit. And then, surprisingly, he struck the granite floor of the banqueting hall with his stick. "Answer me," he demanded.

There was complete silence. For the first time, Nick seemed flummoxed. He stared at Kit. Kit stared back with sightless eyes. Nick averted his gaze.

"I think you are asking about evil," said Prometheus, breaking the silence. "Let me tell you how evil came into the world."

38 Pandora's box

"I have a brother," Prometheus began. "His name is Epimetheus. At one time, we were close." Prometheus seemed to lose himself in memories of a happier past and it was only with some obvious effort that he snapped back to the present. "I'm sorry," he said.

"As I explained before, I did not create Man. Man existed before the gods. But I did play a role in Man's ascendancy, and so did my brother. I restored fire to mankind when Zeus, fearing Man, took it away. My gift to Man angered Zeus beyond reason. Not only did he have me chained to a rock and daily tortured by a ravening eagle, he also determined to punish mankind in a truly dreadful manner.

"My brother was tasked with refining the female of your species. In this endeavour, he had the help of the gods, including Aphrodite, Apollo and Hermes. He took a girl called Pandora, and began to work on her, bestowing on her great beauty, charm and the allure that gives women power over men. He also made her more aware, more sensitive, more devious and more talkative than men. Zeus, who had encouraged his fellow gods to help, approved of Epimetheus' handiwork because he saw it as a way of driving a wedge between men and women, and thereby weakening mankind. There would be an imbalance in the relationship between the sexes which, he supposed, would lead to perpetual conflict.

"Zeus was convinced that if he could ensure irresolvable tension between the sexes, this, combined with human mortality, would ensure his victory over mankind. If they were preoccupied with each other, they would have less time to spend in challenging him. Since they were mortal, time was of the essence.

"Zeus has never been one to rely on a single, simple plan. He's too wily to take such a chance. When Epimetheus' work was almost finished, Zeus gave my brother a box. He told my brother that within the box there was a wondrous gift that he himself had wrought to welcome the new, improved Pandora to the world. He didn't tell my brother it was Man's curse.

"Now I hadn't interfered with the work that Epimetheus was doing on Pandora. I didn't interfere because I foresaw that what Zeus assumed would be a weakness could be turned into a strength. If men and women could work together, they could complement each other, rather than compete. If they could find a way to co-operate, to become partners, they would be more, not less, powerful.

"But I was well aware that Zeus intended otherwise and I therefore warned Epimetheus to take nothing from Zeus, no advice, no suggestions and above all no gifts. But my brother ignored my words, or forgot them, or thought he knew better. When his work on Pandora was finished, he looked at his creation and he fell in love. Not really surprising, since he had crafted the most desirable woman who had ever lived. And what do you do when you are in love? You want to shower the object of your affections with gifts. What better gift than an offering from the king of the gods?"

Prometheus paused. Whether he was thinking of these deeds of long ago, or of his brother's disobedience and what had ensued from it, or of the beauty of Pandora, which was beyond compare, none of the others present knew, but they could see the Titan was momentarily lost in memories.

"If I recall correctly," Rambler prompted, "the box contained all the evils of the world, amongst them disease, disaster, despair, hatred, violence and war. Pandora opened the box and, before she could close it, all the evil had escaped. All that was left in the box was hope."

Prometheus laughed. "I can see the story has been refined a little. The box contained only one gift. Dust."

"Dust?" queried Adam and Rambler in unison.

"Yes, just a pile of dust," Prometheus confirmed.

"So Pandora was a little disappointed," Rambler opined.

"I'm sorry," said Adam, "but I don't understand."

"Well, speaking for myself, I'm not sorry you don't understand," Nick interrupted. "All this is nonsense. Such stories are great fun. But you and Eve didn't come here for fun, did you? You ask unreal questions and it's not surprising the only answers you will find are fairy tales."

Adam ignored Nick. "Why did Zeus give Pandora dust?" he asked.

"That's the right question," said the Titan. "Zeus wanted to punish mankind and he had a plan. The dust was his means of making Man's fate clear. First, when Pandora saw what the box contained, as Rambler surmised, she was disappointed. It told Man, throughout life, he would have to face disappointment and wrestle with despair. While Pandora stared at the dust, Zeus told her and all mankind that this was the beginning and end of every human life, from star dust to earthly dust. When Pandora picked up a handful of the dust, it ran through her fingers and she understood that nothing is permanent, that all things change. And then, finally, she understood the nature of time."

"So there was nothing in the box, except dust," said Rambler, pencil and notebook in hand.

Once again Nick intervened. "Don't forget all the symbolic twaddle that Prometheus here has just dumped on top of the dust in the box which incidentally was not a box but a jar."

"When is a box not a box?" demanded Numpty, before ending triumphantly, "When it's a jar!"

"You're against all symbolism?" Kit enquired of Nick.

"No, not really, so long as all you symbolists understand you're in your own fantasy world," Nick replied. "You can make anything into a symbol, and you can make a symbol mean anything, so it's all a bit arbitrary. Good fun, but meaningless."

"It's certainly funny," said the Storyteller, "that someone who finds the whole idea of meaning rather distasteful should condemn symbolism on the spurious grounds that symbols are meaningless."

"Could be double irony," sneered Nick.

"You said that you would tell us how evil came into the world," said Eve.

"Yes," Prometheus replied. "And I have. It is Man's predicament, as mortal, with memory and foresight. That is his curse. There is the evil men do in exercising free will and there is the evil perpetrated on the whim of the gods, but the essence of the evil Man faces is that he is mortal, with memory and foresight. That is why the cruellest part of Zeus' curse was understanding time; the beginning, the middle and the end; the handful of dust trickling through Pandora's fingers. I know, Eve, you have been driven here by the loss of your daughter. At the heart of your anguish is your memory of Bella, your imagining of what might have been, and her mortality."

"So are you saying, that's just the way it is?" asked Eve.

"At last," said Nick, "At last we're getting somewhere."

"I'm saying that, whether you see life as comedy or tragedy, you must interpret it in the context of one or two fixed points. Death is one such fixed point for everyone. It is a dreadful fate to be able to remember happy times, to look forward to more, to hope and yet to know you must die."

"What happened to hope?" asked Rambler. "Wasn't hope all that was left at the bottom of Pandora's box, or jar?"

Prometheus laughed. "There was nothing in the box but dust. You overestimate Zeus' generosity. The box was all about punishment, nothing else. Hope was a human creation. It was in you. I saw it; I nurtured it but it was Man, not Zeus, who devised it. And I'll tell you a secret. Man's capacity for hope upset Zeus almost as much as Man's possession of fire. When he heard that Man had hope, he asked, 'What must I do to break them?' Yes, that's right. The king of the gods felt threatened and beaten by the puny mortals."

"I don't understand," Eve persisted. "Are you saying the truth is that we just have to put up with everything? That just because everyone dies, it doesn't matter that Bella died? Are you really saying nothing matters?"

"I'm telling you that you matter more than Titans or gods. Surely, that is something. I'm telling you that you put the fear of Man into the king of the gods. I'm telling you that you mortals devised hope and that your hope engendered despair in Zeus. And I'm telling you who have come from the future that, aeons before you were born, Prometheus, the Titan, son of Iapetus, foresaw your destiny and marvelled at it." With that, Prometheus arose and, with his bow in his hand, headed for the mouth of the cave, with Luke, who had been bored to tears by all the talking, loping along at his side. For Prometheus, it was time to fire another flaming arrow into the empty sky.

"All that said," Nick addressed Eve, "all that said, he's telling you that things are the way they are, which is what I've been trying to tell you from the start. That is why your entire quest is a waste of time. You are being misled by my old friend Tel here who is, as I keep telling you, a charlatan."

"Excuse me," Adam intervened, "but that's not what he's telling us at all. And, as I've asked before, what the hell has any of this got to do with you? Don't take this in the wrong way but you are a bit like dog shit. We didn't step into you intentionally, it's a pity it happened and now we just don't seem to be able to get rid of you."

"Adam, what's got into you?" Eve exclaimed.

"It's all right," Nick soothed. "Obviously it's not easy but I'll do my best not to take Adam's abusive canine defecatory simile the wrong way. You know why I'm here, Eve. I'm trying to save you pain and disappointment. I'm not preventing you from pursuing your quest. In fact, Adam, if it hadn't been for me, Eve probably wouldn't have caught up with you at Stoney Cross. I'm just trying to help."

"Were you just trying to help when you sent Gwoat down to Stoney Cross?" asked the Storyteller.

"That was nothing to do with me," Nick responded. "Why would I do such a thing?"

"So you didn't instruct Grimrose to persuade Gwoat to drive away from the Garden? You didn't order Grimrose to kill Gwoat?"

"Have you taken leave of your senses?" Nick asked, clearly outraged. "Why would I do that? Gwoat is unharmed. Indeed, he seems to be in rather fine fettle. Where do you get this nonsense from?"

"From where do you get this nonsense," offered Numpty. Rambler shook his head to discourage his nephew from further stylistic

213

observations but couldn't resist suggesting 'whence' would have been even better.

The Storyteller repeated his accusation. "You instructed Grimrose to lure Gwoat away from the Garden and to despatch him in some isolated spot, thus depriving us of our driver and our van."

"This is silly," Nick replied. "Do you have any evidence for these ridiculous allegations? No, I guess not, since you weren't there, Gwoat is unscathed and I certainly didn't do what you say I did. So I guess evidence is hard to come by." Nick turned to Adam and Eve. "One good thing can come out of this. You must now realise that Tel is an unscrupulous liar who is wasting everybody's time."

"If you are right," said Adam, "there is no point to anything. It's not just the search for truth that is a waste of time. It's all a bloody waste of time. If there's no meaning to a life, what is the point of living one?"

"That's a pretty dumb question," Nick responded, then adding, with a grin, "No offence intended." He explained: "What about fun? What about enjoying life? What about all the pleasures of the flesh? Why do you need a point? Why do you need meaning?" Nick turned to Eve. "Bad things happen. Bella died. It's a pity but it happened. She's dead. You're alive. You don't do Bella any good by grieving. But you do yourself and your self-confessed shit-shod husband harm by wasting your lives."

"So your advice is to go through life having a good time until old age weakens the body and dims the pleasures, until your vital organs decay and, with a degenerating brain and decomposing body, you traipse along a lonely path to oblivion."

Nick laughed. "Lighten up, old chap. It doesn't have to be so bad. And, whatever it is, however bad, believe me, it's better than the alternative. I'm just saying that only a fool wastes precious time in pointless quests."

Adam and Eve looked to the Storyteller. He looked back. He was not going to present a case. He wanted them to make a decision.

"So let's call it a day," Nick resumed. "Tel can take you back to Stoney Cross. If, when you arrive there, Tel wants to get on with pestering a new mark, I can give you a lift back from there to Harrow. No harm done. You won't have the truth but at least you will know there is no truth to be had."

Suddenly, Kit spoke: "What do you think, Numpty?"

Numpty felt flustered and flattered. "Well," he said slowly, "I'm thinking that a life without meaning…" Here he paused because what he was going to say was surely going to sound silly and possibly, heaven forbid, tautological. After the pause, he realised he must finish

214

the sentence and, however silly it sounded, he couldn't think of anything else to say, so he said it. "I was thinking that a life without meaning would mean meaning was meaningless."

"Why don't we leave them to talk things over," said Kit to Nick. "They have an important decision to make." He stood up and waited. "After you," said Nick, and Kit led the way, with Nick close behind.

The Storyteller nodded to Rambler. Rambler rose; "Come, nephew, we have much to do." Numpty looked blank. "I have to write up my notes," Rambler explained, "and I need you to help me for I fear my memory is not as sharp as it was." As soon as they had gone, the Storyteller and Gwoat also took their leave.

39 Turning point

"I think they feel we need to be alone," observed Eve wryly.

"Either that, or one of us is suffering from bromhidrosis. Got that one of Rambler - the word, not the odour," Adam quipped.

Both of them felt slightly ill at ease. "I guess we need to take stock," Eve suggested. "We knew we were taking a risk when we agreed to go with the Storyteller. I hadn't the faintest idea what to expect. I thought he might take us to a philosopher or a scientist or some guru who had some answers. I didn't realise just how bizarre it would be. It's been unreal, that's for sure, but it has also made our normal life seem so superficial. I feel as though I'm in some kind of limbo between two alien worlds, this one which couldn't exist but does and the one we left behind which does exist but seems so mundane and trivial. Do you think we have learned anything?"

"We've learned that there are worlds other than ours, that there are strange creatures very different from us, that there are adventures for those who seek them," said Adam.

Luke padded into the room. He had stood beside Prometheus when he had fired another of his mighty, flaming arrows into the cloud filled sky and he had thought to himself that Titans were just as strange as humans.

"But have we learned the truth, or a truth, or anything?" Eve persisted. "We've seen God exposed as a malignant being who is self-obsessed. And now, here, with Prometheus, we hear stories of gods who seemed bent on tormenting humanity and preventing us from fulfilling our destiny. It's all pretty negative. And no one will answer my question about Bella's death, except for Nick Peters, who just says there is no answer."

Adam pondered Eve's words for a minute or so. "Maybe we have learned something. If you eliminate what is not true, perhaps it is easier to see what is true in what is left. We can certainly cross God, or at least the god we met, off the list. As for Prometheus, well he sincerely believes that Man has some kind of destiny and maybe he's right, otherwise we wouldn't be here, we couldn't be here. It's not an answer to any of our personal questions but, if he's right, it's mildly encouraging. And there's something else. The stories of God and the Garden of Eden and of Prometheus and his ordeal here in the Caucasus, they are great stories. I am beginning to wonder whether it matters if they are true."

"Well that really is progress," said an exasperated Eve. "We set out to find answers to some important, fundamental questions and you've now decided it doesn't really matter too much if what we find is true or not."

"That's not what I mean," said Adam sharply. "Why don't you ever think about what I'm saying instead of immediately jumping down my throat? I'm thinking that perhaps somehow the truth lies in the storytelling, not in the story."

"Is that supposed to make any sense?" Eve was irritated and scornful. "'Truth lies in the storytelling, not in the story'. That's a bit like saying the secret of good food lies in the cooking, not in the eating."

"Well the secret of good food does lie in the cooking," Adam retorted.

"Not if you're the person eating the food. The point of the food is in its eating, not in its cooking."

"The problem with analogies," Adam adopted his pedagogic voice, "is that they depend on finding similar relationships in different cases. For analogies to work, the relationships really need to be identical."

"You are beginning to sound like Rambler," Eve sniffed.

Luke, who had settled at Adam's feet, stirred. This exchange had all the makings of another 'domestic'. When would they learn?

"Let's not argue," said Adam. Luke settled once more. "We need to decide what we are going to do. We either go on with the Storyteller, or we quit and go home. If we go with the Storyteller, it's off again into the unknown. If we take Peters' advice, we make it home in one piece but very little the wiser."

"Nick keeps telling us we are wasting our time," Eve mused.

"That sounds to me like a good reason for going on," said Adam. "The Storyteller warned me he is our enemy, that he will do anything to persuade us to give up. Why? What is he afraid we will find?"

"He says he is just trying to protect us and prevent us from wasting precious time," said Eve. "I don't know why he has involved himself, but the same question applies to the Storyteller. Why is he taking so much trouble with us?"

"We told the Storyteller we wanted to find the truth," said Adam. "He agreed to help us. Nick Peters came out of nowhere, uninvited, and he won't leave us alone. This has to be a joint decision but I vote we go on."

"Joint decision?" Eve queried. "There are only two of us. Who has the casting vote?"

Luke stirred again. This was an argument they were always having. If it was 'a chance to hear again', he was off.

"So you want to quit?" asked Adam.

Eve shook her head. There was the hint of a smile on her lips. "No, I have no intention of giving up. I will not quit until we have answers. I just wondered how joint the joint decision was going to be."

Adam refused to be provoked. The point was they had made a decision. They had both agreed to continue with the quest.

Luke was pleased they were in agreement but sorry they had decided not to return home. He missed the comforts of home, the routine, the walks, the treats and, above all, the warm fire.

On cue, the others returned, Prometheus, accompanied by the Storyteller and Nick Peters, with Gwoat trailing behind; Rambler, with Numpty at his side. Kit was nowhere to be seen.

"Have you made your decision?" Prometheus came straight to the point.

"We have," said Adam and Eve in unison.

"Is it the decision of both of you?" asked the Storyteller.

"Come on," Nick intervened. "Lighten up! This is not a court of law. You'll be asking them to swear on the Bible next."

"That would not be such a silly idea," the Storyteller responded, "given that they are seeking, the truth, the whole truth and nothing but the truth."

"I've never been a great fan of swearing on the Bible, or anything else for that matter," Nick scoffed.

"If you are seeking the truth," hazarded Numpty, "why do you need to say you are not seeking anything else? If I said I am seeking apples, I would not have to add I was not seeking bananas, or pork chops or buses, would I?"

"Yes, my boy," said Rambler.

"Absolutely," said the Storyteller.

Both intended to shut Numpty up but he took their curt but positive responses as encouragement.

"And if I said I was seeking the truth," Numpty continued with enthusiasm, "it would be reasonable to assume I was seeking the whole truth, otherwise I would have said I'm only seeking part of the truth. In fact…,"

Adam had had enough. He cut in: "We have decided to carry on with the quest."

Prometheus and the Storyteller exchanged a look indicating both had guessed correctly that Adam and Eve would not give up. Rambler smiled. He had many more notebooks to fill. Numpty too smiled because his uncle was pleased.

Nick Peters frowned. Two vertical lines in his forehead, rising from either side of the top of his nose, deepened. His eyes hardened.

Eve addressed Nick. "We have given your advice a lot of thought but we have come so far and risked so much, we need to go on."

It was an opportunity for Nick to say that, although he disagreed, he understood. He could have said he appreciated it was a difficult choice; he could have thanked them for seriously considering his advice; he could have wished them well for their onward journey.

But he didn't. Instead, he turned to the Storyteller. "You know well enough what happens now."

"We both have our tasks and know our duty," the Storyteller replied.

Nick turned to Adam. "You have made your choice. I gave you every opportunity to abandon your quest. I demonstrated to you the folly of your search at Fleet. That should have been enough. It seems the salesman lost his life in vain. I even gave your wife, amongst other things, the opportunity to revisit the past in an attempt to persuade her not to waste her future. It was a generous gift and one which merited a little gratitude. Despite all I have done, you both have chosen to ignore my advice. I therefore tell you that I shall do all in my power, and with all the means at my disposal, to frustrate your quest. I shall drive a wedge between you and Eve. If you have faith, I will destroy it. If you have hope, it will be disappointed. If you trust, your trust will be betrayed. You have no idea what I can do to you. You are vulnerable in so many ways. I shall oppose you with such force that you will either quit your search or die. Any who go with you will share your peril. Seek by all means, but I swear you will not find. And if, by any chance, you survive, you will not recover, you will live in fear and disappointment all the remaining days of your short, brutish, meaningless lives."

Eve was pale and shivering.

"Why don't you sod off!" suggested Adam.

40 Deliberations

After Nick Peters had left, there was a general sigh of relief.

"Well that last outburst from Peters was something else!" observed Adam, addressing the Storyteller. "You told me he was our enemy but you forgot to mention he is completely mad. What was all that about driving wedges, destroying faith, hope and trust, a final destiny of death or misery?"

"He seemed possessed," said Eve. "He wasn't the same man...," she was going to say 'I spent time with' but thought better of it. "He wasn't the same man I met at Hook."

"Sadly," said the Storyteller, "he's not mad or possessed. He is, however, dangerous and determined. He will do anything to achieve his goal. You have to understand that. There is no limit to what he will do to frustrate your quest, no limit at all."

The Storyteller waited for his message to sink in: "You say you have decided to continue. Nick Peters has let you know something of what you will face if you persist – but he is your enemy. I am not your enemy, so you can hear what I say, knowing that I am not against you or trying to deceive you or frighten you. If you pursue the truth, I will escort you to other times and other places where you can learn more and where you can ask your questions. But while you embark on these episodes, these insights, these adventures, Nick Peters will be preparing his campaign against you. The more you learn, the more violent and vitriolic will be his assault when it comes. In the end, you will have to face him and what he represents. I am telling you this so that, just as you did at the beginning, you can take an informed decision."

"I'm not sure it was that well-informed," said Eve. "We had no real idea where we were going when we stepped into the camper van."

"I told you what you would face. I told you that you we would have a long and difficult journey, a journey across vast continents and through interminable aeons of time, through the darkest passageways of the mind, on to the peaks of human imagination and, quite possibly, into the depths of hell. The advice may have been a bit light on specifics, but, I can assure you, in general terms, it was spot on."

"I don't understand why Peters is so determined to stop us," said Adam. "I mean I knew the quest would be difficult and you told us it could be dangerous. But I didn't realise we would have to deal with a maniac who will stop at nothing to ensure we fail."

"What does 'stop at nothing' mean?" asked Numpty of his uncle.

"It means he will do anything," Rambler answered, hoping the answer was sufficient but knowing it was not.

"How can 'stop at nothing' mean 'do anything'?" Numpty responded. "In any case, if nothing is nothing how can you stop at it? How would you know where to stop if there was nothing there? Is it the same nothing when you say 'nothing can stop us'?" It would be a shame to be stopped by nothing."

"No, no, dear boy," said Rambler. "When you say nothing can stop us, you don't mean you can be stopped, you mean you can't be stopped."

Numpty looked bemused.

"Moving on," suggested Adam, turning to the Storyteller. "I asked you at the beginning, what were the chances of success? Now we know a little more, I ask the question again."

"It all depends on what progress you make, how much you understand and what help you can get," said the Storyteller.

"That's not terribly encouraging," said Eve.

"There are no guarantees, Eve," the Storyteller responded solemnly. "I can show you events, nodes in time, which will prompt you to think. But I cannot predict where your thoughts will take you. I cannot say what you will make of it all. And I must be brutally frank. You came on this quest because of Bella's death but, if you're honest, it wasn't because you wanted to know why. It was because you could not accept it had happened. Any truth you find may help you see Bella's death in a different way but it will not bring her back."

"We know that," said Adam. "That's not what we expected or hoped for. We just wanted to know if there is a point, a point to anything. Bella died, and for us that is a tragedy and a pain that will never go away. But we know that in the end we all die. Bella's life was ended almost before it had begun; but the rest of us, most of us, have a full life-span. We fill our time. We dream. We strive. If we're lucky, we even achieve. But is there any point? Would it matter if we didn't dream, strive, achieve? When our sun becomes a super nova or whatever it's going to do and planet Earth is scorched to a cinder, will everything Man has done, everything any of us has done, will it all just disappear as though it had never been? Will it, in any way, even matter that it had ever been?"

"All excellent questions," said the Storyteller. "If you really want the chance of finding answers to such questions, we must go on."

"Just on a point of fact," said Rambler, "our sun is not massive enough to become a super nova. I'm afraid it will only manage to achieve red giant status, still powerful enough to char planet Earth but nowhere near as spectacular as a super nova. After that, what is left of our sun will settle down as a humble white dwarf."

"When will that happen, Uncle?" enquired Numpty, somewhat alarmed.

"Not for a very long time," Rambler answered. "I believe we have several thousand million years to go before that happens." Numpty was reassured.

"Unless we suck the planet dry before then," offered Adam, reactivating Numpty's concern.

Eve gave Adam an admonitory look.

"Well, let's face it, a few thousand million years is a long time," said Adam defensively. "We're sure to screw it up long before we become a red giant or a white dwarf. I'm just trying to set young Numpty's mind at rest."

"What!" said Eve. "You're telling him not to worry about the sun exploding on the grounds we'll have destroyed the planet long before it happens."

Rambler, unwisely, decided to try his hand at arbitration. "Your argument," he addressed Adam, "is rather like telling a condemned man he need not fear execution because he is sure to be dead of cancer before they manage to hang him. On the other hand," he turned to Eve, "if we assume that the average generational gap is thirty years and that the Sun will not become a red giant for, say, four thousand million years, we can calculate that there will be some one hundred and thirty three million generations between now (by which I mean the twenty first century of course) and then. Given Man's rather chequered recorded history, which so far consists of a mere two hundred generations, we have to concede that the chances of cataclysmic human abuse of the planet within a hundred and thirty three million generations must be exceedingly high."

"Which is a long-winded way of saying I'm right," suggested Adam.

"That depends on what we were trying to achieve," Rambler replied. "If we were attempting to calculate odds on human survival, you are closer to the mark. If we were trying to reassure a young Numpty here, both you and I are wrong."

"Well, it's the truth we're after," said Adam. "Even if it proves unpalatable to your nervous nephew."

"I think my nephew has adequately proved his courage on more than one occasion," Rambler responded, with a hint of irritation.

"Is there no truth in consolation?" the Storyteller asked.

"What does that mean?" Adam responded sharply to the Storyteller's unexpected intervention.

The Storyteller frowned, shook his head but made no effort to explain.

"I don't know whether there is truth in consolation," opined Rambler, "but let us hope we find consolation in the truth." He preened himself slightly at what he considered to be a fairly neat aphorism.

"I think he means that showing a concern for and understanding of the feelings of fellow humans involves an integrity that is in itself a kind of truth," said Eve.

"A kind of honesty, a kind of decency, sure," Adam conceded. "But not a truth."

Both he and Eve looked to the Storyteller to expand on his comment but clearly he regretted his remark and had no intention of adding to it.

"What about pleasure?" Numpty exclaimed. "What about fun?"

"What about it?" asked Adam, with reluctant curiosity.

"Well, you said 'what is the point of living, if all we achieve can be lost or forgotten when we are dead?" Numpty answered.

"So...," prompted Adam.

"What about pleasure and fun?" said Numpty. "Doesn't pleasure give life a point? Doesn't fun make it worth living?" Something Nick Peters had said had stuck in Numpty's mind.

"I don't know," said Adam slowly. This was the first time he had actually engaged with Numpty. "Pleasure makes life enjoyable and it's certainly preferable to pain but I'm not sure it justifies the living of a life. I mean, pleasure is just a passing sensation. If you have to live, you would prefer life to be pleasurable. But, given the balance between pleasure and pain, joy and sorrow, if you were unborn, would you choose life?"

"That is something of an unreal question," Rambler intervened. "If you were unborn, you would have no knowledge of pleasure and pain, so the question would be meaningless. For those who have been born, the answer to your question is clear since the vast majority decide not only to live out their lives but also seek, to the best of their ability, to prolong them."

"Yes, that's true, but isn't that primarily inertia?" said Adam. "We don't ask to be born. We just find ourselves bounced into the world."

"It's not just inertia," Rambler countered: "Most of us are persuaded by the argument that something is better than nothing."

"Is that why there is a universe?" asked Numpty. "Because something is better than nothing?"

Numpty's ability to pose the unexpected questions remained undimmed.

"Just because something is better than nothing doesn't explain why there is something rather than nothing," said Adam.

"No, I see that," said Numpty, who then added, as an afterthought: "So what does explain it?"

Adam laughed. Eve smiled. Rambler patted his nephew on the shoulder.

"That's a very real question," said the Storyteller.

41 Breaking down

Nick Peters had stormed out of the meeting, with Adam's peremptory 'sod off' ringing in his ears.

So Adam and Eve had decided to continue with their quest. That was both bad and good news. It was bad in that, despite his best efforts, the couple had rejected his advice. He was fairly sure he could have persuaded Eve. He had kept his word with her and had given her a glimpse of an alternative. She had seen her beloved Bella once more. The tragedy had been averted. No cracking bough. No dead child. A fine example of 'what might have been'. Of course it was all unreal but reality was just as much over-rated as truth. Yes, he could have led Eve away from the quest, he was fairly confident.

The problem was Adam. From the outset, there had been some source of antagonism. And the hostility had become worse and worse. Truth to tell, Adam had every reason to be hostile – but why tell the truth? Nick had already done much to frustrate their quest, including getting under Eve's skin and inside her head, but Adam could know nothing of Eve's ambiguous infidelity, unless Eve told him. And he knew she hadn't.

The good news was he could now bring to bear all the might of the Brotherhood of Breakers to ensure final victory. There would be no criticism of his failure to nip the quest in the bud. It was widely recognised that those who persisted beyond Grimrose's fairly crude attempts at dissuasion were, by definition, the harder nuts to crack. Nick knew he had done a professional job but the couple were driven by a potent brew of grief, guilt and curiosity which compelled them to continue with their quest. No, he had nothing to be ashamed of or to fear from the Brotherhood. They would give him every assistance. They would enhance his powers if necessary. Of course, they would hold him responsible for the final outcome but he knew he could count on their wholehearted support on the way.

The final outcome would be something to savour. There would be the feeling of achievement, for a job well done. There would be the satisfaction of knowing that another attempt to transcend the boundaries of a normal human life had been successfully terminated. And, on this occasion, there would be recompense for tolerating Adam's 'sod off'. Really. Some of these questing characters clearly had no idea what they were dealing with.

Nick had reached the mouth of the cave. The brazier where Prometheus lit his arrows was flickering and crackling but there was no

225

sign of the fire's attendants or of Prometheus himself. Nick stood close to the edge of the cave and summoned Grimrose, using elementary telepathic powers. It was time to return to Adam and Eve's epoch, where the dénouement of their quest would take place.

oooOooo

In Nick's absence, Grimrose had spent much of his time deliberating on how best to advise his master of the new terms of the employment contract he wished to negotiate. He had worked out the substantive clauses fairly easily:

- time off in lieu and compensation if projects overran or involved working unsocial hours
- no gratuitous demands for eccentric shape-shifts
- agreed and inviolable holiday arrangements
- regular assessment sessions in which he would be told how well he was doing and where, if at all, he was failing.

He had one further demand and this final demand was the one he thought would cause the most difficulty. He wanted a say in the nature of the tasks they undertook. He accepted that humans could be arrogant and that, from time to time, their vaulting ambition had to be reined in but this obsession with simply stopping them from seeking the truth by whatever means now seemed to Grimrose, following his nocturnal, substellar, Damascene moment, suspiciously unreasonable. It was as though there was some terrible guilty secret that the Breakers were desperate to hide.

All that said, it was not the terms he sought that perplexed him most. It was how to raise the subject with Nick in the first place. They just didn't have that kind of relationship.

It was while he was pondering the best way of opening negotiations that he received the telepathic call from his master for a lift. He disappointed himself by immediately acknowledging the call and replying he would perform the pick-up as soon as he had transformed.

oooOooo

Nick waited impatiently at the mouth of the cave. He knew that Grimrose must make the avian transformation and that interspecies emulations were the most demanding of all shape-shifts. Nevertheless, he suspected Grimrose was taking his time and Peters made a mental note to rebuke him once they had landed safely on the plain.

"It's a miraculous phenomenon," said a voice behind him.

"What the hell!" exclaimed Nick, turning round and pulling back from the edge of the granite platform. "I almost fell off," he complained.

Kit, for it was he, laughed. "First Adam tells you to 'sod off'; then I nearly make you jump off. I'm sorry but I guess it must be time for you to be off."

"I won't argue with you," said Nick. "I'm waiting for my lift." Then he added: "What's miraculous?"

"The ability of shapeshifters," Kit replied. "It must be wonderful to be able to change your appearance, to adapt your form, even to experience the life of other species."

Nick grunted. Shape-shifting didn't seem at all miraculous to him. After all, that's just what shapeshifters did.

"To fly across this land and see the mountains and the plains, that must be something," said Kit.

"Except, in your case, you wouldn't see that much," Nick suggested, "being somewhat visually impaired," he added unnecessarily.

"I can see everything in my mind's eye," Kit replied.

"That must be a consolation." It was unclear from Nick's tone whether he was sympathising or mildly sneering. "Why don't you take a flight now and tell me how Grimrose is getting on?" Kit made Nick feel uneasy. How did the blind man know about Grimrose? How did he know about shape-shifting? How was he able to wander around Prometheus' cave without walking into things?

"You don't like me, do you?" Kit suggested.

"I don't know you," Nick replied, surprised.

"Yes, you do. Of course you do," said Kit. "I'd recognise that voice anywhere. We've crossed swords, or in my case, sticks, several times before."

Nick frowned. He began to think Kit might be mad as well as blind. He had never met the man before, and certainly not several times. "Well, I hope we sorted out our differences," he said cautiously. No point in goading a madman, even if he was handicapped. You never knew how people 'returned to the community' would behave.

"If I remember correctly, we still have unfinished business," said Kit in a tone of affability that rivalled Nick at his most benign.

"Well I'm sorry but any business between us will have to remain unfinished for now," said Nick as he saw Grimrose, now in eagle form, circling above. 'About time too', he thought, just as, without any warning, Kit whirled his trusty stick into the air and, with remarkable precision, struck Nick on the temple with a blow of devastating force. Nick staggered backwards, teetered on the edge of the granite platform, lost his foothold and fell out into space, tipping over and plunging head first down the mountainside.

Grimrose, who was making his final approach for the pick-up, couldn't believe his eyes. Having adopted the form of an eagle, he enjoyed the visual acuity peculiar to the avian breed, so he had been able to see quite clearly Peters and the man with the stick conversing as he circled above them. He had assumed they were exchanging pleasantries. Then, just as he approached, with straps dangling for Nick to grab, the man with the stick thwacked his master on the side of his head and knocked him off the mountain.

A flood of thoughts cascaded through his mind. The first thought, uninvited, was 'Bugger me, I'm not the only one he's pissed off'. His second thought, not invited but somehow irritatingly mandatory, was 'Must save my master'. He went into a dive, driving his descent with a powerful thrust of his wings before tucking them in to achieve a perfect aerodynamic form.

He caught up with the unconscious Nick Peters at about a thousand feet. There was only one chance to save him. As he drew alongside he snatched at his master's body. One talon missed; the other got a firm hold on a leg, so firm it went through the skin, flesh and muscle and bit into the bone.

oooOooo

"You realise I may never walk again," snarled Nick. "You've ripped my leg apart. Jesus, was that really the best you could do?"

"I saved your life," Grimrose returned, with some vehemence. "If you feel the need to be unpleasant, why don't you direct your aggression at the man with the stick who smacked you in the head and knocked you down the mountain?"

Nick grunted. "I would if he was here. I'd do a bit more than direct my aggression. I'd rip his head off."

"I'm afraid the wound is infected," Grimrose observed with just a hint of satisfaction, as he tended Nick's lacerated leg.

"Great! You not only rip my leg apart, you use a germ-infested talon to do it."

"Perhaps I should have let you head-butt the planet. Would that have suited you better?" Grimrose asked bitterly.

"Well let's just think about that," suggested Nick. Even in intense pain, he was able to goad with some finesse. "I guess it's fair to say, if you hadn't intervened, I would have been dead. So I wouldn't actually be in pain now, lying here with a festering wound and the prospect of a slow and lingering death or life with a pronounced limp. So, as things stand, given two unacceptable options, the answer's finely balanced."

"If you want to avoid a slow lingering death…," Grimrose began.

"Are you threatening me?" snapped Nick. "Be careful."

Grimrose backed down immediately. "I was not threatening you," he blurted. He knew what the Breakers could do. They could look into your mind and find what you feared most. Then they would cast you into an altered state, a dream, a trance, where what you feared most threatened to happen. Whatever it was, it never happened but the threatening was worse even than the thing you feared. He had seen a rebellious shapeshifter utterly destroyed by a Breaker. The shapeshifter had a morbid fear of being buried alive, a peculiarly odd terror for one who, with a bit of luck, could indefinitely avoid death by regenerating decaying organs. Anyway, that was the disobedient shapeshifter's nightmare so his Breaker cast him into an undertaker's workshop where the assistants prepared his inert but fully conscious body for a coffin while the funeral director negotiated rates over the phone for a prime burial site in the local cemetery. As soon as the Breaker released him, the shapeshifter took a vast quantity of poison and then immediately shot himself through the head. No one was going to bury him alive.

"Very well," said Nick, satisfied Grimrose had been whipped by fear into a satisfactory shape. "We need to get back to the twenty-first century as soon as possible. Set co-ordinates for Southampton General Hospital. It's a large teaching hospital, I believe. This leg needs serious medical attention."

"Do you not have private health insurance?" Grimrose asked.

"Yes, I do," Nick replied, "but this is something for Accident and Emergency. The rest of it may be a bit dodgy but you can't beat the NHS for A and E."

Grimrose busied himself with fixing the co-ordinates. Not perhaps surprising that Breakers could appreciate the value of Accident and Emergency! After all accident and emergency were tools of the Breaker's trade. This just didn't seem to be the right time to raise the issue of his terms and conditions of work.

oooOooo

"Did you eliminate him?" Prometheus asked.

"Well, let's put it this way," said Kit. "I gave him a fair old whack with my stick. I hit him so hard, he staggered backwards and fell out of the cave and down the mountain."

"If he fell four thousand feet down the mountain, we can assume he's dead," Prometheus concluded. "Your questors can continue their journey without having to face Peters at the end of it. Their task is demanding enough without Peters' malign interference frustrating them at every turn."

"That's the idea," said Kit. "Normally, I'm opposed to violence but, when you come face to face with evil and look it in the eye, metaphorically-speaking in my case, there's nothing like a good thwack with a stick to make your disapproval unambiguously clear."

"You have done the world a considerable service if Nick Peters is dead," said the Storyteller. "I don't doubt what you say for a moment but personally, I should like to see the corpse. He's proved extraordinarily resilient in the past."

"Well, you would have to climb down to the plain," said Kit, "a long, arduous and dangerous venture just for the satisfaction of seeing Nick Peters splattered across a boulder or two."

"Thanks but no thanks," the Storyteller smiled. "We will know soon enough for sure whether he's alive or dead. In any case, even if he is no more, in time the Breakers will send another spoiler. We will have some respite if he is gone but no permanent relief."

oooOooo

The Storyteller gathered the questors together.

Adam and Eve had been in their apartment speculating about the next stage of their journey but, over and over again, one of them would revert to Nick Peters' outburst at the end of their meeting with him. Eve, in particular, could not understand how someone who had gone out of his way to help her, who had looked after her when she was lost, who had even somehow allowed her to revisit her daughter and at least temporarily remould reality and assuage her grief, how such a man could in effect declare war on her and Adam.

Rambler had taken the opportunity to wander around Prometheus' vast cave, taking notes as he went. He was particularly fascinated by the light source, the 'mini-sun' as Numpty had called it. "It's just not possible," he kept muttering to himself. "Nuclear fusion, controlled, contained and safe; it's mankind's dream. That would be as big a gift to mankind in the twenty-first century as fire was at the beginning of Man's journey."

Numpty had stayed in the rooms he had shared with Rambler and played with Luke. Although Numpty could not hear Luke when he spoke, he knew intuitively that Luke was a remarkable dog and always found it easy to communicate with the retriever by non-verbal means.

All had answered the Storyteller's summons, except for Gwoat, who was bidding the delightful Chione a touching farewell. For Gwoat, the sojourn with Prometheus had been a delight. The nectar of the gods gave all the pleasures of an alcoholic drink with none of the unpleasant aftermath, while the Oread Chione had reawakened pleasures he had thought could now be savoured only as memories. He had never felt so relaxed and happy. Furthermore, he had lost his craving for chocolate (which was just as well because there was none) and his terminal digestive problems had entirely ceased.

"Is the camper van ready?" enquired the Storyteller.

"I haven't checked it," confessed Gwoat, "but it was in good order when we arrived and it's not due for a service till July."

"If that's July in the twenty-first century, that's a hell of a long service interval," quipped Adam. Now that Nick Peters had been exposed, or rather exposed himself, Adam felt much more at ease. He had distrusted Nick from the start. At least everyone, including Eve, had now seen him for what he was, whatever that might be.

Prometheus came to wish them well on their way. "I hope I have been of some help," he said. "At least I have made it clear that we gods were not the makers of men and that your destiny transcends the ambitions of mere immortals. Whether you will find what you seek, I cannot tell but I know it is you, not the gods, who may have a chance of success."

Prometheus bent down to pat Luke. After a somewhat shaky start, the Titan and the dog had become good friends.

"We thank you," the Storyteller replied. "All of us thank you, especially Gwoat, who has enjoyed your hospitality to the fullest extent."

Gwoat blushed.

Prometheus smiled. "For sure," he said, "Chione has a soft spot for itinerant Irishmen, and, if truth be told, itinerants from several other countries, too. She is a lovely girl but κορίτσι εύκολη αρετή as we say, or a bit of goer in your quaint vernacular."

"Tank you, sir," said Gwoat in his thickest Irish brogue, although why he was thanking the Titan was unclear.

"Not at all, at all," Prometheus replied in an attempt at an Irish accent. "Not bad for an ancient Greek," he suggested when the others laughed. Then he asked the Storyteller: "Where are you off to now?"

"We are going back to the beginning of everything," the Storyteller replied.

42 'Prune' Leach and Andrew Rimzil

When they left the cave, the sun was shining and the sky was a clear blue. The sun had some warmth in it, enough to take the edge off the cold wind. The questors wound their way back to the van without difficulty, finding the downward path much easier than the unfamiliar upward climb, aggravated by foul weather, which they had faced when they arrived.

The van, which had been parked out of the wind, was enjoying the full benefit of the sun. When all were aboard, Gwoat turned the ignition key and, without any hesitation, the engine roared into life.

"Hold it a minute." This time Adam was determined to elicit at least some details on where they were heading. "The beginning of everything, I think you said? You wouldn't care to elaborate?"

"I couldn't be more precise," said the Storyteller.

"Surely that's not possible?" said Rambler. "Surely we can't go back to…," he tailed off. He was about to say 'the moment of creation' but hesitated because he was not entirely comfortable with the implications of 'creation'.

"Let's just call it 'the beginning of everything'," said the Storyteller. "It's for Adam and Eve, and you and Numpty of course, to determine the best description once you've seen it."

After a moment in which the questors tried to absorb his enigmatic answers, the Storyteller spoke again: "I should perhaps warn you that there will be a moment of discomfort when we arrive at our destination."

"A moment of discomfort," Adam repeated warily. "What kind of discomfort? And, before we set off, how exactly is Gwoat to drive this van off this mountain? Don't we have an insoluble problem before we start this leg of our journey?"

"So many questions," the Storyteller smiled. "Who said anything about problems? We will leave this mountain just as we arrived," he nodded to Gwoat, who put the engine of the van in gear. "As for the discomfort, all I can say is that it will not be painful and, on the sole condition that the van's brakes are in good order and Gwoat applies them judiciously, it won't be in the least dangerous."

"Isn't that two conditions?" enquired Numpty, who had been listening intently while stroking the golden fur on Luke's head.

Before anyone could answer, the van started to move but not in a linear direction. The engine roared as Gwoat took it through the gears and the mountain receded or perhaps more accurately faded away.

Adam had the impression that the van was in fact stationary and it was the Caucasus that was somehow dwindling.

Eve looked out of her window. They were flying. She could see a carpet of undulating white clouds below them and nothing but light blue sky around. Then the blue faded and the sky became black. Although the van seemed steady in its course, it was obvious they were accelerating. They were now deep in space. "Oh my God!" was all she could say.

Adam said nothing but he thought to himself that, however the quest ended, this experience alone justified all the risks.

Rambler, who seemed to have a better grasp of what 'the beginning of everything' meant, spoke to the Storyteller. "Quite remarkable," he observed.

"Just wait," the Storyteller replied, "soon you will see something no one has seen before. You will see the Milky Way from outside the galaxy."

"I was referring to the van," Rambler said. "It is a truly remarkable vehicle. May I ask what kind of engine drives it?" He had taken copious notes on the mini-sun in Prometheus' cave and was curious to know whether the van was somehow using the same source of energy. Whatever the source, it clearly had an unimaginable power.

"Not so," the Storyteller said, as though he had read Rambler's thoughts. "The van has a top speed of about eighty miles per hour, which it reaches in a rather pathetic thirty seconds. It does have an extra gear after top – an exponential drive which enables it to double its speed every thirty seconds. So, at the end of one minute, it's moving away from the starting point at one hundred and sixty miles an hour and at the end of two minutes it's doing six hundred and forty miles an hour. At the end of five minutes it's doing forty thousand nine hundred and sixty miles an hour. Flat out, in space, in just about 10 minutes, it breaks through the light barrier."

"That's not possible," said Rambler. "Nothing can move faster than the speed of light."

"And who told you that?" enquired Gwoat who, while normally reticent, was always more than happy to expound the virtues of the van. "Of course you can go faster than the speed of light. It's simple; once you reach the speed of light, you just need to accelerate. It's true, you can't be seen by others at such a speed. But you're still there, just going faster, out of eyeshot you might say."

"Sounds like a bit of the old blarney," Adam suggested.

"Not at all," Gwoat replied sharply. "Clearly you never met Prune Leach, probably the greatest Irish engineer of all time."

Before Adam could confirm he had indeed never made the acquaintance of Mr Leach, Numpty leapt in: "Why was he called Prune?"

"Well it was to do with his complexion," said Gwoat. "He worked every hour that God sent, much of the time under a car or a tractor, out in all weathers or in his workshop with braziers blazing and splinters of metal flying off his anvil. What with the work and the wind and the oil and the dirt, and the cold and the heat, his whole body, which was not that great to start with, took a hell of a battering. His face, which, truth to tell, was pretty ugly to start with, ended up in his later years like nothing so much as a dried prune. Hence the name."

"What is pretty ugly?" asked Numpty puzzled. "Is it a trick of the light that can make someone look nice one minute and not so nice the next?"

Adam intervened: "What has this Prune Leach got to do with the speed of the van?"

"Ah!" said Gwoat. "He devised the exponential drive. How he did it, I don't know. I asked him many times and he just said it was a bit of Irish magic. He also said it was very simple and he couldn't understand why nobody had thought of it before. He would say, if the fastest you've ever travelled is ten miles an hour, a hundred miles an hour seems impossibly fast but if you're used to doing a thousand miles an hour, two thousand miles an hour doesn't seem out of reach, even though it's 11 times faster than the difference between 10 and 100. I'm not sure what he meant but that's all I could get out of him. Prune could be as tight-lipped as a Scottish spinster's purse. He did say that light was just one way of seeing things and that there was a good deal more to the universe than light would let us see."

"Why would a Scottish spinster have a tight-lipped purse," enquired the ever curious Numpty.

"Leaving aside obscure, contrived and quite possibly tasteless similes," said Adam, "are you saying some wizened, weather-beaten Irish oil-rag came up with a device that can do what we are doing?" Then Adam stopped and turned to the Storyteller. "What are we doing?"

"We are travelling back to the beginning, just as I told you," the Storyteller replied.

"I say," said Rambler excitedly, addressing Gwoat as though he had only just realised the wiry Irishman existed. "What do you mean there's a good deal more of the universe than light will let us see? Whatever you mean, you're absolutely right. According to current thinking, what we know of matter is a relatively small part of what must exist. I've often wondered if there might not be a lot more to the universe than what we can see with our eyes and measure with our instruments. I don't mean some other world or some other universe; I mean in this universe. Just because what we can see and what we can measure is limited by the speed of light doesn't mean there is nothing else to be seen or measured. There might be an awful lot on the other side of the speed of light."

Numpty hadn't followed Rambler's enthusiastic speculation but he could see his uncle was in the throes of a profound personal enlightenment. "Well done, Uncle," Numpty exclaimed with delight several times. "So what do you think of that?" he asked of all, and no one in particular.

"If we are going back to the beginning of everything," said Eve slowly, "where exactly are we going to be to observe the beginning?"

"An excellent question!" exclaimed Rambler. "Where, indeed?"

"You had better explain this one," said Gwoat. "I know how to use it but I don't have the faintest idea how it works." Gwoat put particular emphasis on the word 'it'.

"What is 'it'?" demanded Adam.

The Storyteller sighed, as though the effort of explaining 'it' was almost certainly going to be greater than any benefit his audience would be likely to enjoy from his exegesis.

"Very well," he said reluctantly. "The van has three modes; economy, sport and paradox. Economy gives you the best results in terms of fuel consumption. Sport sharpens up the gear ratios for a more exhilarating drive…"

Adam broke in. "I think we know what economy and sport are for, though why a camper van needs a sport mode is beyond me."

Gwoat looked hurt and indignant. "I don't think you should be so derogatory about a vehicle that can exceed the speed of light."

"All right," Adam conceded, "perhaps I was a little harsh but I was just trying to persuade the Storyteller to abandon the elementary course in driving and get on with explaining the third mode."

"Quite," said the Storyteller. "The paradox mode."

"And what exactly is the paradox mode?" asked Adam.

"It doesn't really lend itself to exact definition," replied the Storyteller.

Numpty was becoming agitated. No one seemed to have acknowledged the extraordinary insight which his uncle had expressed about what was or wasn't in the universe on this or, indeed, the other side of the speed of light. They had all moved on without a word of praise, and now seemed to be engaged in an exchange of gibberish. He was about to launch a barrage of questions but his uncle, who was desperate to find out about the paradox mode, forestalled him: "Numpty my boy, contain yourself."

"I'm sorry, Uncle, but I have so many questions," Numpty pleaded.

"Let the boy ask his questions," said the Storyteller. "We have time enough for him to ask his questions and for you to answer them. Sadly we have even enough time for me to explain, or try to explain, the paradox mode."

Numpty didn't need a second invitation: "How can I contain myself? I am myself so there's nothing of me apart from me to contain myself with. And how can a word lend itself or not lend itself to anything and, even if it did, what use would it be to the borrower who, in any case, had every right to use the word before it lent itself to him? And what is this paradox?" He ended abruptly.

"Well, taking your last question first," said Rambler with benign patience, "a paradox is a statement which appears to be nonsensical but which, upon reflection, reveals a deeper truth."

"Such as...," prompted Numpty, hopeful that an example would make the explanation clearer.

"Well," said Rambler, "the child is father of the man."

He paused. Numpty looked blank.

"I should give up if I were you," suggested Adam, addressing Rambler.

Rambler was undeterred. "The child is father of the man sounds like a contradiction because usually we would say the man is the father of the child."

"Sorry," said Numpty, "but I thought that's what you said."

"If you think about it, there is a sense in which the child is father of the man." Rambler paused expectantly.

"Well," said Numpty slowly, "I suppose it could mean that when the child grows up, if it's a boy, it could have a son who would grow up to be a man."

"That is indeed possible, but that is not the deeper meaning to which I alluded," said Rambler.

Adam intervened abruptly. "For Christ's sake, it means you can see what a man will be like by looking at him when he is a boy."

"That's not always true," said Numpty defensively. "If the child works hard to learn and understand, if he tries his best and is guided well, when he becomes a man he can become much more than what he was as a child, much more than anyone could have guessed."

"I wouldn't bank on it," muttered Adam unkindly.

The Storyteller spoke. "I tell you this, Adam. As things stand, young

Numpty here has a better chance of finding the truth than you. You should listen to what he says before dismissing it."

Adam grunted. On the one hand, he felt a little ashamed of his treatment of Numpty. On the other hand, the young fellow was extraordinarily irritating. To be encumbered with a mentally challenged youth when on a quest for the truth seemed to be a bit of a paradox in itself.

"The paradox mode," said the Storyteller, reluctantly resuming his attempt at an explanation, "is perhaps Prune Leach's greatest invention."

"Not forgetting Andrew Rimzil," Gwoat interjected.

"Absolutely," the Storyteller conceded. "Andrew Rimzil's contribution was crucial. Indeed some say he deserves more credit for the paradox device than Prune himself. Whatever, it was a brilliant collaboration."

"So what is it?" Adam demanded.

"It's a different way of seeing things. It's a way of standing things on their head. It's a way of transcending the obvious and obviating insurmountable obstacles."

"Whoa!" exclaimed Adam. "Enough. I'm as confused as I'm sure Numpty is. What on earth are you talking about? Just tell us what it is and how it's going to help us."

The Storyteller paused, genuinely at a loss to provide a better definition. "Take a brick," he said. "It's a three-dimensional, rectangular piece of material. It might be a piece of rubble or it might be one brick in a magnificent palace. Or it might have been the latter at one time and the former at another. It might be part of a wall to defend you or to keep you in. It might be something that sets limits to where you can go and what you can do; or it might be a reminder that every wall has two sides and there is unknown potential, for good or ill, on the other side."

"So...," urged an increasingly frustrated Adam.

"So," said the Storyteller, "Messrs Leach and Rimzil found a way to choose, to chop and change."

"What, you mean," said Adam, with some contempt, "they were able to see a brick in different ways?"

"No, I mean they developed a device to enable them to choose to make the various options at any time in any situation a temporary reality, at the expense of all the others."

"You probably think you are making sense," Adam conceded, "But, if I'm honest, I think you've lost the plot."

The Storyteller roared with laughter, spluttering, "Lost the plot," over and over again, in between bouts of uncontrollable mirth.

"Well, I'm glad you find it so funny," said Adam both puzzled and slightly worried. After all, they were hurtling through space in a camper van heading for the beginning of everything and their tour guide, who had arranged the excursion, was close to hysterical.

"Sorry," said the Storyteller, eventually gaining control of himself. "I did say it was difficult to explain. Anyway, the point is that, although it might seem impossible and illogical for us to be able to observe the beginning of everything, in that there would be nowhere from which we would be able to observe, nevertheless, by engaging the paradox device, we shall be able to do so."

"It's all so beautiful," said Eve, who had been peering out of her window during the exchange between Adam and the Storyteller. "Just look."

They had left the Milky Way and were now able to see the magnificent spiral shape of the home galaxy. "It is beautiful," the Storyteller conceded, "and it's vast, about a hundred thousand light years across, but it's just one of many, one of billions. It's difficult for the brain to grasp the immensity of space; more than a hundred billion galaxies, with more than a hundred billion stars in each. And that," he added, "is this side of the speed of light."

"So how many stars are there altogether?" asked Numpty.

It was a pointless question but the Storyteller did his best to answer it. "The best estimate I have is ten to the power of twenty-four. That's ten, with twenty-four noughts after it."

Rambler wrote the number out in full in his notebook:

10,000,000,000,000,000,000,000,000

and showed the figure to Numpty.

"What it means," said the Storyteller, who could himself see the figure was meaningless, "is that if we were to share out the stars amongst all the six billion people on earth, every man, woman and child would have one thousand six hundred trillion stars each; that's one thousand six hundred with twelve noughts."

"Why are you showing us this?" asked Adam. "I mean, are we supposed to draw a conclusion?"

The Storyteller smiled. "It's up to you what you do with it," he said. "But, whatever you do with it, it's surely worth seeing. Even if it doesn't prompt you to draw a conclusion, it provides a context for the truth you seek. It's a fact that the universe is unimaginably vast. It may or may not be important, but it's true."

After a moment's silence in which the questors mulled over what the Storyteller had just said, Eve spoke. "Are we really hurtling through inter-galactic space in a camper van?"

"What a question!" the Storyteller exclaimed. "Look out of your window. What do you think we're doing?"

"Yes but, if this was real, wouldn't we need oxygen and suits that would protect us from radiation?"

Adam was stunned. He had never thought of Eve as particularly practical, much less aware of the basic requirements for space travel. She'd always seemed deeply uninterested in space flights and Mars shots and such like.

The Storyteller smiled. "You don't want me to explain the paradox device again, do you?" Without waiting for a reply, he tapped Gwoat on the shoulder; "Do it," was all he said.

The van didn't jolt or shudder but the view out of the windows disappeared. No longer could they see the majestic splendour of the galaxies. Outside the windows was a blank whiteness.

43 A leg up

"How have they been treating you?" Grimrose, in the form of a middle-aged, slightly dishevelled, unshaven working man, enquired of Nick, who was sitting up in his hospital bed in a ward in Southampton General Hospital.

"Well now, let me see," Nick replied affably. "I'm stuck in this room with three other patients. One is quite clearly dying, mainly because no one is bothering to feed him; a second, a man of middle years, in for acute appendicitis, either has premature senile dementia or is professionally stupid; the third snores so loudly that, were I not bed-bound, he would have snored his last days ago. Oh! I forgot to mention, the doctor whom I had some difficulty in understanding, for I fear my Gujarati was not much better than his English, informed me today, mainly using signs and mime, that I shall forever walk with a pronounced limp."

"Oh well," observed Grimrose. "At least you'll be able to walk."

"Isn't it odd," there was menace in Nick's voice, "how easily we can bear other's misfortunes, even, or in your case perhaps especially, when we are the cause of them?"

"Hold on," Grimrose replied, alarmed. "I wasn't making light of your limp. More importantly, I was not the cause of your misfortune. Be fair! I was the one who saved you."

"If only you could have seen your way to saving me without ripping my leg to shreds," Nick carped.

"You were lucky I caught you at all," Grimrose whispered. "I told you it was a mad idea for me to turn into an eagle. I just didn't have enough experience. I thought I did bloody well in the circumstances."

"No need to whisper," was Nick's only riposte. "As I told you, one's dying, another's brain dead and the third, well just listen to that snore."

"Is there anything I can get you?" Grimrose hazarded in an attempt to turn the conversation in a positive direction.

"Well there is, now you come to mention it," said Nick. "You can get me another leg."

Grimrose gave a hollow laugh. He had served his master long enough to know he was not joking. "And how am I supposed to do that?" he asked eventually.

"Not really my problem," Nick returned. "You owe me a leg, so get me one."

"This is silly," Grimrose responded, determined to stand his ground. "You still have a leg; in fact you have two legs. One is damaged but it's

240

still there and is usable. In any case, how the hell would you expect me to get a leg?"

"Well" said Nick, with mock patience as though addressing an idiot, "by my reckoning there are about one thousand patients in here. Most of them have two legs. I guess about half of them are left legs, which is the one I'm after. Now of course I want a good, healthy leg in tip top working order but I'm pretty sure you will be able to find one or two to fit the bill out of five hundred."

It was Grimrose's turn to explain the situation in simple terms. "Well now," he began, "it's pretty unlikely anyone is going to donate you a perfectly healthy working leg, so I assume you're suggesting I wander round the words, find an unwitting donor and hack his leg off."

"Not too much of the hacking," was Nick's only objection. "I want a clean seam when it's grafted on."

"I want a clean seam when it's grafted on," Grimrose repeated. "Are you completely fucking mad? Can you hear yourself?"

"Keep your voice down," Nick urged.

"I thought you said one was dying, one was brain dead and the other asleep and snoring."

"I said there was no need to whisper," Nick snapped back, "that doesn't mean it's fine to shout. There's probably a hospital rule about whipping legs off."

"What do you mean, 'there's probably some rule'?" said Grimrose. "Of course there's a bloody rule."

"All right, all right," said Nick in an effort to calm the shapeshifter. "There's no need to get all uppity. Places like this are lopping off healthy legs all the time. Half the surgeons don't know their right from their left. How many times have you heard stories of people going in to have a left leg amputated and, just as they are going under the anaesthetic, they say "Do make sure you remove the right leg," and before you can say Jack Robinson, or perhaps more aptly Long John Silver, the surgeon's in there slicing and sawing the wrong one off."

"Was that a question?" Grimrose enquired.

"Was what a question?" Nick replied puzzled.

"Were you asking me how often I had heard such ridiculous stories because, if you were, the answer is never, except when you've been concocting such nonsense to try to get me to do something even more stupid than shape-shifting into an overgrown eagle."

"Well it happens oftener than you think," Nick said grumpily.

Grimrose decided to reason with the patient. "Look, even if I could find a leg, and even if I agreed to cut it off (which I won't without the donor's consent, which obviously I won't get), how exactly do you think you are going to get it grafted on? What's the plan? Are you going to grab the surgeon on his rounds and say, 'Excuse me, but I've found a pretty good damn leg going spare by my bed which, in my opinion, grafted on by you in place of the one you recently and not entirely successfully patched up, could serve me exceedingly well'?"

"You're being stupid," said Nick. "Of course we can't ask the surgeon to do it. He'll be too busy trying to explain why one of his patients has inadvertently lost a leg. No, it's going to work like this. First you need to get me out of here. Then you need to put on a surgeon's coat, slip back in here at night and whip off a suitable leg, not forgetting a bagful of anaesthetics. Then you do the business."

"Then I do the business!" Grimrose repeated. "I'm a shapeshifter, not a doctor."

"Well shapeshift into a doctor," suggested Nick.

"It doesn't work like that and you know it," said Grimrose. "Shapeshifters can adopt the form but they don't acquire the skills."

"Quite right," Nick replied unperturbed. "But you do have the power to mould forms. I reckon, if you can get a leg, you can use your powers to meld it on. Many shapeshifters have a healing power in their hands, don't they? It's a kind of extension of the shape-shifting thing. You form your own bodies. I just need a bit of that forming, moulding, melding stuff to ensure a good fit."

"I'm not doing it," said Grimrose flatly.

"My word," said Nick. "Such courage."

"I'm not doing it," Grimrose repeated.

"Have you really thought this through?" Nick asked. "We can't have shapeshifters disobeying Breakers, now can we? Wouldn't do at all! Against the natural order of things."

"I'm not doing it," Grimrose said for the third time, "but I will try some healing on your own leg," he added.

"And what good will that do?" asked Nick sceptically.

"It depends," said Grimrose. "I can probably make it as good as new."

"Well why didn't you say so?" Nick laughed. "No need for all the leg-lopping, sawing and grafting. That's fine by me."

"It will mean considerable risks for me and quite possibly permanent, irreparable damage," Grimrose explained.

"I think we can live with that," said Nick happily.

"No doubt you can; I may not," said Grimrose grimly.

"Don't be so negative," said Nick, determined to maintain his own good spirits. "Even if it kills you, you couldn't die in a better cause."

"What, my death for your leg?" Grimrose grunted, with disgust.

Nick frowned. "You know, I've noticed recently your service has become rather grudging," he observed. "Really, if you can't give willingly, you shouldn't give at all. And then, of course," he added menacingly, "you must expect to take the consequences."

"It will mean I have to transfer some of my essence to you," Grimrose ignored Nick's rebuke and threat. "How much depends on the extent of the damage but, whatever I transfer, is lost to me permanently. At best, it will diminish my shape-shifting abilities and my powers of regeneration. At worst, it will weaken me so much, I shan't be able to maintain my own bodily functions."

"It's only a leg, for God's sake," quipped Nick. "Surely repairing a Breaker's leg will not take so much out of you that it proves fatal." Nick sounded more curious than concerned.

"When do you want to do this?" Grimrose was resigned. Once again, the potentially dire consequences he himself faced were out of all proportion to the benefits for his master. But that was, after all, the Breaker's way.

"Now would seem as good a time as any," said Nick.

44 A singular experience

"Hit the brakes now," shouted the Storyteller. It wasn't panic but it was emphatic, especially the 'now'.

The blank white began to dissolve into lines of a cone which the van seemed to be hurtling into, heading for the vertex.

"You'll have to brake harder," said the Storyteller peering over Gwoat's shoulder, "if you ever want to see Chione again," he added as an entirely unnecessary additional incentive. "The paradox mode won't hold if you overshoot."

Gwoat's foot pressed the brake down as hard as he could. "Use the gears," the Storyteller urged.

All the questors stared through the van's windscreen at the distant vertex of the cone, which they still seemed to be approaching at an alarming rate.

Only Rambler took time to wonder how the brakes in the van could be operating. Since the wheels were in space and had no surface on which to achieve traction, what was the effect of stopping the wheels from turning? He decided not to pursue the matter because when he thought about it, it was probably the same mechanism that allowed the van to accelerate.

The questors were becoming increasingly alarmed since it was beginning to look as though there was no way the van could stop before it hit the vertex.

"We've slowed enough," said the Storyteller. "You can engage reverse and use the exponential drive. I'll activate the paradox mode so we can use the exponential thrust in reverse."

All this sounded like total gibberish to the questors but the Storyteller seemed sublimely confident. Gwoat whacked the gear stick into reverse. There was a judder. The Storyteller hit a button to activate paradox mode. That did it. It was as though they had deployed a massive parachute behind them to drag them to a standstill.

"There's a slip road ahead, or there will be if I tickle the paradox switch a little. As soon as you see it, pull over. We should be able to park just outside the cone, within spitting distance of the vertex." Gwoat followed the Storyteller's instructions and brought the van to a halt in an otherwise empty lay-by. They could see the tip of the cone. It was very small and very black. There was nothing beyond it. It was all very odd but evidently they had arrived safely. There was a general sigh of relief.

"That was a bit like that aeroplane flight when we were both a bit nervous and we landed successfully," Numpty said to his uncle. "When the wheels touched down, we both went 'phew!', didn't we?"

"We certainly did," confirmed Rambler. "And, if you recall, we gave the captain a little clap for bringing us safely home. So why don't we give Gwoat a round of applause?"

And they did, with the Storyteller joining in, although, as Gwoat knew, their successful arrival had more to do with the Storyteller's gifts than Gwoat's driving expertise. Gwoat acknowledged the applause and then said he would rather have a bar of chocolate. They all laughed. Evidently Chione's benign effect on Gwoat was beginning to wear off.

"I'm afraid we are out of chocolate," said the Storyteller. "And if you are going back to your old ways, please restrain any urge to fart. Apart from the appalling inappropriateness of farting when we are about to witness the birth of creation, any gases other than hydrogen and helium at this particular moment could alter the entire development of the universe."

"Can we let Luke out?" asked Numpty. "He's dying for a widdle."

"I'm afraid I'm in the same boat," said Rambler. "Bladder's not what it was."

"Very well," said the Storyteller reluctantly. "We'll all get out and stretch our legs, but briefly. There are no toilet facilities, not surprisingly, so you must make do."

"I don't want to make do 'cos I made quite a big do last thing at the Titan's cave," Numpty revealed, "but I would quite like a widdle."

So it was that the questors, the Storyteller and Gwoat disembarked from the van and split into two groups in the lay-by; one group, the widdlers, including Luke, relieved themselves at one end, while the Storyteller, Adam, Eve and Gwoat chatted at the other.

"Not quite what I had in mind as a prelude to the moment of creation," observed the Storyteller.

"It all looks a bit bleak," said Adam who was peering from the lay-by across to the point of the cone.

"It'll look even bleaker in a minute," promised the Storyteller. When we get back to the very moment of creation, the lateral surface of the cone will retract to the apex until there is nothing there but the point. Then it will begin."

"Should we be this close to the point if it's going to explode into the universe?" Eve asked.

Once again, Eve's practicality in understanding their situation took Adam by surprise.

"If we were in the cone, you would be absolutely right," the Storyteller agreed. "But we're outside the cone; we're outside the point that the cone will retract to. We're insulated by the paradox device. We are about to observe the birth of something that contains everything, including the seeds of something that will eventually evolve, after aeons, into something capable of observing the universe and yet we are able to stand here, long before we have evolved into existence, as observers. It's a unique privilege and one which only the paradox device could make possible."

"Don't think we're ungrateful," said Adam, "but I can't really see how this is going to get us any closer to the truth. I mean all we are going to see is an explosion, isn't it?"

"What I show you and what you see are two different things," the Storyteller replied.

Having completed their calls of nature, the others re-joined them and all the questors climbed once more into the camper van.

Before joining the others, Gwoat took the Storyteller to one side. "Are we sure this is going to work?" he asked, with a clear tremor of nervousness in his voice. Gwoat was far from happy. He had found in the halls of Prometheus a degree of contentment that he had not expected nor indeed ever felt he had deserved. The Titan exuded a benign warmth and that seemed to fill the vast cave and everything within it. Chione had been more than generous with her favours but it was not just the pleasure she had given him. The place itself had made him feel at home and, for an itinerant, Irish camper van driver, seconded to the service of the Storyteller, whose work involved continual travel and, let it be said, risk, the notion of home had an extraordinarily strong appeal. Of course he had no choice but to go where the Storyteller chose, but to leave behind the security and comfort of Prometheus' domain to travel back in time to the beginning of everything, well fairly obviously, the venture was fraught with danger.

"I can't guarantee it will work, nor can I guarantee it will be safe," the Storyteller gave an answer which did nothing to assuage Gwoat's fears. "These quests always involve some risk, as you know," he went on. "It's true that we haven't undertaken this particular exercise before. In theory, the paradox device should enable us to observe without cataclysmic results but we can't rule out unforeseen consequences."

Gwoat began hopping from one foot to the other. "Unforeseen consequences," he repeated. "Cataclysmic results! Be Jasus, you've thrown my guts into a turmoil – there's one cataclysmic result for you already. I feel as though I've got a blender in my stomach."

"Cataclysmic result, perhaps," said the Storyteller, "but not an unforeseen consequence. I have one bar of chocolate which I have kept in secret for just such an occasion." He gave the bar to Gwoat. "Do you know," the Storyteller added, patting Gwoat on the back, "you worry too much."

With that, he climbed into the van, with Gwoat, clutching his bar of chocolate as though his life depended on it, close behind.

"Are you sitting comfortably," the Storyteller quipped, "then the universe will begin. Hold tight!" He then nodded to Gwoat, who started the engine once more but left the gear in neutral. The Storyteller then turned the dial under the paradox switch to maximum.

The lateral surface of the cone began to vibrate. The retraction had begun. The Storyteller explained: "When the lateral surfaces are gone and only the point of the cone remains, or rather the point where the vertex used to be, then you shall see a sight, such a sight, that words will fail you."

And so it was. There was a moment of nothingness. Not nothingness in the sense of completely empty space. No, there was no space. There was nothing, except for the lay-by sustained by the paradox device. Beyond the limits of their observation capsule, there was no space and no time, no light and no darkness. All that existed was the point where the vertex of the cone had been, an inert, non-dimensional position.

And then there was incomprehensible energy. If the van and its occupants had been part of the universe, it and they would have been destroyed in an instant, given that the temperature was about one hundred thousand million degrees centigrade. The only things that could survive at such a temperature were elementary particles such as electrons and positrons, neutrinos and photons. As far as the questors were concerned, as they rode this effusion of energy like surfing a terrifying wave, the birth of the universe was primarily distinguished by the brightness of the light. It was a light such as no one has seen. The entire universe, expanding at unimaginable speed, was a great bowl of brilliant, swirling whiteness.

"Funny thing about the Big Bang," the Storyteller shouted to his awestruck companions, "It created the brightest light that has ever existed, but no one saw it. And, for that matter, the bang itself was a silent bang, for there was no one to hear it."

The Storyteller instructed Gwoat to engage a forward gear. "Lock on to the lay by. We need to take it with us. Then, let's go," said the Storyteller. "We need to fast forward a few hundred thousand years."

45 Gas rules, OK

With some ingenious use of the exponential gear and the paradox device, the van and the lay-by, both still encased in the paradox field, reached the target period in 14 minutes. The view from the van was not easy to describe. The blinding whiteness had resolved a little into heaving, gyrating eddies of elementary particles. The temperature had dropped but, outside the bubble, the universe was about the same temperature as the surface of the 21st century sun.

"What do you see out there?" said the Storyteller.

"Chaos," suggested Adam, "a bright, swirling soup of chaos."

"Not bad," said the Storyteller.

"Might I suggest the soup is hydrogen and helium," Rambler hazarded.

"Very good," said the Storyteller. "Do you see anything else?"

Both Adam and Rambler looked blank.

"There's really not that much to see or to say," said Adam. "I mean, it's been an amazing experience but, at the end of the day, it's a firework display on a cosmic scale."

"Let me give you a clue," said the Storyteller. "What I am asking you to see cannot be seen but, if it wasn't staring you in the face, you wouldn't have a face with eyes to see or a head with a brain to understand."

"That's a clue?" said Adam. "Sounds more like a riddle."

"How do all the gases know what to do?" asked Numpty who was staring at the whirling soup of light outside the paradox bubble. "I mean they are all swirling around but they aren't all going in one direction."

"Good question, my boy," Rambler responded quickly, before Adam could put his nephew down with a sarcastic remark. "I suspect it's a combination of the initial force of the Big Bang driving the particles apart and gravity pulling them together."

"That's good," said the Storyteller, delighted. "That's very good. So what can you see?"

Again all the questors looked blank.

"You've just said it," the Storyteller prompted Rambler – but to no avail.

"You mean gravity," suggested Eve.

"Yes," said the Storyteller, "I mean what we call the law of gravity."

Adam shrugged. "Sure," he said, in a tone that carried an unsaid 'So what?'

"Throughout the universe," the Storyteller explained, "the law of gravity and indeed the other laws of physics, including the force of the Big Bang itself, apply. All matter is governed by these rules."

The questors still couldn't see why the Storyteller was making such a fuss about something so obvious.

"Where are the rules?" asked Numpty. He knew all about gravity. His uncle had introduced him to elementary physics years ago. Yes, he knew all about gravity, but he certainly didn't understand it. His question was greeted by silence, so Numpty said "Sorry," because obviously he had spoken out of turn or had said something silly.

"Well," said the Storyteller, challenging everyone, "where are the rules?"

There was silence. Then Adam said: "I suppose the material that came out of the Big Bang had the rules built into them, so that they knew how to behave."

"I don't think that can be right," Rambler responded. "The original stuff was just a vast number of excited particles. They couldn't have carried all the instructions for the behaviour of all the elements that didn't yet exist. No, the forces we are considering must have come into being at the same time as the Big Bang event took place. They must somehow be part of the fabric of the universe. It is from these forces that we have derived our rules."

"OK," said Adam, "So there are rules and OK I admit it is rather odd these rules exist and that they are universal but I suppose that's just the way it is."

"I don't think we should settle for 'I suppose that's just the way it is' if we are looking for the truth," Eve said sharply. She had no idea what the Storyteller was getting at and she was not particularly interested by the subject but she felt an instinctive revulsion when people answered important questions with 'I suppose that's just the way it is'. That's what Nick had said to her about the death of Bella.

"Did we derive these rules, or did we discover them?" asked the Storyteller. Adam was surprised at the Storyteller's persistence. It was not like the Storyteller to push them in one direction or another when interpreting situations and yet, on this occasion he seemed to be trying to manoeuvre them towards an as yet unrevealed conclusion. "Every object in the universe attracts every other object in the universe," the Storyteller continued, "with a force that is proportional to the product of their two masses and inversely proportional to the square of the distance between them. Rather neat, don't you think?"

"It is rather odd that out of a seemingly chaotic explosion, a universe as ordered as ours should emerge," said Rambler.

"Odd, it is," said the Storyteller. "That's good enough."

It seemed the Storyteller had suddenly lost interest in the discussion.

Adam joined Eve at the back of the van. "What was all that about?" he asked his wife.

"No idea," said Eve. "He seems to think we should be making something of what we've seen, but what it is, I have no idea. I really can't see how witnessing the beginning of the universe or how it really got started with a couple of gases is going to answer any of the questions I have. I certainly don't want a science lesson. That's not going to tell me anything."

"Maybe he just wants us to ponder the fact that order came out of chaos," said Adam. Then he added: "Although I'm not sure that's what he meant because he also seemed to be saying the rules that brought order out of chaos must have been there from the start. Or maybe he's trying to give us a cosmic perspective. You know, setting our short lives into the context of thirteen billion years."

"What, so that we realise how inconsequential our lives are and how trivial the tragedies we have to face?" Eve queried. "I don't think so. If that was what he was trying to do, he could have left it to Nick Peters, who was only too keen to tell me that the past didn't matter and that I should move on."

"Well, I don't think there's any conclusion for me to draw," said Adam. "It's been an extraordinary, outstanding experience and an awe-inspiring spectacle but, when all's said and done, it's really just been a light show – I mean a phenomenal cosmic light show but still a light show. And we don't know why it happened. We don't know what caused it."

Rambler had overheard Adam and Eve's conversation. "It's rather more extraordinary than it appears," he suggested. "I've dabbled a little in cosmology and I am very much aware that what we have seen, both the explosion of time and space together with all those particles at the moment of the Big Bang and now this swirling sea of hydrogen and helium, is the result of a highly improbable series of coincidences." Rambler thumbed through his apparently limitlessly commodious notebook to find the correct references. "You will recall the sketchy account that Angel Rodney gave us in the Garden of Eden of his difficulties in setting up the initial conditions of the universe. Well, his version was, if anything, an underestimate of the precision required in achieving the particular universe we inhabit. No, 'precision' is not the right word. Particularity is perhaps better. Our universe is as it is because of some very particular arrangements, any one of which, if not what it is, would have precluded human life, indeed any life at all. Like you," he spoke to both Adam and Eve, "I don't know what we are supposed to make of it. But it's surely something we can't ignore."

"So you're endorsing Rodney's explanation that they built a sense of direction into the universe," said Eve. "Are you saying that there was truth for us to find in the Garden of Eden? I'll not accept the God we met there. No way will I accept Him as the Creator, nor will I accept the bizarre, sadistic world He ruled. I don't know about a sense of direction. I'm certainly hoping there is some point, some purpose, to it all. But I will not accept we had anything to learn from that psychologically crippled individual who claimed to be God."

"Progress, at last!" interrupted the Storyteller who had been listening intently to the exchange between Adam, Eve and Rambler. Eve took him to mean that he endorsed her savage indictment of the Deity; in fact, that was not what he meant at all.

"Does anyone want a cup of tea?" enquired Numpty. Under Gwoat's supervision, Numpty had mastered the art of tea-making in a camper van and was rather proud of his accomplishment.

So it was, as they sat in a camper van in a lay-by in a paradox bubble at the edge of the speedily expanding universe, which was now a good million years old, the questors enjoyed the uniquely refreshing effects of freshly brewed tea.

46 Comfort break

"We have two more excursions before the reckoning," said the Storyteller, "but, before we set off again, does anyone need to take a comfort break?"

"I should like to stretch my legs," said Rambler, getting up. Numpty gave Luke a pat, and he and the dog joined Rambler, stepping down from the camper van onto the tarmac of the lay-by which, to Rambler's astonishment and delight, had somehow acquired toilets.

"What does 'the reckoning' mean?" asked Adam, who lingered in the camper van.

"Only that when we have completed the trips I have arranged for you, it will be up to you to take stock," the Storyteller replied.

"There's a difference between 'taking stock' and 'a reckoning'," said Eve. Eve felt uneasy. Their journey had certainly provided food for thought; it had, to some extent, distracted her from her grief and from her need to make sense of Bella's death. But the purpose of the journey, as far as she was concerned, was to find answers to precisely those very human, personal questions that perplex people everywhere. So far, the journey had offered much to those endowed with intellectual curiosity but, in her view, it had failed to cater for anyone blessed or cursed with a more holistic intelligence.

"You are right and I must be honest with you," answered the Storyteller. "I must warn you, the reckoning will not be easy. I can't give you a full explanation but I can say there are those who do not wish you to succeed in this quest; there are those who will do anything to ensure you fail. We call them the Breakers. You have met one of their kind, Nick Peters. We may or may not have seen the last of him but whether it is him or another, you will have to face a Breaker before we're through. Don't worry, Eve," the Storyteller added, "you will have your fill of exploring the emotional landscape before our journey is over."

oooOooo

As soon as the Storyteller stepped from the camper van, Rambler grabbed him. "I just wanted to say how grateful I and my nephew are that you have allowed us to accompany you on this epic voyage. I had no idea when we met at Fleet where you might take us but this has, for me, been a life-enhancing experience." Numpty, who had joined his uncle, nodded his agreement vigorously.

252

"You should thank Adam and Eve, not me," said the Storyteller. "It's their quest and it was their decision to let you join them."

"And thank them we will," Rambler replied, "but I thank you too for it is you who is choosing where we go and what we see. And, I suspect, it is you who understands more of what we see than Adam or Eve or indeed I and my nephew. May I ask you a question?"

"Of course you may ask," responded the Storyteller.

"In my somewhat superficial study of cosmology, I have read that the universe is finely tuned to enable intelligent life to evolve. Rodney and Derek's explanation of their work claimed as much and, as I understand it, modern cosmology endorses such a view. Indeed even the Titan Prometheus implied that it was Man's destiny that mattered most in all creation, superseding that of the immortal gods. Is that the conclusion you wish us to draw?"

The Storyteller smiled. "First, it's not for me to lead a questor to any conclusion. There is a good path, and there is a bad path. Nick Peters does his best to persuade my questors to take the bad path. His path has no answers and in the end rejects all questions. I lead my questors to the good path. But the good path has many branches, many highways and byways. The route they take and, in the end, where they go is for them to decide."

"What does 'finely-tuned' mean?" asked Numpty, who felt he was being left behind by his uncle's enthusiasm and the Storyteller's enigmatic response.

"It means 'carefully calibrated to ensure the machine runs smoothly and produces the desired result'," said his uncle, who knew for sure as he spoke that, in the sea of uncertainty aptly represented by hydrogen/helium soup outside the paradox bubble, two things could be regarded as beyond doubt. First, that his explanation left Numpty none the wiser. Secondly, that further questions would ensue.

Encouraged by the Storyteller, who gestured that he should take the floor, Rambler decided to pre-empt his nephew and to adopt his pedagogic persona. This was the first time since joining the questors that Rambler had launched into a full-scale lecture but it was a method of teaching with which young Numpty was familiar.

"In order for the universe to be as it is and for life to have had a chance to evolve, various critical conditions had to be met. It has been observed that all these conditions, which, if random, could have been fulfilled in thousands or millions of different ways, have been precisely set in such a way as to create our universe. For example, if gravity had been a tad stronger, all matter would have collapsed back into a big crunch long before life, much less Man, could have evolved. If it had been a tad weaker, the matter in the universe would have dispersed too quickly and, again, there would have been no chance for life or us. The odds against such a perfect balance would seem to be high. Perhaps even higher are the odds against the creation of carbon, essential for the evolution of life as we know it. To produce carbon it is necessary for three helium nuclei to fuse together at the same time. The only reason that carbon is abundant in our universe is that something called resonance intervenes in exactly the right way to assist the process. The very existence of planets containing all of the elements needed by life depended on the creation of these elements in the furnaces of the stars and then the explosion of these stars to release these elements into space to coalesce under the force of gravity into planets. Had the stars not been of sufficient size and had not gravity been of precisely the right strength, there would have been no explosions and no element-rich planets. There are lots of other examples."

Rambler adopted the lecture mode when he wished to silence his nephew. Numpty preferred to ask questions, rather than to listen to long expositions. He felt he learned more by listening to short answers addressed to whatever was puzzling him. When Rambler lectured, the content prompted so many questions but, because the lecture went on so long, poor Numpty could remember only the first question he had thought of, or the last. All other questions in between were drowned in the inexorable flow of information which Uncle Rambler so generously imparted. On this occasion, when Rambler paused for breath, Numpty simply said: "Thank you, Uncle," which indicated he had heard enough. His uncle had achieved his goal.

"On the other hand," said the Storyteller, "it is scarcely surprising that the universe is set up for us to be here, since we are here. If it wasn't, we wouldn't be."

Numpty had no idea what the Storyteller meant and even Rambler looked flummoxed.

The Storyteller explained: "While you are right that human evolution has occurred at the end of a long chain of highly improbable and certainly, from our point of view, fortuitous factors and events, we should not perhaps read too much into this improbable and fortuitous chain because were it not so, we wouldn't be here to speculate about it."

Rambler was now fully engaged, unlike Numpty who was finding the facts and the discussion of them equally confusing.

Adam, who had heard the last part of the conversation, decided to join in. He had left Eve in the camper van. She was tidying up and chatting to Gwoat, who was browsing through the camper van user manual to find out how to check the amount of power left in the paradox drive.

"I'm not sure I follow that argument," said Adam. "It's true that there wouldn't be anyone to speculate about the odd chain of coincidences if we weren't here, but surely the fact that we are here doesn't diminish to oddness of the chain?"

"There are those," mused Rambler, "who suggest that there must be an infinite number of other universes in which all those variables that have worked out so well in this universe, for life and for us, are different, in which, for example, gravity is actually a bit stronger or a bit weaker. In these other universes, obviously there isn't any intelligent life to do any speculating."

"Oh, really!" Adam scoffed. "You mean in order to explain all those fortuitous coincidences in this universe, somebody is suggesting there must be lots of other universes in which things didn't work out quite so well."

"They are actually suggesting a virtually limitless number of other universes," Rambler conceded. "If you are going to argue all the happy coincidences in this universe happened by chance, the odds are so high against them all occurring in a single universe that you need an infinite number of universes just to produce one like ours."

"Didn't somebody once say that, given various explanations for something, the simplest explanation was the best?" Adam asked. "Is there any evidence for other universes?"

"Not that I know of," Rambler answered. "Indeed I believe such theorists include in their hypothesis the condition that these other universes are irremediably inaccessible to us."

"Well it's not much of a theory if it can't be tested and it's a pretty stupid idea if you have to explain one infinite universe by inventing an infinite number of other infinite universes. Sounds pretty desperate to me!"

"Perhaps they are pretty desperate," said the Storyteller with a smile. "I guess they're worried about the alternative."

"If there's only one universe," said Adam hesitatingly, "and this is it, and everything seems set up to make us possible, then it begins to sound as though we are meant to be here."

"Or it could just be a truly amazing series of coincidences," said the Storyteller.

"Perhaps the universe has a mind of its own?" offered Numpty helpfully.

"It's a thought," said the Storyteller.

47 A successful operation

The sun was setting over Southampton and a warm golden red glow of light poured in through the window of Nick Peters' ward.

Nick now had the ward to himself. The mentally challenged individual had been sectioned and removed after Nick had provoked him to violence by jokingly suggesting the surgeon might have inadvertently removed his brain, rather than his appendix. "Easy mistake to make in your case," he had quipped, "both useless organs likely to do you more harm than good." The ill-nourished dying man had, as Nick had foreseen, died. The snorer too had passed on, when, in the early hours of the morning, Nick, with the judicious use of a pillow, had cured the snorer's blocked nasal passages once and for all, sending the man into an even deeper sleep than that enjoyed at the time by the ward night staff.

"I'm feeling on top of the world," Nick announced when a pale and rather sad looking Grimrose, still in the guise a middle-aged, slightly dishevelled, unshaven working man, entered the ward.

"Where is everybody?" enquired Grimrose.

"We've had a bit of a clear out," said Nick happily. "The thick one has been sectioned. The other two are in the morgue."

"Jesus!" said Grimrose, "There was nothing wrong with the snorer, well nothing that a simple operation couldn't have cured. At worst, he could have undergone uvulopalatopharyngoplasty."

"You never cease to amaze me," said Nick, good-humouredly. "You obviously have far more medical expertise than I had ever imagined. Not only can you pronounce medical terms beyond the range of normal humans, which, of course, you aren't, but, even more importantly and impressively, you have effected a cure of my leg which has far exceeded all my expectations. My left leg is probably the fittest part of my entire corporeal ensemble. Sometimes in the past you have criticised me for failing to appreciate your finer qualities. Well, whip out your diary or your personal information management device and make a note. 'Today, I received fulsome, unqualified praise from Nick Peters, a master Breaker who can now stand tall on two sturdy, fully-functioning legs.' By the way," he added, "the late unlamented snorer was not in for work on his nasal passages. He was going to have a knee operation, I believe."

Grimrose pondered whether he disliked Peters more when, as now, he was full of the joys of spring and even fuller of himself or when, as was more often the case, he was being demanding, critical and sarcastic. He was unable to decide, mainly because he felt really ill.

"You do look somewhat peaky," said Nick. He didn't wait for Grimrose to respond but continued: "Still, it's only to be expected. You said it might take a bit out of you. I guess about a legsworth, eh? Anyway, pull yourself together because we have some work to do."

Grimrose slumped down into a chair beside Nick's bed.

"It's all right," said Nick, with some impatience, "I've done the praising thing. There's no need to milk it."

Had he felt stronger, Grimrose would have tried to kill Peters. It would of course have meant the end of him as well as Nick. The punishment for shapeshifters who rebelled against Breakers was swift and final. But, by God, thought Grimrose, it would have been worth it. For a moment he indulged himself in a happy fantasy, imagining himself in the form of the monster who had despatched Sandy and Maizy. He would strike Peters in the face a few times, more slaps than punches because he didn't want him to lose consciousness. Then he would literally rip Nick's head off.

As it was, he was too weak even to speak.

"By my calculations," Nick continued, "Tel will be about halfway through his cosmological tour, scuttling around the further reaches of space and time. Why he bothers is beyond me. Most of his questors can't work out how to use a smart-phone. Expecting them to get their heads round the birth of the universe and the evolution of life is like explaining the principles of the rotation of crops to a carrot."

Nick glanced at Grimrose to see if he had raised a smile. "We are in a bad mood," he said, when he realised Grimrose hadn't been listening. "Come on," he said. "Shape up, if that's the right expression. There are some things we have to do before the reckoning."

"I thought you had everything under control," said Grimrose, his voice scarcely audible.

"I have," said Nick, "of course I have but that doesn't mean we don't need to put in some effort. We have to make plans. We have to marshal our resources. I have to present an interim report to my regional manager. I've fixed an appointment for tomorrow. We have to be at the regional Breaker's Yard at Cadnam at eleven o'clock. So we'd better get a shift on, if again that's the right expression."

'Still no smile', noted Nick. 'Oh well, fuck him.'

oooOooo

Nick Peters and Grimrose arrived at Cadnam in good time for their meeting with Nigel Vale, Regional Manager of the Breakers for the whole of southern England.

257

Nigel was a bigger, older, heavier version of Nick. His black hair was grey at the temples, giving him a distinguished, authoritative air. He was permanently sun-tanned through all the seasons of the year, sporting a bronze skin colour which contrasted rather well with the bright white shirts which he invariably wore. His rich baritone voice, which seemed well suited to his skin tone, exuded bonhomie.

"Nick, how good to see you," said Nigel, "and I see you've brought your shapeshifter with you." Nigel's brow furrowed a little when he saw the seriously debilitated Grimrose. "You'd better sit down," he suggested, addressing the shapeshifter. Grimrose slumped gratefully into a chair to the side of Nigel's desk. Nick took the seat facing his Regional Manager. He kept his sunglasses on.

"Now fill me in," suggested Nigel. He didn't like the look of Grimrose, who had retained the form of a middle-aged, slightly dishevelled, unshaven working man, mainly because he didn't have the strength to attempt a shape-shift of any sort.

"Well," Nick began, "things have gone pretty well so far. I've managed to talk to Eve, explained the pointlessness of her quest and given her a taste of what we can do for her. I can't claim she's persuaded."

"That's fairly obvious," Nigel interrupted, "since she and her husband are still with the Storyteller, gallivanting around space and time. The more he shows them, the harder it is for us to close them down. I was hoping you could have persuaded at least one of them, the woman Eve perhaps, to have given up before they went to the Caucasus. He's no fool, the Storyteller. After the Garden of Eden, which most of his questors find rather dispiriting, he hurries them off to meet Prometheus. I'll say one thing for the Titan; he knows how to treat his guests. And the visit to the Caucasus opens up new vistas for the questors. Sets them up for the Storyteller's cosmological extravaganza. It's always best to nip these quests in the bud."

"I did my best," said Nick. "I'm pretty sure I got to Eve. Gave her a glimpse of her dead daughter and how things might have been, and a taste of more carnal delights but, unfortunately, my plan to eliminate the camper van failed. I was, I fear, let down by Grimrose here. I ordered him to abduct Gwoat and the van and dispose of them both. Sadly, he failed. If we had destroyed the van and the driver, there would have been no trip to the Caucasus or indeed anywhere else."

"There's a couple of things I should make clear," said Nigel. His voice had a harder edge. "But before I do so, do you think you could remove your sunglasses? I like to see the eyes of my subordinates when I'm talking to them."

258

Reluctantly, Nick took off his sunglasses, grimacing as he did so. The brightness of Nigel's white shirts was quite extraordinary.

"Good," said Nigel. "My first point is that Breakers do not make excuses. They certainly don't try to dump blame onto shapeshifters. I was surprised when you brought Grimrose with you. As you know, strictly speaking you are not supposed to mention the name of subordinates at these debriefings. Grimrose here is part of your team and your responsibility. If he failed, you failed. You can sort his failure out with him. I will sort your failure out with you. Do you understand?"

"Yes," Nick replied. This was really embarrassing. He was sorry he had brought Grimrose along to the meeting. He had hoped to deflect any criticism onto the shapeshifter. As it was, he had simply exposed himself to a reprimand in front of his subordinate.

"The second point is rather more important," said Nigel. "These particular questors – by which I mean Adam and Eve, not their fellow travellers – are a special case. It is even more important than usual that they are broken. I can't give you a complete explanation but I can say there is concern at the highest level."

"What kind of concern?" asked Nick.

Nigel frowned. "There is a fear that Adam or Eve, or both of them, might initiate a Beginning. It is our job to make sure that doesn't happen."

"Our job?" queried Nick.

"Yes, our job," replied Nigel sharply. "Just as you are responsible for Grimrose here and what he does, so, for my sins, am I responsible for you. You are going to front run on this but I can tell you now that I will make sure you have whatever you need. If it's within my powers, you will have whatever support you request. There is no budget limit on this one."

Nick's eyes widened briefly before the reflective light from Nigel's shirt compelled them to resume their erstwhile squinting configuration. He had never heard of such a thing. No budget limit! Wow! This was something else.

"So, what do you need?" Nigel asked.

Nick paused. He was going to have to think about this but he felt he should make a start. "When the questors return at the end of their itinerary, I want a complete and indefinite lock-down in a place of my choosing." Then he added: "In fact, I want a mysland."

The creation of a mysland (pronounced like 'island' with an 'm' at the beginning) was extremely rare and outrageously expensive. It involved fabricating a space where the Breaker had total control of all events and from which those inside (who had no idea they were trapped

259

in a fabricated world) could not escape. It gave the Breaker power of life and death over the prisoners of the mysland and the freedom to manipulate his victims at will. Well, Nigel had said 'no budget limit'. We would see.

"No problem," said Nigel. "What else?"

Nick could scarcely conceal his surprise. "I would like the assistance of a Dawk, the best we've got."

Dawks were the Breakers' backroom boys who dealt with some of the intellectual challenges that questors posed at the end of their journey. They were reductionists, trained in logic, general reasoning, analogy, rhetoric, emotional blackmail and all forms of sophistry.

"I guessed you would need a Dawk," said Nigel. "I have made arrangements for Despiro Nihilopificus to be on call, day and night, from the moment the questors return until they are broken."

Despiro Nihilopificus, generally known affectionately as Sparrow to the Breakers and, rather less affectionately as Razor by the Storyteller, was legendary amongst the Dawks. He had taken the most committed questors, the most convinced truth-seekers and, within a few days, had brought them to their senses. He didn't shout; he didn't rave; he didn't threaten: but he always won.

"Now why is Grimrose so ill and what can we do about it?" asked Nigel. "He's part of your team and he needs to be fully operational. Why is he so weak?"

Before Nick could dismiss such concerns as of no importance, Grimrose managed to speak.

"Mr Peters sustained an injury to his leg. I used my healing powers to repair the damage but, as I told him at the time, his cure could cause me permanent harm. I had to use part of my own shapeshifter essence to effect the repair. As you can see, I have been weakened. I have consulted my own people. It is their view I have only a fifty:fifty chance of survival."

"That was very brave of you," said Nigel. "Is there anything we can do to restore your health? Shapeshifter physiology is beyond me but, if anything can be done, we will do it."

"Sadly, there is only one way for me to restore at least some of my vital essence," said Grimrose, "and that way will probably be unacceptable. To restore Mr Peters' leg, I had to use most of my shape-shifting reserves of energy. If I withdrew some of the essence I used for the repair, I could at least recover some energy. This would give me a better chance of recovery."

Before Nigel could respond, Nick spoke: "Probably unacceptable! You're kidding. If fixing my leg took so much out of you, what the hell do you think would happen to my leg if you try to grab some back. You really are a drama queen. OK, so you're feeling a bit low. Tough. Pull yourself together. You heard the man. We've got a major project on our hands. Let's stop whingeing and get on with it."

Grimrose looked to Nigel for support. He had seemed sympathetic so far. He had at least acknowledged the sacrifice he had made. "I'm sorry," said Nigel, "I'd like to help and, if there's anything else we can do, name it – but we can't risk debilitating Peters. Not now, when he is charged with preventing a potential Beginning. Just can't risk it."

"Quite," said Nick to Grimrose, and then added in a voice redolent with sympathy, mainly for Nigel's benefit, "you do understand, don't you? Perhaps in other circumstances but not when so much depends on how well I perform."

It hadn't turned out so badly after all, Nick thought to himself. Yes, Nigel had rebuked him but there was no doubt he retained his fellow Breakers' confidence. After all, a 'no budget limit' project was unprecedented. And free call on the services of Despiro Nihilopificus settled it. His career was on the move, despite Grimrose's disappointing and mildly disloyal performance.

48 No worries

When the Storyteller climbed back into the camper van, he paused for a moment to talk with Gwoat.

"How are we doing for fuel?" he asked.

"We're OK," Gwoat replied, "so long as we don't spend too much time at our next stop. We've got half a tank left but, as you know, engaging the paradox device drinks fuel."

"We'll make a move immediately," said the Storyteller, leaning back out of the van and summoning Adam, Rambler and Numpty, all of whom were, in their own way, pondering the Storyteller's recent pronouncements.

Once all were aboard, Gwoat hit the accelerator.

"I guess there's no point in asking where we're going?" said Adam, as the vehicle shot along the lay-by, which seemed to extend in length, however fast the van moved.

"Well, we've done the birth of the universe. We storytellers call that the first great Beginning. Now we're going to the place and time of the birth of life. That is the second great Beginning; it is the moment that inanimate matter became animate. It is the first step the universe took to understanding itself. And what a step it was! I have to warn you, it probably won't look that momentous. No fanfare, no applause and, of course, no witnesses except for us, but what a moment! Billions of years in which the seething sea of gases coalesced into stars and planets; in which the only movement was that driven by the laws of physics; in which nothing that happened was registered by anything else; a dead, unheard, unseen, unfelt wasteland, and then, and then, the second great Beginning."

For the first time since Adam and Eve had met him, the Storyteller seemed profoundly moved.

"I don't know how much progress we have made but our guide certainly seems to be enjoying a moment of enlightenment," Adam whispered to Eve.

"If we are truly to witness the birth of life, it will be a moment for all of us to treasure," said Rambler, who had overheard Adam. "It will mark the beginning of a great adventure."

"I shouldn't get too excited," said Adam, who found Rambler's involvement in the quest slightly intrusive. "As I understand it, what we will see, if anything, is some kind of bacteria swimming in a puddle. Like the man said, it won't look momentous."

"Hold tight everyone," called Gwoat. "I'm uncoupling the paradox device." While they had been talking, the ever-extending lay-by had disappeared and they had continued their journey through a pure blank whiteness. There was no sign of movement outside the windows, no wisps of cloud scudding past, no features at all but evidently they were travelling at great speed because Gwoat had the engine of the camper van running flat out.

"Do as Gwoat says," urged the Storyteller. "Everyone back in their seats with seat belts on."

There was a clunking sound and a judder which shook the van and its occupants.

"Bugger," said Gwoat.

"Problem?" enquired the Storyteller with some urgency, sufficient to alarm the questors.

"We need to disengage the exponential gear," said Gwoat. "We're going too fast. We'll overshoot the solar system. I don't want to use reverse. It would probably damage the gear box at this speed and it would use an enormous amount of fuel."

"How far out are we?" asked the Storyteller.

"Well we passed the solar system about three minutes ago," said Gwoat.

"How could this happen?" asked the Storyteller. "I set the co-ordinates myself."

"I'm sorry," said Gwoat, beginning to exhibit once again the signs of extreme nervousness.

"For goodness' sake, calm him down," urged Adam. "We can't risk him breaking wind, not in a confined space with locked windows."

"Does he mean farting?" enquired Numpty of his uncle.

"He does indeed," Rambler responded. "I should however mention, young nephew, that 'farting' is a vulgar and colloquial expression not to be used in polite company."

"So what is the polite word for farting?" was Numpty's reasonable riposte.

"It's funny," said Adam. "There isn't really a single word. You'd think we would have dozens."

"There is 'flatus'," suggested Rambler, "though it is not in common use. I believe it is the past participle of the French flare, meaning to blow. 'Fart' itself is interesting. I'm not sure where it comes from."

"Out of your bottom," squealed Numpty, who, delighted at his wit, was unable to control a burst of hysterical laugher.

"Perhaps we should concentrate on the matter in hand," suggested the Storyteller. "Gwoat, calm yourself. I'm sure you are not to blame. It's possible Peters interfered with the van in the Caucasus. He had plenty of time on his own. When we arrive at our next destination, we will recalibrate the navigation instruments. In the meantime, I suggest you cut the engine and we calculate a decaying orbit. It will take a little more time but it will save fuel."

Gwoat continued to shuffle nervously but, with a falling orbit to calculate and then achieve, he was occupied and therefore less stressed.

"Have we got the time right?" asked Adam. He didn't really understand what was going on but it had crossed his mind that, if they were to see the birth of life, they not only needed to be in the right place, they had to be there at the right time.

The Storyteller smiled. "Time and place, it's much the same thing," he said, "but yes, we're good for time. Nine billion years after the birth of the universe and four billion years before your present day, give or take."

"There's definitely a problem with the navigation system," said Gwoat. "I've entered the course for a decaying orbit twice but it seems to have a mind of its own. Insists on misreading the figures; seems to want to put us in a permanent orbit around the solar system. I'll have to steer manually; it might be a rather bumpy ride but at least we should end up in the right place."

oooOooo

'Rather bumpy' turned out to be a bit of a euphemism. After an extremely rough approach which had taken a good deal longer than expected, they landed safely but severely shaken. Gwoat had held together really well as he guided the van in through Earth's atmosphere. He had taken the vehicle in at a shallow angle to reduce friction but that had meant two complete circuits of the planet before they could touch down. Throughout all that time Gwoat had been totally focused on the job in hand and had been a paragon of determination and fortitude.

"I told you we couldn't have a better driver," the Storyteller declared on landing, amidst the sighs of relief from the other passengers. Gwoat's own relief from tension, combined with the Storyteller's words of praise, produced a not entirely unexpected reaction. His bowels began to loosen. "Out of the van, I should be going," he declared as he threw the driver's door open, stumbled from the van, dropped his trousers just in time and relieved himself.

"He's beginning to sound like Yoda," was all Adam managed to say before the hot air from outside the van hit him.

"Oh dear!" said the Storyteller, "this is most unfortunate."

"Is the air breathable?" Eve asked, alarmed.

"Oh yes," the Storyteller replied. "The air is acceptable and, in any case, we have a dispensation on that front."

"So what's the problem?" asked Adam.

"I'd have thought it was obvious," said the Storyteller, clearly somewhat upset. "I brought you here to see the birth of life. Up till this moment, the entire universe had not contained one ounce of organic matter. I was planning to show you the first inklings of life. Instead, and I'm not blaming him because he did a wonderful job landing us here and because obviously he hasn't complete mastery of his digestive system, the universe does now contain a sample of organic matter but sadly not of the type I had hoped."

Gwoat returned to the van, having completed his motions: "Sorry about that," he said as he tightened his belt, "but I feel so much better. Hope I haven't caused offence."

What began as a chuckle from Rambler built into a full-bodied torrent of laughter as first Numpty, then Adam, then Eve and then both the Storyteller and Gwoat saw the funny side of it.

"So the first sign of life on Mother Earth," screamed Adam, as the tears streamed down his cheeks, "was a liquid dump from Gwoat's flaccid anus. You don't suppose," he added, "that there's some kind of hidden meaning, some symbolic message, some kind of subtle subtext?"

Luke, who had not enjoyed this leg of the journey at all and who had thought he was going to die when they drove through earth's atmosphere, had leapt from the van as soon as Gwoat had opened the driver's door. He was now exploring the unfamiliar landscape and sniffing vigorously. There were many smells to be savoured, chemical and metallic, but none of organic origin, except of course for Gwoat's contribution. It was simply second nature for Luke to find the source of the only organic odour in the universe and to mark it by raising a leg and taking a much needed leak.

"In the beginning was the turd," said Numpty suddenly. "Could I say that?" he asked his uncle.

"Well you have said it, my boy," said Rambler, "but I have to say it's rather indelicate and quite possibly blasphemous, so personally I would have preferred it if you hadn't."

"Things just aren't going your way," observed Adam to the Storyteller.

"It's not what I had in mind," conceded the Storyteller, "But I'm still here to show you something extraordinary, something unique, something for you and Eve to ponder on."

"What are we going to see?" asked Rambler, now eager that they should concentrate on the momentous event they were privileged to witness.

"We have a little further to go," said the Storyteller. "We have to drive beneath the ocean."

This proposition raised some serious issues. They were on a shore so they could see the ocean easily but it was not like any ocean they had ever seen before. It was hot and it was turbulent. Beneath a vibrant orange and purple sky, waves writhed and huge clouds of steaming spray swelled up out of the water. The sea was chaotic.

Then of course there was the whole idea of 'driving beneath the ocean'. The camper van had proved itself to be a truly remarkable mode of transport and Adam was prepared to accept it might have the capability to perform under water but, given the violent inhospitable roiling breakers that crashed onto the shore, he felt the need for reassurance.

"We don't have to go far," said the Storyteller, "and we won't stay under too long." He might have added that they couldn't stay under too long because, outside the bubble, they would be dependent on the camper van's cooling system to prevent the passengers from cooking, and the cooling system used fuel, rather a lot of fuel.

"So it's perfectly safe?" asked Eve.

"Little in this life or any other is perfect," said the Storyteller. "But it's certainly safe enough."

"And why do we have to drive into the ocean?" asked Adam.

"Because," said the Storyteller, "that's where life began. I am going to show you where the precursor of all life on this planet first appeared."

"And that's under the ocean?" queried Eve.

"Yes, under the ocean," replied the Storyteller. "Most of the planet is covered in ocean at this time so it's not perhaps surprising that life began in the sea. What is surprising is that life began in what is going to seem to us an extremely inhospitable place. We are going to visit a place where the ocean floor is cracked and the water boils in a maelstrom of steam, sulphur and hydrogen."

"Is that where life began?" asked Adam. "Sounds more like the gates of Hell."

"Well you didn't seem too impressed with Rodney and Derek's account of the birth of life, so I'm hoping you'll find this explanation more to your liking," said the Storyteller.

"Hold on," said Adam. "We're seeking the truth. You're talking as though we can pick and choose. Are you going to show us where life began or not?"

"Yes," said the Storyteller.

Adam still felt uneasy. The Storyteller was always evasive. Why couldn't he give a straight answer? Even his 'yeses' seemed to carry an air of ambiguity.

"Let's go," said the Storyteller.

Gwoat was not happy. He had been checking the engine of the camper van and had found some anomalies. He spoke to the Storyteller. "Someone has been fiddling with the van. I've recalibrated the navigation system. Someone had shunted the dial round by almost one degree."

"Have you fixed it?" asked the Storyteller. Gwoat nodded. "Then let's go," urged the Storyteller.

Gwoat was still unhappy. "I checked the oil in the gearbox," he said. "That was low. Lower than it should have been. I topped it up before we set out. We should have had more than enough for the complete itinerary. And someone's tried to access the paradox device."

"Really?" said the Storyteller, obviously concerned by the last revelation. "They didn't succeed, I hope?"

"No, they failed," Gwoat answered, "but they tried. They tried really hard. Fortunately they didn't understand how Prune Leach and Andrew Rimzil had set the device up so the harder they tried to access it, the more resistance they faced."

"Well, if you've successfully recalibrated the navigation system, topped up the gearbox and the paradox device is unharmed, perhaps we can go," said the Storyteller with a hint of impatience.

Still Gwoat was uneasy. "What's the matter with you, man?" asked the Storyteller.

"This ocean you want us to drive into doesn't look exactly camper van friendly," said Gwoat. "Given somebody's has been fiddling with the van, and given that we've never gone submarine before, I'm just a little worried about this leg of the journey."

The Storyteller asked Gwoat to step outside the van for a private word. "I know you are of a nervous disposition," he said to Gwoat, who had resumed his habit of hopping from one foot to the other. "But it is very important you don't communicate your nervousness to our questors. If they give up on the quest, it's a victory for the Breakers – and an easy one at that. They win without firing a shot. Now, if you have legitimate concerns, you tell me but not in front of Adam and Eve. I will decide what action to take. I promise I will not expose you, or Adam and Eve, or anyone, or indeed the van, to any unnecessary risks. This particular foray into the ocean is an important part of the quest, not because of what they will see but because of the questions it will raise.

Now let's get on with it. And, one other thing, if you can, get a grip on the fidgeting. It makes the questors nervous and me irritable."

"Yes, sir, certainly sir," said Gwoat, still hopping, but slightly less vigorously. "I'll do my best." Then he added; "I could do with a bar of chocolate or, better still, some of that nectar that Chione gave me."

"I fear that chocolate and nectar, both being of organic origin, are not available in this pre-Achaean, prebiotic aeon," said the Storyteller. "But, happily, Chione gave me a phial of concentrated nectar for just such an eventuality and, if you promise to control your worrying and get on with the quest, I will give you a shot now." With that, the Storyteller produced a curiously-wrought metal bottle from his jacket pocket, poured a measure into the bottle's cap and gave it to Gwoat.

Gwoat drank the nectar and immediately felt more relaxed. He looked around at the landscape and, although the turbulent air was extremely warm and the ocean extraordinarily restless, bubbling away beneath a vivid blue, livid purple and angrily orange sky, everything seemed somehow less threatening. "To be sure, I'm feeling better already," said Gwoat. "I'm sorry for making a fuss."

"No problem," said the Storyteller. "Just stop worrying. We'll give the van a full service as soon as we get back."

The Storyteller and Gwoat climbed back into the van and, after some soothing words of reassurance from the Storyteller, the questors settled into their seats. Gwoat, now mildly sedated and slightly euphoric, drove the van towards the ocean.

It's true Gwoat, under the influence of titanic narcotics, was not fit to be in charge of a vehicle, especially one with five passengers, but since he had only to aim for the vast ocean, driving across a long, wide beach, any risks attributable to the condition of the driver were as nothing compared with those involved in the nature of the journey and their intended destination.

49 That's life

The van entered the water. The seabed inclined downwards gently for three hundred metres. The water was only up to the windows when suddenly the van dropped below the surface and continued to fall. They had driven off the shelf and were now sinking. There was general alarm amongst the questors, alarm only partially allayed by the evidence that the van was watertight.

It was several minutes before the van came to rest. "I hope that's it," said Adam. "I really don't think we should go any further or any deeper."

"No need," said the Storyteller.

Eve was gripping Adam's arm fiercely. "Are you all right?" Adam asked turning toward his wife. Only then did he see what Eve had seen. The van had landed on the edge of a great fissure in the sea bed. Out of the fissure spewed fire.

All the questors were terrified.

"This is it," said the Storyteller proudly. "This is where the story of life began."

"Great," said Adam. "Could we just back away from the edge?" he appealed to Gwoat.

"In a minute," the Storyteller replied. "But first, I want you to understand what you are witnessing. For some nine thousand million years, the universe had been forming itself. First stars, then galaxies and, somewhere along the way, planets to orbit stars. The universe had energy, it had heat, it had matter and it had the laws of physics. It was magnificent in scale and power. But it was inanimate. For nine thousand million years, that's what it was. Energy, matter and the rules that determined how the energy and matter behaved. Nothing else.

"Then life began. Who would have thought it? Obviously no one, because there was no thinking going on. Who would have guessed it? No one, not even if there had been a means of guessing. Nine thousand million years is a long time. The universe is a big place. If something like life was going to happen, surely it would not have taken nine thousand million years?

"And yet here, at the edge of this fissure which you are so eager to escape, here, on this planet far out on an arm of the Milky Way galaxy, here at this time, something unprecedented happened. Some chemicals took it into their heads, not of course that they had any heads, literally or indeed metaphorically, to kick start life. There was nothing organic for this new life to feed on, obviously. So it decided to make do with sulphur. I need not tell you how unlikely the event was. In nine thousand million years, it hadn't happened. The odds against it happening were astronomical, literally. It would, one might say, be infinitely less surprising if it hadn't happened. It was at least as momentous as the birth of the universe. It was the moment when the universe began to show just what it could do and, possibly, where it was heading. It was the Second Beginning.

"Anyway, without labouring the point, I am suggesting you add this truly epoch-making fortuitous event to your list of happy but highly improbable coincidences."

The Storyteller seemed satisfied at last. "We can go," he said to Gwoat.

"What, that's it!" said Adam. "You brought us here to see an underwater volcano. And now we go. No samples, no proof. What was the point?"

"I thought you were keen to leave," the Storyteller replied.

"I am," Adam retorted. "I am particularly eager to move back from the rim of this fissure. I have no wish to be boiled like a lobster. I'm simply expressing surprise that you would take so much trouble to put us in such danger without, apparently, any justification."

"I have samples, thermocytes I call them, the first form of life," said the Storyteller, "and you are welcome to observe them through a microscope but, as I said, they are unlikely to inspire you. What should inspire you, what I hope has inspired you, is what I have said to you in this place. We take life for granted because we are part of it, because we are familiar with it, because it is, for us, the most important feature of the universe. I wanted you to see the universe as it was before life, to imagine just for a moment, how utterly unlikely the Second Beginning was and to appreciate the time and place where something invisible to the human eye elevated the world of matter to an entirely new and unexpected level of being."

The temperature inside the van was rising and Gwoat was shifting in his seat uneasily. "Very well," said the Storyteller. "Let's go."

Gwoat seemed to be struggling with the controls. "I can't get any lift," said Gwoat, with scarcely concealed panic in his voice. "The vertical drive isn't working." A great bubble of flame and steam spewed from the mouth of the fissure and the van shook violently.

"Try the ancillary motor," said the Storyteller calmly. "We still have power. Divert all the power to the ancillary motor."

"It's not firing," said Gwoat, with a choking, squeaky voice.

Adam was staring out of the window on Eve's side of the van. "The fissure's widening", he said. "If we don't move soon, we are going to fall into it."

"A rather ironic turn of events if our lives are to end at the very spot where all life began," Rambler remarked.

"We're not going to die, are we?" asked Numpty.

"I very much hope not," said Rambler, "but we seem to have some serious mechanical problems."

"No, we're not going to die here," said Eve. Adam looked at her. She never ceased to surprise him. How could she be so cool and so sure in the face of imminent disaster?

"Why is that?" asked the Storyteller.

"Because it wouldn't make a good ending," said Eve.

"Not by any stretch of the imagination," added the Storyteller.

Before Adam could ask Eve what she meant, another bubble of steam rose majestically from the fissure. This was the mother of all bubbles for, as it spilled over the rim of the fissure, it wobbled outwards and entirely enveloped the van. Gwoat started to pray. The precise nature of his prayer remained obscure but Adam was sure he heard an appeal to Prune Leach and Andrew Rimzil, as well as to other, no doubt greater and lesser, entities.

"I'm feeling really hot," said Numpty to his uncle. "I don't think I'm going to be very well," he added, grabbing his uncle's hand.

The gigantic bubble began to rise majestically and it took the van with it. "Now," shouted the Storyteller, "try the vertical lift again. Use the main engine." There was a loud whistling noise. The van continued to rise but at a slightly accelerated rate and the temperature in the van fell to a more tolerable level. Although still faulty, the drive was working.

"Be ready to head towards the shore as soon as we clear the top of the ledge," said the Storyteller. Gwoat didn't have time to point out that such an instruction, encapsulating the blindingly obvious, was redundant. He was solely concerned with maintaining vertical lift, which it seemed was dependent on a symbiotic relationship between the van's vertical drive, now at least partly operational, and the steadily ascending submarine volcanic bubble.

When they reached the shore, Luke was the first out of the camper van. He had spent the whole oceanic venture lying close to Numpty's feet, whimpering, convinced that this time death was not merely probable but certain. His back legs were shaky from fear and his mind in turmoil but, as he felt the sand beneath his paws, he realised they had all been given a last minute reprieve and were still alive, albeit in an alien world. "I'll say this," he said to no one in particular, no one that could hear him anyway, "I'll say this. If Nick Peters is still alive and he

271

wants to persuade someone to give up this insane quest and go home, he will find in me at least a receptive audience."

50 The Sparrow

Before leaving Cadnam, Nick Peters was told to attend a planning meeting with the Dawk, Despiro Nihilopificus. On leaving Nigel Vale's office, Nick told Grimrose to wait in the reception area of the building while he met with Despiro.

The master Dawk was a tall, grey-haired ascetic looking man in his middle years. His manner was reserved, some said cold, and, most agreed, haughty. His lips were thin and pale. His speech precise and clipped. "You are the Breaker I am to assist," he said when Nick Peters entered his office. "I have been expecting you."

This was not a welcome. It was simply a statement of fact.

"It's a great pleasure to meet you," said Nick. Nick rather liked the idea that the great man acknowledged his role was to be merely an assistant to Nick in the neutralisation of Adam and Eve. "It seems we are to carry a heavy responsibility," he suggested. "As I understand it, the consequences of failure would be extremely serious." Nick was choosing his words carefully. He needed some feedback from the Dawk. Reading others was an essential weapon in the Breaker's armoury and, although Despiro Nihilopificus was not an enemy, Nick still felt the need to tread cautiously.

"I am unaccustomed to considering the consequences of failure," Despiro replied. It was not a rebuke. Once again, it was a simple statement of fact.

Nick paused and pondered how best to proceed. While still less than halfway through his ponder, the Dawk spoke. "There is a chance, albeit a remote one, that Adam or Eve might trigger a Fourth Beginning. That cannot be allowed to happen. We are to stop it."

This succinct account of their purpose left Nick in a quandary. He was confident of his own ability to break Adam and Eve. He had already probed Eve's weaknesses and, unless he was much mistaken, given the right circumstances, Adam would be an even easier target than his wife. In addition to his own skills, he had the support of the most renowned Dawk of all, and an unlimited budget within which the outrageous costs of a mysland could easily be accommodated. It all seemed fine. Except he had no idea what the Fourth Beginning was, nor why it was so important that he and the Dawk must prevent it.

"Ah yes," he probed, "the Fourth Beginning."

Despiro nodded.

This was like getting blood out of a stone, Nick thought. Never mind. If that's how he wants to play it, so be it. "What exactly is the

Fourth Beginning?" he asked. The question sounded cruder and slightly more desperate than he had intended but what did it matter? He wanted to know what he was up against and, after all, Nihilopificus had been instructed to assist him in any way.

"The Fourth Beginning," said Despiro, without any emotion in his voice, "is an illusion." That was it. That was all he said.

Nick began to feel frustrated and not a little irritated. "So we are to prevent an illusion. Images of sledge-hammers and nuts come to mind. Why is it so important we prevent an illusion? Does it really require my not inconsiderable skills as a Breaker and your undoubted competence in deconstruction to prevent two seemingly mediocre individuals from triggering an illusion?"

"It is an illusion that could remake the world," said the Dawk. There was no emotion in his voice. "It is not for us, Breakers and Dawks, to understand such things. Our role is to prevent them. Beginnings are disruptive, unpredictable, uncontrollable. They are dangerous. And the Fourth Beginning will be the most dangerous of all because it will be the most disruptive, the most unpredictable and the most uncontrollable. That is all we need to know. We would be spending our time more usefully in planning our strategy and tactics rather than in speculating about an event it is our task to ensure does not take place."

Nick grunted. No one really liked Dawks. They were too…what was the word… grey. No sense of humour. No fun. No curiosity. Just into stating the obvious without feeling. He and Despiro could work together. They would almost certainly make a powerful and ultimately highly successful team. But Nick had the feeling, at the end of it, he would not know the Dawk any better than he did now.

"I will deal with any rational questions they may have at the end of their quest," Despiro stated baldly. "You can rest assured I shall bring them back to reality. But, as we know, regrettably, grounding them in the real world is not sufficient. There are features of questors that only Breakers can destroy."

Nick smiled. He was on home territory. "No need to worry. I'm pretty sure I could break them on my own but, with your help and with the resources of a mysland, success is guaranteed. I shall demonstrate to them the pain of life, the despair at the heart of it, the reality of death. I shall erode their hopes, decry their aspirations, sap their spirit. I shall destroy their trust, their faith and their love. To be honest, by the time I've finished with them, I'll be amazed if there are any residual questions of reason or philosophy left in their troubled minds for you to deconstruct."

51 Mind over matter

After their submarine venture and what seemed to them all to have been a pretty close shave with death, the questors felt the need to compose themselves. The Storyteller and Gwoat busied themselves with a thorough check of the camper van, its bodywork and, in particular, its engine and drives. Gwoat remained concerned that someone had tampered with the vehicle and, now the effects of the shot of nectar were wearing off, the signs of returning worry were evident to all. The Storyteller himself was also perplexed but showed no sign of it since he was determined not to alarm the questors.

"That's the second event the Storyteller has shown us that doesn't make any sense," said Eve. "First he shows us the start of the universe, which seems to burst out of nothing. Now he shows us how life begins, or rather where life begins, but again there's no explanation. It's all so improbable. I mean, once life has happened, it seems plausible that you boil up the right mixture of chemicals and this thing called life happens – just because it did happen. But, before it happened, no one could have predicted it."

"Well that's certainly true," Adam laughed.

"You know what I mean," Eve pursued her line of thought. "Life happened. It hadn't happened before, not as far as we know. It hasn't happened since. When you look at what existed before there was life, there was no reason whatsoever to imagine that life would emerge."

"That argument applies even more to the creation of the universe," said Adam. "At least with life, there was a range of material elements that you could keep tossing in the air, or swirling in the water, to see what happened. But the creation of a universe out of nothing, that's something else."

"The thing that worries me," Eve continued, "is why life? I mean the emergence of life was so improbable that it seems perfectly reasonable to ask why it wasn't something else, something as unimaginable as life."

Adam looked blank but Rambler, who had been listening to the exchange between Adam and Eve, joined the conversation. "I see what you mean. If the emergence of life was so improbable and unpredictable, something else, indeed perhaps anything else, could have occurred."

Adam seemed puzzled. "Yes, but life happened, not something else. So what is the point of speculating? It's a bit like winning the lottery. If you win, however extreme the odds, you have won. Of course someone

275

else could have won, but they didn't. Just because one thing happens against the odds doesn't mean other equally improbable things will happen."

"No," said Eve, "that's true. But it does mean any of the others in the lottery could have won."

"What others?" asked Adam. "Obviously life was the only thing that could happen. The odds against might have been astronomically high, but the bet came off."

"Why is it obvious that life was the only highly unlikely thing that could have happened?" asked Rambler. "The creation of the universe was another highly unlikely event. So there's already two highly unlikely events. It's beginning to look as though the universe is, if not full of, at least capable of, some deeply profound improbabilities."

Adam decided to let the matter drop. They seemed to be going round in circles. Yet again, Eve had surprised him. She had never before expressed any particular interest in matters scientific or philosophical. Her goal in the quest was to find an answer to the seemingly random nature and utter pointlessness of Bella's death. Yet, on the basis of their excursions through space and time, she seemed to be working her way to some obscure realisation.

The Storyteller climbed back into the camper van, followed by Gwoat. "We've checked as much as we can and everything seems to be in order," said the Storyteller. Gwoat, recently fortified by the Storyteller with another shot of Chione's nectar administered outside the van, nodded enthusiastically. "We can now embark on our third and final excursion," the Storyteller announced.

"Not much point in asking where and when," observed Adam.

"Of course there is," the Storyteller responded. "We're off to the Middle East, to a place not far from modern day Beirut. The time? Well I can't give you a precise date because there weren't any calendars around but it's about fifty thousand years before your century."

"May I add a 'why'?" Adam probed.

"For the 'why' you must wait and see," said the Storyteller.

At a nod from the Storyteller, Gwoat slammed the van into gear. The vibrant orange and purple sky began to fade into gentler pastel shades. The van appeared to be moving but not at the interstellar speeds they had attained on their journey to the singularity where everything had begun and on their journey back from the singularity to earth.

"This trip involves traversing more time than space," the Storyteller explained. "Our last port of call is on earth, not too far from where life started. But, in time we need to cover just under four billion years in which life has been doing what it does best."

oooOooo

When they landed in what is today Lebanon, the world looked much more familiar.

"Perfect," said the Storyteller, as Gwoat manoeuvred the van into a grove of cedars. "The trees will shade us from the heat of the midday sun and, in any case, it is best we do not draw too much attention to ourselves."

Adam laughed. They were back on familiar territory, back on the home planet, back on a recognisable earth. They had journeyed to the birth of the universe when the temperature had been several trillion degrees centigrade. It had been almost impossibly hot when they had glimpsed the birth of life. Somehow they had survived. Yet now, when thankfully they were on home ground in a temperature not dissimilar to the weather they had left behind at Stoney Cross, now the Storyteller felt the need to find shade for the van.

The Storyteller explained: "No observation capsule. No paradox device. We are here. On our last two excursions, we could observe but not interact. It may have seemed we were part of what we saw but it was not so."

"What about Gwoat's dump just before the birth of life?" asked Adam. "Surely there was a significant bit of interaction there." Numpty giggled. Eve gave a look of disapproval.

"Happily, although Gwoat certainly needed to evacuate his bowels", the Storyteller answered affably, "and his motions seemed real enough to us, too real in many ways, nevertheless, from the point of view of the universe, it was a purely notional dump."

"And Luke had a notional widdle, then," said Numpty thoughtfully, before asking his uncle: "What does notional mean?"

"It means 'theoretical', 'not real', 'imaginary'," offered Rambler.

"Is that a paradox?" enquired Numpty. "I mean there's nothing more real than a poo, so a notional poo is a paradox, isn't it?"

"The lad's right," the Storyteller intervened. "That's exactly what it is."

"A notional dump, courtesy of the paradox device, at the birth of life," mused Adam.

"We have come to this precise spot," said the Storyteller, who felt the need to move on from matters excremental, "because I want you to meet a rather special person. He may not look terribly impressive to you but looks can be deceptive. He's a quite remarkable individual. I've named him Albert. Of course that's not his name. We probably couldn't

277

pronounce his real name because it's a series of clicks which to our ears sound indistinguishable but I've named him Albert for convenience and he seems happy enough to respond to the name. Albert is special and I am pleased to count him amongst my friends."

Adam's brow furrowed and he looked towards Eve, who simply shrugged. It was obvious the Storyteller had been to this place and this time before, perhaps on his previous quests.

"If we leave the van and walk towards that clearing, I'm pretty sure we won't have to wait long," said the Storyteller. All disembarked except Gwoat, who preferred to stay with the camper van. He thought it most unlikely anyone would attempt to tamper with the vehicle again but you could never be too sure.

The ground was soft with lush green grass growing where gaps in the cedars allowed the copious sunlight to reach the forest floor. Luke kept close to the humans, scampering off for a quick sniff but returning promptly. This might be more familiar than the singularity or the ocean bed where life began but it was still strange enough to warrant caution.

When they reached the clearing they saw the figure of a man. He had the face and the physique of a modern man, except he was below average height. To Adam, he looked to be no more than 30, a young man still in his prime, with dark hair, suntanned skin and bright blue eyes.

"Albert," shouted the Storyteller, obviously delighted to see his friend. "How are you?"

Albert clicked several times in quick succession and then, to the astonishment of all except the Storyteller, he said in almost perfect, if slightly stilted, English: "I am good; it is fine to see you."

The Storyteller laughed delightedly. "I thought you might have forgotten what I taught you but you have an excellent memory. Small point but it might have been better to say 'I am fine; good to see you'."

Now they both laughed and embraced each other.

Adam shook his head in disbelief.

"These are my newest questors," said the Storyteller to Albert. "This is Adam and this is Eve. They have been joined by Rambler here and his nephew Numpty. Not forgetting, of course, Adam and Eve's dog, Luke."

"If anyone says 'not forgetting' as a way of introducing me again, a truly benign, well-behaved golden retriever is likely to morph into a raving Cerberos."

"Only if you can sprout another two heads," suggested the Storyteller, who alone could hear what Luke said.

"Why would I need another two heads?" asked Albert, who assumed the Storyteller's remark had been addressed to him. You have always told me the head I have is more than sufficient."

"And it is, believe me!" the Storyteller reassured his protégé before addressing the questors. "On my last visit, Albert informed me he had discovered the principle of the lever. He did not call it a lever obviously because there was no word for it but it was a lever nonetheless. More important, he showed me the relationship between the fulcrum and the power of the lever."

Albert was more interested in Luke than in the Storyteller's praise. "I like dogs," he explained. "They help us hunt; they keep guard; they let us sleep safely at night. And this is the most unusual, the most beautiful, dog I have ever seen."

Luke nuzzled into Albert's clothing, a simple tunic of animal skin. The smell of the skin was rather appealing, exuding the aroma of an animal that, had Luke been hunting, would have signalled an attractive prey, but there was another reason for the nuzzling. Luke felt an immediate rapport with Albert who, although he could not hear the dog talk, nevertheless seemed entirely in tune with his mind.

"You mean Albert here invented the lever," said Adam.

"Well, more discovered than invented," said the Storyteller. "You could say he invented a particular lever but, much more important, he discovered the principle of the lever. He worked out how to determine how much a lever could lift, depending on its length and the position of the fulcrum."

"Extraordinary!" exclaimed Rambler. "What period is this? Surely this is long before civilisation?"

"You're right," said the Storyteller. "This is long before even elementary technology became widespread. That is why I brought you here. And that is why I wanted you to meet Albert."

Albert seemed entirely absorbed in playing with Luke, whom he obviously found more interesting than his human visitors.

"So, what are you saying?" whispered Adam. "Are you saying Albert here is a precocious freak? And, if he is, why didn't civilisation get going much earlier? I mean, if primitive men had a genius like Albert to help them, what was stopping them?"

"Why did you bring us here?" asked Eve. "Yes, I know you wanted us to meet Albert. But, really, why?"

The Storyteller smiled. "The start of the universe took place at a particular point at a particular time. Life also began in a specific place and at a specific time. The Third Beginning, the birth of human consciousness, well, that was more diffuse. Albert was not the only man to invent or discover the lever. It happened many times in many places. Sadly Albert's contribution was short-lived, as indeed was Albert. I brought you here to give you some idea of just how great a leap and just how extraordinary the emergence of human consciousness was."

"I think we all appreciate how special we are," said Adam.

"Each of us is the proud possessor of what may well be the most complex organic device in the universe," Rambler added.

Numpty, who was a little disconcerted by the rapport that had sprung up between Albert and Luke, felt powerfully consoled by his uncle's observation. Obviously he was included in Rambler's eulogy of the power of the human brain.

"Yet again I have to ask you to view this event from a point in time before it happened," the Storyteller explained. "Because we live in a time much later than the development of human consciousness, we take it for granted. Indeed, because we know it happened, and because we are ingenious, curious creatures, we are clever enough to work out more or less how it happened. But I want you to shed all those preconceptions. Just as I showed you the complete absence of everything before the singularity, and just as I showed you the turbulent but utterly lifeless mix of minerals and chemicals before the birth of life, now I want you to consider the extraordinary improbability of that sulphur-eating elemental life-form developing into us."

Adam frowned. They seemed to be covering familiar ground. "Well it didn't just happen," he said a little dismissively. "It took a few billion years. A lot can happen in a few billion years."

"Why do you call the things 'Beginnings'?" asked Numpty out of the blue.

Again the Storyteller smiled. "I cannot answer that," he replied.

"Obviously it is a metaphorical way of explaining these major events in the history of the universe," offered Rambler, intending to assist the Storyteller. "It would be like describing the emergence of a butterfly from a caterpillar as a Beginning," he continued uncertainly. "Or like the formation of an ice crystal. Or like the symmetrical crown of drops that rise from still water if you drop a drop of water on to it...," He trailed off, hoping the Storyteller would confirm he was on the right lines.

The Storyteller said nothing.

"Why do you keep showing us these events?" asked Eve. "What happened to all the stories?"

That was a good question, thought Adam. They had set out with the Storyteller as an act of trust. After the incidents at Fleet, they had visited the Garden of Eden and then gone on to the Caucasus to meet

Prometheus. The Garden of Eden had been a nightmare; the visit to Prometheus had been more comfortable and less dangerous but equally challenging and disturbing. Adam had struggled to make sense of both experiences but at least they had one thing in common. They offered explanations. Not the type of answers that Eve sought but at least attempts to make sense of it all. These recent excursions on the other hand, which Adam knew it was a privilege to have shared, these excursions were events. They offered no explanations. And, apart from emphasising the inherent improbability of each event, the Storyteller had failed to explain them, except for calling them 'Beginnings', which, as Rambler had discovered, prompted more questions than answers.

"I know a story," said Albert, who, although seemingly absorbed with Luke whose tummy he was tickling, had nevertheless heard and understood the conversation. "One day, some travellers from far away visited the land of sand and cedars. They brought with them a golden god with floppy ears and a wagging tail. The travellers met with a stranger who was not really a stranger because he lived in the land of sand and cedars and they asked if they could share his food and water. The stranger who was not a stranger willingly agreed, saying he would give them fruit and nuts and juice from the grape, which, if left for a while, could have an interesting effect upon the one who drank it, but he made one condition – that when the travellers departed, they must leave the golden god behind"

"That was an exceedingly complex sentence for someone who has only recently learned the language," observed Adam, "and who has no one to practise with when the teacher is absent travelling."

"With whom to practice," suggested Numpty.

"We're not leaving Luke behind," said Adam.

"But one of the travellers refused to allow the golden god to stay with the stranger who was not a stranger," Albert continued with his story. "That was a serious mistake because a curse fell upon the travellers. From that time on, for all eternity, they were doomed to wander the world, always seeking but never finding what they sought."

"That's a bit harsh," suggested Adam. "He's our bloody dog."

Albert looked alarmed and checked Luke for any signs of injury.

"I've not introduced him to swearing," explained the Storyteller.

"Did someone mention food and drink?" enquired Rambler hopefully. "I'm sure we can resolve any proprietorial issues as amicably on a full stomach as on an empty one."

Albert smiled, having assured himself of Luke's well-being. "Yes, of course. Come with me and I will give you all the fruit and nuts you can eat and the magic grape juice to wash them down."

"Hospitality was one of the first matters we discussed," said the Storyteller. "Albert really liked the idea. He said he could see that offering hospitality was justified by self-interest in that it gave the host a psychological advantage. Of course he didn't use the word psychological because I hadn't explained the word to him at that time."

The questors followed Albert to his home, a finely constructed shelter of woven branches covered with leaves from the luxuriant plants that flourished on the banks of a nearby stream. When all were refreshed with the promised food and drink, Adam took the Storyteller to one side.

Before Adam could ask a question, the Storyteller began to explain: "Albert is not unique but he is exceptional. After Man, Homo sapiens, began to develop consciousness, there was vast potential, the potential to achieve what Man has subsequently achieved and more, but at the time when consciousness began, little of that potential was realised. As it is today, so it was at the beginning of human consciousness, there were ordinary people, clever people and, occasionally, outstanding geniuses. If Albert had been born in your times, he would have been an Aristotle, a Leonardo Da Vinci, an Albert Einstein. But he was born tens of thousands of years before the earliest human settlements. I brought you to meet Albert because I wanted you to understand the Third Beginning. I chose Albert as its representative. If you observe him closely, you may learn something of interest."

Adam shrugged. It was an answer of sorts to his unasked questions. "Why did you pick Albert?" he said.

"Two reasons," the Storyteller replied. "First, he really is exceptional and a willing learner. He has an open mind and quickly takes on board whatever I choose to teach him. Even as a genius in our time, Albert would be exceptional. He has no preconceptions. And he has a truly adventurous, fertile, creative mind."

"And the second reason?" Adam prompted.

"Ah, the second reason," said the Storyteller, "the second reason is that, within the year, Albert will be dead. This is important. Albert, without my interference, would have been an outstanding individual. He would not have been recorded in history because he lived in pre-historical times but, had there been a dictionary of biography in his era, he would have merited an exceedingly lengthy entry. That would be true without my interference.

"But with my interference, although I have been careful, he might have changed the course of human development. I've tried not to prompt him or help him, but simply providing him with access to the complex and subtle syntax of a modern language has given him a massive advantage. So I picked him because I know that in the next few months, he will cut himself in a fall and the wound will become infected. He will die."

"So you are simply using the poor fellow," said Eve, who had joined them. "Just to prove what?"

"I'm not trying to prove anything," said the Storyteller, clearly pricked by Eve's accusation. "You set out on a quest for the truth, or for at least your truth. If you are to find a truth that makes any sense, it must take account of, fit in with, the fundamentals of reality. I started by showing you a couple of explanations for reality. You were dismissive of the God who inhabited the Garden of Eden and, although you found the Titan Prometheus more congenial, he failed to answer your questions. So I decided to show you the three great Beginnings – the birth of the universe, the birth of life and the birth of consciousness. The selection of these events is not subjective or arbitrary. They are three markers of existence. In passing, I should mention that very few questors have had the chance to witness any of the Beginnings. As far as I know, you are the first to witness all three. Anyway, now you have seen them, I am hoping you have found some bearings for your pursuit of the truth. The Beginnings are not the truth, but no truth will stand that does not fully accommodate them.

"As for the accusation that I have simply been using Albert, I refute the charge absolutely. Albert was fated to die in a few months whether or not I intervened in his life. I have made his short life far fuller than it would otherwise have been. I have enabled him uniquely to glimpse the potential of the more gifted of his kind, even to see, by your presence here, what his descendants will become.

"That, I suggest is fair recompense for the use I have made of him."

"Why is there no one else here?" Eve asked abruptly. She did not apologise to the Storyteller. "Does he live alone?"

"No, Albert is a highly respected member of his tribe," the Storyteller replied. "He has three surviving children, two by the same woman. Three offspring for a man of twenty at this time is well above average. He is allowed a high degree of freedom and privacy because, having demonstrated the use of the lever to his people, none of whom really understood how it worked, he has been accorded the status of a shaman. He himself chose this place for our meetings and has forbidden all members of his tribe from entering this wood."

"And what are we to make of this prodigy?" asked Eve.

"By now you must have realised that I cannot tell you what to make of the things I show you," the Storyteller replied wearily. "It is what you make of them that matters."

At this moment an agitated Numpty joined them. "Have you seen Luke?" he asked, close to panic. "One minute he was with us; the next, nowhere to be seen."

Adam, Eve and the Storyteller looked around the cedar grove. The trees were well spaced and the strong sun sent shafts of light through the branches to the ferny forest floor. There was no sign of Luke.

Adam called Luke's name and then whistled. Luke always came to the sound of Adam's whistle.

Still no Luke.

Albert joined them. "Don't worry," he said. He can't have gone far. He will be safe."

"Yes," said Numpty. "But where is he?"

"He is safe," said Albert.

"How can you know he's safe, if you don't know where he is?" Numpty persisted.

Albert frowned. After a moment, he said: "Because there is nothing here to harm him."

"But perhaps he's had an accident," said a tearful Numpty. "Perhaps he has a thorn in his paw or perhaps he's broken a leg."

Again Albert paused. "I don't think so. There are no thorns in this grove and there are no places where the golden god could break a leg. He is safe. He can stay here. He will be safe."

"He can't stay here," said a distraught Numpty, a sentiment immediately endorsed by Adam.

"Luke is our dog. He stays with us." There was a combination of determination and irritation in his voice.

Albert was upset. "The tall man has forgotten my story. In my story, the travellers enjoyed the fruit and nuts and juice of the grape but they had to leave the golden god of the floppy ears and wagging tail with the stranger. The golden god lived happily ever after in the land of the cedars and the travellers went on their way. Otherwise," Albert added solemnly, "otherwise, if the travellers would not release the golden god, as soon as they leave, they will be cursed through all eternity."

"I think your protégé has lost the plot," said Adam to the Storyteller. "He seems to think he really is a shaman. Perhaps he's not as bright as you think."

"What people believe is not a matter of intelligence; it is often a matter of circumstance and always, by definition, a matter of faith," said the Storyteller. He then took Albert by the hand and led him away from the others. "You must return the dog."

"But in my story…," Albert began.

"I know, I know," said the Storyteller. "But the questors too have a story, and Luke, the golden god, is part of it. You must give him back."

"Perhaps he doesn't want to go back with them," said Albert. "Perhaps he would prefer to stay here. Here he is a god. With the questors, he is just a dog. He is just the 'not forgetting Luke' dog."

"Then perhaps we should ask him," suggested the Storyteller.

Albert said nothing.

"If we are to ask him, we have to know where he is," the Storyteller added.

Albert looked a bit sheepish. "He's in my shelter. He's asleep. He drank some of the juice of the grape."

"You mean he's drunk," said the Storyteller accusingly.

"That's what I said," Albert replied. "He's drunk of the juice of the grape."

"Never mind," said the Storyteller.

The Storyteller explained to the others what had happened. He suggested that Albert had simply been extending hospitality to Luke, just as he had to the humans, but they all suspected Albert had known exactly what he was doing.

It was a good hour before Luke stirred. When he awoke, his head hurt. He padded out of Albert's shelter into the sun. His eyes hurt. The shafts of light seemed to shift around between the trees in an entirely successful attempt to make him feel giddy and sick. "I don't feel too good," he said to the Storyteller.

"You have a hangover," the Storyteller explained.

Adam patted Luke. "Why the hangdog expression?" he enquired happily.

"Adam is my master," said Luke to the Storyteller, "and of course I love him but there are times when I could happily bite the hand that feeds me."

"You must be feeling as sick as a dog," Adam continued. "Guess a hair of the dog might help." Adam had not heard Luke's rebuke and, in any case, would not have been deterred.

"Drink some water," suggested the Storyteller. "You will soon feel better." The Storyteller turned to Albert. "You have many dogs in your tribe. Why did you want to keep this one?"

"Look at him," said Albert. "He is beautiful. He has golden hair. He is a god amongst dogs."

Luke was feeling better already. Respect! No, this was beyond respect. This was, at last, recognition of his outstanding qualities. How odd it should be Albert, a human living long before the modern period, should be the first to recognise it!

They spent the rest of the afternoon eating the fruits and berries.

Albert busied himself preparing a fire. Rambler approached the Storyteller, who was sitting a short distance from the others, resting on a convenient tree stump.

"Is fire one of Albert's discoveries?" asked Rambler.

"No," the Storyteller laughed. "Our forebears were using fire at least two-hundred thousand years before Albert's time. Albert is, however, developing his cooking techniques. Watch him. He is going to give us some meat to eat. Instead of roasting it on a spit, he will wrap the meat in damp leaves and steam it in the embers of the fire. He tells me the meat remains moist and tender when cooked this way."

Rambler had more questions. "I understand you wished to bring us here to show us how Man had developed from the elementary life form we saw on the ocean bed," said Rambler. "And don't misunderstand me, it's absolutely fascinating. But Albert's quite a long way down the line of human development. I'm no expert but Homo sapiens had been around for a million or more years before Albert. Why did you pick him and now?"

"I will try to explain to you," said the Storyteller. "But first let me ask you a question? What have you noticed about Albert?"

"Well, if he invented or discovered the lever, he is extremely intelligent," Rambler suggested.

"No," said the Storyteller. "That was not an observation; I told you how clever he was. What have you yourself noticed about his behaviour?"

"He seems extraordinarily fond of Luke," Rambler hazarded. "I have read somewhere that dogs played a crucial role in human development. Because of the mutually beneficial relationship between us and dogs, we were able to rest more securely at night. The dogs kept watch and warned us of any approaching danger."

"I have heard that too," said the Storyteller. "I have also heard that, because dogs have a superb sense of smell which they were prepared to use on our behalf, Homo sapiens was able to reduce his olfactory arrangements, thereby leaving much more room in his cranium for the further development of the brain."

Rambler started to scribble furiously in his notebook. "Careful," warned the Storyteller, "I'm not saying the 'nose reduction; brain enhancement' theory is true. It's just what I've heard."

Rambler paused, frowned and then resumed note-taking.

"Have you noticed anything else?" the Storyteller probed.

"Well, he came up very easily with his story about the travellers, the golden god and the importance of our leaving Luke behind."

"Good," said the Storyteller. "He finds it easy to invent a good

286

story. It was a story designed to persuade us to do what he wanted. But note how he did it. He made the deal he wished to strike part of the story – his hospitality, food, drink, rest and recuperation in return for the dog. Then he added the curse to encourage us to accept the terms of the deal. Incentive and threat. Carrot and stick. What else have you noticed?"

"He's pretty unscrupulous in trying to have his own way," suggested Rambler. "I'm pretty sure he lied to us about Luke. In fact I'm sure he did. He tried to give us the impression that Luke had run off, when he knew he was asleep in a drunken stupor in his shelter."

"That's right," said the Storyteller. "He lied. That is perhaps the second greatest gift of language. It enables us to lie. Before language, there was just the way things were. Language gave us an infinite number of alternatives. It allowed us to speculate about how things might be different and then, if we so wished, to pretend they were different."

"So I've learned that he loves dogs, finds it easy to concoct a tale, is manipulative and ruthless, and will lie to get what he wants," Rambler summed up.

"That's just about right," the Storyteller smiled. "Not a bad general description of humankind."

Rambler shook his head and wrote several more sentences in his notebook. When he had finished, he looked up and asked a final question. "By the way, what's the greatest gift of language?"

"The ability to tell stories," the Storyteller answered. "Obviously."

Rambler looked puzzled.

"Something extraordinary happened when human consciousness emerged," the Storyteller continued. "It was as significant as the birth of the universe. In fact, it was the birth of a universe or, even, many universes. There was no need for life to reproduce; no need for life to evolve. Let's face it, life was made from inert stuff. Where do you think the inert stuff got the urge to arise, reproduce, evolve? Even viruses have this obsession with reproduction. The drive to reproduce is exceedingly odd. It's only not amazingly odd if you start from where we are, and say: 'That's just the way it is'. If you start from before there was life, the sudden appearance of life would be an unbelievably astonishing development. It didn't happen for thousands of millions of years. It was an event that, if there had been anyone around, no one would have predicted. Indeed the emergence of life is only plausible because it did happen. We take too much for granted. Just because it happened. We forget the far more likely scenario where it didn't happen, and we don't bother to ask why it did.

"Then we have an even more extraordinary development. The human mind. Suddenly, in a universe empty of such things, there is consciousness, there is awareness of time, there is hope and fear, there is imagination. We can begin to make sense of our universe. Our minds find that the universe obeys rules and we can discover these rules. We can test them and we can exploit them. We can tell stories that, at some level, explain the predicament in which we find ourselves; and we realise there is no limit to what we can imagine. If consciousness cursed us with awareness of our mortality, it compensated us with a precious gift, the ability to think whatever we wish to think, to explore worlds of infinite possibilities and to seek eternal truths.

"So, out of that maelstrom of gases, we somehow end up with Euclid, Plato, Shakespeare, Mozart and Einstein. Just think about it. You and the others have been uniquely privileged. You have seen the universe as it was before life and consciousness. You even saw the birth of the universe itself. You have been able to see the inherent improbability and unpredictability of it all. You witnessed the three Beginnings. It will not be easy but Adam and Eve's search for truth will have to accommodate all you and they have seen."

While the Storyteller and Rambler had been talking, Adam had wandered over and had heard the last part of their conversation.

"No one's denying the emergence of human consciousness was an extraordinary event," he suggested, "but, as I said before, so is winning the lottery. The odds may be a million to one against, or even a billion to one, but if your number comes up, that's it. You've won. The fact that the odds were against it doesn't mean it was fixed. It just means you've been lucky."

"Of course," the Storyteller conceded. "But if you win a second time, eyebrows are surely raised."

"It could still happen. Coincidences happen," said Adam, sticking to his guns.

"What about a third time?" the Storyteller asked. "After all, the emergence of human consciousness was the Third Beginning."

52 The Breakers' preparations

After his meeting with Despiro Nihilopificus, Nick collected Grimrose, whom he had left in the reception area of the Breakers' offices, and marched off to Internal Resources. The Internal Resources Division was housed in a long, separate, one storey block. Nick took Grimrose along because he wanted the shapeshifter finally to grasp just how important his Breaker master was.

"I'm Nick Peters," he announced to the rather pretty receptionist. "I think I'm expected."

The girl slowly put her nail file away after a few more desultory strokes of a red painted finger nail. She looked down the list of routine appointments. "Sorry," she said. "What was your name?"

Obviously she was a new girl (Nick had known her predecessor rather well) but, new or not, the girl's incompetence was bordering on impudence. "My name was and still is Nick Peters," said Nick with a hard edge to his voice. "I won't be on your list."

"Well, if you're not on the list, you will have to phone to make an appointment," said the receptionist, picking up her nail file with the obvious intention of resuming her former occupation.

"I don't need an appointment," snapped Nick, "and, if I did, I'd expect you to put the bloody nail file away and give me one now."

The girl looked at him with a mixture of anger and fear. "I could report you for sexual harassment," she declared.

"What are you talking about?" Nick was genuinely puzzled.

"Look, dear," Grimrose intervened. "We're here to make arrangements for the commissioning of a mysland."

"I'm not 'your dear'," said the receptionist. "I could report you too – for being a patronising old fart."

Grimrose subsided into silence. He felt awful, weak and dizzy. It had taken all his strength to try to save the girl further embarrassment and she had peremptorily dismissed him and his well-intentioned intervention.

"How dare you insult my associate!" said Nick. Then he changed his tone, exuding concern for the girl. "But let's talk about you for a moment. How are you feeling? A little sick? You must expect some discomfort in your condition."

"What condition?" the girl asked.

"It's fairly obvious you're pregnant. I would guess about five months," said Nick.

289

"Well that would be a surprise," said the girl, "because I wasn't pregnant at all when I came in this morning."

Nick shook his head as though taken aback. "But look at yourself," he said. "Look at your distended belly."

The girl looked down. He was right. Her belly was distended. Now she felt sick.

"But I can't be," she said. "I've been so careful. Sid'll go mad. We can't have a baby now."

"Well I'm afraid it's too late to get rid of it," said Nick. "But don't worry about Sid," he added consolingly. "It's not his. No, the father is the black drummer you had a one night stand with a few months back at the Pembrey festival."

The girl broke down in tears.

"Now could we get back to why I'm here," said Nick, satisfied the girl's life was comprehensively ruined. "I need to see the head of the Technical Department and I need to see him now. Just give him my name – yes, it's still Nick Peters – and I'm pretty sure he'll be here in person before you can get back into any kind of rhythm with the nail file."

After some sobbing and choking, the girl managed to regain sufficient self-control to inform the office of the Chief Technician that Nick Peters was in reception. Almost immediately an assistant appeared and conducted Nick and Grimrose to the Chief Technician's office.

"Have you any idea what is involved in constructing and maintaining a mysland?" asked a gruff Scots voice.

Joaquim McCardle, known to all as Joaq (pronounced Joke), was not a man with an overly developed sense of humour. He was none too keen on the nickname Joaq and he certainly couldn't understand why others found it so amusing. But then others were stupid and superficial and found amusement in the silliest of things.

"I'm sure it's extremely demanding," said Nick tactfully. He had no interest in how hard McCardle and his team would have to work. That was not his problem. On the other hand, he might as well humour the Chief Technician.

"You shouldn't have done that to the girl," Grimrose muttered. "She was rude and incompetent but you've destroyed her life."

"What!" said an exasperated Nick, turning on Grimrose. "What the hell is the matter with you? Why do you care about the silly little bitch? We have probably the most important assignment ever entrusted to a Breaker, and you start burbling on about some stupid tart."

"What about the baby?" Grimrose persisted. "Single mother with a mixed race baby, what kind of a start in life is that?"

"What baby?" asked Nick.

"The one the girl is carrying," answered Grimrose.

"You know I really think your mind is decaying faster than your body," snapped Nick. "There is no baby. I just made that up."

"Thank goodness!" said Grimrose.

"No," Nick continued. "There was no way I could make her five months pregnant. I didn't have any sperm to hand and the time factor would have been a problem. No, she's got stomach cancer."

"You can't mean that," Grimrose's pleading was tinged with horror and anger.

"I don't know what has got into you," Nick replied. "What does it matter and what do you care? Anyway, I did it for you. She insulted you. Called you a senile old fart or some such. Couldn't let that pass. So I taught her a lesson."

"With stomach cancer! You taught her a lesson with stomach cancer!" said Grimrose incredulously.

"Have you two finished your little chat?" enquired McCardle, "because if you haven't, perhaps you wouldn't mind buggering off. We work here."

"I'm here to arrange a mysland to deal with the questors Adam and Eve," said Nick indignantly, stung by the Chief Technician's rebuke.

"I know why you're here," snapped McCardle. "The only reason you're in my office is because I know why you're here. Now, if you've finished your domestic, perhaps we can get something done."

'Wow!' Nick thought. Everyone seemed so edgy and grumpy. Still, that's the way people in head offices tended to be. They didn't have real jobs, proper jobs, so they resented anyone who did. What made it worse, insofar as they did anything, it was to service field operatives, and obviously they resented what was essentially a subordinate role. He would explain all this to Grimrose when they left in case the shapeshifter had gained a false impression.

"What size of area do you have in mind?" McCardle pressed on.

"It's got to be faultless," Nick replied. "I may have to hold them for some time and I need to keep them apart. It's crucial that both of them believe they are back in the real world. I'll need a fully functioning virtual world that is utterly convincing. If they have the slightest inkling the mysland is a construct, the whole project could unravel with dire consequences."

McCardle's eyes looked heavenward momentarily. "I think we have a problem," he said. "I asked you a question. What size of area do you have in mind? You come back with some blather about how you intend to operate. That would make sense if I had asked you how you intend to operate. But I didn't. I asked you what size of area you had in mind. The correct answer to that question should have been in the form of a number of square metres, kilometres or miles. Not some drivel about the need to convince your subjects. I don't have time for this."

Nick began to feel his hackles rise. "Whoa!" he said. "Take it easy. Loosen up. You are going to have to work with me whether you like it or not. That's right, isn't it, Joaq?"

Now McCardle's eyes blazed.

"Oh come on," Nick goaded. "You're so keen on straight answers to straight questions. I just asked you a straight question. You have to work with me, don't you?"

McCardle scowled a 'Yes'.

"Right then, Joaq," Nick continued, pronouncing the name carefully to ensure it was indistinguishable from the word 'joke'. "Maybe we got off on the wrong foot," he adopted his most conciliatory tone. "Let's start again. When the Storyteller brings the questors back, they will touch down at Stoney Cross off the A31. I want a mysland that replicates the area around Stoney Cross. I suggest the boundary should be Cadnam to the east and Fordingbridge and Ringwood to the west."

"A couple of things," said McCardle. "First, don't ever call me Joaq again. It's overly familiar. Secondly, you cannot be serious about the area. We can stretch to Cadnam. We've done one or two constructs before using Cadnam as a starting point. But taking in towns is a nightmare. It takes time, an enormous amount of effort and vast amounts of money."

"Sorry," said Nick with fake contrition. "I wasn't asking you a question and I certainly wasn't inviting you to tell me how you need to operate. I was telling you what I want. Thought that was what we agreed. Straight talking; no nonsense."

"Your friend looks unwell," observed McCardle, ignoring Nick's jibes.

Nick turned to look at Grimrose, who was beginning to lose form involuntarily, a deeply worrying sign in shapeshifter circles. "I think you'd better get him some help."

"Call this number," Grimrose wheezed. "Tell them I'm losing register."

Help was summoned. It arrived surprisingly quickly. Two ambulance men ran into the Chief Technician's office, loaded the dwindling Grimrose into a wheelchair and were gone. The explanation for their speedy arrival was simple. When Nigel Vale had reported his conversation with Nick to the Board of the brotherhood, they had instructed him to do something about Grimrose. They could not have been more emphatic. "Peters may not value the shapeshifter but he's an indispensable member of the team. He needs to be revived, at least for now. Don't care how you do it. Just get it done."

"He seemed to be in a pretty bad way," observed McCardle.

"Always difficult to tell with shapeshifters," Nick replied. "They can adopt some forms that look pretty unhealthy but it doesn't mean there's anything wrong with them."

"I'm no expert on shapeshifters," said McCardle, "but your friend was seriously ill. Looked as though he'd had all the strength drained out of him."

"He's not my friend," said Nick. "He's seconded to help me on breaking assignments. That's all. I'm sure he's fine. If he isn't, there's plenty more where he came from. Could we get back to the mysland?"

"I'll be honest with you," said McCardle. "I know your assignment is important and you know I've been told to give you my fullest co-operation but, even if I tell my people to drop everything else, it would take us months to create a mysland of that size. I also know you've been told you can have an unlimited budget. But even unlimited budgets have limits. Even if we could construct a mysland of the size you suggest, we couldn't maintain it for long. The drain on our resources, in manpower and energy, would be enormous, unsustainable."

"You won't need to maintain it for long," said Nick encouragingly. "And the questors don't know the area that well so you won't need to be one hundred per cent accurate in replication."

"Even so, the area's too big," McCardle persisted.

"Most of it is forest," Nick responded.

"It's the towns," McCardle explained. "We have to replicate the buildings, the homes, the main streets, the side streets. And then there's the people. In one day, each virtual person takes the same energy as an average house uses in a month. The logistics alone…,"

"All right, all right, I get it," Nick cut him off. "Drop Fordingbridge but I must have Ringwood. I must have one plausible town. Ringwood's the obvious choice. It's on the A31. If they go to any town from Stoney Cross, it's most likely to be Ringwood."

McCardle could see that Nick had gone as far as he was prepared to go.

"Very well," he said reluctantly, "from Cadnam to Ringwood east to west, up to Godshill and Bramshaw to the north, and up to but not including Bisterne Close and Brockenhurst in the south. That's it. It'll be the largest mysland we've ever attempted. I just hope it's worth it."

"Let's put it this way," said Nick. "If it prevents the Fourth

Beginning, it will be more than worth whatever it costs."

McCardle squinted at Nick. He had no idea what the Fourth Beginning was but he was not about to reveal his ignorance to Nick.

Which, from Nick's point of view, was just as well.

oooOooo

After Nick had left, McCardle received a call from Nigel Vale.

"How did it go?" asked Nigel.

"What he's asking for will drain our resources to the limit," McCardle answered. "We will have to drop everything else and concentrate on Peters' mysland. He wants us to include the town of Ringwood within the boundary. Why he needs a town is beyond me. If he can't break the pair of questors within a normal size mysland, I can't see how incorporating a town will help."

"Did he say why he wanted such a large construct?" Nigel asked.

"Not really," McCardle answered. "He blathered on about the importance of credibility but, given he has total control over the mysland space, I don't see why he can't get all the credibility he needs in a more reasonably sized mysland without draining all our resources."

"I'm afraid you'll have to give him what he wants," Nigel replied sympathetically. "I've been told by the Board we must give him whatever he asks. It seems there's a serious risk of a Fourth Beginning and he's been charged with making sure it doesn't happen. It seems the consequences of failure are incalculable."

"What is this Fourth Beginning?" McCardle asked. He hadn't been prepared to expose his ignorance to Peters but Nigel Vale was a decent fellow.

"I haven't the faintest idea," Nigel replied. "All I know is the Board is very much against it." Then he added: "By the way, what did you think of Peters?"

"I thought he was a self-centred, conceited prick," McCardle replied.

"Couldn't agree more," Nigel responded.

"When this is over, I'd like to take him down a peg or two," said McCardle.

"Splendid idea," said Nigel, "but unfortunately, if he succeeds in preventing the Fourth Beginning, his position will be unassailable, at least in the short term. If, on the other hand, he fails, I suspect Nick Peters will be the least of our worries."

53 Taking stock

The questors spent just one night in Albert's cedar grove in the Lebanon of 50,000 years ago, enjoying Albert's food and wine, and his restless, enquiring and creative wit. That night, Albert came close to inventing the wheel, anticipating a discovery for which mankind had to wait at least another 40,000 years.

That night, Albert also became reconciled to the need for Luke to leave with the travellers. The Storyteller promised that, if Albert still felt the same, he would return within the year with a golden retriever that Albert could keep.

When the questors awoke, after a good night's sleep in Albert's shelter, the Storyteller announced that they would be returning to their own time that afternoon.

Adam and Eve spent the morning talking together, each of them trying to make sense of their journey since leaving Harrow and the extraordinary excursions that the Storyteller had arranged.

The sun was shining and a gentle breeze was blowing in from the sea. It was the most pleasant of mornings and Adam and Eve both felt refreshed by Albert's generous hospitality.

Adam spoke first. "So we are coming to the end of our quest. I guess we are supposed to make something out of what we have seen but, to be honest, I'm more confused than when we started. It's all been a bit crazy. I mean, the Garden of Eden, Prometheus in the Caucasus, the birth of the universe, life and consciousness. It's been fascinating, amazing. We'll have some great stories to recall when you and I are in our dotage, sitting in our rocking chairs in front of a log fire. But are we supposed to be any closer to the truth?"

Eve was thoughtful. "I think the Storyteller has been trying to show us different ways of looking at things. Right from the start, he asked us what kind of truth we wanted. I don't think he ever intended to show us the truth – or even a truth, unless, somehow, the truth is in the stories."

"What does that mean?" asked Adam.

"I don't really know, except that I can see that only stories can make sense of it all," Eve replied. "I'm not sure I know the difference but there's truth and there's meaning. I think I've been looking for meaning and, if that's what I'm looking for, I need to look in a different way."

"What, in stories, like make-believe?" Adam sounded dismissive.

"No, not make believe," Eve answered. "No, the story has to accommodate reality. That's why the Storyteller took us on those excursions. But, after you've got a grip on reality, you need a story to make sense of it because, on its own, reality doesn't have any meaning. That's not to say it's meaningless; just that it needs a narrative to make any sense."

"I might have to give that some thought," said Adam, with a smile.

oooOooo

Far away, in time and space, in Cadnam in the present day, in the boardroom on the top floor of the Breakers' offices, a light in one corner of a flat screen monitor flickered green and then turned amber. It then oscillated between green and amber for several minutes before reverting to green.

54 Welcome back

The journey back from Lebanon of 50,000 years ago to the Stoney Cross of today proved to be the easiest leg of the questors' journey.

Gwoat had stayed with the van throughout the questors' meeting with Albert and had usefully employed his time in servicing the van as far as he could and checking and rechecking all the settings, recalibrating instruments over and over again. It was clear that someone had interfered with the van but the protection that Prune Leach and Andrew Rimzil had built into the system had done its job and the damage seemed to be superficial.

On arrival at Stoney Cross, not surprisingly the questors had a feeling of anti-climax.

"So is that it?" Adam addressed the Storyteller.

The Storyteller didn't answer him. He seemed to be preoccupied. Eventually, after surveying the surroundings for a minute or so, he spoke: "I'm very much afraid it's not over. No, it's far from over."

"What does that mean?" Eve asked.

"It means…," but before he could finish, the sound of police sirens coming at them from all directions drowned out his words.

"Wow! That's quite a reception," said Adam, trying to make a joke of it.

Six police cars skidded to a halt on all sides. Armed police in body armour leapt out of every car, taking cover behind their vehicles and aiming their weapons at the questors.

"Step out of the vehicle," one of the officers ordered.

"We're out of the vehicle," Adam called back, his voice a little shaky.

"All of you, lie face down with arms outstretched," the officer continued.

"What's going on?" Adam asked. "What have we done?"

"If you do not lie down with arms outstretched immediately, I shall give the order to open fire," said the officer.

Rambler and Numpty were already obeying the officer's orders. The Storyteller began to kneel and whispered to Adam and Eve that they should follow his example.

Why Gwoat felt the need to shut the van's door before obeying the officer's command is unclear. It is possible he realised he was about to be separated from his precious vehicle and was fearful an open door would invite vandals. Or perhaps it was simply habit. It is even possible that, although he was of a nervous disposition, the barking orders of the police officer called forth the innate rebelliousness of the Irishman and he wanted to show he was not utterly cowed by the unnecessary and excessive show of force. Such speculation is futile.

The first bullet – which entered through the back of his skull and exited through his right eye – killed Gwoat outright. The subsequent hail of bullets which jerked his body this way and that before it could fall to the ground and which peppered the side of the van was totally unnecessary.

"My God!" shouted Adam, who, following the Storyteller's advice, was kneeling before lying down. "Are you insane?" He started to get up, his anger overcoming his fear. "You have just killed an unarmed man. You shot him in cold blood."

"Do not fire," the officer ordered his men. "This one and the woman we have to take alive."

Four officers, still carrying semi-automatic weapons, ran out from behind their vehicles. Two of them knocked Adam to the ground. The other two tied Eve's arms behind her back. When both Adam and Eve were secured, the officers turned their attention to Rambler and Numpty. Rambler, who was traumatised, offered no resistance except that the uncontrollable shaking of his limbs made it difficult for the police to apply their handcuffs. Numpty was also terrified but he could not stop himself from protesting at the barbarous slaying of Gwoat. "You murderers," was all he could manage. He was struck on the side of the head by one of the officer's guns, rendering him unconscious.

The four questors were then forced into the police cars, each in a different car.

"Clear this mess up" the leading officer ordered the police from the two remaining cars. He then strode over to where the Storyteller lay prostrate, with Luke vigorously licking his face. The Storyteller sat up. The officer addressed the Storyteller. "You really are a fucking nuisance," he said. "I don't understand you people. You can never leave well alone. And you don't give a toss what it costs because it's not you that pays for it. Who has to clear it up? We do. What thanks do we get? None. You make me sick. I'd prefer to put a bullet through you now but, for some reason no doubt well above my pay grade, my guv'nor told me not to."

"Why did you shoot Gwoat?" the Storyteller asked, choking as he spoke. "What possible purpose did it serve to kill an unarmed man in cold blood? He was my friend. You murdered him. Why?"

"You're going to have to learn a helluva lot quickly," said the officer. "First of all, you've hit the jackpot this time. You are going to face the full power of the Breakers and I can tell you now, they intend to destroy you, all of you. Second of all, your runty little driver didn't do what he was told. I warned you all what would happen if you didn't obey my orders. He didn't obey my orders. He asked for it; he got it. Third of all, you troublesome little shit, you don't ask the questions. I do."

"I thought so," the Storyteller responded. "I thought so but I wasn't sure. These are the ones. At last. It's hard to believe but the Breakers must be sure. If they are right, they can use all their power, they can marshal all their resources, they can commit themselves totally to the coming conflict, but they will not win."

"I don't think you're in any position to predict the outcome of this little episode. One of you is already dead. The rest of you are under arrest."

"On what charge?" the Storyteller enquired.

"We don't have to charge you. We're holding you on suspicion of terrorism. We can hold you indefinitely while we question you. Because of the nature of your offences…,"

"Alleged offences," the Storyteller corrected.

"Because of the nature of your offences, we need time to build the case against you," the officer continued. "And even when we've built the case against you, we probably won't charge you. For security reasons," he added. "We'll just deal with you. We won't bother with the judicial system. You gave up any rights to a fair trial when you decided that a futile pursuit of the truth was more important than stability and maintaining the status quo."

"If the pursuit was so futile, why are you so scared?"

The officer laughed. "Scared! I'll show you scared. By the time we've finished with your precious charges, they will be so scared, so anxious, so neurotic that pursuit of the truth will be the last thing on what's left of their minds."

"You have killed a good man," the Storyteller said, "a friend who worked with me for more years than I can remember. When this story is told, he will be remembered as a loyal and brave warrior who helped all those who set out on the quest. You will be exposed as a callous murderer."

"That's where you're wrong," the officer responded. "Your story won't be told, at least not by you. It's the victors, not the victims, who write history and, let's face it, you and your rabble will be lucky to get a mention."

55 Divide and rule

As soon as Adam was seated in the police car, a bag was placed over his head. He protested but quickly realised there was no point. None of this made any sense. The only thing in his mind was the shooting of Gwoat. They had travelled with the wiry, nervous Irishman to the beginning of time and back again to the present. They had faced the furnace of the Big Bang and the seething, sulphurous ocean where life had begun. They had faced a tyrannical, malicious God in the Garden of Eden. And yet none of them had been harmed. The moment that they set foot in the present, one of their party is brutally slain and all of them are arrested without charge or any explanation.

It was difficult to judge but Adam reckoned the car journey took about 20 minutes. When the car stopped, he was bundled out of the car and marched, still hooded, by two policemen for about 100 yards. He heard doors opened. He was marched another few yards. He could hear the sound of a lift in motion. Lift doors opened. He was pushed in. He felt the lift descend. One of the police officers removed the hood.

"Where am I?" he asked.

"No talking," said one of the two officers.

"But why am I here? What is going on?"

The other police officer whacked the butt of his semi-automatic weapon into the side of Adam's head.

oooOooo

When Adam awoke he was in a small room, no more than 10 foot square. There were no windows. Instead, a harsh light came from cylindrical neon bulbs set into the coving. Two cameras were fitted to ensure complete coverage of the room. Adam could see the cameras were live because small red lights blinked every time he moved. The walls of the room had been freshly painted. He could smell the faint aroma of drying paint. The colour of the walls was magnolia. The floor was concrete. It had been skimmed roughly so there were ridges and it felt rough to walk on. Adam realised his shoes had been removed.

There was no furniture in the room, only a mattress lying on the floor abutting one of the walls, and a bucket. Adam looked into the bucket. It was empty. He looked around the room more carefully. There was no door. He felt sick.

Then the lights went out.

oooOooo

Eve was driven away westwards, in the opposite direction to the one in which Adam had been taken. Eve's escort drove down the A31, pulling off just before they reached Ringwood. The car followed a winding lane that squirmed its way quite deeply into the New Forest.

The two officers who accompanied Eve treated her courteously but seemed unable to answer her questions. Not that Eve asked many questions. The butchering of Gwoat had unnerved her. She did ask where they were taking her. One of her escorts said: "You'll like it. You'll be comfortable enough."

The car stopped at some iron gates. One of the officers punched a code into the numerical keypad on a gate-post and the gates swung open. They then drove some 200 metres along a winding drive before stopping in the forecourt of a pleasant, three-storey, brick built house. A candy-coloured awning covered the terrace, which was furnished with some rather expensive garden seating. In one corner of the terrace was a modest barbecue.

One of the policemen opened the car door for Eve and invited her to step out. Eve looked around. The garden was beautiful; close-cropped lawns undulated away to the edges of impeccably kept flower beds which were ablaze with roses of every variety and colour.

"It's really good to see you again," said a voice that, for Eve, was at the same time familiar and sinister.

"It's you," was all Eve could manage.

"Welcome to my home," said Nick Peters. He waved expansively, taking in the house and the gardens in a sweeping gesture.

"I thought you lived in Hook," mumbled Eve.

Nick laughed. "The cottage," he said. "Oh yes, that's just a watering hole. I have a number of safe houses; that's just one of them. I call them safe because, when I've had too much to drink, I can walk to them from my favourite pubs without fear of losing my licence."

For a moment Eve thought of questioning whether anyone bought houses near to the pubs they liked, just to avoid using a taxi or minicab but she thought better of it. There were rather more urgent issues.

"What is going on?" she asked.

"At least come in and sit down," said Nick, affable as ever.

Eve was tempted to refuse. She didn't want to go anywhere. She didn't want to sit down. She wanted answers. But Nick took her gently by the arm and propelled her into the house.

"First of all," said Nick as soon as they were seated in the large, welcoming kitchen diner, "let me say how sorry I am about the fiasco at

Stoney Cross. No one should have been hurt. It should have been a simple matter of arresting you. Someone was trigger happy. They will be severely disciplined."

"It wasn't just one officer," Eve objected. "They all opened fire. They shot Gwoat in cold blood."

"You can't be sure it was all of them," said Nick soothingly, "but rest assured whoever was responsible and however many were responsible, they will all be held to account."

"But why were we being arrested anyway?" Eve demanded. "What were we supposed to have done?"

"You've been arrested on suspicion," Nick replied. "If you ask me, the whole thing is an idiotic mistake and I'm pretty sure I can sort things out. Apparently someone with a name similar to yours has been involved in some kind of terrorist activity, or terrorist planning at least. I think it's a case of mistaken identity but, with all the secrecy, it's difficult to be sure."

"It's obviously difficult to be sure about anything," said Eve, recovering some of her spirits. "You think it's an idiotic mistake. It might be a case of mistaken identity. Of course it's an idiotic mistake. Of course it must be a case of mistaken identity. You know where we've been and what we've been doing."

"Yes," said Nick slowly, "that's part of the problem. From the police's point of view, you've been missing for almost two weeks, under the radar as they call it. They don't know where you've been and, given their suspicions, when a couple of suspects suddenly disappear, well panic buttons tend to get pushed."

"But you can tell them," Eve persisted.

Nick's brow furrowed, then his mouth resumed it's almost habitual smile. "Let's just give that some thought. At the moment, you are merely suspected of being terrorists. If I tell them, or indeed you tell them, where you've been and what you've been doing, you're likely to end up in a mental institution. Let's face it, as terrorists, you'll probably only get life, which means you could be out in nine years. As lunatics, well, you could face a real life sentence. You know, one where 'life' means life."

"Don't be ridiculous," Eve said angrily. "We haven't done anything. Where have they taken Adam? Is he here?"

"No, he's not here," said Nick. "He's being questioned by the police at their interrogation centre at Cadnam."

"Interrogation centre?" Eve exclaimed. "He can't be interrogated. He doesn't know anything."

"Calm down," Nick urged. "If he doesn't know anything, they will find that out. That's what they do. They find out what people know. And they find out what they don't know. Assuming he doesn't know anything, they will let him go."

"I don't understand," Eve was becoming increasingly worried. "Why is this happening? Why are you involved?"

"Well, I suppose I am in charge of your case," said Nick in an entirely matter of fact tone.

"You're what!" Eve exclaimed.

"Hold your horses," Nick cut in quickly. "I'm not the police. I'm just an agent. But I'm your agent or at least one of your agents. I'm one of the people who've been tracking you and, in my case at least, trying to make sure you don't get yourselves into trouble. I was against your arrest, let me make that absolutely clear. I told them it would be counter-productive. I'm on your side. I know you're not a terrorist. I know you're not crazy. On the other hand, you have to see it from the point of view of the security services. We can't just take people's word that they're not terrorists. We have to investigate and interrogate."

"So you're responsible for this," said Eve with ill-concealed anger.

"Now just wait a minute," said Nick, with more than a hint of irritation. "I have done everything to help you and Adam from the start. I made it abundantly clear at every opportunity that you were wasting your time with Tel, your Storyteller. I told you that, at best, you would be disappointed. At worst, well, you can see the mess he's got you into. What were you thinking? What did you know about Tel? What did you really know? Why on earth did you decide to go off with him, a stranger, on a hare-brained quest which was doomed to failure from the start. We've had our eye on Tel for years. He's a menace. He picks on vulnerable individuals, fills them with hope of finding the truth or discovering meaning or some such nonsense, and before they know it, they've lost all sense of proportion, all sense of reality, in fact all sense altogether."

"He didn't promise us anything," said Eve. Nick's account sounded quite reasonable but Eve wanted to hold on to how she saw things, to assert how things had really happened. "We wanted more from life than we had. We wanted to understand why bad things happen. We wanted to find out if there was any point. The Storyteller didn't try to persuade us to do anything. It was our decision, our choice."

Nick laughed. "If you knew how many people have sat where you now sit and have told me the same thing, you might be a bit less sure of yourself. Especially when I tell you that after a gentle debriefing and a little time and space to think about what happened, every single one of his victims has accepted that the Storyteller is a dangerous confidence

303

trickster and, if the security services are right, probably something much worse."

"What do you mean by 'something much worse'?" Eve interrupted. "What has he done to arouse suspicion and what is he suspected of?"

"We think he is trying to subvert the state," Nick replied, his tone grave. "We think he is the mastermind behind a terrorist plot to bring down the establishment."

It was Eve's turn to laugh. "You think the Storyteller could bring down the establishment. Perhaps you don't know him as well as you think. He's about as likely to change the world as I am. He's more a dreamer than a revolutionary. And he's extraordinarily vague. Adam asked him lots of questions and I don't think he got one straight answer. It's going to be a very ambivalent, diffident revolution if the Storyteller is to lead it."

Nick seemed a little troubled by something Eve had said. He decided to change tack. "Listen. I'm prepared to accept you are entirely innocent in this affair. And no doubt Adam is innocent too. I am your best hope of clearing your names and going home. You will have to stay here for a few days. I've been instructed to vet you and I have to appear to be obeying my orders. There's a very comfortable guest wing along the corridor which has been prepared for you. You can move freely around the house and the gardens but please don't try to leave. If you do, I shan't be able to help you. While you're resting and recuperating here, and hopefully managing to find a better perspective on recent events, I will go to the Interrogation Centre at Cadnam and see what I can do to help Adam."

"You mean I'm a prisoner," said Eve.

"You're my guest," Nick countered. "Come on, Eve. I'm trying to help you. All I've ever done is try to help you. Yes, it's true I'm advising you not to try to leave but, if you accept my advice, you are my guest, not my prisoner."

"You say all you've ever done is try to help," Eve sneered. "I haven't forgotten what you said in Prometheus' cave. You said if Adam and I had faith or hope or trust you would destroy it. You threatened us with fear and disappointment, if I remember correctly, fear and disappointment all our days."

"Yes, I said that," Nick replied. "It was a final desperate effort to persuade you to abandon your quest. I had tried reason and persuasion but you were under Tel's spell. So I decided to use threats. It was wrong, I know that. But I was desperate. And I still stand by what I said. All I've ever done is try to help you."

Eve said nothing.

"You will not be alone," Nick went on. "Your two travelling companions will be staying here with you, Rambler and the lad Numpty."

Still Eve said nothing. She was pleased and relieved to hear that Rambler and Numpty were safe. After the extraordinarily brutal behaviour of the police at Stoney Cross, she had feared the worst. But she had nothing to say to Nick. She needed to think.

"Now, if you'll excuse me, I'll go to Cadnam and do my best to help your husband," Nick continued, with just a hint of hurt in his voice.

56 Reunion

When Nick arrived at Cadnam, he went straight to Nigel Vale's office. He was eager to update his superior on progress to date. He knocked politely on Vale's door. The sound of laughter within stopped and he was immediately invited to enter. Nick went in and was surprised and none too pleased to find Grimrose lounging in the chair opposite Nigel's desk.

Unusually for Nick, he felt awkward and was uncertain what to say or do. He had assumed that by now Grimrose was either dead or grimly hanging on to life by a tenuous thread. He certainly had not expected to see the shapeshifter in rude good health and apparently on friendly terms with senior management at Cadnam. What was more, there was an issue of etiquette. Grimrose was sitting in his chair – or rather the seat where the most senior person visiting Nigel Vale should sit, and indeed the seat where Nick had quite rightly sat on his recent visit. The only alternative would be to sit where Grimrose had previously sat, on a much less comfortable chair to the side of the office in a clearly subordinate position.

"Well, come in and sit down," Nigel ordered, when he saw Nick hesitate.

Grimrose resolved the situation. "You'd better sit here if you're doing a debrief," he said, in tones as affable as any Nick had ever employed. "I'm not one to stand, or rather sit, on ceremony." With that he moved to the other chair.

Nick frowned. Grimrose had adopted the shape, clothes and demeanour of a highly educated, rather smooth member of the middle class, clearly an articulate professional of some sort. Giving up his chair and resolving a potentially embarrassing situation had somehow seemed to give Grimrose an advantage. And what had he meant by 'not standing on ceremony'? Surely that was something Nick could have said if the situation had been reversed. Grimrose had somehow implied it was entirely appropriate he should have the best chair but, because Nick had to be debriefed, he would graciously waive his right.

All these thoughts flashed through Nick's mind in a second. The frown faded and he smiled an acknowledgement to Grimrose. "Good to see you," he said. He then turned to Nigel: "I told you he was making a fuss about nothing," he said with a laugh. "Look at him. He's fitter than me now."

"Only after the Breaker's Board took a hand in the matter," Vale corrected, "and provided him with the best healthcare that money could buy. It was decided that it would be foolish to pit you against the truth-seekers without the aid of your shapeshifter. After all, he has frequently played a crucial role in your past successes and prevented some of what would otherwise have been failures."

Nick was stunned. Evidently Cadnam had got the wrong end of the stick, no doubt deceived by Grimrose. So while he had been preoccupied setting up a mysland, with all the organisational complexities involved, Grimrose had been comfortably convalescing at enormous expense and misrepresenting his own modest role in Nick's outstanding record of success.

"Yes, I owe the people here more than I can say," said Grimrose, "and the leaders of the shapeshifters. So many have made sacrifices to put me back together."

Nick shook his head. Of course, the prevention of the Fourth Beginning, whatever that might be, was incredibly important. And it was perfectly reasonable that the Board should decide it would be better if Nick, in dealing with the threat, had the support of a shapeshifter. But why go to all the trouble of patching up Grimrose when they could have assigned any other competent shapeshifter to serve him?

"Yes, it was a pretty tough job," Nigel Vale continued. "We had to persuade the shapeshifter community to put together a *disturba*. Yes, you heard right. A *disturba*.

Disturbae were so rare that many of the younger Breakers thought they were just fanciful stories. To save a particularly important member of the shapeshifter community who had been injured in the line of duty, very occasionally the leaders of the shapeshifters would declare a *disturba* and call for volunteers. It was a tough call. Those who stepped forward knew they were risking their lives. When the quota of 27 volunteers had been met, the ceremony, or perhaps one should call it the operation, could begin. The volunteers would form a circle around the sick shapeshifter. Then each in turn would step forward and place both hands upon the patient and would give what they could give. It was a matter of pride for each to give as much as he or she could. It took a massive amount of shapeshifter essence to restore a shapeshifter. A single shapeshifter could mend a human on his own but it took a good deal of the essence of 27 shapeshifters to restore a single shapeshifter. Not infrequently a volunteer would give too much. It would be a fatal mistake. The over-generous healer would die, his consolation the title of *disturbyr*, or *disturba* martyr.

Nick was dumb-founded. Why the Breakers and the shapeshifters had gone to so much trouble over Grimrose was beyond him. Grimrose was now a *disturbatim*, one of the highest ranks open to shapeshifters, the title given to those who had been deemed worthy of a *disturba*. No wonder he was so relaxed when socialising with Breaker management. Why the Breaker Board had thought such measures necessary remained obscure. Nick could only assume the Breaker Board had felt it was important to keep the established team together and felt the absence of the very junior member of the team, even if replaced by an equally competent substitute, was a risk they did not need to take.

"Well who's a lucky fellow?" was all Nick could say.

Grimrose shook his head. "Two shapeshifters died in the *disturba*. If I had been conscious, I would have refused the curing. I was not worthy of a *disturba* – and certainly not worthy of the martyrdom of two of my brothers."

"Nobly said," declared Nigel, "but there are more important issues here than the survival of any individual. You are deemed an important component in our response to the impending threat. Any of us may be called upon to make sacrifices, even the ultimate sacrifice. And we all stand ready to respond to the call."

'What a nerve!' thought Nick. 'Bloody typical. These suits sit in their offices, with all the comforts of modern technology, expensive furniture, lavish carpets, air-conditioning, security and, of course, a pool of attractive naive young girls to pander to their egos and their appetites, and they have the gall to talk about the ultimate sacrifice! Running out of coffee in the espresso machine is about the gravest danger people like Nigel ever had to face'.

"Would you like me to tell you how things are going?" Nick enquired rather brusquely.

"Of course," Nigel replied. "That's why you're here."

Even that sounded slightly insulting to Nick. Was Vale suggesting that, if he didn't have something to report, he wouldn't be entitled to be there, even though Grimrose, who had nothing to report, was clearly a welcome visitor? Nick shook his head. He was letting things get out of proportion. He was the lead Breaker in the most important project the Breakers had ever faced. It was time he acted with the authority the Board had given him.

"The questors returned to Stoney Cross as expected yesterday," Nick announced. "On arrival, they were greeted by a number of police and security personnel. All the questors were arrested. They were not charged with any specific offences but were advised they were being detained under anti-terrorism legislation. The operation went smoothly and, apart from one small glitch, everything went precisely as planned."

"One small glitch?" queried Nigel.

"Nothing that affects the plan," Nick replied reassuringly. "The driver of Tel's van refused the order to lie down. When he persisted in refusing to obey orders despite a second warning, he was shot."

"Gwoat has been shot?" Grimrose asked.

"That's what I said," returned Nick. "Certainly not part of the plan. The offending officer will be disciplined. Fortunately Gwoat's death is not a problem. He had no part to play in our little drama."

"Are you sure?" Nigel Vale asked. Nick was probably right but had he thought through the possible effect of Gwoat's death on the questors and, most of all, the Storyteller. Gwoat and the Storyteller had worked together for more years than anyone could remember. The Storyteller would not take Gwoat's death well.

"It's fine," Nick reassured Nigel. "In some ways, it's a benefit. It wasn't part of the plan but Gwoat's death has certainly impressed on the questors just how serious the situation is, and how precarious is their predicament. It's softened them up quite a lot – and that will save time."

While this exchange between Nick and Nigel was going on, the keen observer would have noticed several almost imperceptible tremors running through Grimrose. One of these, a momentary loss of corporeal focus indicated a high level of stress. A subtle change of skin tone, a quivering oscillation between marginally lighter and darker shades, was a sign of some emotional turmoil. A single tear, a general indicator of sorrow in Breakers, shapeshifters and humans in general requires no exegesis.

Neither Nick nor Nigel noticed the effect on Grimrose of the casual announcement of Gwoat's death.

"Eve is settled in the safe house on Poulner Hill," Nick continued. "She's frightened, confused and angry, which is precisely how I want her. I've left her with Rambler and Numpty for company and with some firm advice she should not attempt to leave."

Nigel nodded approval.

"How is Adam doing?" Nick asked.

"As well as could be expected for someone who's traumatised by arrest without charge and incarceration in the box without water, food or light," Nigel replied. "We have done exactly as you asked. He's not been questioned. He's not even been allowed to speak. In fact, you can see how he's doing on the monitor. We can show him through the infrared camera. There he is. Terrified. And, it's fair to assume, extremely thirsty."

"Excellent," said Nick, happily. "We'll leave him for a few more hours. I'm going to get a bite to eat. Bring him to the Number One interrogation room at three pm." Nick then added: "Nigel, are you free for lunch?"

"Sorry," said Nigel. "Another time. I'm sure Grimrose here will keep you company. In fact, he'll be keeping you company all the time until this project is successfully concluded."

Nick got up, shook Nigel Vale's hand and left. Grimrose followed him.

Nick tried to assess his own feelings about the meeting. He wasn't unhappy. The plan – really his plan although he had checked everything out with Despiro Nihilopificus – had been approved by the Board. He'd been given all the resources he needed, including the full extent of the mysland he had negotiated. So far everything, except the killing of Gwoat, had gone to plan, and Gwoat's death was irrelevant. Eve was simmering away nicely at Poulner Hill. Adam was being tenderised in a cell in the bowels of the Breakers' offices. So all was going well. No, he wasn't unhappy, but he was slightly uneasy. When he analysed the cause, he realised his concerns centred on Grimrose. Given the shapeshifter's parlous condition after he had healed Nick's leg, it was astonishing the Breaker Board had gone to such lengths to save him. Now here he was, entirely recovered, on seemingly friendly terms with Cadnam senior management and a *disturbatim* to boot. Nick didn't begrudge Grimrose his revival, his resurrection, or whatever a *disturba* ritual was, but he was uneasy about the meteoric rise in status the shapeshifter had achieved. Clearly the Breaker Board considered Grimrose considerably more important to the project than seemed to Nick appropriate or justified.

"It's good to be back," said Grimrose. "I thought I was finished. When I passed out in McCardle's office, I thought that was it."

"I'm very happy for you," said Nick in a neutral tone that left Grimrose wondering whether his master was being sincere or sarcastic.

"So what's the plan?" Grimrose asked.

Nick brightened up. So Grimrose didn't know the plan. Perhaps he had overestimated the shapeshifter's success in ingratiating his way into the confidence of Cadnam management. Perhaps Nigel had just been kind, indulgent and informal merely to encourage and motivate the recently restored Grimrose. After all, the title of *disturbatim* might be highly regarded amongst shapeshifters but it wasn't a rank recognised by the Breakers.

"I'll fill you in over lunch," said Nick. Now he sounded positively cheerful.

57 Destiny

As soon as Nick left her, Eve decided to explore. She wanted to know where she was, the layout of the building and grounds and, if possible, how to escape if she needed to.

The building was a fine Edwardian structure, built of grey stone, with hand-carved mullion windows, set in stonework, recently repointed with lime mortar.

If the house was fine, the gardens were outstanding. Beautifully laid out, the lawns led to individual miniature landscapes of exquisite composition. A group of five silver-birches stood to one side of the main lawn, like a group of benign sisters presiding over the beauty of the land. Rose bushes splashed vivid colours across the flower beds. Water gurgled in a small pond, not far from the house. It was idyllic.

Suddenly Eve heard her name called. The caller's voice was charged with emotion but whether it was joy or desperation was unclear. "Eve! It's you!" It was Numpty, who ran across the grass and almost jumped into her arms.

Numpty was followed by Rambler. After an exchange of greetings and many expressions of relief that the three of them were unharmed, Rambler gave voice to the thoughts upper-most in all three minds. "Why have we been arrested and why did they kill Gwoat?"

"I have no idea" said Eve. "This is Nick Peters' house and he's got something to do with it. He says he's an agent, part of the security services, and we've been arrested because Adam's name is similar to someone on a list of terror suspects. He says he thinks it's a case of mistaken identity and he said he would try to sort things out."

"I thought we had seen the last of Nick Peters in the Caucasus," said Numpty. "I thought he had an accident and fell off the mountain."

"I wouldn't trust anything Peters says," offered Rambler. "Is he saying that they killed Gwoat because of a case of mistaken identity? You don't shoot a driver because you think one of his passengers just might be a terrorist suspect. It's true the state tends towards paranoia but shooting unarmed civilians in the back goes too far."

"But that's exactly what they've done," said Eve. "And we're not on one of the Storyteller's excursions. This has nothing to do with our search for the truth, unless we are to find the truth in the fact that the police can kill an innocent man and then detain all the witnesses without charge."

"Where's Adam?" asked Rambler, prompted by Eve's reference to all the witnesses.

"According to Nick, he's being held in the Interrogation Centre at Cadnam, in the main offices of the Breakers," Eve answered. "Nick has gone to Cadnam to try to sort things out."

"If Adam's in the hands of the Breakers, then we must be in the hands of our enemies," said Rambler. "The Breakers are the ones who are determined to prevent us from finding the truth. And clearly our enemies have the backing of the state, which means we persist in our quest at our peril."

"We can't give up," said Numpty, with a firmness that surprised himself as well as the others.

"I'm not suggesting we should," Rambler replied. "But it would be good to talk to the Storyteller, to have his advice."

"He's always been a bit wary of giving advice," Eve observed. "And he's disappeared anyway. I haven't seen him since Cadnam and, to be honest, I was so worried about Adam, I forgot to ask Peters."

"Well, with or without the Storyteller, we know we're back in our own time and our own place now," mused Rambler, "and we are all agreed we are still on the quest. We have to try to make sense of what we've been through and this may be part of it."

"I'd rather get out of here," said Numpty. "What they did to Gwoat was terrible and that was in a public place. They could shoot any of us here and no one would know."

By chance, as he spoke, in the distance a gun was fired. Although they could not see it, in a neighbouring property a rabbit rolled over and expired, peppered with shot-gun pellets. All three of them jumped.

"We can't leave," said Eve. "Or at least that's what Nick says. He says if we try to leave, he won't be able to help us."

"Nick says," muttered Numpty, resentfully. "Nick says. Do we have to do what Nick says?"

"The boy's got a point," added Rambler. "We have no reason to trust Peters. Indeed we have several reasons not to trust him. What about his outburst in Prometheus' cave?"

"He says that was a desperate attempt to persuade us to abandon the quest," said Eve. She felt uncomfortable, as though, inadvertently, she was slipping into the role of Nick Peters' apologist.

"And why was it so important we abandoned the quest?" Rambler returned. Although it had not been his quest in the beginning, Rambler was now as committed as any to pursuit of the truth. Indeed, in his own way, he had always been on such a quest, as evidenced by the copious notes he took on every event.

"Yes," said Eve thoughtfully. "Why is he so against a search for the truth?"

Rambler shook his head. It was a good question but he had no obvious answer.

"Because he's afraid," suggested Numpty.

Both Eve and Rambler could see Numpty might be right. "But afraid of what?" Eve asked. "Afraid of the truth? Or afraid of us? Or afraid of us finding the truth? And why was he so worried? We haven't found the truth. Adam had some big questions. Why are we here? Is there any point? Is it all just a great big messy pot of serendipity? I had a question which to me was much more important. Why did Bella die? The only person to answer that question was Nick. And his answer was simple enough. 'It was an accident. Get over it. Move on.' That was his answer."

"The funny thing is," said Rambler, flicking through his notebook, "although we didn't find the truth, there was a kind of theme to all our adventures with the Storyteller."

Eve thought, frowned and then asked: "Which was?"

"Well," said Rambler cautiously, "they all had some point to them. I'm not explaining myself very well. In the Garden of Eden, we met a really appalling God who was made in the image of Man, the very worst man you could possibly imagine. Self-centred, insecure and sadistic, I won't go on. Even so, if we are to believe Rodney and Derek, this pathetic excuse for a supreme being set in motion the creation of Man. And the man and woman Rodney and Derek designed and made had a destiny. We were not sure what the destiny was but Kit gave us some idea of how Man could somehow transcend God, that God anyway. God was powerless before Kit.

"And then we visited Prometheus. What a relief after God! He was very kind and hospitable. He told us not to fear the gods. He told us our destiny was to outlive the gods. Just as he had stood against Zeus and given us fire, he expected us to vanquish the gods of Olympus. He said we had a destiny."

"That's all very well," said Eve. "But just because the gods, or one of the gods, believed we had a destiny doesn't make it so."

Rambler pondered Eve's words. "I wonder if that's true. If I believe I have a destiny, maybe I make a destiny. I certainly make myself a person who has a destiny."

"No you don't," said Eve. "You just make yourself a person who believes you have a destiny. In any case, that's not really the issue. The quest was to find the truth. If we have a destiny, what is it?"

Rambler shrugged.

"Where's Luke?" asked Numpty who was bored with the conversation.

"I don't know," Eve answered. "The last time I saw Luke, he was licking the Storyteller's face. I guess he's with the Storyteller."

"Is destiny something you have or something you make?" Rambler pursued his own line of thought.

58 Interrogation

"So," said Nick, leaning back after a rather heavy lunch, and sipping the most expensive brandy that the Breaker Board dining room could provide, "that's it. That's the plan. We undermine Adam and Eve individually and we deconstruct their relationship until they are so disturbed and demoralised that they no longer feel the need to seek the truth. A bit of fear, a soupçon of insecurity, a tad of jealousy, a generous portion of doubt and, to top it off, lashings of despair. If there's any residual spirit in them when I've finished with them, if they still have any appetite for asking questions, we can call on the services of the master Dawk, Despiro Nihilopificus. Finally, we have the full backing of the Breaker Board – and we all know what they are capable of. That just about wraps it up, don't you think?"

Grimrose, whose lunch at Nick's insistence had been light ('Can't condone over-indulgence while you're recuperating!', Nick had said) and who had not been offered any brandy at the end of the meal, nodded. He nodded, but he was not entirely convinced. Nick made a good case but, if it was going to be as easy as Nick suggested, why was there a need for all these resources. Why had Nick been told success was not just desirable but crucially important? Why had Despiro Nihilopificus been assigned to assist? Why had the Breaker Board gone to the extraordinary expense of allowing Nick a mysland? It all seemed far too much unless there was something Nick didn't know, something which the Breaker Board knew but hadn't told him.

On top of all the resources, there was the unprecedented interest the Breakers had taken in his own well-being. Their efforts on his behalf, while not quite in the same league as the resources given to Nick, were still extraordinarily generous. To save Nick's leg, Grimrose had risked complete dissolution. On his first visit to Cadnam, his deteriorating condition, which had reached a critical point in the office of Chief Engineer McCardle, showed he had given a little too much of his shapeshifter essence to help his master. He had certainly assumed, as he lost consciousness in McCardle's office, that he was dying. Then the Breakers' medics had swept in and delivered him with amazing speed to the shapeshifter medical facility. Before he arrived, as he learned later, a *disturba* had been arranged and he was treated immediately.

No, Nick might think that this was a done deal but there was too much riding on this assignment for any complacency. The Breakers' management understood that, even if Nick didn't.

There was another wrinkle. Grimrose himself. There was often tension between a Breaker field operative and his shapeshifter. It was inherent in the relationship. The Breaker was in charge but was dependent on the extraordinary abilities of his shape-shifting assistant. The Breaker could achieve a good deal on his own, especially in the handling of vulnerable or susceptible women but, in other circumstances, where an entirely different approach by a different type of person was called for, the shapeshifter was just what was needed. So, in any partnership between a Breaker and a shapeshifter, there had to be a negotiation, a way of somehow reconciling the absolute authority of the Breaker with the extraordinary abilities of the shapeshifter. The key to that reconciliation was respect. A shapeshifter would tolerate the most outrageous demands on condition that the Breaker making the outrageous demands showed his shapeshifter respect. That was the problem. Nick had lost the key. He failed to show respect. He had broken the covenant.

"You're very quiet," said Nick.

"I was just thinking," Grimrose replied. "Taking it all in," he added, to pre-empt Nick asking 'What about?'

"It's time for our first interview with Adam," said Nick. "You might as well sit in. You can be the Warden of the interrogation facility. Be as mean and hard-looking as you like. I'm here to help Adam. You can make sure I'm not too successful."

Nick and Grimrose made their way to the Number One interrogation room, a large, well-lit space with a rectangular table in the middle, and four chairs, two on opposite sides. Adam was already seated at the table, still blinking in the bright light, still clearly disorientated and terrified.

"You'd better stand up in the presence of the Warden," Nick suggested quietly.

Adam couldn't see the faces of his visitors but he recognised the voice. He staggered to his feet, leaning on the table to maintain his balance.

"Sit," ordered Grimrose, now a powerfully built man in his mid-forties, with a broken nose and a scar running down one side of his face from the corner of his right eye to the corner of his mouth.

Adam fell backwards awkwardly into the chair.

"The Warden has very kindly allowed me to see you for five minutes," Nick began, "but, for obvious security reasons, he has insisted on being present throughout the interview."

Adam began to focus his eyes. He could now see the faces of the two men facing him. One, the intimidating fellow with the florid scar, he had not met before. The other was Nick Peters right enough.

"Where's Eve?" were Adam's first words.

"Don't you worry about Eve," Nick replied. "She's in good hands and much better shape than you. I think we had better use the limited time available to talk about you. You are in serious trouble. I guess you've worked that out."

"What have I done? What am I supposed to have done?"

"Well," said Nick slowly, "you are suspected of conspiring to overthrow the establishment and you are being held under the Prevention of Terrorism Act, which allows the Warden here to hold you until either he has sufficient evidence to charge you or he concludes you don't pose a risk to society."

"That's ridiculous, and you know it. You know what I've been doing. We've been on a quest. I'm not interested in overthrowing anything. I just wanted a few answers. You can tell them."

"Whoa!" Nick interrupted. "It's not that simple. For a start, you've certainly been associating with the one you call the Storyteller. Terry Torrance, to give him his real name, has been under suspicion and observation for years. We've not been able to charge him with anything specific but we are absolutely certain he's a subversive. Furthermore, I'm not sure you would want me to tell the Warden here all about your alibi – that you've been on a quest through space and time, looking for the truth. I think he might conclude you were either insane or taking the piss."

"Where's Eve?" Adam asked again. What had they done with Eve? He knew they had killed Gwoat without a second thought and they had thrown him into a cell without light, water or food for what seemed like days. He shuddered to think what she might be going through.

"Eve's fine," said Nick. "I think she's beginning to see things in perspective, you know, getting back to reality. She's not going to be a trouble. No, you're the problem. If you want to get out of here, you will have to co-operate fully with the Warden and his people. It's no good denying everything. You need to admit you've made some mistakes. Meet the Warden halfway and things will be easier for you."

"What do you want me to admit? Of course I've made mistakes. Who hasn't? But I've never, ever been remotely involved in any kind of terrorism and I've certainly never tried to overthrow this state or any other."

"Well, obviously you need to give it some thought," said Nick. "I'll come back when you have."

With that, Nick stood up. "When you put him back in his cell, would you consider allowing him some light, and perhaps some bread and water?" he asked of the Warden. Grimrose nodded his assent. The

317

shapeshifter even tried to encourage Adam with a benign smile but, unfortunately, the side of his face with the scar did not respond, so what set out as a smile ended as a rather sinister grimace.

"Wait," Adam shouted. "You can't just go. Where's Eve? Where's my wife?"

Nick left. Two warders took Adam, now shaking uncontrollably, and dragged him out of the interrogation room. When he was gone, Grimrose joined Nick.

oooOooo

"Thought that went rather well," said Nick as soon as they were out of the building. "He's obviously disorientated and frightened, and let's face it, we've hardly started. I reckon he's about as much chance of undermining the establishment as the proverbial snowflake has of extinguishing the fires of hell."

"Nice simile," observed Grimrose, before adding: "Do you mind me asking why we're doing all this? I agree with you. Adam is terrified. If this goes on, I've no doubt you can cause a complete mental breakdown. But why are we doing this? He's not a threat to anyone, is he? Why are we going to all this trouble?"

Nick decided to be honest. The Breakers considered Grimrose was an important element in this venture and there was no point in keeping anything from him. "Have you ever heard of the Fourth Beginning?" he asked.

"I've heard of the three Beginnings. It's one of the stories we tell our children. It's about a wizard who grants a child three wishes. If I remember correctly, each time the child wishes for something, the wish is granted but there's always a catch. Is that what you mean?"

"I doubt it. No, this is about the Storyteller and those he takes on quests. The Storyteller persuades his punters there's some grand scheme of things, or at least encourages them to think there might be. He tells them there have been three great Beginnings; the start of everything; the birth of life; the arrival of consciousness. It's all completely arbitrary, of course. Anyway, that's not the point."

"And the point is…?" Grimrose prompted.

"The point is the Board seems to think there is a risk of another Beginning."

"And what would that be? What kind of Beginning? What are we looking for?"

"That's just it. I don't know. I don't think they know. All we do know is it's our job to stop it. Whatever it is, the Breakers don't want it.

In fact, they don't want it so much that they are prepared to do whatever it takes to stop it. And that, Grimrose, means we have to do whatever it takes."

"It's a bit difficult to prevent something when you don't know what the something is," said Grimrose. "And what has all this to do with Adam anyway?"

"Adam and Eve are the key. If we can break them, if we can persuade them to abandon their quest, not only abandon it but accept that the quest was pointless, would always be pointless, apparently we can stop the Fourth Beginning, at least for now. I know it's all a bit vague and obviously it would be easier if we knew exactly what is was we had to prevent. But at least we know how to stop it and, for the purposes of completing this project, that's good enough."

"When you say we have to break Adam and Eve, what does that mean? What you're doing to Adam seems crazy. You've put him in solitary confinement in a tiny cell. You've starved him, deprived him of light, terrified him. Why? He doesn't even know what you want him to do."

"Oh dear!" said Nick wearily. "I thought you understood. It's perfectly simple. With the help of the Storyteller, Adam and Eve have come close to activating the Fourth Beginning. Now I don't know why it should be them that's done this; I don't know how they've done it; and I don't know why they've done it. Most of all, I don't know what it is they've done. I'm the first person to admit there are all these things I don't know. But I do know one thing and I really want you to know it too. We have to destroy them. We have to destroy them completely, partly because we don't know any of the answers and the only way to be sure we've stopped them is to destroy them."

"So why haven't you killed them? Surely you don't have moral qualms? After all, you had your people take out Gwoat without a second thought."

"Of course I don't have moral qualms!" Nick snapped. "Killing them won't do. If we kill them there will be others. This is a test case. We have to demonstrate that the Fourth Beginning isn't going to happen, that it's an illusion dreamt up by the Storyteller and his ilk. If we can reduce Adam and Eve to despair, others will be deterred and the Storyteller will find it more and more difficult to find punters. And, since you raise the subject, I didn't order my men to kill Gwoat. That was just an accident, a happy accident because I couldn't stand the little Irish git, but an accident nonetheless."

"You say we have to demonstrate the Fourth Beginning is an illusion. Is it?"

319

"How the hell should I know? I guess if we prevent it and it doesn't happen, in will be an illusion."

"So what do we do now?" Grimrose could see his master was in no mood to fail to answer any more questions.

"We make a start on Eve."

59 Observers

The Storyteller patted Luke on the head.

They were sitting outside the Elm Tree pub in the sun. The Storyteller was drinking a cool pint of Guinness. Luke was seated beside the Storyteller, his golden coat gleaming in the sunlight.

"So what do we do now?" Luke asked, unknowingly echoing Grimrose's question in the mysland.

"We wait and see," the Storyteller replied. "It's out of my hands."

"But why can't we help them? Where are they? And how did we get here? And where is here?"

The Storyteller smiled. "So many questions. Now let me see. The questors are trapped in a mental construct, put together and sustained by the Breakers' technical division. They call it a mysland. It will be a replica of a real area, an exact replica of the landscape, the buildings and the people. The only difference between this construct and the real world is that the Breakers have complete control of everything that happens within the mysland."

"So it's not real. Does that mean Gwoat isn't dead? He was killed in the construct thing."

"No, I'm afraid Gwoat is dead," the Storyteller replied sadly. "Whatever happens to real people in the mysland, happens for real. Gwoat is gone."

"So where is this mysland and how do we get into it? Or are we in it now?"

"No, we're in the real world or, at least the world we were in when we set out on the quest. This Elm Tree pub is just inside the New Forest and not far from Nick Peters' house on Poulner Hill. But there's an exact replica of this pub and the house on Poulner Hill within the mysland. And it's in that replica house that Eve and the others are being held. We can't access the mysland because no one can enter or leave without the permission of the Breakers. They control the boundaries. It's their construct."

"We can't just sit here in the sun while Adam and Eve are being terrorised by those thugs," said Luke with evident frustration. "We must be able to help. How did we get out if no one can leave without permission?"

"We had permission. Indeed, they threw us out. They know I'm irrelevant now. Even if we could find a way in, I can't help. I've already given Adam and Eve everything I have to offer. Now it's up to them."

Luke was very unhappy. He liked to be close to Adam and Eve at all times but now, when they were obviously in danger, when they had most need of him, when even their lives could be in peril, he was not there. "Well, at least tell me what is happening to them. Tell me why they have been seized."

"It's not easy to answer you," said the Storyteller. "There is a chance that Adam and Eve will find the truth, will complete their quest successfully. How that would be, I don't know. What that might be, I can only guess. But it is a possibility. It is still not likely – but, for the first time for a very long time, it is possible.

"As a result, Nick and the Breakers are determined to stop them. I tried to warn Adam and Eve that this is how the quest would end. They would have to face the Breakers. But when I warned them, I had no idea how seriously the Breakers were taking the challenge. Setting up a mysland is horrendously expensive. Even the Breakers will find their resources are quickly depleted. If they are to destroy Adam and Eve, they will have to do it quickly, simply because the costs of maintaining the mysland are insupportable for any length of time."

"Destroy Adam and Eve!" Luke exclaimed. "Is that what these Breakers are planning to do?"

"I'm afraid so. They need to make sure they will never try again. If they break them, it may well be another thousand years before we get this close."

The pub where the Storyteller and the golden retriever were sitting was not full but there were two other tables occupied in the garden of the pub, a man and a woman at one table and two young men at another. All four looked over to the Storyteller from time to time. He seemed to be talking quite earnestly to the dog. He also seemed to be leaving gaps between his remarks, as though he were allowing time for the dog to respond. The two young men stared once or twice and then laughed before returning to their drink and conversation. The man with the woman also laughed until chided by his companion, who said something about it being inappropriate to mock those who clearly had been 'returned to the community'.

"Does it matter?" Luke enquired after pondering the Storyteller's last remark. None of this made any sense. From the very beginning, he had been of the view that no one in their right mind would leave all the comforts of home to go in search of something indefinable, unknown and probably unknowable. A bone covered in juicy meat was worthy of some effort. A chase across open ground to catch or retrieve game justified the expenditure of energy. But pursuit of the truth was about as sensible as chasing your own tail or fighting your own shadow. "Does it really matter?" he asked again.

"Some, most, almost all, think not," the Storyteller replied. "But for a very few, it is the only thing that matters."

60 Softening up

Nick and Grimrose said little on the journey from Cadnam to Poulner Hill. Nick was busy calculating the best way to begin his destruction of Eve. He had a clear overall plan but he still needed to think through the tactics he would need to deploy on the way.

Grimrose was trying to work out what he was doing and how he felt about it. For years he had helped Nick to frustrate quests. That was his job and he did it well. He had always assumed that, although they might from time to time need to use questionable methods, at the end of the day what they were doing was right. The questors might not always understand; they might not always agree; but Grimrose had taken as a premise that he and Nick would not be employed to do such work unless it served some useful, beneficial purpose.

For the first time in his long career as a Breaker assistant, Grimrose was seriously questioning what they were doing, not merely in this particular instance (although that certainly concerned him) but in a general, fundamental sense. Whose side were they on? Were they doing good or harm?

Of course, shapeshifters were not supposed to ask such questions. The idea that a creature that could adopt any form it chose including, at a stretch, that of an animal, should have a coherent moral sense was generally thought by both Breakers and shapeshifters to be palpably absurd. Why, even on this recent quest, Grimrose had adopted the forms of a recalcitrant fairy bent on murder, and a huge psychopath who had despatched hitch-hikers Maizy and Sandy with such brutal force, and without a second thought.

No, Nick was right. They had a job to do. They had their orders. Best to get on with it.

Nick dropped Grimrose off at the gate and told him he wouldn't need him for an hour or so. He then drove up the winding drive to the house. Eve was sitting on the patio at the back of the house.

"Good to see you enjoying the sun," said Nick in his most affable tones. "It's a lovely garden, isn't it?"

Eve was in no mood for pleasantries. "How is Adam?" she asked immediately. "How is he? How are they treating him? Have you explained things?"

"I've done everything I can and I think I've persuaded the authorities to improve his living conditions."

"Is that it?" snapped Eve. "What exactly have you done? I thought you were going to Cadnam to sort things out."

"It's not as simple as that," Nick replied, adopting his hurt voice. "I've done my best but I can't wave a magic wand. There are procedures. He has to be interrogated."

"Interrogated about what?" Eve almost screamed with frustration. "He hasn't done anything."

"I'll be honest with you," said Nick. "He's not in good shape. Physically he's fine. But mentally, well he seems disturbed and depressed."

"We're all disturbed and depressed," said Eve. "I'm disturbed and depressed. Rambler and Numpty are disturbed and depressed. We all want to go home. We've all witnessed a brutal murder by the same people who are holding my husband. So I'm not only disturbed and depressed, I'm pretty desperate. And desperate people do desperate things. I'm sure Adam feels the same."

Nick studied Eve. She was being totally honest. She was frightened and she was angry. And she was strong, that was clear. But she didn't seem like someone capable of triggering a cataclysmic event, not one to initiate the Fourth Beginning, whatever that was.

"Adam seems to have something on his mind," said Nick carefully. "The interrogators have picked something up. He's holding back. They're very good at what they do. They can tell when someone is trying to hide something. That's why I haven't been able to do more. Until they find out what he's hiding, there's no chance they will release him. Sorry."

"Whatever he's hiding, if he's hiding anything, it's certainly nothing to do with terrorism," Eve responded.

Nick's face remained impassive but he smiled inwardly. She's half taken the bait already. She must be wondering, if Adam's got a secret and he's not a terrorist, what can the secret be about? "I've promised to do all I can and I will keep my word," he said. "Now I need to get some rest. It's been quite a day."

oooOooo

Rambler and Numpty joined Eve on the patio, eager to hear any news Nick had brought from Cadnam. Eve gave them a summary.

"So not much progress," observed Rambler.

All three were silent. Then Numpty spoke: "They seem to be going to an awful lot of trouble," was all he said.

Rambler picked up his nephew's thought. "That's true. It's as though they are afraid of something, perhaps even afraid of us. But why? We have been on a quest but we haven't discovered anything to

325

make them fearful, have we? Or have we? We've seen the inadequacy of the God that underpins Abrahamic monotheistic faiths. I suppose that's quite something. And Prometheus told us a little about our destiny, although since he was making predictions thousands of years before the present, his forecasts seemed less prescient to us than they were no doubt when he made them. What else?"

"We've witnessed the three Beginnings," offered Numpty.

"That's right," said Eve. "And in each case, the Storyteller was keen for us to have a sense of the way things were before each Beginning. He seemed to feel that looking back on a Beginning gave us a false perspective."

"Yes," Numpty jumped in. "Like winning a lottery despite outrageous odds against winning and then, just because you've won, forgetting about the outrageous odds and all the other outcomes when you wouldn't have won, which were in fact much more likely simply because you did win, and then thinking that it was perfectly reasonable that you won and that winning despite the outrageous odds doesn't need any explanation at all because that's just the way it is."

"Quite," said Rambler, fearful that Numpty might never be able to find an end to the sentence.

"It's interesting that Nick Peters has been so keen from the start to stop us from seeking the truth," Eve mused.

"He told you there wasn't a truth to find, didn't he?" Rambler reminded her.

"Yes, but if there was no truth to find, why try to prevent us from looking? I don't think he's the altruistic type – to put in all that effort just to stop us from wasting our time. And if it wasn't altruism, what other motive could he have had?"

"Perhaps he was afraid you would succeed," said Rambler. "After all, he's part of the security services, isn't he? He's involved in all this, perhaps even behind all this. There must be something in what we've seen or heard whilst in the company of the Storyteller that constitutes a threat. I don't know what the threat is or who's threatened, but whoever Peters represents is scared. I'm sure of it."

"They think Adam knows something, is holding something back," said Eve. In her summary of her conversation with Nick, she hadn't mentioned Nick's explanation for Adam's continued detention.

"Perhaps he's worked something out," said Rambler. "Perhaps he really has discovered something that constitutes a threat. What else did Peters say?"

"Nothing. He just said they won't release Adam until they find out what they think he's hiding."

"That sounds ominous," said Rambler, "especially if he isn't hiding anything."

oooOooo

Seated in his office on the top floor of the house, Nick Peters switched the monitor to record. He would skim through the rest later. The first part of the conversation between Eve and her fellow questors had been a little worrying. He'd been hoping their current predicament would have driven thoughts of the quest out of their minds. Instead, that irritating old fart Rambler seemed intent on trying to make something of it. At the end, however, all had turned out well. Evidently the possibility of Adam having a secret had lodged in Eve's mind and, despite Rambler's irritating suggestion that Adam might have discovered something really dangerous, there was no indication that Eve agreed. Eve remained convinced Adam's secret, if he had one, was certainly not the sudden discovery of the truth.

oooOooo

That evening, Nick hosted a dinner party for his guests in the house's rather imposing dining room. Adopting his most affable persona, he entertained his guests with studied courtesy in a determined effort to persuade them they were not being held under duress. Despite his best efforts, the meal was not a complete success. Eve took every opportunity to remind him that they all knew well enough they were prisoners and none of them would be satisfied until they and Adam were free to go.

After the meal, Nick despatched Rambler and his nephew to the games room where he urged them to have a game of snooker. Eve he held back.

"You want me to do everything I can to persuade Cadnam to release Adam but you have to help me," he began. Eve looked puzzled. Adam continued: "Have you given any thought to what Adam might be hiding?"

"He's not hiding anything and, even if he was, it certainly has nothing to do with terrorism," Eve replied.

"Do you think it could be something to do with Bella's death?" Nick asked.

Eve was stunned. Why should it have anything to do with Bella's death? That tragedy had happened years before. And why would the security forces want to know about the accidental death of a child?

"Perhaps he is blaming himself for Bella's death," Nick suggested.

"What would that have to do with anything?"

"Of course, it wouldn't be of any interest to the security forces," Nick conceded, "but it might explain why they think he's holding back. Perhaps he feels guilty and that's what the interrogators are picking up."

"You mean another misunderstanding, just like arresting him in the first place."

"It's a possibility," Nick suggested. Then without waiting for Eve to question why Adam should feel guilty, he continued. "How is your relationship with Adam?"

Eve couldn't see where this was going and, in any case, it was certainly none of Nick's business. "It's fine," she said.

"Fine?" said Nick. "That's a pretty measured response. You've been married a good few years. Must have had a few ups and downs?"

"Well, obviously Bella's death was what you might call a down." Eve was angry. She was a prisoner, albeit a well-treated one. And her captor was asking personal, inappropriate questions. "What exactly do you want?" she snapped.

"I don't want anything," said Nick, "except to help you – and Adam. You see, I know he's hiding something and I know Cadnam won't release him until they find out what it is. You want him released. So we have to find out what he's hiding."

"I don't think he's hiding anything," said Eve, exasperated, "but, if he is, you won't find out what it is by asking me. You'd have to ask him."

"That's precisely what they're doing," said Nick. "At Cadnam."

oooOooo

In the games room, Rambler and his nephew were practising their snooker. Rambler was trying to explain the rules to his nephew. After a few trial strokes, Rambler set up the balls for a game, explaining the potting sequence the players must follow.

Numpty was fascinated.

"You can start," said Rambler. "Just disturb the triangle of red balls."

"Should I try to put one of the red balls into one of the holes so I can start scoring?"

"Well you can try," said Rambler, "but it won't be easy."

"But it is possible?" Numpty persisted.

"Well, I suppose so," said Rambler.

"Could I put two red balls down the holes with my first shot?" asked Numpty.

"It's just possible, I suppose," said Rambler "but very unlikely. And, in any case, your second pot should be of a different colour."

"How unlikely?" asked Numpty undeterred.

"I really don't know," said Rambler. "Very unlikely."

"What about putting all the red balls down the holes with one shot?"

"No," Rambler tried to end Numpty's questions. "No," he said emphatically, "that would not be possible."

"But if you could put one ball down and maybe two, why not three, and four, or even all of them?"

"The odds against it are incalculable," said Rambler.

"Do you mean the odds are very high, or do you mean it's impossible?"

"I think I mean it's impossible," said Rambler. As often happened, his nephew was making him think. "I suppose something could be theoretically possible if you tried to do it enough times but there might not actually be enough time in the universe for you to be able to do it enough times."

"So are you saying that something could be possible but, because it's so unlikely, there wouldn't be enough chances for it to happen?"

"Yes," said Rambler slowly. "I think that is what I'm saying."

"So you're saying that something that is possible is impossible," said Numpty triumphantly. "Is that what you call a Pandora's box?"

"Not quite," said Rambler patiently. "I think you mean a paradox."

61 Further softening up

The following morning, Nick and Grimrose left early for Cadnam. It was a gloriously sunny day and the New Forest looked at its best. This part of the forest was open moorland and the golden landscape rolled away for miles on either side of the A31. In some of the dips in the land morning mist hung like delicate lace veils, provocatively concealing further imagined beauties.

"Eve is simmering nicely," said Nick, as they reached Stoney Cross. "I can bring her to the boil as soon as we've marinated Adam for a bit."

Grimrose was mildly puzzled by Nick's culinary allusions but not sufficiently to comment on them.

"I shall need your help with the marinade."

Still Grimrose failed to respond. He had reconciled himself to his role in this major project and yet something in a corner of his mind kept nagging away at him.

"Hello," said Nick. "Is there anybody there?"

"Sorry," said Grimrose. "I was miles away."

"That's a bit worrying," said Nick. "I thought you guys had a saying 'a shifter and his shape should never be parted'. I've never really understood what that meant unless it's saying that you need to pull yourself together. I'm hoping that's what it means and that's what you are going to do."

Grimrose nodded.

"Good," said Nick, "because today you are going to be Eve."

"Now wait a minute…" Grimrose began.

"Yes?" said Nick.

Grimrose frowned but did not speak. That was the problem. Of course he would do what Nick required. There were problems. Sex change shifts were always demanding. Shifting into a shape and adopting the persona of someone who was intimately known to the person you were trying to deceive was a major challenge. But that wasn't why Grimrose had started to object. It was something else. It was that nagging thing in the corner of his mind.

"Well…," Nick prompted.

"What do you want me to do?" said Grimrose.

"That's better. I'm not asking you to change into Eve, so you can relax. I just want you to talk to Adam. I'm going to tell Adam that the Warden has agreed to allow him a brief telephone conversation with his wife. In that conversation, we are going to sow some seeds of doubt in Adam's mind. It shouldn't be too difficult. He's frightened, disorientated and insecure. This is what I want you to do."

Grimrose listened to Nick's instructions. It would be easy. All he had to do was adopt Eve's voice. If what Eve said sounded strange to Adam, he would assume it was because of the pressure they were both under.

oooOooo

When they reached Cadnam, Nick parked and left Grimrose in the car. "I'll call you in about twenty minutes," said Nick. "Then you talk to Adam for a few minutes. When you've finished, I'll have Adam put back in his cell – and you and I can get a decent breakfast in the canteen."

Adam, looking pale, tired and drawn, was already seated in the No. 1 interrogation room.

"We meet again," said Nick, with entirely inappropriate jocularity. "How's it going?"

Adam produced something between a grunt and a groan.

"Look," said Nick, now concerned, "I know things are difficult for you but I'm doing my best to sort something out."

"How is Eve?" Adam asked.

"She's fine. In fact I've got some good news for you on that front. But first, I need to talk to you about whatever it is you are trying to conceal from the security services."

"I can't keep repeating myself," said Adam, trying to energise himself. "I'm not hiding anything. I've nothing to hide. I'm not a terrorist. I don't know any terrorists. I've never even been on a demonstration. Until now, I've always had the highest respect and regard for the forces of law and order."

"So you admit you are hostile to the establishment now?" said Nick.

"No, I wouldn't say that."

"I thought you just did."

"No," Adam explained wearily, "I said until now I had always had the highest respect and regard for the forces of law and order. I admit that respect and regard has been somewhat shaken by the security forces deciding to murder an entirely innocent and unarmed man in front of me."

"Murder," Nick picked on the word. "There's a lot of aggression in you."

"In me!" exclaimed Adam. "I'm not one of the bastards who mowed down Gwoat."

"No, quite right," said Nick. "Anyway, moving on. We're here

331

together alone because I persuaded the Warden that, if you were treated better, you'd be more likely to co-operate. They still think you're hiding something. I know you're not a terrorist but I'm pretty sure there's something troubling you. You can talk to me. It's just you and me. So what is it?"

"The only thing troubling me is being held by you and the security forces without charge for something I certainly haven't done."

"Eve thinks it might be something to do with Bella's death," Nick suggested.

"What!" said Adam.

"Yes, she thinks it might be some kind of guilt over the death of your daughter. She thinks the quest with the Storyteller may have stirred up memories of what happened and that you blame yourself. She could understand that."

Adam shook his head. This was madness. What had Bella to do with any of this? Of course, he was always thinking of Bella. You don't ever forget the loss of a child. It's with you every day. But why should Eve think he was hiding something to do with Bella? And why should she think he might feel guilty about the accident? After all it had been a freak accident and, if there was any blame (which there wasn't), it was hers as much as his.

"I don't know what you mean," was all Adam could say.

"The good news," Nick made no effort to explain, "the good news is that I have persuaded the Warden to allow you to talk to Eve on the phone."

Adam's eyes brightened.

"There are one or two rules," Nick continued. "You must not say anything that could reveal where you are being held and, if at any time, I feel that matters of security are being compromised, I have to pull the plug. I shall be listening to you and Eve throughout so be careful. Do you understand?"

Adam nodded. Nick produced two mobile phones, dialled a number and handed one of the phones to Adam. Grimrose answered promptly, speaking with Eve's voice. Both Nick and Adam heard him say: "Hello."

"Is that you Eve?" said Adam, with a crack in his voice.

"Adam, are you all right?" Eve's voice answered.

"I've been better," Adam replied. "I don't know why they're holding me. I'm in solitary confinement except when Nick Peters visits me. He's here now. Everyone here seems to think I know something or I'm hiding something. I don't know what to tell them. I don't know anything. But how are you? Where are you? What's happening?"

"I'm fine," said Eve's voice. "Rambler, Numpty and I are staying in a house somewhere in the New Forest. I think we must still be fairly close to the A31 because sometimes I can hear the sound of traffic."

Nick interrupted. "I've told both of you to steer clear of questions about location. If you raise the subject again, this conversation will be ended and it's very unlikely the Warden will agree to a second."

"Are they treating you well?" Adam resumed.

"We're all in good shape. Nick has made sure we are comfortable and, except for the fact that we can't leave, there is nothing to complain about. It's a fine house, lovely gardens and the food is good. Nick has been really kind and he's doing everything he can to help you."

Adam was silent for a moment. Had Eve forgotten Nick's outburst in Prometheus' cave? Surely she hadn't started to trust the man again.

Eve's voice continued: "Nick says they think you're hiding something. He says they won't release you till they know what it is."

Adam felt deeply unease. 'Nick says.' 'Nick says.' Why did she keep saying 'Nick says'? After another silence, Adam spoke with undue emphasis on the first two words: "Nick says you think my secret may be that I feel guilty about Bella's death?" He waited for a response.

"It has crossed my mind," said Eve's voice. "If that is what is worrying you, just tell them. If they're satisfied, they will let you go. They will let us all go."

"Why do you think I would feel guilty about Bella's death?" Adam said sharply.

"I'm not saying you should feel guilty," Eve's voice replied. "I was just trying to think of something that you might want to keep to yourself, something the security forces might misinterpret."

"Bella's death was an accident. No one's to blame. I'm not to blame. You're not to blame. If we need to blame someone, it's the psychotic God we met in the Garden of Eden."

"I'm not blaming you," said Eve's voice.

"Thanks," said Adam.

Once again Nick intervened. "Come on you two. You're surely not going to spend these precious minutes arguing. Eve has a point. They won't let you go, Adam, until you tell them what it is you're holding back. If it's not about Bella, you had better come up with something else."

A buzzer went off in the interrogation room. "I'm sorry," said Nick. "That's it. I have to terminate the call." With that, he pressed a button on his mobile and Eve, or rather Eve's voice, was gone.

"I don't know what you're playing at," said Adam. "You may have

Eve fooled but I am absolutely certain that, whatever you're doing, it's much more likely to harm Eve and me than do us good."

"You don't have so many friends you can be profligate with them," Nick chided. "And you should listen to Eve. She's a smart, intelligent, attractive woman. You're lucky to have her."

"Don't tell me to appreciate my own wife." Adam was angry. How dare this man who had sworn to destroy them proffer advice on Adam's relationship with his own wife? It was offensive, intrusive and, yes, somehow menacing.

oooOooo

Nick collected Grimrose and they repaired to the Cadnam canteen for a full English breakfast. "Well done," said Nick graciously. "Beautiful impression! Impossible to tell your voice from Eve's."

"Shapeshifters don't do impressions. If you need a word, I'd prefer you to use impersonation. We adopt the persona of the individual. That is how we can not only simulate the voice but also the way in which the subject uses language and the type of things they would say."

"Fine," said Nick. "Just trying to give you some well-deserved praise."

They both tucked in to the bacon, eggs, sausages, black pudding, tomato and fried bread. Half way through the meal Nigel Vale joined them.

"Good morning Grimrose; good morning Nick," Nigel began. "Do you mind if I sit with you for a moment?"

Nick nodded agreement while wondering why Nigel had greeted Grimrose first.

"How is it going?" said Nigel, evidently eager to get straight to the point.

"It's going rather well," said Nick quickly, unreasonably fearful that Grimrose might seize the initiative. "Adam is close to breaking. Eve has been prepared. The next stage of the plan should effectively end their relationship. In the ensuing emotional turmoil, we can be certain the last thing on their minds will be the pursuit of truth or the initiation of the Fourth Beginning or any other cataclysmic event that seems to be worrying the Breaker Board."

Nigel seemed relieved. "Good. I know you are already under some pressure and I've no wish to add to the strain but I have been asked to remind you there is a time limit on the operation. Maintenance of the mysland is draining our resources at a phenomenal rate so the sooner you can bring the project to a satisfactory conclusion the better."

"Everything is in place," Nick assured his Regional Manager. "If it's that urgent, I will bring things forward. We'll leave for the house as soon as we've finished our breakfast."

"I think you have," said Nigel. "No time to lose," he added.

62 Revelations

Nick and Grimrose spoke little on the return journey, both keeping their thoughts to themselves.

Nick oscillated between euphoria at how well everything was going and concern that the Breakers and Nigel were pressing too hard for a speedy resolution. The only possible cause for failure was, in Nick's view, this pressure to bring things to a head prematurely. Both Adam and Eve needed time to adjust to the divergent realities he was creating for them. If he engineered the confrontation and the breakdown too quickly, his plans could unravel.

Grimrose was more concerned to identify the emotions that were burbling away inside him, an extremely odd preoccupation for a shapeshifter. By their very nature, shapeshifters were adept in adopting foreign personae and all the cultural and moral attitudes they brought with them. Of course, it was assumed, at least by shapeshifters, that each shapeshifter had his own core of being, his own unique essence but, given they spent most of their working lives in alien forms, it was an assumption considered rather esoteric and certainly one that was rarely tested. So why, Grimrose asked himself, should he be so keen to identify and put a name to the unease he felt? After all, surely he could get rid of any feeling by shape-shifting into a being that didn't feel it, that didn't have such a feeling of unease in its emotional repertoire? And yet that thought didn't help. There was a small insistent voice inside his head which kept telling him that even if he changed into an elephant or an ant, the core of Grimrose which held together all such transformations would still feel ill at ease. Suddenly Grimrose knew the name of the feeling. The unease was guilt.

When they arrived at the house on Poulner Hill, Grimrose was relieved when Nick told him to take the rest of the day off. He stayed in the car for a few minutes after Nick had parked and left. Opening the vanity mirror in the sun visor, Grimrose studied his face. He was in relaxed mode, which meant, as far as he could tell, he was himself. So who was he? He was a man in middle years, of medium height and build, not handsome but not unpleasant-looking. His face was marked with the lines of one who has experienced much in life, which, given the many forms he had been required to adopt, was not in the least surprising. His eyes were grey, a little washed out but enhanced by laughter lines that radiated from the outside corners of his eyes like the spokes of a wheel. Grimrose pondered his reflection for some moments.

In Nick's absence, Eve, Rambler and Numpty had not been idle. They had divided their time between planning a method of escape and trying to fathom what was going on, why they had been detained and why the authorities seemed to be afraid of them – and especially afraid of Adam.

Their efforts to explore the possibility of escape had enjoyed mixed results. The good news was that they had found the yellow camper van. It had been left in a corner of one of the barns located not far from the house. The bad news was that it looked as though it had been knocked about a bit. While it had never been in tip-top condition, the van now looked rather sad and dilapidated. Numpty had suggested they should try to start the vehicle but, while they debated whether they dared, one of the guards arrived and ushered them out of the barn into the meadow. "Best to leave the equipment alone," he suggested. "You'd be surprised how many accidents happen when novices play around with farm machinery."

As for fathoming the reasons for their predicament, Rambler felt they had made some progress. "After thinking hard about our amazing experiences with the Storyteller, it's fairly clear to me that he was trying to point out that our universe has developed with a sense of direction. I'm not saying there's a God, benign or otherwise, but I am saying there are far too many particularities in the making of the universe and life and us for it all to have happened purely by chance."

"So you're saying that, in the grand scheme of things, there's some kind of purpose," said Eve, without any great enthusiasm. She was not really interested in the great scheme of things. Humans didn't lead their lives by reference to the great scheme of things. They lived in a particular time and place, with a small number of nearest and dearest. Their lives were made up of routine daily living, punctuated from time to time by the small great events of individual births, marriages and deaths. There might be some over-arching purpose for the universe, divine or otherwise, but for Eve it was about as interesting and relevant as movements of money on the international money markets.

"No, I'm not saying there's a purpose," Rambler responded. "I'm just saying there is a direction. The more I think about it, the more obvious it is. In fact, speaking as a scientist, albeit an enthusiastic amateur one, I would say the evidence is everywhere. Of course, evolution has taken place. From the birth of the universe to the world we know today, evolution has been the mechanism. But is has not been random. The odds were very much against a universe being capable of supporting life. And when life came along, there was no reason why it should have sought to replicate, to multiply, to evolve. And, even when it evolved, the emergence of human consciousness was again against all the odds, unless that was where evolution was heading from the start."

Eve shrugged. Rambler was disappointed. He felt he had made a breakthrough.

"You may very well be right," said Eve. "But that's not the kind of answer I was looking for. I wanted to know if there was any point to our own, individual, short lives. To be honest, I don't really care about the universe or where it's headed. I want to know about the lives of ordinary people, people like me, and people like Bella, whether they have any point or meaning."

"Where do you think it's headed?" asked Numpty, attentive throughout but happily generally silent in recognition of a conversation to which he could contribute most by listening rather than talking.

Rambler was slightly taken aback. "It was Eve who talked about where it's headed," Rambler responded. "I don't know where it's headed but, if I'm right and it has a sense of direction, I guess it's perfectly reasonable to ask, 'What next?'"

oooOooo

On leaving Grimrose in the car, Nick headed straight for his office. In front of the mirror in the en suite bathroom he rehearsed once more what he was going to say to Eve. When he was satisfied with both the words and the tone, he sat behind his desk and summoned Eve over the intercom.

When Eve entered his office, Nick presented a suitably serious countenance. He asked Eve to be seated. "I have some news," he began. "I think, in the long run, it will be good news but I'm afraid you may, no you will, find it upsetting."

He paused to give Eve plenty of time to speculate and for the tension to build.

Nick continued. "I have found out what Adam has been holding back. I have found out why he feels guilty."

Again a pause.

"Well?" said Eve. "Are you going to share Adam's guilty secret with me?"

Nick sniffed. "Very well," he said. "Adam has been unfaithful to you."

Eve had not been convinced Adam had a secret but she had given the possibility some thought. That his secret was a sexual infidelity had never crossed her mind.

"I thought you said he was feeling guilty about Bella's death," Eve said eventually.

"I was wrong."

"And what makes you think he's slept with someone else?"

"He told me so. I have just come from a meeting with him. He's close to a mental breakdown. In the end, he blurted it all out. He begged me not to tell you but I have no choice because, if he is to be released, the interrogators have to be told and to believe this infidelity is the reason why their stress detectors have picked up clear warning signals. You will have to know so you can confirm his story."

"And when is this infidelity supposed to have taken place?" Eve asked.

"It was when you were with Prometheus. Adam made love to Pandora."

"But I never met Pandora. She was just part of one of the stories that Prometheus told."

"It is not necessary for you to meet someone before your husband can make love to them. Pandora lives in Prometheus' cave. While you and he were staying, Pandora, whose sexual morals are lax to say the least, hit on Adam and he succumbed. I should say, in Adam's defence, Pandora is extremely beautiful and a mistress of the art of love-making."

Eve felt angry and betrayed. They had set out together in search of the truth and, if Nick Peters was to be believed, at the first opportunity, Adam had abandoned the quest for a quick piece of tail. And, of course, Nick's excuse for Adam, that Pandora was irresistibly beautiful, didn't help in the slightest.

Nick's faced expressed understanding and sympathy. Inside, he was smiling broadly. They had wanted a quick result. Well, by tomorrow, all the pieces should be in place. It had been risky but then great feats often involved risk.

Nick's satisfaction suffered a minor jolt when the telephone rang and, when he answered it, he heard Nigel Vale at the end of it. "I thought you said everything was under control," said a disturbed voice.

After dismissing Eve from his presence, Nick said "It is. What's the problem?"

"Rambler's the problem. He's still thinking about the quest. He's on the wrong track but it would be best if he wasn't thinking about the truth at all. The more he thinks about things, the greater the risk he will start a line of thought we really don't want."

"He's not a problem," Nick asserted. He was genuinely surprised that they should think the senile old fool a threat of any sort to anyone. "I'll have a word with him myself. I'll give him something else to think about."

"No," said Nigel emphatically. "I'm sending Despiro Nihilopificus. I'm not saying you couldn't handle it but this is too important to take any chances. This is the Sparrow's forte; it's his territory."

"You really don't need to send a Dawk," said Nick petulantly. "You're just wasting his time. By tomorrow it should all be over."

"Despiro is on his way," said Nigel Vale and, without waiting for a response, he put the phone down.

63 Friends reunited

The Storyteller and Luke had taken to spending most days in the Elm Tree pub. Although they were in the real world and Adam and Eve were in the mysland, Luke insisted they should stay as close as possible to his master and mistress. He continued to press the Storyteller to think of some way of gaining access to the mysland.

"It's just not possible," the Storyteller told him. "And even if it were possible, what could we do? The mysland is entirely under the control of the Breakers. They can make anything happen there, anything at all. They could have the police arrest us as soon as we set foot inside the boundaries. We could be shot on sight, like poor Gwoat. It's ironic that after years of working with me undertaking the most hazardous of adventures, it should be Gwoat, the greatest worrier of all time, who should be the one to lose his life."

The Storyteller would sink into a mire of sadness, dwelling on the loss of his driver and friend but Luke was undeterred. Day after day, as the Storyteller slowly drank his pints of Guinness, Luke would persist in urging the Storyteller to think hard and think again about how they could help Adam and Eve.

One early evening, their routine was interrupted. "Do you think I might join you?" said a warm, sonorous voice.

The Storyteller stirred himself and looked up at the tall figure standing in front of him. He couldn't see the stranger's face because the sun was behind him. The Storyteller hesitated. There were several empty tables nearby.

"You never know," said the stranger. "I just might be able to help."

Luke recognised the voice and saw the white stick at the same time. "It's Kit," he minded to the Storyteller.

"It's Kit?" repeated the Storyteller incredulously.

"Don't sound so surprised," said Kit. "This is my old stomping ground. Anywhere between Fleet and the World's End pub at Almer. I thought I might run into you again."

"Ask him about the excursion to Prometheus' cave," Luke prompted the Storyteller.

"You can ask me yourself," Kit pointed out. Luke had forgotten that, like the Storyteller, Kit could hear him. "Yes, that was quite a trip, a bit out of my way, but well worth it. It's always a pleasure to see Prometheus again. Of course, he's a Titan but I feel a natural rapport with him. The trip also gave me a chance to cross swords, or should I say sticks, with Nick Peters. Always a special pleasure to give him a wallop."

"It was a bit more than a wallop," Luke observed, while wagging his tail vigorously and enjoying the welcoming pats that Kit was liberally bestowing on him. "You knocked him off Mount Strobilos into oblivion."

Kit laughed. "It takes more than a thwack with a stick and a tumble down a mountain to put an end to Peters. He's like dog poo. Once you've trodden in it, you just can't get rid of it."

Kit shook the Storyteller's hand warmly and resumed his patting of Luke. "Anyway, how are you? I'm surprised to find you lazing around in the Elm Tree, delightful drinking hole as it may be. I thought you were questors, man and dog of action. Incidentally, where are the others?"

The Storyteller recounted the events when they had returned to the present. "They killed Gwoat," the Storyteller ended. "They killed Gwoat in cold blood. They've detained the others. That's all we know but, given the way the security forces behaved at Stoney Cross, I shudder to think what is happening to them."

"Well shouldn't we find out?" said Kit. Luke wagged his tail even more vigorously.

"It's not that easy," said the Storyteller. "They set up a mysland, and a massive one at that. It's a mental construct…,"

Kit laughed. "It's all right. I know what a mysland is."

"In that case, you know we can't enter without permission and there's no reason on earth why they should let us in."

"We won't need permission," said Kit confidently. "I've entered a mysland many times before on my own, and this time, we are going to have some help."

"What help?" asked the Storyteller and Luke in unison.

With a flourish, Kit waved an arm and said: "Allow me to introduce Prune Leach and Andrew Rimzil, the engineers who modified the camper van, turning it from a rather mediocre touring vehicle of the twenty first century into an intergalactic charabanc."

Two ill-assorted figures approached. They had been chatting outside the entrance to the Elm Tree, waiting for Kit's signal. The taller of the two was a slim, distinguished looking man with a neatly trimmed, white moustache. He looked like a military man, straight-backed, disciplined and smartly dressed in a grey suit, white shirt and unexceptional tie. The other figure was shorter, squatter and really rather ugly. The brown skin of his face was wrinkled to the point where it seemed as though it must have been entirely folded and crushed at some time and then rather roughly and only partially re-inflated.

The newcomers were striking in their own right but, had anyone failed to notice them, the small creature that waddled between them would surely have caught the eye. "Isn't that a penguin?" asked Luke unnecessarily for it was unambiguously a penguin. "It's Optimius, their pet. Treat him well. Prune is very fond of him," minded Kit to Luke.

"Pull up some chairs and join us," said Kit. Once the newcomers were seated, Kit spoke. "It is always a mistake to judge by appearances. It's an error that it is easy for me to avoid," he said, tapping his white stick, "but one that so many others frequently make. Seated at this table are two of the greatest minds of their generation, both hailing from the Emerald Isle, one from the north," (he indicated Andrew Rimzil), "and one from the south," (Prune grinned and nodded an acknowledgment). "Gentlemen, I give you the inventors of the exponential drive and," he paused for effect, "the paradox device."

The Storyteller shook both men by the hand. "Gwoat told me so much about you. I owe you so much. I am truly delighted to meet you at last."

"I'll have a Guinness," said Andrew Rimzil.

"Make that four," said Prune. "Just giving the exponential drive a warm up," he explained. "And could you see whether they might have any raw fish going for nothing in the kitchen," he added. "Opt hasn't eaten since this morning and, although he always looks on the bright side, he needs fish even more than I need Guinness."

The four men and two animals settled down for a convivial evening. News of Gwoat's untimely and brutal death upset both Prune and Andrew but, as the Guinness flowed, they began to recall the good times they had shared with the camper van driver and gradually the pain of grief softened at least a little.

Luke tried to make conversation with Opt but he either didn't understand or had a savagely restricted vocabulary because, whatever Luke said, the penguin would just flap his flippers and declare "Yep, yep."

64 Understanding power

Adam was no longer held in solitary confinement.

The reason for this improvement in his treatment was odd. He had become angry. Sitting in his small cell he had started to think about the last few weeks. He had tried to make some sense of what he had been through, obviously no easy task but one for which, being in solitary confinement for most of the day, he had plenty of time. He had meticulously gone through each stage of the quest, from the ringing of the bell by the Storyteller at his home in Harrow, through the trip down the M3, M27 and A31, including the diversion to Hook, on to the Caucasus and then through the three extraordinary excursions to witness the three Beginnings. Whether he was any closer to the truth was far from clear but beyond doubt he had been given a new and uniquely privileged perspective.

That is the point at which anger replaced fear, the realisation that his enhanced perspective somehow went far beyond the confines of his imprisonment.

When the guard brought him his next meal, he had put the tray to one side and demanded to see the governor. The guard seemed confused. Adam was insistent. The guard said 'No'. Adam felt anger rising inside him and spreading out until it filled the whole of his cell. He did not shout. He did not threaten. The anger alone was sufficient. The guard said he would ask whether the governor would see him.

Within five minutes, Adam was in the governor's office. Adam had thought the governor and the Warden would be one and the same person but the governor was very different from the man who had sat in at Adam's first interview at Cadnam with Nick Peters. The governor was a thin, pallid, rather nervous looking fellow, one of nature's bureaucrats, ill-suited to dealing face to face with suspected terrorists or intergalactic questors.

Before the governor could speak, Adam took control. "You will treat me with respect," he said. "I will not return to my cell. If you have genuine concerns for the security of the realm I will stay and answer your questions. But you will listen to my answers and, if you have no evidence to contradict what I tell you, you will let me go. Do you understand?"

Adam felt at least as surprised as the governor at his boldness. "We have a job to do," the governor responded, "but, if you are prepared to be reasonable and co-operate, we can certainly conduct your cross-examination in a more civilised manner."

"Then that's settled," said Adam, "but I must warn you that, if you show any signs of reverting to the barbaric way in which I have been treated to date, you will regret it. Am I making myself clear?"

"You are a prisoner," the governor responded lamely.

"Am I?" said Adam. The answer made no sense. Then he added: "Stone walls do not a prison make," as though that made his position on the matter crystal clear.

oooOooo

After Adam had been conducted to a reception room on the prison floor where he could relax in a comfortable chair and pour himself a passable cup of coffee from the drinks vending machine, the governor picked up the phone. He spoke hurriedly to Nigel Vale. Nigel in turn phoned the Board Room. The room was full. All the Breaker directors were present and all eyes were on the flat-screen monitor. The light in the corner of the screen had turned amber. It flickered between green and amber several times while they watched but it settled in the end for a weak amber.

Nigel phoned the governor. "It's amber," he said. "A weak amber but definitely amber, not green. We must hope Nick Peters knows what he's doing."

65 Deconstruction

The Chief Dawk, Despiro Nihilopificus, arrived at Poulner in the early evening of the day when Nick had revealed Adam's infidelity to Eve.

He was greeted politely but coldly by Nick Peters. "How do you want to handle things?" Nick asked. "As I understand it, you're here to sort out Rambler. Do you want to deal with Rambler on his own, or do you want Eve and Numpty to be present?"

"I will take all three together," said Despiro, "but before I begin, I should like some light refreshment and an hour to gather my thoughts and prepare myself."

'Great,' thought Nick. 'It's a matter of extreme urgency. It's so urgent Nigel Vale has to terminate my breakfast half way through. And when the Master Dawk arrives, what does he do? He decides he needs light refreshments and an hour to prepare himself.'

"Of course," said Nick.

Despiro made himself comfortable in the study, a quiet room, well-suited to the undisturbed contemplation he required, and sipped a cup of tea. Dawks (Deconstruction Administered With Kindness) were a humourless lot. They provided the intellectual under-pinning of the Breakers' operation and ultimately the justification for their existence but Dawking was, in many ways, a dull and uninspiring profession.

Unlike Nick, Despiro was conscious of the scale of the challenge he faced and the very serious, possibly cataclysmic, consequences of failure. He was certainly not going to underestimate his assignment or the individuals whom he needed to deconstruct.

The Chief Dawk decided to start work after Eve and her fellow questors had finished dinner. He wanted them to feel replete and relaxed. When they were seated in the drawing room, Despiro made his entrance and introduced himself.

"I have only one purpose in being here," he said after the exchange of names. "It is to help you to return to your normal lives as soon and as easily as possible."

"And how are you planning to do that?" Eve asked.

Despiro allowed the hint of a smile to replace the otherwise permanently serious and solemn expression which had years before taken up more or less permanent residence on his face. "I suppose my real task is to sort out misunderstandings. I'm an analyser and a clarifier. Give me a complex problem and I will tease it apart until anyone can see, however impenetrable it might seem, it is just made up of simple components which anyone can understand."

"Interesting," was Eve's only response.

"So how can you assist us?" asked Rambler. Anyone who suggested he could help them back to their own lives deserved a hearing and, in any case, this Despiro Nihilopificus had a certain air about him, a quiet confidence and, most encouragingly, an aura of sincerity. Rambler took some pride in his ability to judge a man by his demeanour. The moment the Chief Dawk had introduced himself, Rambler had felt confident the stranger was an honest man.

"I think it best to start from the point when, as I understand it, the problem began. Adam is under suspicion of involvement in terrorism or at least some involvement with those who are suspected of being terrorists. This suspicion seems to be based on two interconnected factors; first, the one you call the Storyteller, who has been under surveillance for years; second, your disappearance from our view for the last two weeks. If you could tell me about the relationship you have with the Storyteller and what you have been doing for the last two weeks, I'm sure we can make real progress in clearing this mess up."

"Clearing up this mess," said Numpty.

"Quite," said Despiro.

"Quite right," said Rambler.

"I understand you have been on some kind of journey," the Chief Dawk prompted.

"Before we tell you anything," Eve responded, "I have a question. In this country, in any decent country, a person is innocent until proved guilty, or at least can't be treated as though they are guilty until some evidence of wrongdoing has been produced. There is no evidence against Adam or any of us. So why should we have to answer your questions? Why are we being held? And, for that matter, why on earth did the security people shoot an unarmed man? Why did they murder Gwoat?"

"I do not have sufficient information to answer all your questions," said Despiro, "but I'll answer those I can. In normal circumstances, you are absolutely right. Innocent until proved guilty. Absolutely. But these are not normal circumstances. The authorities have reliable information that there is a plan, a plot, to subvert the government, to destabilise the status quo, to overthrow all the pillars of the state. If the plot is successful, there will be no chance at all of due process, no chance at all of a fair trial, no chance of any kind of justice. So, in these extraordinary circumstances, we have to take extraordinary measures."

"So to preserve our system of justice, we have to adopt unjust methods. That sounds a bit contradictory to me," said Eve. "And who decides? I'm suspicious of you. I'm suspicious of Nick Peters. I am suspicious of everyone we've met since we returned to Stoney Cross. What's more, I've some incontrovertible evidence, evidence of a cold-blooded murder, evidence of kidnapping, evidence of abusive treatment. So why aren't you under arrest?"

"I have come here to help," Despiro replied. He had known it would not be easy but he had not expected such hostility, such aggression, such incisiveness. "I represent the authorities. You cannot draw a parallel between your position and mine."

"So those in power decide, that's what you're saying," said Eve. "I just hope you realise how dangerous that is. Anyone in authority can decide to suspect anyone they don't like and their victim can then be arrested, detained, interrogated without charge and without legal representation. It's a tyrant's charter."

"Your point is nicely made but sadly your objections are not really helping us with the matter in hand. If I am to facilitate your release, I need to know who you have been with and what you have been doing for the last two weeks, since you set out from your house in Harrow."

"Whom," said Numpty. "With whom."

"We set out to find something," said Eve. "We thought we were looking for the truth but I think we were looking for meaning. I wanted to know if there was any point."

"Any point?" Despiro queried.

"Yes, any point, any point to anything. I mean we didn't ask for any of this. We arrive here involuntarily. We're born as a particular person and at a particular time in a particular place. We are stuck with who we are. What's the point?"

"Yes, that's right," said Numpty. "I've often wondered why we are born clever or stupid, beautiful or ugly, strong or weak. It doesn't seem very fair but that's just the way it is. And that's the way it is, not for one day, or for one month or one year, but for all the days of our lives. We don't get a chance to be beautiful if we're ugly; we don't get a chance to be clever if we're stupid. Not even for one day. Not even once. We're stuck with what we are, even though we didn't ask to be here and we certainly didn't agree to take pot luck when the brains and the looks were handed out."

"That's not quite true," Uncle Rambler objected gently. "We both know what extraordinary progress one can make with effort and diligence. You, my boy, have earned everyone's admiration with your determination to better yourself in every way."

Numpty preened himself a little but then objected: "Yes, but for some people it is easy and for others it is so hard."

"I'm sorry," Despiro interrupted, "but I think we are drifting away

348

from the matter in hand. Eve, you said you wanted to know if there was any point. I need to understand what you mean by that question."

"I think it's self-explanatory," Eve responded. "Is there any point to anything? Does it matter whether I live or not? Do I matter? Did my daughter Bella matter? If Bella had been alive today, she would be a beautiful ten year old girl, with all her life before her. She might have done anything, become anything, achieved anything. As it is, she died. She won't fulfil any of the promise she showed, or any of the ambitions she had or might have had. Does it matter that she died? Does it matter that she lived? So I say again, is there any point?"

"I see," declared Despiro, seemingly relieved. "Of course there is a point. Almost everything has a point. The point of ploughing land is to prepare it for sowing seeds; the point of sowing seeds is for crops to grow; the point of growing crops is to provide food to eat; the point of eating is to sustain life."

"Yes, of course," said Eve. "But these are little purposes. They are things we do to achieve little goals. They make sense for us in particular circumstances. But I am asking why bother?"

"Because, if you did not, you would starve."

"You don't understand," said Eve. "Of course we wouldn't want to starve because we are alive and starving would be horrible. That's not what I'm suggesting. What I'm asking is this. Would it matter in any sense if we weren't here to eat or to starve?"

"I still don't understand fully what you mean." Despiro seemed genuinely puzzled.

"Perhaps I can help," Rambler offered. "As you may know we have been on a quest, a rather epic quest by all accounts. We've all been looking for something. We can call that something the truth, or a truth, or meaning, or purpose. It doesn't really matter what we call it. Whatever we call it, it is, in the final analysis, simply a justification for existence, all existence, my existence, your existence, this table's existence, the planet's existence, the existence of the universe and everything in it."

"I see," said Despiro. He had dealt with this kind of problem before. There was a cast of mind that really felt at home only when pondering the largest abstract questions. The best way to deal with such ideological speculators was to rein them in, bring them back to earth, compel them to be more precise in use of language and in their definitions of questions. "And in the course of your epic quest," Despiro prompted, "what did you find?"

"We found that some of the standard attempts to explain and justify existence were wholly inadequate. We found God to be a rather considerable disappoint-ment. We were better received and advised by the Titan Prometheus but he was behind the times, so to speak, and told us little we did not already know."

"So are you saying you learned little from your quest?" Despiro asked. Clearly it was best to go along with their account, resisting the temptation to point out the impossibility of their claimed encounters with mythic beings.

"We went on three excursions," Numpty spoke. "We saw the three Beginnings. My uncle learned something very important." He knew that his uncle had discovered something but was not sure exactly what it was so he decided not to elaborate.

Despiro looked to Rambler for an explanation.

"I am of the view," said Rambler, "that existence has a sense of direction." He paused for the significance of his pronouncement to sink in.

After the silence, Despiro Nihilopificus, the master Dawk, responded. "I have no wish to be disrespectful but surely you can see you are attributing a human characteristic to a largely inanimate phenomenon. Things don't have a sense of direction. Seen by humans, we can conclude that things fulfil a function but they themselves don't have a sense of anything, let alone a sense of direction."

Rambler seemed a little taken aback at the Dawk's peremptory dismissal of his theory. "You think that I am simply projecting my own perception of purpose on to reality."

Numpty too was disappointed. His uncle was always ready to listen to the opinion of others but he rarely ceded any ground. He never conceded defeat.

"Let me be absolutely honest with you," Despiro began.

"Excuse me, sir," Numpty interrupted. "Have you been less than honest with us before? You said you were here to help us, to facilitate our release. Was that true? Were you being honest? And if you were being honest, were you being absolutely honest? Are there degrees of honesty? Is absolutely honest more honest than just honest?"

A rare smile hovered on Despiro's lips. "I know you went on three of the Storyteller's excursions. I know you witnessed the three Beginnings – the creation of the universe, the birth of life, the emergence of human consciousness. All very impressive, I don't doubt. He took you to these events in chronological sequence but collapsing thirteen thousand million years into fewer than thirteen days, he gave you a false impression. He performed rather a lot of ruthless existential editing, if you like. By omitting the aeons of trial and error, the laborious process of evolution, he gave you the impression of a purposeful sequence."

"We're not disputing evolution," said Eve, "nor how long it all took."

"Of course not," Rambler confirmed what Eve had said: "but I at least am suggesting that, however long it took, it had a sense of direction. The events we saw need not have happened. The fact that they did happen and that they all seemed to be part of a process, whereby the universe is becoming more self-aware, has to be significant."

"What do you mean by a sense of direction?" Despiro asked. He was more than happy for Rambler to pursue this line of thought. He might have some difficulty in proving Rambler wrong. He might even have difficulty in sustaining his own position. But at least, if they stuck to this line of speculation, there would be no risk of a Fourth Beginning. "Are you suggesting some divine purpose, a creator, a God?"

"No," said Rambler. "I like to think of myself as a man of reason. I cannot infer from a sense of direction that there is a divine navigator but I can dispute the notion that the history of the universe is a random sequence of events. If it was, there would be no direction and the odds against us arriving where we are today would be beyond computation."

Despiro frowned a little. "No one is suggesting an entirely random process. As you will know, the evolution of life is predicated on a mechanism, the survival of the fittest. It's not random. Those best fitted to survive in a given environment outbreed those less well fitted."

"Was Bella ill-fitted to survive?" Eve asked.

"That was an accident," Despiro responded gently. He knew from briefings and his own research he was treading on sensitive ground. "The survival of the fittest relates to species, rather than individuals."

"The problem is that you don't seem to understand what we are saying," said Eve, weary of what seemed to her to be a fairly meaningless discussion. "Rambler is asking you why any of this happened. Why did nothing become something? Why did dust become animate? Why did our ancestors develop self-consciousness? Do you have an answer? Are you going to say that that is just the way things are because, if that is your view, you're wasting your time and ours. As for me, I'm not really interested in any of these universal questions. I just want to know why my Bella died. And don't tell me it was just an accident. Of course it was an accident. I'm not stupid."

Eve was angry and Eve was confused. Had Adam really slept with some woman while they were in Prometheus' cave? As far as she could remember he had been with her most of the time. And wasn't Pandora supposed to have been the source of all the evils that beset Man? With that kind of reputation he would have to be a moron to embark on an illicit relationship with such a woman. But then men were capable of imbecilic behaviour in some circumstances, especially when the slut in question was 'irresistible'.

"I really don't see the need for an explanation," Despiro responded to Eve's challenge, "except to determine, step by step, how things moved from where they were at the beginning to where they are now. There is no other kind of explanation. Any other type of explanation is pure speculation, unprovable, untestable and therefore irrelevant."

"Why do living things wish to survive and reproduce?" asked Numpty. "I mean why do they bother?"

"Because it is in the nature of living things to do so," said Despiro.

"That's just the way things are?" Eve mocked. "That's pathetic. Numpty asked why. Either you don't understand the question or you don't have an answer."

"I think our friend means that certain features, certain qualities of reality are given," suggested Rambler, trying to help out the Master Dawk. "For example, all the rules of physics; the qualities of the chemical elements; and the survival instinct in living things."

"What! They're all just given," said Eve. "No explanation. That's it."

"You persist in asking 'why' questions," said Despiro almost petulantly. "We know how things happen and often, when we know the 'how', we can see the 'why'. But no one can answer the ultimate 'why' questions."

"But they are the ones we're asking," said Eve.

"They are, after all, the most important questions," Rambler added.

"You know the reason for everything and the meaning of nothing," said Eve.

Eve was upset and angry. She felt the need to release her feelings. This grey man who claimed he could help them to freedom but seemed far more interested in finding out what they had learned on their quest, this Despiro Nihilopificus, was a perfect target. "You don't seem to be a particularly stupid man," Eve began, "but I have to say that your inability to grasp the questions we are asking suggests your vision is severely restricted. You're the type of person who seriously believes that the true nature of a painting is best understood by studying each dab of paint on the canvas. You believe the best way to appreciate a building is to point out is it made of a large number of bricks. You think the secret of a Shakespeare sonnet is best understood by counting the number of syllables in each line. You look down rather than up; you look in rather than out; you look back rather than forward. You tell us everything happened by chance and then you think you prove your point by explaining how one thing led to another. But you don't ask why there should be one thing; you don't ask why it led to the next thing. Why it didn't just stop or lead to something else. I've no doubt you could explain in meticulous detail how van Gogh painted a wheat field, how he mixed his paints, chose his colours, applied his brush. But you can't say why he painted that wheat field; why he became a painter; what he intended when he chose to paint."

Despiro shook his head, in the manner of a parent trying to deal with a fractious child. "I can see you are emotionally disturbed," he said. "We can continue another time when you are more," he paused to choose the right word, "settled."

Eve's eyes blazed. "Don't patronise me. I'm no more emotionally disturbed than the situation warrants. I thought you were going to help us to get out of here. I'm not planning on settling."

"Looking back rather than forward," said Rambler, addressing the Chief Dawk. "That's a really important point. Your explanations make sense looking back, simply because whatever happened, happened. You don't have to explain why, of all the things that could have happened, only that one thing actually happened. The problem becomes clearer when you look forward. It's rather like the weather. We can have a detailed and entirely accurate account of the weather for every day over the last ten years. But we still cannot predict what the weather will be in the next ten days, although we know, in ten days' time, the weather in those intervening ten days will become part of our entirely accurate historical record. Looking back is one thing; looking forward is a different story."

Numpty, who had fallen behind the conversation a little but was keen to catch up, suddenly spoke: "All these things that are 'given', you know, the physics and the chemistry and the survival thing. Given by whom?"

When the Chief Dawk left the questors, he was not displeased. There was little if any sign of the threatened Fourth Beginning. The only thing that troubled him was Eve's remark that he knew the reason for everything and the meaning of nothing. Despiro was incapable of formulating aphorisms himself but he knew one when he saw one, or heard one. It was just that type of glib formulation that inexplicably could do so much damage to the Dawks' cause. People liked that kind of thing. They would repeat it to each other in pubs and parks and at dinner parties. They would say, "You know those Dawks; they know the reason for everything and the meaning of nothing." It was really irritating, especially because, as far as Despiro could see, if you took the statement apart, it didn't mean a bean.

66 Rebound

The following day, early in the morning, Nick and Despiro drove up to Cadnam together. Nick left Grimrose at Poulner, with instructions to keep a general eye on things.

"I hope everything went well," said Nick to Despiro as they drove out of the grounds of the house.

"From my side, I am confident the problem can be contained," said the Chief Dawk. "There is no sign that Eve or indeed any of them is in a position to trigger a Fourth Beginning. Eve seemed preoccupied with other matters and in a rather emotional state. Rambler can be quite challenging but he is no threat. He is marching with considerable determination in the wrong direction. As for his nephew Numpty, well, far from sniffing around the Fourth Beginning, I'm not sure he's even fully reached the Third. If you are playing your part, I think we can be well-satisfied with progress to date."

Why was it, Nick thought to himself, that everything the Chief Dawk said, however seemingly positive or polite, somehow put him down? Nick considered challenging Despiro to explain what he meant by 'If you are playing your part' but thought better of it. He knew what the Dawk would say: 'I am simply stating the fact that you and I are jointly responsible for this operation and that since I have been successful, we only need to make sure you are equally successful for us both to know we have both been successful'. In that way, by treating him as though he was stupid, Nihilopificus would add a second insult while in effect confirming the first. So Nick tried a different tack.

"Eve's preoccupation and her emotional turmoil, both as you say pivotal in the satisfactory outcome of your session with them, were my doing. Earlier yesterday, I revealed to Eve that Adam had been unfaithful to her. On this visit to Cadnam, I shall put the last piece of my strategy in place and we should be able to report to the Breaker Board that the job is done."

"Before we report success," said Despiro, ignoring Nick's crude attempt to appropriate credit for the Dawk's achievements, "we had best ensure there are no loose ends. As I understand it, the Breaker Board had reason to be seriously concerned. We would be wise to ensure we have entirely closed off the possibility of a Fourth Beginning before any premature triumphalist claims."

He's done it again, thought Nick – the effortless put down. Must have been to Balliol.

On arrival at Cadnam, Nick was surprised and then enraged that

Adam had been allowed out of his cell. He questioned the prison governor, who explained that Adam had agreed to co-operate with their investigations if treated better and, in the absence of any explicit instructions to the contrary, the governor had decided to give it a try.

"And what have you gained by adopting this benign approach?" Nick demanded. "What valuable information has Adam divulged?"

The governor conceded that they had learned nothing new but added that, since they didn't know what type of information was sought, lack of progress was not entirely surprising.

Nick's anger did not abate. "I decide how the prisoner is to be kept. Your decision was inappropriate. I shall report your conduct to the Board. What can you have been thinking?"

The governor decided not to mention that Adam had unexpectedly asserted himself and to some extent had somehow compelled the governor to release him from his cell. Compelled was too strong a word. Persuaded was better, except that it was persuasion by force of will rather than by word. "If we knew why we were holding him and what we wanted from him, it would be easier," said the governor, part question, part excuse.

"You don't need to know," Nick snapped. "All you need to know is that you don't do anything without my permission and, when I've finished with Adam today, you put him back in his cell and leave him there until I tell you to release him. Is that clear?"

The governor nodded.

When Adam was brought to Nick in the interrogation room, Nick immediately noticed that Adam had acquired a new self-assurance. His success in persuading his keepers to allow him out of his cell had clearly increased his confidence. Not at all what Nick wanted.

"I see you are in better shape," said Nick.

"Not surprisingly," said Adam. "I don't know who you people are but it cannot be legal to treat me the way I have been treated and, when I get out of here, I'm going to make sure there is an investigation and those who have broken the law are punished. I'll be surprised if anybody here has a job by the time I've finished."

"If you've finished, or even if you haven't, I suggest you shut the fuck up!" said Nick. "We need to get one or two things straight. First, we haven't finished with you yet, not by a long chalk. You are suspected of involvement in terrorism and, unless or until we can clear your name, you will stay here. Do you understand?"

Adam's eyes blazed. He said nothing.

"If your name is cleared, you will not be released unless you sign the Official Secrets Act, which will prevent you from talking to anyone about your treatment here. Let me explain something very clearly. If you don't sign the OSA, you will not be released. If you sign it, but we suspect you are thinking you can do what you like once you are freed, you will not be released. If you are released and make any effort to talk to anyone, you will be found dead, in circumstances which strongly but wrongly suggest suicide. Am I getting through to you?"

Nick was pleased to see Adam's courage was giving way once more to fear.

"I thought you were here to help me," said Adam.

"My job is to get to the truth. If the truth will help you, I'm here to help you."

Despite all his concerns, Adam noted the irony in Peters' claim that he wanted to get to the truth. After all that's what he and Eve had been trying to do from the start, and it was what Peters had done everything possible to prevent them from finding. Clearly, Peters' truth was different in kind from what they had been seeking. "How is Eve?" asked Adam. "Is she still being held? Can I talk to her?"

"Ah," said Nick, "Eve. I'm afraid Eve is a little upset."

"Upset?" Adam choked. "What have you done to her?"

"We have done nothing to her, at least nothing to harm her. I'm afraid I had to tell her something that she found upsetting, that's all."

"What did you tell her?"

"I told her I was hopeful you would be released soon," said Nick.

"And that upset her?"

"No, of course not," Nick laughed. "No, it was the reason why you might be released. I explained to her that I was pretty sure I knew what it was you felt guilty about, what it was that was making the interrogators suspicious you were hiding something."

"Which was?"

"Your brief affair with Pandora," said Nick. "You made love to Pandora when we were in Prometheus' cave. If I can persuade the interrogators that is what you felt guilty about, they are much more likely to release you."

Adam was stunned and disturbed. How did Nick know about that strange experience with Pandora? And it wasn't an affair, anyway. Somehow Eve had turned into Pandora. It had not been his intention. How had Nick known and why had he told Eve? He asked only the last question.

"I had to explain why I was optimistic they would release you. When you spoke to her on the phone, you made it pretty clear you didn't accept blame for Bella's death. She knows you're not involved in terrorism. There had to be some other reason for your guilt. So I thought 'Why not tell the truth?'."

"But it's not the truth. I was with Eve. I was making love to Eve and then somehow she turned into this other woman."

Nick laughed. "I've heard some pretty rum excuses from errant husbands in my time but that's a new one. I wasn't screwing someone else dear; it was really you. You just didn't happen to be there at the time. I've heard of men making love to their wives while thinking of some else. This is the first time I've heard of someone making love to someone else and imagining it's their wife."

"What did she say?" asked Adam.

"Well, as you can guess, she wasn't best pleased."

"I need to talk to her, to explain what happened."

"I'd give that a miss if I were you. I don't think telling her you mistook Pandora for your own wife is likely to cut it. Anyway, don't worry. I'm sure it'll blow over. After all, if it doesn't, it would be rather like the pot calling the kettle black."

It took a moment for Nick's last remark to sink in.

"What do you mean by 'the pot calling the kettle black'?"

"It's just an expression. It means the accuser is just as bad as the accused."

"I know what it means. Why did you say it? Are you suggesting Eve has been having an affair."

"Come on," said Nick. "We're all adults. It's no big deal."

"What are you saying?" Adam's voice carried a mixture of trepidation and revulsion.

"What I'm saying is this", said Nick, his tone changed. "I'm sick of you, your hypocrisy, your insecurity and your whining. I've decided it's time you had a taste of hell. You think you were ill-treated in your cell. Well now you will find out what the Breakers can do, what Breakers do best. I'm sending you into the bowels of this building where Breakers perform their finest work. If you survive, you will be interrogated when hell has finished with you. If the interrogators are satisfied you are irreversibly damaged mentally or simply have nothing useful to tell them, they will ask me what to do with you. I will then decide. I will be frank with you. In many ways it would be easier, neater, tidier if you disappeared, or never emerged from hell, so, if it comes to it, it's up to you to persuade me that you should live."

Adam was taken away. He didn't struggle. He didn't resist.

oooOooo

Nick went straight to the office of the Chief Dawk. He knocked and entered. "I think that will do it," he said as he flopped down into the chair opposite Despiro. Eve is disturbed. Adam is distraught. They are both utterly confused, as of now. I'm giving Adam a spell in hell, just to make sure. When they meet, they will have so many misunderstandings to resolve, so many doubts, uncertainties and fears to work through that, even if their relationship survives, they are unlikely to do any more questing this side of the grave."

67 Intent on rescue

The six of them, four men, a dog and a penguin, sat around the table outside the Elm Tree pub, conspirators planning the boldest and most dangerous of ventures.

"You say you know how to break into this mysland phenomenon," said the Storyteller to Kit. "Pray tell how."

"It's not so difficult," Kit replied. "A construction of that size has to have seams. The mysland holding our friends is particularly large. It will have several seams. What do you think Prune?"

Prune Leach was on his fifth Guinness of the evening. He was in an unusually benign mood but otherwise unaffected by the alcohol. "If the mysland stretches from Ringwood to Cadman, it's my guess there would be maybe twelve seams. And I'll tell you this for nothing, or for another Guinness when this one's done, given the drain on the Breakers' power supply in maintaining a mysland of this size, I'd be surprised if we couldn't get in through any one of the twelve."

"We will need to pick our time carefully," Andrew Rimzil added. "The Breakers will be using reserve generators to maintain the mysland. If we wait for a change-over to the reserves or back to the main generators, we should be able to slip through a crack. What we need is an imperfect seal."

"This is really good news," Luke whispered to Optimius, the penguin, who, although unable to communicate with humans, except for 'yepping', could understand the dog without difficulty.

"Yep, yep, yep", said Opt, as the penguin was known to friends.

Of course, as a sanguine penguin, Opt had from the start assumed they would find a way into the mysland. Indeed, despite the absence of any evidence on which to base his optimism, he had assumed the venture as a whole would be a total success. But his enthusiastic yepping related not to the favourable omens for the venture but to Rimzil's reference to an imperfect seal. In their natural habitat, penguins and seals were not particularly close but, given the inevitable loneliness that goes with being the pet of humans, the possibility of meeting a creature with a similar background and common interests was very exciting. The descriptive adjective 'imperfect' could be seen as either intriguing or worrying but, given his sanguine disposition, he put out of his mind the thought that the seal might be in some way mentally or physically disabled and chose to focus on the possibility that she, for he assumed the seal would be female, would have enjoyed a rich and interesting life, with many marine stories to tell of errors of judgement and some minor misdeeds.

The Storyteller, who could hear Opt's thoughts, made a mental note of the penguin's expectations.

"So when do we start?" asked Prune.

"There's no time like the present," Kit answered.

A few weeks ago, Luke would have quipped, for the benefit of the Storyteller and the penguin, since only they could hear him, 'There's no time but the present'. Two weeks on and much the wiser, Luke now knew there were many times other than the present, some pretty-much fixed in the past, others, unknown and unknowable in the future.

"We can't go anywhere till I've finished this drink," said Prune.

So they waited for Prune to down his fifth pint. Then Kit spoke. "Men, and animals, we can enter the mysland, I am sure. But I have to warn you that, once inside, we will be in a world entirely under the control of our enemies. Everyone within the mysland is compelled to fulfil the will of the mysland master. We will find no friends; no one will help us. What is more, if the mysland master decides to imprison or kill us, we will not even have the satisfaction as we languish in jail or dangle from a noose that he may eventually be brought to justice. Within the mysland, his is the only justice. So, if any of you, man, dog or penguin, wish to excuse yourselves, now is the time to do it. I would just like to say no one will think any the worse of you. But I can't because, if you do decide to drop out, the rest of us will inevitably think of you as cowardly little shits."

"I'll drink to that," declared Prune, putting the now empty glass to his lips and then whacking it down on to the table in disappointment.

"Very well," said Kit. "One of us must stay here. We need an anchor in the real world. Someone we can trust and who will help us to escape the mysland when we have rescued the prisoners. That is your job," he addressed the Storyteller.

The Storyteller nodded his acceptance.

"Let's go," said Prune, who rose to his feet with remarkable alacrity. He then added, with just the hint of a slur: "Gentlemen, the first thing we need to relieve on this epic venture is my bladder."

When Prune had made himself comfortable, the rescue team set off for Ringwood, which offered the nearest approach to the perimeter of the mysland. "We are close," said Kit, who evidently was using a sense other than sight to locate the mysland boundary.

"That's it," said Andrew Rimzil, indicating a large chestnut tree. "Look at the trunk. It's just a little blurred."

Sure enough that trunk was just a little frayed at the edges. This was one of the many points at which the mysland had been stapled to the real world and, although it was almost exact, there was a slight mis-registration between the real chestnut and the mysland version.

"I don't think the gap is big enough," said Prune. "I'm the smallest and even I couldn't squeeze through."

"You're not the smallest," said Kit.

Opt padded forward towards the slit between the real and the fabricated tree. "Be careful," advised Luke.

'No,' thought Opt, 'I'm going to be extraordinarily reckless. Why do people and articulate dogs always say things like that? They say: "Take care" or "Drive carefully". Oh thanks, if you hadn't said that, obviously I was going to drive like a total maniac, eyes tight shut, pissed as a newt. Without your salutary advice I was almost certainly going to drive straight into a brick wall at around a hundred miles an hour. No, of course I'm going to be careful and there's no need to worry. 'Worry' has no place in the vocabulary of a sanguine penguin. I know what to do and I know I shall succeed.'

These were Opt's thoughts. What he said was: "Yep, yep, yep."

The penguin slipped through the crack with ease but, on reaching the other side, he encountered a large, soft, grey mound which blocked his path. Using his flippers, he slapped the mound to determine its nature and whether it might be possible to peck a hole in it.

"Don't do that again," said a rich contralto voice.

Opt jumped back a little disconcerted. He could now see that the mound was a living creature, a big fat, living creature.

"Sorry," said Opt, "I just need to pass."

"Who are you and why should I let you pass?" said the deep, soft voice. Unlike Prune and Andrew, this creature understood him, not at all like the humans who apparently heard only 'Yep', whatever he said.

"I am Optimius, widely known as Opt, the sanguine penguin. And you are?"

"I am Elsa the seal, and don't ask me why I am here. I feel very much like a fish out of water, except obviously I am not a fish but a marine mammal."

That explained Opt's enhanced communication competence. Elsa was of his kind, an aquatic creature, with almost certainly a similar background and cultural reference points.

"Well Elsa," said Opt, joyful at having met a kindred spirit, "I'm really sorry to have bumped into you in one sense; but I'm delighted in another. I love my masters but they are human and therefore largely insensitive to the needs of aquatic life forms. For example, they do not seem able to hear what I'm saying. Indeed, whatever I say, all they hear is 'Yep, Yep, Yep'. With you, I can be myself. Are you not the renowned imperfect seal, the very creature we seek who, although morally flawed, could nevertheless be of crucial help in our venture and thus become the stuff of legends which, serendipitously, brings to mind the subject of leg ends? I've always wondered about the flippers of seals which are, I assume, vestigial legs rather like my flippers are vestigial wings. It's odd how both of us started out as creatures of other elements but both found a way to convert what enabled us to move on land or through the air into flippers that have given us mastery of the oceans. I suppose, in a way, one could say your leg ends constitute a crucial part of your legend." Opt was so excited at the opportunity to converse with a fellow seafarer that the words gushed out like an incoming tide.

"You say your masters cannot understand what you say," said the seal in a languid voice. "Is it possible that you say so much so quickly that their ears have become impaired?"

Opt's enthusiasm for his new friend was a little unrealistic. The disparity in size alone was sufficient to impede what Opt saw as their burgeoning relationship. Opt himself was a modest half a metre in height, weighing about four kilos. Elsa was a large earless seal about three metres long and 1000 kilograms in weight. She maintained her considerable bulk by consuming a varied diet, including penguins, which, had she not been recently well-fed, might have constituted a further impediment to the deepening of their friendship.

Being perfectly suited to aquatic life, Elsa found movement on land difficult and onerous. She had therefore been deemed ideal by the mysland designers as a sentient means of blocking any weak or defective seams in their construction. Massive in size, unable to move, her only duty was to report any attempts to interfere with the mysland boundary.

"I have to report your incursion," said Elsa. "Sorry," she added, for she could see the penguin meant no harm.

"Don't do that," said Opt. "We've come to rescue some people who have been unjustly imprisoned by the authorities. You can help us."

"I have a duty to report you," Elsa replied. "And who is 'we'?"

"I have some friends with me, all good people."

At this moment, Luke stuck his head through the tear in the seam, now slightly enlarged by Opt's passage. "How's it going?" enquired the dog. "Any problems?"

"None at all," replied the ebullient penguin. I've located the imperfect seal and, if we can persuade her not to report our incursion, I'm pretty sure she could become a valuable ally."

"Give me one good reason why I shouldn't report you," demanded

Elsa.

"Let my friends through and I guarantee they will be able to give you half a dozen," urged Opt.

Two factors worked to the rescuers' advantage. First, Elsa was curious. She had been put on guard duty at the edge of myslands before and nothing had ever happened. No one had tried to get in and no one had tried to get out. Each shift had been mind-numbingly tedious. The second factor was a non-conformist, rebellious streak in her which had frequently led her to misbehave. Hence the soubriquet 'imperfect'.

"Very well, they can enter, on condition that they give me at least one good reason why I should be so co-operative with you and disobedient to the mysland masters."

With that, Elsa heaved herself round and sliced down through the defective seam with her tail, opening up a slit long enough for Kit, Prune and Andrew to squeeze through.

"Put the flaps back together," urged Kit. Andrew and Prune held the flaps in place. Kit ran his hand down the join and it seemed to meld together. "That'll do," said Kit. "It won't hold for long but it will prevent the alarm from sounding and we should be out of here before it splits. If we're not, they will have caught us, so it won't matter very much."

"Well?" said Elsa expectantly. As with Luke, so with Elsa, the blind man was able to hear and understand the language of animals.

"Well what?" asked Kit. Luke explained to Kit that Elsa wanted something in return for her compliance. "So you want a reward?" said Kit.

"We are giving you the opportunity to do some good," suggested Andrew

"Virtue is its own reward," offered Prune helpfully.

"I will tell you your future," said Kit.

"Oh, yes?" said a sceptical Elsa. "So what are you? A fortune teller? A seer? A wizard?"

"I'll tell you little of your past. If I am right, you will believe I can see the future."

"That's not very logical," said the seal, "but, if you get every detail right, I'll give you the benefit of the doubt."

"You have quite a few brothers and sisters; you have little recollection of your early years, perhaps because they were so happy that few specifics registered; you have a small scar under your right flipper; and sometimes, about every four hours, you fall asleep for a few moments, lulled by a gentle buzzing sound."

Elsa was stunned. Being a fairly unimportant element of the

364

mysland, the Breaker engineers had provided no more than a rudimentary memory store for the seal. Kit was therefore precisely correct in suggesting she had only a hazy recollection of the past. He was also right in telling her she was one of many siblings. The engineers had used all her brothers and sisters as sentient guards. She hadn't seen the scar which was concealed under her flipper but there surely was a small sore area where he had predicted the scar to be and it was certainly true that, regular as clockwork, she nodded off briefly every four hours to the sound of a gentle buzzing.

"Fair enough," said Elsa. "Don't know how you did it but you've got me down to a tee! I think you know more about me than I know myself."

"If you help us, I know I can give you something as valuable to you as life itself," said Kit.

"Well, you seem like someone I can trust and you passed the test with flying colours, so let's give it a go. What do you want me to do?"

"In about an hour, you will have one of your drowsy spells. I want you to stay awake until the buzzing stops."

"That's it?"

"Yes, that's it. If you can do the same four hours later and then again once more, after another four hours, you will give us enough time for us to rescue the prisoners and for me to reward you for your help before we leave."

"I think I can do that," said Elsa. "I shall probably be very sleepy by the end but, for something as precious as life itself, whatever that might be, it's worth the effort."

"To help you and bolster your resolve, Opt will stay with you," said Kit.

Elsa was unimpressed but raised no objection. Opt was less happy. "It won't be much of an adventure if you leave me here at the edge of the mysland," he minded to Kit.

"What's a mysland?" asked Elsa.

Kit ignored the seal's question. The less Elsa knew the better.

"I'm giving you perhaps the most important part to play in the entire venture," said Kit to Opt. "If Elsa nods off and transmits our arrival to the Breaker monitors, there is no way we can succeed. It is therefore fair to say your role is pivotal."

Opt was mollified, his natural positivity quickly reasserting itself. He was, after all, a very sanguine penguin.

"Very well, that's settled," said Kit. "No time to lose."

68 Conflict and resolution

While Kit and his companions were breaching the mysland boundary, Nick was reporting to the Breaker Board. He had explained the situation to Nigel Vale, who was satisfied the threat of a Fourth Beginning had been averted. Nick also had the tacit support of Despiro Nihilopificus, who endorsed the view that the danger had been eliminated but mainly because, in his discussion with Eve and Rambler, he had seen no real evidence of any danger in the first place. Eve had been feisty and Rambler had been curious; but Eve seemed confused and wrapped up in her own problems of death and betrayal, Bella's death and Adam's betrayal, while Rambler's quest for understanding was taking him down a blind alley.

"I think I can say with confidence that the project has been successfully concluded." Nick was making an heroic effort to conceal his self-satisfaction. "When Adam emerges from hell, I propose to release him and reunite him with his wife."

"Is that wise?" asked a Breaker Board member. "Would it not be better to hold Adam for a while longer or dispose of him altogether?"

'Do you have to be thick to become a Board member or does being a Board member make you thick?' Nick wondered. He had explained to them precisely how he was going to take Adam and Eve and their relationship apart. He'd told them how he was destroying the trust that underpinned their marriage; how he had carefully invoked guilt about Bella's death and then thrown confused resentment about sexual infidelity into the mix. Even the Board must see that, if all this preparatory work was to reach the intended climax, Adam and Eve had to be reunited, rather like firing two packages of uranium at each other to produce a nuclear explosion. That was the whole point. To fail to reunite the couple or, worse, to eliminate one of them altogether, would jeopardise the entire project. It would allow the survivor to process the experience, to reflect, even possibly to understand. Was that what the Board wanted?

Nigel Vale intervened before Nick could deliver a reply resonating with ill-concealed scorn. "I think we can take it that the danger is over and the project has been successfully completed," he said, indicating the monitor which had resumed a steady green colour. There was a general murmur of agreement from the Board members and a joint sigh of relief. "If I may, on behalf of the Board, extend my congratulations to Nick Peters here and Despiro Nihilopificus, who is celebrating with the Dawks but who will join us later. Congratulations on a splendid job."

There were many 'hear, hears', and a rippling round of applause. Nick bowed extravagantly.

oooOooo

Nigel and Nick left the Board Room together. As soon as the Board Room door was closed, the Chairman of the Board spoke for all when he expressed heartfelt relief that the threat of a Fourth Beginning had been eliminated. "Of course," said the member who had suggested holding on to Adam, "absolutely, no question, but I have to say I really can't stand that ghastly Peters fellow." There was some chuckling and many nods of agreement. "Don't know how Nigel puts up with him," said one of the others. "I have a question," said a third. "Why did we have to authorise a mysland of such vast dimensions? I can't for the life of me see why he couldn't have managed with a much smaller construct? Most of it wasn't used. Why did he want Ringwood included? All just wanton extravagance if you ask me. Just Peters exploiting the situation to satisfy his own vanity." There were several more 'hear, hears'.

"Say what you like," the Chairman intervened. "Whatever the price, it was worth it. This was a job well done."

oooOooo

Nigel and Nick walked together back to Nigel's office. "So what are your plans now?" Nigel asked.

"When hell has finished with Adam, I'll collect him, take him back to Poulner Hill to enjoy the ensuing fireworks."

"What about the mysland?" Nigel knew the Board was keen to see the construct powered down as soon as possible.

"I need another twenty four hours," Nick replied. "No loose ends, I think we agreed. I just need to make sure everything, and I mean everything, is sorted."

367

69 Hell

When Adam awoke, he found himself in a vast subterranean cavern, lit only by flickering torches, held in rusting iron holders embedded in the scaly, limestone walls. The air was warm, damp and malodorous. Adam couldn't identify the smell, although it reminded him of the sweet, sickly aroma of rotting flesh. He peered into the depths of the cavern but the light of the torches was too weak for a clear view and its constant flickering created illusions of movement where there was none – and, Adam speculated, concealed movement where there was.

The floor of the cavern was rough, rock-strewn and pitted with holes, most of which were filled with water and a noxious brew of corrosive chemicals. Overhead, there were several undulating black clouds which Adam could scarcely make out in the gloom but which he surmised might be millions of bats. Ahead of him, Adam could see the glow of a fire but he was unable to judge its size because distances were extremely difficult to gauge in such circumstances.

Adam decided to make his way towards the fire. The cavern was damp and he guessed that the air around the fire would be drier. The fire also generated light and, if he approached, he thought he might be better able to take in his surroundings. After walking for several minutes, Adam paused. The fire was now bigger and certainly the air was warmer, but the fire had not grown in size as much as he had expected. He reassessed the size of the cavern. It must be miles across, he thought to himself.

It took him the best part of half an hour to reach a point where he could clearly see the fire and its source. Although the fire was still some way off, heat from the flames spewing from a fathomless fissure in the floor of the cavern felt hot on Adam's face.

"Welcome to hell," said a smooth, cultured voice.

Adam whirled round. Standing beside him was a tall, slim young man, dressed smartly in a grey business suit, with a red tie.

"Bit of a shock, I guess," the young man continued. "Some of those sent here crack up immediately. You're doing rather well. My name is Archy, Archy Stonx; I know your name. Any idea what you're in for?"

Adam pondered the meaning of the question. Did he mean what crime had he committed? Or was he asking whether Adam knew what he now had to face?

"None at all," said Adam, since that seemed to answer both questions satisfactorily.

The young man produced a smart-phone from his jacket pocket, touched the screen a few times and said; "Now let me see." He read for a moment, scrolling down several times, and then added: "Wow, you're getting the works. Somebody up there really doesn't like you."

"What am I doing here?" Adam asked. Of all the crazy experiences of the last few weeks, this seemed the most bizarre.

"Desperately trying to get out," Archy suggested. "If you could see this screen, you'd definitely be making a break for it. I'm sorry, but I've never seen an ordeal quite as harsh as this."

"I mean why am I here?" Adam tried again.

"Sorry, we don't answer questions like that," the young man laughed. "And, to be honest, if you don't mind, I should like to get on with the business. Normally it's my role to keep company with our guests throughout the action – not to help them, you understand, but to witness events and how they handle their ordeal. In your case, however, given what it says on this screen, I think I might dip out now, if you don't mind."

"What does that mean?" Adam asked, becoming increasingly frustrated.

"You have to perform one simple task to escape from here." The young man ignored Adam's question.

"And that is?" said Adam.

"You have to find the quickest way to turn lead into gold. That's it."

"That's it?" Adam repeated incredulously.

"Well there's a few dangers you have to avoid, a few hardships you have to bear and, of course, you have to work out how to perform the 'lead to gold' thing, but in essence that's it."

Adam shook his head. "Are you crazy? How can I do that?"

The young man laughed again. "I can't help you. That would be very much against the rules. But I can give you this piece of paper with a few bits of advice and one or two clues written on it. That's all I can do."

"And I have to stay here until I find an answer? In other words, I have to stay here for ever."

"It does look that way," said the young man. "Oh and I should mention something else. 'Ever' won't be all that long. For every hour you spend here, you will grow one year older. I see you're thirty-five. Assuming you live to be eighty, that gives you a little under two days – maybe less, because eighty is rather optimistic in the context of the list. I have to leave you now."

With that, the young man sauntered off into the darkness, muttering something that sounded to Adam like "Poor bugger".

Adam slumped on to a rock. He was sick with worry and with

breathing the hot, fetid air. He tried to take stock of the situation but it was so weird and so terrifying he made little progress. The fire from the fissure in the cavern floor would suddenly spew out more heat as though the belly of the earth was belching. Clouds of acrid smoke drifted up towards the roof where the bats hung. Adam had no idea how he had reached this hell and therefore no idea how to escape. Was there a door or gate? Peters had said something about the bowels of the building, so he was probably in the Breakers' Head Office at Cadnam or rather under it, but then he could be anywhere. The cavern was vast and, having walked some distance without seeing any end to it, he had no idea whether he was in the middle of the cavern or close to the edge. He had passed out when the guards had escorted him from the interrogation room at the end of his last conversation with Nick Peters so he really had no idea for sure where the cavern was or where he was within it.

And was he really going to age a year in every hour? Was that possible? If so, Peters had, in effect, condemned him to a two-day long execution. Why? Peters knew he wasn't a terrorist. Peters must want him out of the way for some other reason. Did Peters have something going on with Eve? Peters had said something about infidelity being 'no big deal'; he had said they were all adults; he had said that, if Eve was upset about Pandora, it would be like the pot calling the kettle black. Even if Nick hadn't started an affair with Eve yet, perhaps he intended to, in which case, Adam's disappearance would be rather convenient. Adam felt sicker. When Peters had said he was sending Adam to hell, he had meant it.

After about 20 minutes, Adam felt what he took to be the first twinges of arthritis in the wrist and the joints of the fingers of his right hand. It was probably his imagination but who knew what effects an accelerated ageing process might entail.

70 Rescue

"So now we're in, where do we go?" asked Prune. They had left Opt with Elsa and started to walk through the mysland version of Ringwood.

"I think Andrew is the best person to answer that," said Kit.

Andrew produced a small satnav device from his pocket.

"How's that going to help?" asked Prune, who now felt he should either have had one pint of Guinness more or one fewer at the Elm Tree.

"It's an ordinary satnav," Andrew explained, "which I have tweaked just a little. In addition to telling us where we are, it also picks up hotspots inside the mysland."

"Hotspots?" Prune frowned, although given the deep lines and profound wrinkles in the skin of his face, the imposition of a frown was almost imperceptible.

"The mysland is a construct. In some parts it's fairly crude. As we've seen there are weaknesses at the boundary. In other parts, the Breaker engineers have put in a great deal of effort and the result is so good it's almost impossible to tell the mysland version from the real thing. But all that engineering work and the energy needed to sustain these almost perfect replications show up on the satnav as hotspots. Look."

He showed the satnav to Prune. Sure enough, there were three clear markers. One simply showed where they were. Another marker, larger than the other two and pulsating, indicated Cadnam. The third marker, also pulsating but with lower intensity, not far from the first, showed the house on Poulner Hill where Eve, Rambler and Numpty were being held.

"So we have two targets," said Kit. "We'll take the nearest first."

Only Luke wondered how Kit had known there were only two hotspots. He thought of asking the blind man but decided against it. Since Kit could hear a dog talk and understand what a penguin thought, guessing the number of hotspots on Andrew's satnav was not a particularly remarkable feat.

The three men and their dog walked through Ringwood, turned right at the main roundabout on to the A31 and started to walk up the hill.

"So what's the plan?" asked Prune.

"Break into the castle, rescue the fair maiden and her friends, and effect our escape," said Kit.

"Nice plan," observed Prune. "Bit light on detail."

371

"There will be some guards," said Kit. "They will be armed. They have been ordered to prevent Eve from leaving the house, even if it costs them their lives. They are highly trained in weaponry and hand to hand combat. They are utterly fearless and equally ruthless...,"

"Enough!" said Prune. "I think we should go back to the Elm Tree and consider our options."

Andrew looked expectantly at Kit.

"There is a possibility," said Kit slowly, "that we might achieve our ends without bloodshed, theirs or more likely ours. We could use guile instead of force."

"Sounds good," said Andrew. "What have you got in mind?"

"Well, if we could impersonate Nick Peters, we could issue the order for the release of the prisoners and the guards would obey without question."

"Hmmm!" came from Prune. "Well if it's impersonating a tall, slim Englishman, in his thirties, I'm probably not first choice. I think my accent might give me away."

Kit laughed. "Accent, height, build, age, colouring. You're right. Not the ideal candidate. Indeed none of us is ideal. Or even possible."

"So?" prompted Prune.

"We can't do it. But I know someone who can. Whether he will be willing to do it is another matter."

Both Prune and Andrew were puzzled. Kit had told them that no one in the mysland would help them but, since neither of them had any idea of how best to proceed, Kit was offering the only plan in town so they went along with him.

Luke, on the other hand, knew what Kit was thinking. "You cannot be serious," he minded to Kit.

"Never more so," Kit minded back.

Halfway up Poulner Hill, they turned right into a winding tree-lined lane and walked as far as they could go. When they reached two iron gates, they stopped.

"You're not just going to ring the bell?" Andrew Rimzil queried. Given Kit's description of the strength of the opposition, such an approach seemed to fall somewhere between foolhardy and insane.

Kit rang the bell. After a minute a man's voice answered.

"This is the Environment Agency," said Kit. "We have reason to believe you may have a rare newt on your property, a great crested newt to be precise. We need to conduct an inspection."

There was another pause. Then the same man's voice said: "What?"

Kit repeated his message. Prune and Andrew looked at each other and then back to Kit.

"Wait a minute," said the voice on the intercom. After a wait of at least two minutes a new voice spoke. "What do you want?"

For the third time, Kit explained, delivering his message with the ponderous authority of the seasoned bureaucrat.

"Wait where you are," said the voice. "I will come down to the gate."

A few minutes later a middle aged man walked briskly down the drive to meet them. He was wearing country casual clothes, tweed jacket with leather-patched elbows, cavalry twill trousers and sturdy walking shoes. When he reached the gate, he scanned the faces of three men, focused his attention on Kit and said: "I thought it might be you."

"Hello Grimrose," said Kit. "Good to see you. Delighted you've fully recovered from your venture into avian territory."

"What do you want?" Grimrose asked. "I very much doubt if the mysland engineers thought to replicate the great crested newt. A bit obscure and totally unnecessary I would have thought, until of course you arrived."

"I wanted to have a word with you," said Kit. "Indeed rather more than a word. These are momentous times. What happens in the next few hours could change the course of history. You have a part to play but exactly which part is not yet settled. Let us in and we will talk. We promise not to make any moves while we are talking and, if at the end, you are not persuaded by what I have to say, we will leave peacefully."

Grimrose looked doubtful. "I can't think what you can say to persuade me of anything. We are in a Breaker mysland. The Breakers made this bubble of unreality; they control every aspect of it; you can't change any of it. So what are you hoping to achieve? What exactly do you want?"

"Let us in and I will tell you," said Kit.

"That's not good enough," said Grimrose, turning away.

"When Nick Peters plummeted from the ledge on Mount Strobilos, you caught him. You saved his life. It did cross your mind to let him fall, because you were unhappy working for such a man, but you didn't let him crash to his death. You caught him and saved him. Was he grateful? Then, when he complained about the wound he had sustained to his leg when you saved him, he called on you to use your shape-shifting essence to restore the limb. You complied and, in so doing, came so close to death that only a *disturba* could save you. Was Nick Peters grateful? When the questors arrived back from their travels and Gwoat, with whom you had struck up a friendship, was brutally slaughtered, was Peters contrite? When you look in the mirror and ask yourself who you are, how pleased are you with the answer?"

Grimrose had stopped to listen. The blind man saw too much. "Very well," said Grimrose, "you can come in but keep your word. If you make any moves at all, the guards will kill you and, even if I wanted to stop them, I couldn't."

Grimrose pressed an electronic key and the gates swung open. Kit, with Prune on his left and Andrew on his right, followed Grimrose up the drive. Luke kept close to Kit, trotting along quietly behind. If the guards would kill three unarmed men without scruple, obviously they would think nothing of despatching a dog.

When they reached the house, Eve was making coffee in the kitchen. Luke was so excited to see his mistress that, contrary to all his training when a puppy, he leapt up to lick her face, almost knocking her to the ground. Eve was so astonished to see Luke, whom she had feared dead, that for a moment she failed to recognise Kit.

"I know," said Kit when recognition dawned, "I keep turning up out of the blue."

At that moment, Rambler and Numpty appeared, curious to find out the cause of the commotion. "Kit," squealed Numpty, "have you come to rescue us?"

Kit smiled. "I've come to have a chat with Grimrose, that's all," said Kit, shaking hands with Rambler and then returning Numpty's enthusiastic embrace. "Just a friendly chat. No talk of rescues, otherwise the armed guards might feel compelled to take drastic measures."

"It is good to see you once again," said Rambler.

"And you," said Kit. "Why don't you introduce yourselves to Prune, this is Prune, and Andrew Rimzil, this is Andrew. These are the ones who built the camper van, or rather modified the vehicle with the exponential drive and the paradox device. Without them, the quest would have been impossible. While you are getting acquainted, Grimrose and I will take a turn around the gardens and have our little chat."

Kit and Grimrose walked out into the gardens. It was a beautiful day – brilliant sunshine, with wispy white clouds widely dispersed high in the otherwise uniformly blue sky. Kit spoke. "These are momentous times."

"As you said before," Grimrose responded. "Would you care to be a little more specific?"

"There is a chance that we shall witness a Fourth Beginning. This couple, Adam and Eve, offer the best chance for millennia. They do not realise it yet, but they are close. In fact they are so close that panic has broken out amongst the Breakers. Hence the mindless extravagance of this overblown mysland. The Breakers will do anything to prevent the Fourth Beginning because, almost certainly, it will end their power. They are desperate to deconstruct Adam and Eve, not just because the pair could trigger the Beginning, not just because deconstruction is what they do, but, most of all, because they fear the Fourth Beginning will expose deconstruction itself as negative, simplistic and destructive."

"I have heard talk of this Fourth Beginning, but no one seems to know what it is," said Grimrose thoughtfully. "I assume the Breakers are simply erring on the side of caution in trying to prevent something that could have such far-reaching consequences when the nature of the consequences is unknown."

"So would you have prevented the three previous Beginnings, on the grounds that, before they happened, no one knew where they would lead? That would have meant no universe of matter and energy, no life and no consciousness. And do you not see a progression? Is it not obvious that the universe is designed to become conscious of itself – from nothing to something, from matter to life, from life to consciousness? We are not at the end of a process. We are close to a time of the Fourth Beginning."

"I am just a humble shapeshifter," Grimrose interrupted. "My role and my duty is to serve the Breaker Nick Peters. What do you expect me to do?"

"I am asking you to be honest with yourself. You have known for a long time that Nick Peters is evil. I don't mean in any grand archetypal sense. I just mean he is destructive. He takes pleasure and pride in discouraging creativity, in ridiculing aspiration, in defiling what is good. You know this to be true. So my question is this. When you look back on your life, do you wish to see yourself as the menial servant of an evil person, or would you rather be the shapeshifter who helped to change the world?"

"Have you ever thought of becoming a salesman?" Grimrose asked.

"It's funny you should ask me that," said Kit, entirely unfazed by Grimrose's response. "One of the reasons I'm a traveller is that I'm really rather good at selling. But I don't sell things. I sell ideas. It has been said," and there was a hint of pride in Kit's voice, "that I could talk the world and his wife into handing over all their money just to join me on my wanderings. But I don't and I wouldn't. Why anyone would wish to embark on an uncertain future with a blind wanderer is beyond me unless it's my undoubted charm, wit and charisma. And frankly, I'm not sure I would wish to spend my time with a bunch of penniless layabouts, especially if I had become disproportionately wealthy at their expense. On the other hand, an ability to sell is undoubtedly useful. It enabled me to escort the questors out of the Garden of Eden, despite the delusional deity's desire for vengeance."

"If I helped you," said Grimrose, "I would be an outcast from my own people and an enemy of the Breakers – and, as we all know, the Breakers are intolerant of enemies."

"If you don't, you will regret it all the remaining days of your life."

"Of which there are unlikely to be many more if I decide to help you," observed Grimrose wryly.

"It's time to decide," said Kit. "I know it's difficult. I know I'm asking you to abandon what you have seen as your duty and to embark on a course of action which I admit is full of danger. But I have watched you for years. There is goodness, honesty, integrity in you which even years in the service of Nick Peters has failed to erode. The Breakers are holding consciousness back. Their reductionism is sterile. Help us and I promise hope will replace regret."

Whether Kit understood it or not, he was asking Grimrose to choose between life and death; life as a servant to Nick Peters, or death trying to help these questors. When a shapeshifter was allocated to a Breaker, it was for life. There was no release clause for the shapeshifter. If the shapeshifter failed his Breaker, the Breaker could dismiss him but the shame of such a dismissal was worse than death and the failed shapeshifter would be expected by his own community to terminate himself. If a shapeshifter betrayed his Breaker, the punishment was death, imposed by both the Breakers and the shapeshifters. Death was really the only way out. On the other hand, living a life in the service of someone you hated and despised was really no life at all. The shapeshifters had a saying that you could put a value on a life only when you knew how it ended. So Grimrose asked himself what value would his life have if he spent it and ended it in the service of Nick Peters.

Kit said no more. There was no more to say. There is a time for talking and a time for waiting patiently in silence. Almost despite himself, Grimrose grew a little taller. His jaw became firmer and his eyes acquired a glint of determination. The shapeshifter was finding himself.

"Welcome aboard," said Kit.

oooOooo

Nick Peters, or a figure so closely resembling him in every respect that even his own mother could not have told them apart, strode back into the house with Kit at his side.

The guards, who had in Grimrose's absence been keeping an eye on the questors and their visitors, were somewhat surprised to see Nick back so soon. They leapt to attention and waited for instructions.

"I'm pleased to be able to tell you," said Nick, addressing Eve, "that Adam has told us everything. I'm really sorry about the delay but, if he had only been honest with us from the start, we could have sorted this out days ago. You are all free to go. It's all been an unfortunate misunderstanding, a case of mistaken identity compounded by Adam's failure initially to co-operate but all's well that ends well."

"Not for Gwoat," said Numpty.

"Let's not dwell on the past," said the semblance of Nick. "If I were you, I'd pack my things and leave. After all that's what you want, isn't it?"

"There's something we should do before we leave," said Kit. "If we have your permission. We would like to take the camper van with us. After all, it belongs to the Storyteller and we would like to return it to him. He has lost his driver; he need not lose the van."

"You may take the van, if you can make it work," said Nick. "I believe it is in a state of disrepair."

"I think we can deal with any problems," said Kit. "We have a couple of engineers with us. The van is very much their brain-child. It probably just needs a little TLC."

"And some filler compounds for the holes," suggested Rambler, recalling the spray of bullets which had hit the vehicle when Gwoat had died.

Numpty escorted Prune and Andrew Rimzil to the camper van. Prune pulled a small case out of his pocket and produced a set of hex keys. "I'll have this sorted in no time," he said and, true to his word, within minutes the van had coughed into life.

"Now we have wheels," said Kit, "let's hit the road. We have some more rescuing to do."

Prune drove the camper van to the front of the house. Eve, Rambler and Numpty were packed and ready to leave. When they were all aboard, Prune drove slowly down the drive behind Nick, who insisted on walking them to the gate. Nick opened the gate and the van went through.

Kit leant out of the window. "Perfectly done."

Grimrose still in the semblance of Nick smiled and replied: "I should be able to replicate Peters. I've spent long enough with him. I'll wait here in the house. Either you will succeed, in which case I will see you again; otherwise, I shall have to make my own arrangements. One thing is certain. My time as Nick Peters' acolyte is well and truly ended."

They left Grimrose behind.

"I've got a question," said Prune as they turned on to the A31. "What was all that about newts?"

Kit laughed. "I had to think of something odd. Anything normal, like a parcel delivery, and the guards would have simply told us to leave. Newts were outside their zone so I knew they would refer it to Grimrose. And I knew Grimrose would realise it was us because no one who was part of the mysland would have come up with newts."

"But how did you know Grimrose was here?"

"And that Nick Peters wasn't?" added Andrew.

"The Storyteller told me," said Kit.

"I thought so," said Eve.

71 Back in hell

Adam tried to shake off the pain by straightening his fingers and exercising his wrist.

"That won't do it," said a voice. It was Archy.

"I thought you'd buggered off, couldn't face my ordeal," sneered Adam.

"Apparently I have no choice. Orders from those on high. Have to stick with you to the bitter end. Anyway, that's a bit of arthritis," Archy continued. "It doesn't get better. In fact it gets a lot worse but not till about midday tomorrow when by my reckoning you will be about seventy years old."

"There must be some way out of this," said Adam, more in desperation than hope. The sulphurous smell of the fire was beginning to irritate his nose and his lungs. "What is the benefit to the Breakers in putting me through this? If they want me out of the way, why don't they do to me what they did to Gwoat?"

"If that's a question," said Archy cheerfully, "I'm not allowed to answer it. But I can tell you they have their reasons. As for a way out, I've already told you. Lead into gold, by the shortest route."

"So you say, lead into gold, but I'm not an alchemist. I'm not even a chemist. I have no idea where to start. It's just crazy."

"Well, if I were you, and thank heavens I'm not, I would start by looking for some lead."

Adam was about to say there was no point since he wouldn't recognise lead even if the noxious smoke filled cavern was full of it when he noticed what he thought was a thin snake working its way towards him. It was only when it reached the rock on which he sat that he realised it wasn't a snake, it was a crack, and in the centre of the crack there was a red and gold thread running through it like a brilliant spine.

"I should start moving if I were you," said Archy backing away. The crack widened a little.

Adam leapt up. The ground was shaking. Slivers of fire and gas were spurting out of the fissure.

"This way," shouted Archy, bounding off into a darker part of the cavern. Adam chased after him. Behind him there was an appalling shriek as the rocks, riven by heat and pressure, split, ground into each other and then exploded. Adam felt the blast go through him, as though a giant heat-exuding fist had thumped him in the back. The force from the explosion accelerated his run and he was unable to prevent himself from bumping into Archy, who, having reached safe ground, had turned to watch the fireworks.

"Sorry," said Adam, as the two of them picked themselves up. "What the hell was that?"

"Happens all the time. The cavern floats on a lava lake. That's why it's so warm. From time to time, the release valves, like the one where we met, fail to relieve the pressure so the lava finds another way."

Adam shook his head. Just how bad could things get?

"So are we looking, or sulking?" asked Archy.

Adam was beginning to despair. His body ached. He might have aged only two or three years since he had found himself in the cavern but the accelerated ageing process was in itself debilitating.

"It's up to you entirely," Archy continued, "but, if you want any chance of surviving, you had better move yourself. Trying may not succeed, but despair guarantees failure."

Adam started to move forward, with Archy at his side. They walked for another two hours until Adam, utterly exhausted, called a halt. "I can't go on," he said. "I need water. The heat and the exertion are drying me out. And I ache."

"Have you read the piece of paper I gave you?" asked Archy.

Adam hadn't looked at the note Archy had given him. It was difficult to see anything in the gloom.

"OK," said Archy. "Since I'm here, I can tell you what it says. You're entitled to three 'comforts'. That's comforts, not wishes. I'm making the distinction clear because we get some smart-arses who confuse the two and think they can wish for immediate release. No sir. That's not on at all. A comfort is very different from a wish. It's something to make your journey through hell just a little easier for a little while. If it's a wish at all, it's a kind of heavily qualified, strictly regulated, really rather limited wish. Now, do you want to spend one of your comforts on some water?"

"I shan't live to enjoy the other two if I don't."

"Quite right," said the ebullient Archy. "Good thinking."

With that he produced a hip flask and offered it to Adam.

"Why didn't you just give it to me instead of all this comfort nonsense?" asked Adam after taking a swig.

"I'm not here to help. I'm really just supervising and observing the Breakers' plan for you. You want water as a comfort, I can provide it. You just want water – sorry, no can do."

Adam took another drink from the flask, emptying it.

"Shall we move on?" asked Archy.

Before Adam could answer, Archy screamed "Look out!"

Adam looked down to the cavern floor expecting to see a crack sneaking its way towards him but the ground looked solid. There was no golden-spined snake heading his way.

Archy dived into Adam knocking him to the ground, as a bat with a wing span of at least 12 feet flew past. "Vampire bats. Best to keep out of their way," said Archy. "They have a sensor called a pit organ on their muzzles, which is sensitive enough to pick up body warmth. It's so sensitive, they can locate veins precisely. And let me tell you, bats the size they reach in here can drain a pint of blood in the blink of an eye. By the way, it's a complete misconception that vampire bats go for the neck. They're much more likely to home in on an arm or a leg or, much-favoured by these big 'uns, the anus. They pick on sleeping animals or knock one out with a blow to the head, land on the ground, creep up and lock on. They use an anti-coagulant in their saliva to make sure the blood keeps flowing. I'll be honest with you. If you give up or collapse, that's most likely how your life will end. They do a lot of cleaning up round here."

"What animals?" asked Adam. Apart from the bats, they had not seen any living things within the cavern and Adam had assumed the environment was so hostile no creature would choose it for its home.

"Mainly dogs," said Archy.

"There are dogs down here?" said Adam.

"Yes," said Archy, "but they're not your average dogs. Let's put it this way, the dogs down here make wolves seem like pussycats, if you'll forgive a bit of taxonomic hooliganism."

"Are we likely to meet any?" Adam asked.

"'Fraid so," said Archy. "They have a taste for human flesh. But no need to worry yet. Despite the fact that a pack of these hell dogs could easily kill an elephant, they prefer to attack the old and weak. You should be OK for a few hours."

For a moment, Adam was struck by the absurdity of the situation. While being put through some kind of fatal ordeal by a group of demented security officials who, despite knowing his innocence, seemed determined to destroy him, here he was conversing with a Breaker employee in a place as close to hell as Hell itself about the terrifying fauna that somehow survived in a cavern floating on a lake of lava.

"Let's move on," suggested Archy.

"You just saved me," said Adam. "You pushed me out of the way of the vampire bat."

"That's all right," said Archy, a little embarrassed. "No big deal."

"Are you sure?" asked Adam. "I thought you weren't supposed to help me."

"Oh, I see what you mean. Well, I'm allowed a bit of latitude. It's not as though I'm helping you to escape. They might be a bit pissed off but it's not a serious transgression, so long as things end up as they should."

After another two hours, Adam announced he needed to rest. Archy accepted Adam's decision without argument although he did suggest that Adam shouldn't rest for too long. "You're over forty already," he said.

Adam lay down on the flattest piece of rock he could find. So Archy reckoned he was over forty. That felt like an underestimate. His whole body ached and he was still feeling sharp piercing pain from time to time in his right wrist. His lungs were congested and his head felt as though it was being compressed by a vice.

So Adam rested and, despite his many discomforts, slept. When he awoke, Archy greeted him. "I didn't know whether to wake you. I could see you needed the rest, but I could also see you were growing older. In the end, I left it to you, mainly on the grounds that I shouldn't interfere. How do you feel?"

"How long did I sleep?" Adam asked.

"Just over four hours or, in your case, four years."

"Look, Archy," said Adam, "I know you can't help me to escape this nightmare but can you at least give me some idea how to change lead into gold. I guess it must be possible. If it is, I need some help."

"No can do," said Archy. "You have to work it out for yourself. All I can say is this. Ask yourself who makes the rules. That's all."

Adam shrugged. He had the feeling that Archy was trying to help but if so, sadly, without success. Adam pulled himself to his feet. He felt like crap. The aches and pains had subsided a little and his head felt better but his lungs were still heavily congested. He coughed and brought up some mucus. The atmosphere was thick with dust or soot or other noxious particles which seemed to waft through the cavern like malign, low-flying clouds.

"I think we should move on," said Archy. "If you're still looking for lead, you won't find it in this part of the cavern. And let's not forget about the dogs. They live in the west, back where we have come from. The greater distance we can put between them and us the better. They have an amazing sense of smell and they can pick up the scent of human disease and despair from miles away."

They trudged on through the cavern for another two hours. Adam stopped. "I must eat," he said.

"Time for your second comfort then," said Archy.

"Is there any chance of a drink to go with it, I mean without using my third comfort?" Adam asked.

"I think we can stretch to some water," Archy replied. "I like you," he added. "You're taking all this rather well. And I like a man who bargains."

72 The beginning of the endgame

As the camper van, driven by Prune, approached Cadnam, Eve asked Kit if he had a plan. After all, they had no idea where Adam was being held within the Breaker complex.

"I suppose we should do a reccy?" Rambler hazarded. Amongst his many careers, he had worked for some years in the film industry and still liked to use words from his old trade.

Andrew Rimzil was tapping on the screen of his modified satnav device. "He's in there somewhere," he said, "but something is interfering with the signal."

"Is all this part of the mysland?" asked Numpty, looking out of the camper van window.

"It's incredible," said Rambler. "It looks so substantial, so real."

"The Breakers must be feeling the strain. The energy requirements to sustain this construct are astronomical," said Andrew.

"We're going straight in," said Kit, answering Eve's question. "This is the endgame. The time for subtlety, to be honest never my strong suit, is over. In through the front door and face up to the enemy. Now is the time, Eve. For you, it's now or never."

Eve knew what Kit meant. She was on the verge of something. What it was, she didn't know. She thought that, quite possibly, she was about to have a complete mental breakdown. She and Adam had set off on what most would see as an entirely ludicrous quest to find the truth, whatever that meant. In the course of the quest, she had realised not only that she and Adam were looking for different things but that the search itself was changing them. It was opening up understanding. The journey was an end in itself. But it was not the final end. That final end, she had enjoyed glimpses of, but that was all.

And throughout the quest, Nick Peters had tried to impede them at every turn. There was no point to the quest because there was nothing to find. There was no point to Eve's questions about Bella's death; it was just an accident. In fact, there was no point to asking 'why' about anything because there were no answers. Or the answer was because that's just the way it is. That fellow Despiro Nihilopificus had been the ultimate proponent of the 'that's just the way it is' school of thought. If she and Adam had learned nothing else, they had grasped that satisfaction with that kind of explanation only worked looking back. What had happened, had happened. No one could argue with that. But what about what might happen in the future; what about what could have happened in the past? Peters and his Dawk friends were silent.

They took the clock apart and, when what had been the clock lay in pieces in chaos on the table, incapable of telling the time or of any other useful function, they said, "There you are; that's all there is to a clock."

As for what had happened to her relationship with Adam, well, at the moment, that seemed to her to be a bit like the disassembled clock. All the bits were there but unless they could find a way to put it back together, it just wasn't going to work.

All that said, Kit was right. There was unfinished business. They had to rescue Adam. God alone knew what they had been doing to him. And they had to have justice. Throughout, the Breakers had been determined to stop the questors from succeeding. None of them knew what success meant but no one had the right to stop the questors from trying. Nick Peters had tricked and troubled them throughout; the security forces, under Breaker control, had murdered Gwoat and had abducted and abused Adam. There had to be a reckoning.

Prune parked the van in a vacant parking space in front of the Breakers' Head Office, a space reserved for the Managing Director. When Eve queried his choice of space, Prune laughed and simply said he could be as unsubtle as anyone.

Kit led the way into the building, with Luke padding alongside. Eve, who was unable to pick up Luke's lucid instructions, was surprised that a blind man should be able to find his way into a strange building without help. She followed Kit, with Prune on one side and Andrew on the other. Rambler and Numpty brought up the rear. Eve was even more surprised by the absence of any security. "Must have caught them during a tea break," said Kit, answering Eve's unasked question.

Kit made his way to the office of Nigel Vale. Without knocking, he marched in. Nigel's office was a good size but by the time the entire party had entered it was full. Nigel, who had been putting the final touches to his own report on recent events, startled by the invasion of his space, stood up.

"Sit," said Kit. Nigel sat. "Send for Peters," Kit ordered. Nigel's brow furrowed but he pressed a button on his intercom and said: "Nick Peters to Nigel Vale's office – now."

"Excellent," said Kit, offering the best visitor seat to Eve.

"Who are you?" Nigel managed eventually.

"For you, I'm rather hoping we are the beginning of the end," said Kit. "For the world at large, I'm hoping we are the beginning of the Beginning."

"You realise that you need an appointment to see me," said Nigel, regaining a little composure.

"It'll take a little more than an appointment," Kit laughed, tapping his stick.

"You're blind!" Nigel exclaimed, as though blindness was in itself an offence.

"There's none so blind as those who won't see," Kit replied.

"What does that mean?" Numpty asked of his uncle.

"Not now," Rambler replied.

"We've come for Adam," said Eve. "Where is my husband?"

Nick Peters entered the room. "Hello, Eve, good to see you." Nick was puzzled by the arrival of the guests from the house on Poulner Hill until he saw Kit. It was that man again, the blind man with the stick who was forever interfering, the man who had knocked him off Mount Strobilos. It was a good thing Nick was a forgiving man.

"Where's Adam?" Eve ignored Peters.

"He's undergoing a small endurance test, prior to his release," Nigel Vale replied. "We're just making sure he's up to facing the world outside."

"I want to see him," Eve demanded.

"Of course you do," Nick intervened. "And just as soon as he's finished the course, you two will be reunited."

"I think we would like to see him now," said Kit.

"Well, if Eve really wants to join Adam now, it can be arranged, but I really wouldn't advise it," Nick sounded genuinely concerned. "It's a tough course and you really need to work your way in gently. If we just insert her where Adam is now, it might not produce good outcomes."

Eve bridled. What right had Peters to tell her when she could or couldn't see her husband? And why was he adopting this pseudo-management speak? What did outcomes mean? Mud on her shoes, or summary execution? Why couldn't he say what he meant?

"I'll go," said Kit.

"What?" said Eve.

"I'll go," said Kit firmly. "I'll go on your little endurance test. I'll make sure Adam is all right. And then you can bring both of us back and Adam and Eve can be reunited."

"I don't think a blind man can undergo one of our endurance tests," said Nigel. "I think it's specifically ruled out. Health and safety."

Nick smiled. "Oh I think we might make an exception in this case. If this particular blind man wishes to go, I'm prepared to authorise it, on my responsibility."

"And me," said Luke to Kit. After all, Adam was his master and Kit was his good friend. He had missed Adam from the moment they had been separated so he felt it was important he should reach him as soon as possible. As for Kit, they had proved a rather successful team of adventurers before, so why not again?

"And I'll take the dog," said Kit.

Nick shrugged. "And the dog then," he conceded, "but that's it. We can't have all and sundry interrupting our test."

"Who is Sundry?" asked Numpty.

"Shhh!" came from Rambler.

Nick summoned a guard and instructed the man to escort Kit and the dog to the Breakers' endurance test in UnderHall No. 1.

73 Who makes the rules

When Kit suddenly appeared in the cavern beside Archy, Adam was just finishing the meal Archy had provided as his second comfort. In the gloom of the cavern, Adam was scarcely better sighted than his blind visitor.

"Hello, Adam," said Kit.

Luke let out a whine. "I don't know what they've done to him but he looks awful. He must have aged twenty years," Luke minded to Kit.

"How are you feeling?" Kit continued.

"Is that you?" asked Adam, struggling to make out the form of the man and match it to his voice.

"The answer to that question must always either be yes or silence," said Kit gently. "If you mean, am I Kit, then yes, I am Kit and this is your faithful dog, Luke."

"How did you get here?" asked Adam, uncertain whether Kit and Luke were there or whether he was hallucinating. Luke had nuzzled into Adam's legs and Adam was tentatively patting his dog.

"Good question," said Kit. "I've got a question too. Where is here? The air is rank. All I can smell is sulphur and methane. And it's so warm. Where the hell are we?"

"Good guess," said Archy.

"This is hell," said Adam.

"I'm not going to argue with you on that," said Kit. "If it looks like it smells, it's hell sure enough. What are you doing here?"

"Peters sent me here, I don't know whether as a punishment or a test. I've been given an impossible task and, unless I can perform this task, I can't leave. And there's something else. I'm growing old. For every hour I'm here, I age one year. I didn't believe it at the beginning but look at me. My body is falling apart. In a few hours I'll be too disabled to walk and too senile to think. Then I'll die. You have to understand; Peters is the devil incarnate. Why would anyone do this to another human being? Why is he doing it to me? I've never done him any harm."

Kit interrupted Adam's flow. "Let's take one step at a time? First of all, I think you should introduce me to your companion."

"I'm Archy Stonx," said Archy, saving Adam the trouble. "I work for the Breakers. I handle arrivals down here."

"You handle arrivals? What exactly does that mean?"

"I receive people thought to be dangerous. I check them in. Give them some instructions. Tell them the nature of the task they have been allocated. And let them get on with it."

"So why are you here with Adam?"

"Orders. Direct orders. To be frank, when I saw what had been planned for Adam, I was keen to leave him as quickly as possible and I did. But I was sent back. To observe."

"I see," said Kit. "And what is the task that Adam has been set?"

"He has to turn lead into gold by the quickest possible means," said Archy. "And the tasks here are not impossible, although I have to admit almost no one completes them."

"And why is that?" asked Kit.

"Well, the tasks are admittedly pretty difficult and sometimes rather tricky. And then of course, there's the bats and the dogs – that's the giant vampire bats and the hounds of hell."

As though on cue, a blood-curdling howl echoed through the cavern. Adam shivered. The hairs along Luke's back rose up. "They're still some way off," said Archy. "Sounds are deceptive in the cavern. Weird acoustics. The dogs are probably about three quarters of a mile away."

"What are the dogs likely to do if they find us?" asked Kit.

"Oh, they'll find us," said Archy. "Amazing sense of smell. They can pick up a scent from miles away. And, of course, a ravening appetite. When they find us, it's kill or be killed. In the circumstances, it tends to be the latter rather than the former."

"So let me summarise," said Kit. "Adam here has been cast into this noxious place to perform an impossible or near impossible task, while ageing at a phenomenal rate and under threat from vampire bats and rabid dogs."

"They're not rabid," said Archy defensively. "Just hungry. Always hungry."

"It's a neat summary," said Adam to Kit, "but is there anything we can do about it?"

"As I understand it, the only thing we can do is perform this impossible task. I guess we need to find some lead."

"But even if we find lead, I can't turn it into gold."

"Equally you can't turn lead into gold unless you first find some lead."

"Would you like your third comfort?" enquired Archy, addressing Adam.

"I don't know. Would I?" said Adam.

"It might help," said Archy.

"All right," said Adam. He knew Archy wanted to help him, within permitted limits. "What is it?"

"There is no lead," said Archy.

"What do you mean there is no lead?" gasped Adam, who felt cheated. "No lead. No lead in this entire cavern. Great. How exactly does that help?"

There was another howl from a hound of hell. The pack had picked up a strong scent of three or four warm-blooded creatures and the saliva was already mingling with their breath as they padded ever closer over the warm stony floor of the cavern, avoiding the flaming, sulphurous fissures with practised ease.

"No lead," mused Kit.

"So it's not possible," said Adam despairing.

Luke had taken up a position between Adam and the approaching hounds. He realised he didn't have a chance. From Archy's account, just one hound would have made short work of him. A pack of such animals would be unstoppable. Nevertheless, Adam was his master and Luke was determined to do his best. The memory of resting comfortably at home on warm carpets in front of crackling winter fires passed fleetingly across his mind. He determined to die with that memory in his mind when the time came.

"Archy has said all the tasks are possible," said Kit. "We just need to think about the problem in a different way."

"Well, we'd better think of a different way pretty damn quickly," said Adam.

Kit rubbed his chin, thoughtfully. "If there is no lead in the cavern, the lead in your task is just a word without any correlation with a material substance. So, if we treat the task as a word game, all we have to do is turn the word lead into the word gold."

"By the shortest possible route," said Archy.

"I don't understand," said Adam.

"It's easy," Kit seemed quite excited. "He took it from Archy's response that he was on the right lines. "Lead, read, mead, meld, mold, gold," he declared triumphantly.

Adam looked at Kit as though he had taken leave of his senses. With death ferociously padding towards them, why was Kit speaking gibberish?

"You just change one letter at a time to convert one word into another, making sure each letter change produces a real word," Kit explained.

Adam was unsure what was happening. Kit was suggesting he could fulfil his task by seeing it as word game. Could that be right? Could he escape this nightmare, this entire replica of hell, with its fissures and fires, its exudations of sulphur and methane, its vampires and hounds, simply by playing a word game?

He would never know. A ring of overgrown dogs surrounded them, red eyes blazing, white saliva dripping from their jaws. Some of the hounds stood on the cavern floor; others had climbed onto rocks to give themselves a better view of their prey.

"The quickest way," whispered Archy.

Adam hadn't the faintest idea what he meant. Was he saying the dogs would put them out of their misery quickly; it would soon be over. Or was there a way of escape, a tunnel into which they could flee and where they could hide but where the dogs couldn't follow?

There was a strange silence. "Why aren't they attacking?" Adam asked Archy. Archy shook his head. He had no idea.

Only Luke knew why. The dialect of the hounds was obscure, old-fashioned, even medieval but Luke could understand the gist of what they were saying. Luke was the reason the hounds had stopped. They were looking on a dog with golden hair. They were looking on a dog which in their eyes was the most beautiful representative of their kind they had ever seen. He was what they should have been, could have been, perhaps what they had once been before the environment and ecology of the Breakers' hell had made them what they were. Before them was the archetypal god of dogs, the golden dog of ancient stories when, long ago in the mists of time, man and dog had first formed their pact to link their fates together. Before them stood the god dog of canine legend who had once appeared to an ancient shaman and who had promised, one day, to return. "The quickest way," Archy repeated. "You're almost there."

"What?" said Adam, his mind preoccupied with the prospect of imminent dismemberment.

"Lead to gold, the quickest way," Archy explained.

"You can do it," said Kit.

Adam thought. One letter at a time. Can't be that hard. After all, one letter is common to both four letter words and is already in the right place at the end. "How about *lead, load, goad, gold*?" he said. "Can't be any shorter route than that."

A claxon sounded. The hounds looked at each other, bowed their heads in deference to Luke, turned around and loped off into the darkness.

"Bugger me!" shouted Archy. "You've done it. I'm amazed. I just love it when one of you guys makes it. It happens so rarely. They'll pick you up in a few minutes. Well done."

"Thank you," said Adam. "I think you have taken a few risks to help me and, for that, I thank you. Answer me one question. Was that what this was all about? A silly word-game?"

"As I said to you, it's a question of who makes the rules," Archy replied. "You, or rather you and Kit, made it into a word-game. You set the rules. And then you won by those rules. I shouldn't say this, I really shouldn't say this, but no one can stand against the rule-maker, the Breakers least of all. First you have to set the rules. Then you can win."

74 Freedom

When Adam was brought back up from the cavern, he was in bad shape. The sunlight, after hours in the sepulchral darkness of the cavern, blinded him. His body felt as though it had been to hell and back, as indeed he was convinced it had been. He had aged some 15 years and, although now released from the cavern, the ageing process had not been reversed. The arthritis in his wrist had spread to other joints and, although he was not permanently in pain, he was in a state of continual trepidation, not knowing when or where he would feel the next spasm.

Throughout the night before he had been thrown into the Breakers' pit, he had been recycling a series of thoughts through his brain. What was Eve thinking? How had she reacted to the news of his infidelity? Had he really been unfaithful anyway? And why had Nick told her he had? How did Nick fit into all this? How had Nick become involved in the quest? Just how plausible was it that a random biker should turn out to be a time traveller and also an important member of British security services? What were Nick's plans for him? Could they really eliminate him without charge, without trial, without legal representation? Most of all he kept asking himself, what had Nick meant by 'the pot calling the kettle black'?

Now his thoughts were different. His spell in hell had given him a new perspective. First, he realised how good it was to be alive, even if suffering with pain and infirmity. Secondly he understood how trivial were most of the worries that troubled him. The quest, in the company of the Storyteller, had given him new perspectives. The Breakers had inadvertently added another dimension. In their efforts to weaken him, they had actually empowered him. What was it Archy had said? 'No one can stand against the rule-maker, the Breakers least of all. First you have to set the rules. Then you can win'. Although he didn't yet fully understand how, the Breakers had exposed their own weakness.

"He's been through a lot," said Kit as he helped Adam into Nigel Vale's office. Eve gasped when she saw her husband but then embraced him. Adam acknowledged Rambler and Numpty. Prune Leach and Andrew Rimzil both shook his hand warmly as Kit introduced them.

"I have some good news for you," said Nick Peters as he swept into the crowded office. "Adam, you are free to go," he announced. "You've been given a clean bill of health by the interrogators, although, to be honest, you don't look too healthy to me," he laughed. "That last little test seems to have taken a good deal out of you. Anyway, the interrogators are confident you know nothing of interest to them."

There was a general sense of relief in the room. Nick was all smiles. "I suggest your friends wait for you outside in the famous camper van. There are just a couple of formalities for us to complete, Adam, and then you can be on your way."

Adam went to the nearest washroom to clean himself up. He washed his face and then stared at himself in the mirror. The face that looked back was that of a man of around fifty. It was still his face. In fact, in some ways, it was a better face. It seemed to be both tougher and more compassionate than the face of Adam in his mid-thirties. But it was a face that told him his life had been significantly shortened. The Breakers had stolen years of his life. Some of his aches and pains were subsiding now he was clear of the noxious vapours of the cavern but, without doubt, his body had aged.

"Just a bit of paperwork," said Nick when Adam joined him in the spacious reception area. Nick had been chatting to the new receptionist, a pretty brunette with green eyes. 'They go through receptionists here quicker than I do,' thought Nick. "Yes just a couple of forms," he said to Adam, "one to say we've returned all your possessions; the other, the Official Secrets Act. As I mentioned at our last meeting, you should take the second form very seriously. If you talk to anyone about your stay with us, you are likely to find yourself back here very quickly, if you're lucky. If you're not so lucky, you'll be found in a wood, leaning up against a tree with your wrists cut."

"You're not going to win," said Adam. "You've tried everything. You've given it your best shot. You've gone to the limit and beyond. But you're not going to win."

Nick's expression darkened. "We've already won, son," he sneered. "Why else do you think we would let you go? You can now go back to your normal, humdrum life. You've been on your quest and you have found nothing but trouble. You have lost years of your life and, in those years that remain, you will feel pain in your bones, aches in your muscles and fear in your heart. Your questions remain unanswered; your hopes frustrated; and your love compromised. I think it's fair to say that you have been satisfactorily and comprehensively put back in your box."

"I don't believe you," said Adam. He felt old and ill but he didn't want Nick, the author of his woes, to have the last word.

Nick laughed. "What does it matter what you believe? What makes you think what you believe is a matter of any importance?"

"I solved the riddle you posed for me in hell. 'Lead, load, goad, gold'. I made it into a word game. It wasn't a word game until I chose to see it as a word game. Was that a matter of any importance?"

"No idea, old boy," said Nick. "Yes, you came up with an answer to the challenge. But it was irrelevant. I intended to release you anyway. It was always part of my plan that you should be reunited with Eve. Never come between a man and his wife, eh?"

"I will not sign your forms," Adam declared. He might be weakened, ill, and older than his years but his spirit was not broken.

"No matter," Nick laughed. "I'll sign them for you."

oooOooo

Adam joined his friends in the camper van. Thick clouds were rolling in from the west and the entire landscape had taken on a grey sheen.

As Prune drove them out of the grounds of the Breakers' Head Office, Eve said to Adam; "We need to talk."

Adam nodded but he was so tired, he could scarcely keep his eyes open. "Yes," he said, "we need to talk – but not now."

"Drive back to Poulner," said Kit. "We need to have a word with Grimrose before we leave the mysland. And then we need to sort out Elsa when we finally return to the real world."

"I really don't understand about Sundry," said Numpty. "Surely Sundry is part of all. He can't not be part of all because all includes everyone, so, when someone says 'all and Sundry', surely 'and Sundry' is redundant? It is like saying 'All and Numpty deserve credit for the success of our recent rescue attempt', which doesn't make sense, unless you put in an 'especially'. You could say 'All, and especially Numpty, deserve credit for the success of our recent rescue attempt'. That would mean I was part of 'all' but, because of my particularly remarkable contribution to the recent rescue attempt, I was worthy of special mention."

"You have to admire the lad's tenacity of purpose," said Rambler to the others. "In our studies, we have recently been concentrating on logic, which, I'm sure young Numpty will admit, has not come easily to him. But, as in so many other areas, the lad has demonstrated that determined effort can often surpass the attainments of natural aptitude."

Encouraged by his uncle's favourable remarks, Numpty decided to pursue his quest for understanding. "When someone says 'There's none so blind as those who won't see', what does that mean? You can't be more blind than somebody who is blind, so surely somebody who won't see can't be more blind than a blind person? And, if you're not blind, how can you not see? I mean seeing is involuntary, isn't it? I can't not see unless I shut my eyes." Numpty was about to pursue his line of thought when it crossed his mind he might be treading on sensitive ground. "I don't mean any offence," he said, addressing Kit, "but I think it was you who said this thing about some people being blinder than a blind person."

"Don't mind me," Kit laughed. "It's just a saying. It means that, if you are dealing with really stubborn people who are not prepared to change their minds however much evidence you produce to change their view, you're wasting your time. They refuse to see the evidence. Take Despiro Nihilopificus, the Chief Dawk. You could present evidence to him that evolution has some general sense of direction till the cows come home and he still wouldn't accept it."

'Oh dear!' thought Rambler. 'Here we go.'

"Would he be more likely to accept it after the cows had come home?" asked Numpty. "I mean on such an important issue, why should we set a limit on the time we spend trying to persuade him, and why pick such an odd and arbitrary cut-off? After all, the cows might come home early or late. It's not a very accurate sort of indicator of time."

Kit laughed again. "I think you misunderstand me."

"Sorry, if I have misunderstood you," said Numpty, full of contrition. He knew that sometimes he jumped to conclusions without sufficient forethought. "Did you perhaps mean that evolution has a sense of direction till the cows come home, and that after they have come home, evolution may well lose its sense of direction? Like cows which have been grazing in a meadow and then, with a clear sense of direction, follow a well-worn path back to their cow shed until, once there, they lose their sense of direction since they have arrived at their destination. Or did you mean," said Numpty excitedly, as though the light had dawned, "that the arrival of the cows at their home marks the end of evolution, that somehow the home-coming of the cows fulfils the purpose of evolution?"

"Help!" said Kit.

In the sky, directly above the van, storm clouds like the heads of bearded giants crashed into each other in violent irreconcilable argument. As the van approached the top of Poulner Hill, the heavens opened and the rain fell. It fell at first in large widely spaced drops, like cupfuls of water. Then the number of drops increased until they merged into continuous sheets, as though water was spilling out from a limitless lake in the sky. The windscreen wipers did their best but they made little impression on the deluge that coated the windscreen and obscured Prune's view.

"It's like being back in the Emerald Isle," said Prune.

396

"I should slow down," said Andrew Rimzil, "if you ever want to see the Emerald Isle again."

Prune gently applied the brakes and the van slowed, enabling him to pull gracefully into the slip road off the A31. The rain continued to hammer on the roof of the camper van as Prune drove up the lane.

"Someone has to get out, press the button and ask them to open the gate," said Kit. "I'd do it but I might have some difficult in locating the buzzer."

"Well, I'm not doing it," said Prune, "because I'm the driver. I need to drive the van through when the gates open."

"There's plenty of time for someone to press the buzzer, explain who we are and get back into the van before the gates close," said Andrew helpfully.

Prune glared at his old friend. Andrew, eager to calm Prune, whose temper had been likened to the wrath of God, hurriedly added: "I'm not suggesting you should be the one to face the elements. I'm just saying that there is no insuperable obstacle if you wanted to."

"He's saying that being the driver doesn't give you an excuse for not getting out and pressing the buzzer," said Numpty helpfully, eager to show his grasp of the meaning of words was improving by the minute.

"Indeed, given that your seat is closest to the buzzer on the gate," Rambler made his contribution, "you, as the driver having the seat in the front on the right and the buzzer being on the right post of the gate, there is a strong case for arguing you are ideally placed to be the one."

"Well, how's this for an even stronger case?" said Prune in measured tones, "You can all go away and fuck yourselves because I'm not getting out into this monsoon for love nor money."

A frisson of alarm suffused the van. "No one's suggesting it should be you," said Andrew hastily. "At least, I'm not," he added, realising that his blanket denial didn't quite cover Rambler.

"I don't think anyone was proposing to bribe you or have sexual relations with you," said Numpty, responding to Prune's emphatic refusal.

"I'll go," said Eve. "I just need to get past Adam."

As Eve tried to reach the door on the right, Adam awoke.

"Where are we?" he asked.

Eve looked at him. What had they done to him? He looked like an old man. There was fear behind the tiredness in his eyes, lines of worry had been etched deep into his forehead, his hair had receded. "We're at a house near Ringwood," said Eve. She had almost said 'We're at Nick's house' but, given what Adam had been through on Nick's orders, she decided to be less specific.

"Can't we go home?" Adam pleaded.

"We will all go home, as soon as we've sorted out one or two matters," said Kit. "It won't take long."

Eve tried to open the door beside Adam.

"What are you doing?" asked Adam. "Where are you going? We need to talk."

"I'm just going to push the buzzer on the gate."

"I'll go," said Adam, "it's raining."

Before Eve could remonstrate, the gates swung open.

"Magic!" exclaimed Numpty.

"I doubt it," said Andrew and Prune in unison.

They pulled up in front of the house, as close to the entrance as possible. Then all eight of the car's occupants, Adam and Eve, Rambler and Numpty, Prune and Andrew, Kit and Luke, made a run for the door. Even though the distance was only a few yards, all were thoroughly soaked by the time they reached the house.

"If this carries on, we will need to build an ark," said Andrew. The rain was still falling heavily and showed no signs of abating.

At the door, to greet them, stood Grimrose in default form. He had shifted back to his own form as soon as the van had left. There was always a chance Peters would decide to come back to the house unexpectedly and obviously two Nicks would be at least one too many. "I saw you on the monitor, sitting at the gate, as though wondering whether to come in or not. Anyway, I opened the gate for you."

"Thanks," said Kit. "What's happened to the weather? It was sunny, with blue skies yesterday."

"Must be something the Breakers are doing," Grimrose replied. "They control the weather, as well as everything else, in the mysland."

"It seems a bit odd," observed Kit. "All the extra effects cost money. Still, I guess that's their problem."

"How did it go?" asked Grimrose. "I see you've succeeded in liberating Adam, which is certainly no mean achievement, although he does look rather the worse for wear."

"They put him through a terrible ordeal," said Kit. "He survived. That's about all we can say."

"You could mention how we ventured into hell, you and I," minded Luke. "You could mention how the hounds, with blood-red eyes hunted us, found us and were ready to rip us apart, limb from limb. It might just be worth recounting how they were stopped in their tracks by a golden retriever (that would be me) whom they recognised as, if not divine, at least a cut above your average ravening mutt from the nether regions."

Luke was rather put out by Kit's failure to tell anyone the extraordinary role the dog had played in Adam's rescue. After all, had he not halted the hounds of hell, they would have destroyed Adam before he managed, with Kit's help, to solve the riddle.

"You'll enjoy full recognition of your heroic contribution," Kit minded back, "just not yet. Adam would find such a recounting distressing."

"So what's your plan?" asked Grimrose.

"We will rest here for an hour or two. Adam needs to regain his strength. Indeed, we've all been through quite a lot. We'll gather again before evening."

Grimrose showed the visitors to a large sitting room. Adam and Eve he then took to a private suite of rooms so that Adam could rest in peace and quiet.

As he left them, there was a flash of lightning, quickly followed by a guttural rumble of thunder. "What was that?" asked Adam, his nerves severely frayed.

"Just a storm," said Eve.

"Don't worry!" added Grimrose. "It's not the end of the world."

75 Flickering

As the camper van, with the recently freed Adam in it, drove out of the car park of the Breakers' Head Office at Cadnam heading for Poulner, Nick took a moment to indulge wholly and unashamedly in an orgy of self-satisfaction.

Some people had a gift for planning, based on experience, foresight and an ability to analyse complex situations, devising the best response to all likely eventualities. The master schemers, in whose number Nick very much felt himself to be, explored all possible unwelcome unintended consequences and avoided them. Indeed, Nick saw himself as pre-eminent amongst this elite company.

All that said, it had to be understood that the best laid plans could always be frustrated by the utterly unexpected, the unforeseeable, the inexplicable, so, however skilled the planner, he or she could never be certain of success until the plan had been fulfilled. Therefore, when it was over, even the most proficient planner could not help but feel a flush of relief.

Now that success was assured, Nick felt he could savour the glory. Yes, he had enjoyed the backing of the Breakers and the assistance of the Chief Dawk but no one could deny that he, N. Peters, Esq., had been the author and prime mover of the entire enterprise.

The Fourth Beginning had been comprehensively pre-empted. A broken man and a confused woman in a ruptured marital relationship were not the stuff of which beginnings of any sort are made. No, siree!

After a few delightful moments of unadulterated self-congratulation, Nick pulled himself together. He must assume a patina of humility. No one likes a narcissistic smart-arse. He would adopt, albeit with some difficulty, the guise of a modest man. The Breaker Board and Management would then feel compelled to go out of their way to praise and reward him. He had saved them from something they most feared and, although what it was that they feared remained obscure, the importance of his success could not be overestimated.

Nick re-entered the building and wandered in the general direction of the Board Room. One or two Board members might still be there and it would be good to take a sounding of the depth of their relief and gratitude. When he reached the Board Room, it was deserted. A little disappointed, Nick was about to leave when he noticed the monitor. It was showing amber. Nick frowned. It should be green or the light should at the very least be oscillating between amber and green. And yet it was firmly amber. Evidently the sensors were not as responsive as they should have been. He decided he would come back in an hour and, if the light had not reverted to green, he would talk to the engineers about recalibrating the sensors. Strictly speaking, such issuing of instructions to Engineering was well outside his competence and above his pay grade but, once his success in frustrating the Fourth Beginning had been acclaimed, he suspected there were very few limits in the Breaker Head Office that would apply to him.

He pondered for a few moments how his relationship with Nigel Vale was likely to change. He wondered whether the manager would decide it best to apologise immediately or whether he would think it better simply to show Nick the respect he deserved in future and hope that Nick would show magnanimity. That was a tough one for Nick. Magnanimity was not a dominant aspect of his character but clearly there would be more long-term pleasure in seeing Nigel squirm, unsure whether he had achieved a sufficiently abject level of obsequiousness to earn Nick's forgiveness, rather than allowing him to clear the decks immediately with a full up-front apology for previous slights. Of course there was always the possibility that matters would be taken out of his hands. If the Breaker Board learned that Nigel had in some way offended the hero of the hour, they might well decide peremptorily to dismiss him.

Then there was Grimrose. Nick really felt quite antagonistic towards his shapeshifter. Yes they had worked together for years and, for sure, they had made a good team. But there was a very senior partner and a very junior partner in the team and sometimes, especially recently, the junior partner seemed to have forgotten which one he was. Lounging in the prime visitor's chair in Nigel's office when he, Nick, had been left standing, albeit momentarily, might not have seemed a grave offence to Grimrose. Indeed an outsider might not have understood the enormity of the outrage. But to Nick, it was a blow at the heart of the working relationship between a Breaker and his shapeshifter. It was deeply, inexcusably impolite.

There was something else. Grimrose had done the right thing in restoring Nick's leg. It was his duty as Nick's assistant, doubly so in that Grimrose had been responsible for the injury. But somehow, this perfectly appropriate and proper act which any Breaker might legitimately expect from his shapeshifter had been projected as an act of selfless heroism and had apparently impressed the Breakers as such in Head Office. The consequence was that he, as the beneficiary of this selfless and heroic act, was expected to feel gratitude. In the undoubtedly complex relationship that developed between a Breaker and his shapeshifter assistant, there was certainly provision for gratitude but the gratitude was meant to be felt by the shapeshifter, not the Breaker. In any relationship, benevolence frequently generates resentment in the recipient. So Nick's kindness to his inferior had clearly generated inappropriate responses from Grimrose – on top of which any expectation of gratitude harboured by a shapeshifter clearly undermined the essential structure of the Breaker/shapeshifter relationship.

No, Grimrose would have to go. In normal circumstances, eliminating a shapeshifter was relatively easy. On condition that the Breaker did not have too bad a record in dealing with shapeshifters, few if any questions would be asked. Grimrose was, however, a special case. Grimrose was a *disturbatim*, the highest rank amongst shapeshifters, the holder of their highest honour. If Grimrose were to meet an untimely death, there would be grief and no doubt some anger in the shapeshifter community. More than that, Grimrose had somehow ingratiated himself with the Breaker Management at Cadnam. It was the Breakers who had sent Grimrose back to his own people and urged them to organise a *disturba* to save him. The Breaker Board would be none too happy if their shapeshifter protégé was snuffed out so soon after his miraculous recovery, especially as they were under the impression he had made a contribution, however modest, to Nick's success in aborting the Fourth Beginning.

So, although it was imperative that Grimrose be despatched, the method required some serious thought. It must appear to be an accident, an unfortunate consequence of the job every shapeshifter had to accept as a possibility. It worried Nick that, if Grimrose died while performing his duties, his death would simply confirm the shapeshifter's heroic status as a *disturbatim* who had helped prevent the Fourth Beginning and who had then selflessly given his life in the line of duty. What was it about this particular shapeshifter that, the more you tried to put him down, the more insistently and energetically he bobbed up?

There were two obvious ways of despatching his seemingly irrepressible assistant. He could either instruct Grimrose to adopt a form from which he would be unable to return or simply put him in harm's way until he sustained injuries from which even a shapeshifter could not recover. How to adopt one or other course, while at the same time diminishing Grimrose's burgeoning reputation, required further thought. However he achieved his end, it would be no bad thing if the shapeshifter community was reminded that, at the end of the day, the shapeshifter role was to serve his Breaker, whatever the cost.

Now he came to think of it, it would be best if Grimrose joined him at Cadnam. It would look odd to some if he appeared without his shapeshifter and, in any case, it would be much easier to keep an eye on him and indeed engineer his demise if he were, so to speak, to hand.

As for Adam and Eve, well that was really finished business. They were well and truly stymied. The only paths open to them were recrimination, distrust, alienation and, most probably, loneliness. There really wasn't any more he could do to them directly.

Their dog was a different matter. Nick was well aware of Luke's gifts. The animal might even be smart enough to hold his family together. He also knew how consoling the loyalty and affection of a dog for its master and mistress can be. At the least, he would probably provide some comfort for one of them. It was standard practice amongst Breakers to kill the pets of targets, especially dogs. An accident, ideally one for which the owner held himself responsible, was favourite – a dog inadvertently crushed by the owner when carelessly reversing his car was much favoured – but a fatal disease would do almost as well. Another conundrum for Nick – a quick accidental death or months of pain and anxiety while Luke wasted away from an inevitably fatal disease.

Still, wrestling with such problems was grist to the Breaker mill, so to speak. Wasn't life fun!

76 Conversations

Adam sank into the settee in the room Grimrose had allocated him and Eve. Eve sat beside him and looked at her husband. Adam looked back. Neither knew where to begin.

"How do you feel?" asked Eve. It was a silly question and the old Adam, or rather the younger Adam, would have replied with humour or sarcasm but not today. Today was different.

"I feel confused. I feel threatened," he said, and Eve nodded to indicate both that she understood what he meant and that she shared his state of mind.

They were silent for several minutes. Then Adam spoke. "Nick Peters told you I had been unfaithful to you. With Pandora. In Prometheus' cave."

Eve waited.

"I'm going to tell you exactly what happened," Adam said and then stopped.

"Well," Eve prompted, "do you want to tell me or not?"

Adam described to Eve how he remembered the incident, how he and Eve had been together and somehow, as his thoughts had turned to the act of sex, Eve, his wife, had been replaced by Pandora. It sounded crazy but that is what had happened.

Eve shook her head a little and shrugged. What could she say? Adam's account was unbelievable but clearly he at least believed it.

"When Nick Peters told me he had told you of my supposed fling with Pandora, I said you would be upset, angry. He said that would be the pot calling the kettle black. What did he mean?"

"I don't know," said Eve.

This time Adam waited. He knew his wife and he knew she was lying. Her denial had been a little too quick, too sharp, too defensive.

"When we became separated at Hook, I found myself alone outside the gates of the Garden of Eden. You and the others were trapped inside and I couldn't find my way back. I couldn't even find the gate. It had all disappeared."

"Yes, I know," said Adam. "Nick Peters turned up and took you under his wing." He reflected for a moment, and then added: "For God's sake don't tell me he took you to his bed as well."

The thought of Eve being unfaithful sickened him but, if she had been unfaithful as soon as they had become separated, that would mean either he didn't know his wife at all or there had been something so seriously wrong with their marriage before the infidelity that it must have been then, and must be now, irreparable. On top of that, there was their subsequent knowledge of Nick Peters' true nature. Adam found it impossible to express his loathing of the man who had done everything in his power to frustrate their quest and to destroy his life. The thought that Eve had hopped into bed with such a man was enough to drive him mad.

"No," said Eve. "It wasn't like that." As soon as she had said it, she regretted it. She hadn't meant it in the way Adam understood it.

Adam groaned. He was so angry that he felt some of his old strength returning. "My God!" he said. Before he could say more, Eve tried to explain.

"I didn't mean I slept with him, Adam. Listen to me. Listen. He seemed to know everything. He knew about our quest. He knew about you and where you were. And he knew about Bella. He promised to give me a chance to see Bella again."

"What do you mean?" Adam interrupted. "How could you see Bella again? Bella is dead. What's the matter with you?" Surely she wasn't going to try to persuade him that she had been seduced on the spurious promise of a temporary reunion with their dead daughter?

"I had a dream. I tried to tell you about it," Eve continued. "We were back on the day of the accident but it was different. You told Bella to keep away from the tree. The lightning struck but no one was hurt. We all went home safe and sound. That night, with Bella tucked up in bed, we made love."

"Well?" said Adam. "What else? You had a dream. Peters told you that you could see Bella again. That suggestion triggered a dream. And you gave the dream a happy but unreal outcome. So?"

"The man in the dream was you," said Eve uncertainly.

"Yes," said Adam. "It would be. If it was the day of the accident, I would have been there. As your husband and Bella's father, I guess I would have to be part of the dream."

Eve said nothing.

"Come on, Eve. If we have any hope of getting through this, we have to be honest. What else? Why would it be the pot calling the kettle black?"

"The man in the dream was you, but the man had Nick's voice. It was you, but it was him."

"So in your dream, you slept with a man who had my body but Nick's voice. Well, I'm not over the moon, but since it was just a dream and since it was at least my body, I guess I can just about live with that."

That was more like the old Adam. She decided not to tell Adam that

405

she was convinced her dream was not the result of suggestion but had been created in every detail by Nick; that, to her, the dream had seemed far more real than any experience in her waking life; and that the man with whom she had made love that night might have had the physical appearance of Adam but she was certain at the time and even now it had in fact been Nick.

He decided not to tell Eve that he had realised the substitution of Pandora for his wife just before, not during or after, he had engaged fully in the sexual act.

Some things are best left unsaid.

Much of the tension between them dissipated. In both cases, their infidelities had been ambiguous, not quite real and not quite illusory, difficult to define, slightly blurred at the edges.

There was a knock at the door. Eve opened the door. It was Kit.

"How's Adam?" Kit asked. "I've brought a cordial, the last of the nectar. The Storyteller had some in a small bottle to give to Gwoat in an emergency. Must have been a gift from Prometheus. Sadly Gwoat won't be needing it, so the Storyteller gave it to me. It won't give Adam back his lost fifteen years but it will help and it will certainly make him feel pretty good for a man of his age."

"I'm getting better," said Adam. He drank the offered glass and at once the favoured tipple of the gods began to warm his blood. "Is there any chance of some food?"

Kit laughed. "I'm sure we can find something and I know Grimrose will be happy to lay on a good spread, as soon as he returns from Cadnam."

"Grimrose has gone to Cadnam," said Eve. "Is that wise?"

"Nick Peters sent for him," Kit answered. "He asked me whether he should go. I said he should. If he refused, Nick would know something was wrong. For the moment, Nick is convinced he has won. We don't want to do anything to disabuse him. We need more time. You need time to process what you have been through. We all need time to take stock and to plan our exit from the mysland."

Kit used his stick to find an armchair and settled into it.

"I'm really pleased to see that you two have been talking things through," he began. "Peters has done everything he can to destroy each of you and your relationship but you mustn't let that happen. Not now. Not when we are so close."

"We have some personal issues to sort out," said Adam. It was a fairly blunt hint that he and his wife were in the middle of a difficult intimate discussion.

"I know," said Kit. "And I think you're almost there. Eve, your dream involving Nick was designed, constructed and directed by Nick. You had no say in it, although at the time you seemed to be an active participant. Nick wanted you to take just two things out of the experience, Eve. Uncertainty and guilt. Your experience with Pandora, Adam, was a cheap and shoddy piece of magic, a tawdry sleight of hand and eye by a devious illusionist, again to create in you a sense of guilt. He put just enough reality into each situation for your feelings of uncertainty, remorse and guilt to divert your attention from your goal. That was his purpose, but I'm hoping both of you will have understood something else."

"I understood there were no lengths to which Peters wouldn't go to break us," said Adam.

Eve was thoughtful. "It made me think about reality. What is real? What makes something real? My dream when I saw Bella was a dream but it had more reality in it than my normal life. It was so vivid. How could something so false be so powerful? I suppose it's the power of the imagination."

"Imagination is the most powerful phenomenon in consciousness," said Kit. "It can be used for good or ill. It can be used to escape reality or to heighten it. Sometimes it can even be used to create it. Nick, of course, uses it perversely. He uses it to persuade people to look back rather than forward, to look down rather than up, to look in rather than out. But there is another way."

Adam and Eve spent the next hour talking, reviewing all their experiences since they had set out with the Storyteller. Occasionally Kit, who listened intently throughout, would throw in a comment, a word of encouragement, a suggestion. Most of his interventions took the form of an invitation to expand on a theme which Adam or Eve had already raised.

At the end of an hour, Kit excused himself, leaving Adam and Eve to pursue their animated conversation. He walked into the main reception area of the house and listened. The rain was falling as heavily as ever. The flashes of lightning were more frequent and the gap between the lightning and the thunder shorter.

"I like thumbles of runder," said Numpty, as he and Rambler joined Kit. "It's exciting."

"So exciting evidently," said his uncle, "that you have inadvertently perpetrated a Spoonerism, or would have done, had either 'thumbles' or 'runder' existed as words." No sooner were the words out of his mouth than he regretted them. He decided to pre-empt his nephew. "'Inadvertently' means 'without intending'; 'perpetrated' means 'doing something, usually rather bad'; and Doctor Spooner was a dean of an

Oxford college who was in the habit of transposing the initial letters of words in common phrases." He hoped he had said enough.

"Sorry?" said Numpty who had found the explanation more puzzling than the sentence it purported to explain.

"You said 'thumbles of runder'," Rambler explained. "You meant 'rumbles of thunder'."

Numpty remained confused.

"It's like saying 'flocks of bats' instead of 'blocks of flats'," Kit offered.

"What have blocks of flats or flocks of bats got to do with the storm?" asked Numpty.

"Although Spooner always denied it, he is supposed to have said 'Is the bean dizzy?' when he meant 'Is the dean busy?' said Rambler. "He complained bitterly that others made up Spoonerisms to mock him." Why, Rambler wondered, did he still find himself in these extended but generally pointless exchanges with his nephew? The lad had made outstanding progress but through formal, structured lessons, not by means of eclectic questioning. When they returned to normal, he resolved to reinstate the disciplined teaching method he had always used to such good effect before he and his nephew set out on their travels.

Then Numpty smiled. "Sounds to me as though the good Doctor Spooner was a shining wit."

Rambler was stunned. Either that was the most extraordinary coincidence, or his nephew was having a little fun at his and Kit's expense. If the latter, then it would seem the pupil had just put the master in his place.

Kit just smiled and said softly to Rambler. "Don't be hurt. I think we may have to add a blushing crow to our menagerie of dog, penguin and seal."

"Do you think he meant to say that?" Rambler asked.

"I do," said Kit. "And I think we had all better prepare for some extraordinary changes."

Kit asked Rambler and his nephew to sit down and converse with him. As with Adam and Eve, he invited them to reconsider all their experiences whilst in the company of the Storyteller.

Rambler confessed he could not resolve the mystery of what the angel Rodney had called ektropy. It was not a question of *how* things seemed determined to become more complex and sophisticated; it was a question of *why*. The Chief Dawk had no answers; indeed he didn't seem to understand the question. He didn't seem to understand that simply saying 'because that's the way things are' is no more satisfactory than saying 'because God said so'. The more Rambler thought about it, the more he felt both explanations were totally unsatisfactory. Invoking God was pretty pathetic. They had met God in the Garden of Eden and a less likely and less likeable Creator it would be difficult to imagine – on top of which Rodney and Derek's account revealed a mind-boggling level of incompetence and extravagance in the process of creation. It had been a botched job from start to finish. As for Despiro Nihilopificus, he had turned out to be extraordinarily stupid for such a clever fellow. When you boiled it down, he was the frustrated parent who, when asked by an intelligent child why something is the way it is, replies 'because I say so'.

At the core of the problem, Rambler surmised, was the issue of time. It all depended on whether you were looking back or looking forward. Things in the past seemed to make sense because you could find patterns in events. But looking forward, there was little to go on. You could try to predict the future by extrapolating trends from the past but it was obvious that every major development in existence – from the creation of the universe, through to the birth of life and the emergence of consciousness – had been entirely unpredictable.

Numpty listened with rapt attention to his uncle's musings. He was so lucky to have such a wise and patient mentor. When Rambler had finished exploring his own thoughts, there was a silence. Then Numpty, who loved a good story and had hoped for a clear and happy conclusion, asked: "So what happens next, Uncle?", to which Kit, who had said nothing during Rambler's ruminations, replied; "With luck, young Numpty, the Fourth Beginning."

77 Alarm bells

When Grimrose set out from Poulner for Cadnam in one of the fleet of house cars, the rain was still hammering down. The sky looked extremely angry. Lightning bolts were randomly cutting through the almost black clouds with remarkable frequency, each time briefly exposing the snarling outline of the battling mountains of wind and rain. As Grimrose started up the A31, he shivered.

He had driven no more than three miles, just a couple of miles beyond Picket Post, when, quite abruptly, the rain ceased and the skies cleared. Grimrose peered into the rear view mirror. He could see behind him the storm which seemed to be centred over Poulner. He pulled into a lay-by and stopped. He stepped out of the car so he could take a good look back down the A31. It was quite a sight – a boiling, roiling storm hung like a mighty cowl over the whole of Ringwood. That in itself was strange, that the storm should be so localised. All around the storm, the sky was blue. Stranger still was something Grimrose noticed after a few minutes. The storm wasn't moving. Where he stood in the lay-by, he felt the light movement of warm air on a summer's day. That was at ground level. Higher up, it was reasonable to assume a brisk breeze was blowing. And yet that storm seemed to be anchored somewhere between Poulner and Ringwood.

When Grimrose arrived at the Breakers' Head Office, he felt nervous. There shouldn't be a problem, he told himself. Peters is convinced he's won. He has no reason to be suspicious and, even if he did have doubts about his shapeshifter, it was a matter of little consequence because the danger of the Fourth Beginning had been emphatically averted. And yet Grimrose felt nervous.

"Good to see you," said Nick enthusiastically when Grimrose entered the spacious reception area. "Glad you could make it."

'What did that mean?' Grimrose asked himself. Nick had summoned Grimrose. Of course he had come because that was what a shapeshifter did when summoned by a Breaker. Indeed that was precisely why Grimrose had come, to make everything seem normal. So why should Peters say 'Glad you could make it'? As though there was a real possibility he might not have come.

"Good to see you too," said Grimrose. He was being too sensitive, too suspicious. It must be guilt, although why anyone should feel guilt in their dealings with Nick Peters was surely a mystery beyond the comprehension of the brightest shapeshifter.

"I think we can confidently prepare ourselves for a period of intense adulation," suggested Nick happily. "The honourable members of the Breaker Board were excreting rectangular solids of the excremental kind over this Fourth Beginning nonsense. I've no idea what the Fourth Beginning is or was but, apparently, it meant the end of the line for the Breakers, or at least the Breaker establishment. So you and I, Grimrose, are the blue-eyed boys, the heroes of the hour, the main men, the head honchos. What we want, we will get."

"I don't really want anything," said Grimrose.

"You're a strange one," said Nick to Grimrose but loud enough for the new receptionist, the pretty brunette he had been chatting up before Grimrose arrived, to hear. "Is there really nothing you want? Take Sally here," he said indicating the girl. "I certainly wouldn't say no to a romantic evening with this young lady."

Sally blushed and was clearly embarrassed.

"I'll leave the sexual marauding to you," said Grimrose. 'Oh dear', he thought, 'shouldn't have said that.'

Nick laughed. "That's fine by me." He winked at Sally. "I wonder about you shapeshifters. I think all this shape-shifting must affect your libido. If you're a man one minute and a woman the next, your hormones must be in a state of perpetual confusion. I mean you're a man now but, if I give you the order, you could turn yourself into a replica of Sally here in the blink of an eye. So I don't really see how the sex thing works. You might be horny as hell for Sally here one minute and then have no interest in her at all the next. Unless of course, you were a lesbian. But then you wouldn't be an exact replica of Sally, at least I hope not because I've got plans for Sally that assume she has a healthy heterosexual appetite."

"I'm not going out with you," said Sally. It was an unnecessary and slightly pathetic response to Nick's assumption of her availability but she felt she had to say something.

"That's a pity," said Nick, "because rejection brings out the worst in me." He walked over to Sally and took a position behind her chair. She tried to swivel round but Nick locked the chair with his foot. She tried to get up; he pushed her down. "Listen to me, sweety," he said, holding her by the shoulders. "I can really do what I like with you or any of the young ladies in this building." He slipped one hand down and cupped her right breast. Sally turned her head round and up to remonstrate with her tormentor. "If I wanted to," Nick continued, "I could lay you out on this desk, whip off your knickers and fuck you into the middle of next week, and no one would stop me. You might complain, which would be inexplicably ungrateful, but no one would take any notice. Because I am Nick Peters, saviour of the Breaker breed."

"Leave the girl alone," said Grimrose.

"Whoa!" exclaimed Nick, releasing the girl. "What have we here? Surely not a disobedient shapeshifter? I don't know. What is the world coming to? An uppity little tart and a dysfunctional shapeshifter in the reception area of the Breakers' Head Offices, both at the same time. What's going on? Is there rebellion in the air? That would be a pity. No sooner have I disposed of the Fourth Beginning problem but we start to see the breakdown of respect for the natural order within the Breaker establishment. Threats from within as well as without!"

"Sexual assault on an innocent girl is not part of the natural order," said Grimrose. He knew he shouldn't be arguing with Peters but he was so sick of the man he couldn't help himself.

Nick was now staring into Grimrose's eyes. "You pompous little shit," he said with a laugh. "It's a good thing I'm a forgiving man or I might take offence."

It was at that moment that a claxon sounded. Then a voice over the speaker system said: "Nick Peters to the Board Room. Nick Peters to the Board Room. Now".

"You wait here," Nick ordered. "You can keep little Miss Frigid company. Maybe you can warm her up. Anyway, I've got a job for you when I've finished upstairs."

With that, Nick Peters, Breaker First Class, set off for the top floor of the Breaker Head Office. What he saw when he reached the Board Room was not quite what he had expected. The room was full but the directors were not seated ready to deliver an encomium. Rather they were standing, milling round, and talking to each other in excited, possibly, fraught tones.

The Chairman and the Managing Director were standing in front of the monitor. Nick peered round the not insubstantial bulk of the Chairman to see the screen. It was amber and it was flickering, but it was flickering from amber to red, not amber to green.

"What the hell is going on?" said the Chairman as soon as he saw Nick. "I thought the problem had been resolved. You even let the subject Adam go free."

"Lighten up," said Nick. "The monitor is faulty. I came in here a few hours ago and I noticed the system needed recalibrating. I was planning to have a word with Engineering."

The Chairman's face, always of a ruddy inclination, now looked positively apoplectic. "Lighten up!" he spluttered. "Lighten up! How dare you, you arrogant, incompetent idiot! There is nothing wrong with the monitor. We had Engineering check the system immediately. Do you think we are imbeciles? It's flickering between amber and red

412

because the risk of a Fourth Beginning is growing not diminishing, much less entirely obviated."

"That can't be right," Nick asserted, although now there was the hint of uncertainty in his voice. "Neither Adam nor Eve is capable of opening a village fete much less a new Beginning. It's all they can do to hold themselves together. Adam's suffering from premature senility, bodily if not mentally, and Eve will be trying to determine whether her predominant feeling towards her husband is pity or anger, possibly laced with a trace of guilt."

"You really are a complacent prat," said Nigel Vale, who had been submitting his report to the Board when the monitor had started flickering redward. "There is nothing wrong with the monitor. We know this because the Chairman had the system checked immediately and because there is a huge storm over your house at Poulner. There is a deluge of rain falling on Ringwood and the accompanying lightning is providing an extraordinary celestial firework display. What is so odd about that, you might ask. Well, I'll tell you. That storm has got nothing to do with us, which is rather worrying because, as you know, we control everything that happens in a mysland."

Nick frowned. "What do you mean it's got nothing to do with us? If we control everything, it must have been programmed by us, unless a piece of code has become corrupted."

"No," said Nigel, as calmly as he could. "We have checked the code. Given the immense expense of maintaining a mysland, all code is routinely checked and tested and checked again. The storm which is centred over your house and which is now threatening to wash our mysland replica of Ringwood away completely, is not of our doing. In that respect at least, we have lost control of our own creation. You will therefore understand the Board's concern."

Nick considered arguing that the Board was over-reacting, that there must be a simple explanation for the anomaly, that, in any case, freak weather conditions didn't in any way imply that Adam or Eve was about to initiate a Fourth Beginning, that any precipitate action now would jeopardise all his work in deconstructing Adam and Eve and their relationship, that the whole point had been to make an example of the pair and that, for them to fulfil their destiny as sad reminders of the futility of questing, they had now to be left alone – but he thought better of it. It would be deeply disappointing to see all his brilliant scheming unravelled but he could turn the Board's irrational fears to his advantage. If they thought there was a really major problem and he solved it, he would gain even more kudos. Then we would see which one of them was the 'incompetent, arrogant idiot' – N. Peters, yet again

413

hero of the hour, or the flatulent, panicky Chairman, who thought a bit of bad weather heralded the end of the world. He would exact a terrible revenge from that overblown fart. And Nigel Vale, who seemed to be encouraging the Board's over-reaction, would fare no better. This, Nick Peters vowed.

"I'll get onto it right away," said Nick. "I swear I'll have this sorted before the end of the day."

When Nick rejoined Grimrose in reception, he took him by the arm and led him outside into the parking area. "When you left Poulner, what was going on?" he asked.

"What do you mean?" Grimrose responded.

Nick tightened his grip on the shapeshifter's arm. "You wouldn't be holding back on me, now would you?" He gave an extra and now painful squeeze. "For example, was there anything odd about the weather?"

"It was raining," said Grimrose, squirming a little in an effort to escape Nick's iron grip.

"It was raining? Would that have been a light shower or something heavier?"

"It was quite heavy," said Grimrose. He thought it odd that Nick should be so concerned about the weather. It was, after all, his mysland.

"Quite heavy, was it?" said Nick. "Like heavy enough to submerge Ringwood, making the old market town the new Atlantis?"

"It was a storm," Grimrose conceded.

"Jolly good," said Nick. "We got there in the end. Now why, when I asked if there was anything odd about the weather, couldn't you have said, 'My word, yes. There was a fucking phenomenal tempest', because that's what it was, wasn't it? Was there anything else odd at Poulner? And let's get straight to the point this time."

"What do you mean odd?" said Grimrose, shaking off Nick's hold on his arm. "Adam and Eve arrived at the house with that fellow Kit and a couple of strangers who, I assume, were his friends. I guess you knew they were heading for the house when you released Adam and sent them back down the A31. Adam was in pretty bad shape. When I left, they were resting. They were all tired, especially Adam. How's that? Clear enough?"

"The monitor in the Board Room seems to be suggesting that our work is not entirely complete," said Nick. "The Chairman is panicking. So I think we must consider drastic measures."

"Drastic measures?" Grimrose repeated.

"Yes, drastic," Nick confirmed, "and my drastic is, as you well know, nothing short of biblical in its proportions."

78 More conversations

Back at the house on Poulner Hill, Eve was engrossed in a conversation with Kit.

Adam was resting and Eve had decided to sit quietly in the well-stocked Library to give herself time to think things through. She had been in the Library for about a quarter of an hour, when Kit, who had left Rambler and Numpty chatting away in the reception area, came in and asked if he might join her.

"I was just trying to sort things out in my head," she had said.

"How's it going?" he asked.

"I'm trying to make sense of everything."

"Everything! Quite a challenge!" Kit laughed.

"We set out to try to find answers, but I'm not sure we knew what the questions were. I think mine were personal. I wanted some explanation of why dreadful things happened. Adam wanted answers to more general questions."

"The meaning of life?" Kit suggested.

"Are you making fun?"

"Not at all. I think you may have been asking the same questions but just in different ways or with different emphases. Did your quest produce results?"

"I'm not sure. We had some amazing experiences. We met some amazing individuals. We saw some amazing things."

"So I take it you were amazed."

"You are making fun."

"I've known the Storyteller for many years, and I've seen the work that he does. He can't provide answers but he does show questors where to look. He provides new perspectives. I have to ask you a question."

Eve waited expectantly.

Kit seemed momentarily to be somewhere else. Then he said: "I am blind. The things I see are not the things a sighted person sees. I am without one of the great sensory faculties. My world has no colour. The sun for me is not a magnificent burning golden globe; it is simply warmth on my skin. The sea for me is not a vast expanse of rolling waves; it is the spray of salt water on my face. The storm is not the majestic battle of mighty clouds but the sound of rain upon the roof and thunder rumbling in my ears. That said, there are compensations. I am a wanderer and, in my wanderings, I have found ways to touch reality which are generally denied to those who are sighted."

Eve did not ask but Kit could feel her curiosity in the silence.

"There are many ways," he said with a smile. "For example, I see patterns everywhere, in the words of common conversation, in the events of everyday life, in the history of our planet. Then again, I can often feel what others are thinking. That particular gift I have learned to use with care. It is certainly open to abuse but it can be used for good. When your husband and the others were trapped in the Garden of Eden, I could persuade God to release them because I could feel God's weakness, His terrible guilt and His insatiable desire for forgiveness. He did as I wanted because, quite irrationally, more than anything else He wanted me to acknowledge Him as my father. I also have a heightened sense of the power of language and, in particular, metaphors, how you can find truth in a metaphor that would otherwise remain concealed. Metaphors provide passageways between different worlds. And yet, when all this is said, I am blind. I still cannot see the sun, or the sea, or the storm."

"You were going to ask me a question," Eve reminded. Kit seemed to have drifted off into a personal contemplation.

"What has struck you most in your adventures with the Storyteller?"

Eve thought long and hard. Then she spoke slowly. "I think I have realised what a story is. It is a way of making sense of existence. A story gives a jumble of events some kind of coherence."

"That is very perceptive," said Kit. "Ponder the word 'gives'. You imply the adding of something that is not there. That is the key. Converting events into a story is not just rearranging elements; it is adding to them."

"It is adding meaning," said Eve.

"Isn't that what you were looking for?"

Eve wanted to pursue this thought but was interrupted by the arrival of Rambler and Numpty. Uncle and nephew too had been debating the significance of their experiences since joining Adam and Eve, and Rambler in particular was keen to have Kit's view on a matter of some importance.

"May we join you?" enquired Rambler.

"Of course you may," said Kit, "although I think Eve came here to be alone."

Eve smiled to indicate the arrivals were welcome.

"Uncle Rambler has come up with an interesting question," said Numpty excitedly, eager to put his uncle centre stage as quickly as possible.

"Much of what we have seen," said Rambler, unashamedly taking the opportunity presented by his nephew, "has been about aspects of

416

evolution. For me, the most significant feature of what we have seen is this sense of direction which seems to permeate existence. Now Despiro Nihilopificus couldn't see it, but it seems obvious to me that you have to explain why things have developed from nothing into inert matter, then into life and then into consciousness. I think what I'm saying is that the Chief Dawk's answer that 'things are as they are because that's the way things happen' is post hoc reasoning. In other words, his explanation of why things are as they are would be the same whether things were as they are or were totally different. He tells us what has happened and sometimes how things have happened but he can't explain why, of all the things that could have happened, these particular things did happen."

Rambler paused for breath, wondering whether he was making himself clear.

"So?" Kit prompted.

"Well, my worry is that we may inadvertently be interfering with the process."

Frowns of incomprehension all round.

"Let's leave aside the 'why' and concentrate on the 'how'. Let's assume for the moment that the Chief Dawk is right and the mechanism for evolution is the survival of the fittest and the drive to procreate, to 'pass on one's genes' as they say nowadays, is paramount. Well, that's just not happening. We do everything we can to enable even the least viable babies to survive and, when mature, even to procreate. All the old mechanisms for destroying the weak and encouraging the poor have been dismantled. Even the patriarchal system that allowed the powerful king, or chief, or sheikh to have many wives and mistresses and thus many offspring has to a large extent been swept away. The most successful, who pay for their children's education and provide for them in many other ways, now have far fewer children because of the cost whereas the indigent on benefit find themselves better, or at least no worse, off if they have more children. For the first time in the history of life we are favouring the weak."

"Is that not the measure of a civilised society, how it treats the weakest amongst us?" asked Eve, rather shocked by what Rambler seemed to be arguing.

"The meek shall inherit the earth," said Kit.

"That could just mean that the meek are going to outbreed the strong," suggested Numpty.

"I don't think that was what was meant," Kit responded.

"Anyway, what's that go to do with anything?" asked Eve, still perturbed by Rambler's drift.

"Well," said Rambler, "I was thinking about this Fourth Beginning. It must be another big step in evolution, comparable to the creation of the universe, the birth of life and the flowering of consciousness but, if we are systematically interfering with the evolutionary process, what chance is there for such a leap?"

"If there is to be a leap," said Kit, "it could be, it almost certainly will be, of a difference in kind. That's what we should expect because all the others have been. There was no reason to expect the singularity at the beginning of time would produce a three or four or ten or twelve dimensional material universe. There was no means of predicting that a jumbled mass of elements would take it upon itself to generate life. And, after billions of years of life where evolution seemed to be quite content with simply permuting the various physical biological forms, it was entirely unforeseeable that, quite suddenly, human consciousness should emerge. I think we can be confident that a little benign interference with the survival of the fittest mechanism is most unlikely to prevent the occurrence of something as momentous as the Fourth Beginning, whatever that may be."

"So the Fourth Beginning could be anything," said Numpty. "It could be something, anything we least expect."

"Except that there has been a sense of progression in the Beginnings to date," said Rambler. "You know, this sense of direction, the direction of travel, that I talked about. Existence seems determined to become more aware of itself."

"Perhaps taking care of the weak and disadvantaged is part of it," said Eve, still upset by Rambler's apparent objection to even well-intentioned interference with the rules of evolution.

"As you sow, so shall you reap," said Kit.

"That's a metaphor, isn't it?" asked Numpty, and Uncle Rambler nodded his approval. "By the way," Numpty continued: "Where are your friends Prune and Andrew? I haven't seen them for a while."

"They are working on the camper van," Kit replied. "It took a bit of a battering when they killed poor Gwoat. Most of the damage is superficial, just holes in the bodywork, but they're checking to make sure there is no serious damage to the clever bits, the exponential drive and the paradox device. They seem to be taking their time but, once those two get together, they will happily spend hours tinkering."

"When we leave," said Rambler, who was still pondering the implications of meddling with the natural order of things, "you said we would reward Elsa, the seal. How can you reward something that will cease to exist when the mysland is terminated?"

"I'm hoping to take her out of the mysland into the real world," Kit replied.

"It would be really excellent if Optimius and Elsa could be together," suggested Numpty. "Do you think they have become good friends? They could swim off into the ocean together."

"It's possible but that would mean Optimius would have to leave Prune and Andrew. I guess it depends on how well Optimius and Elsa have been getting on."

"They'd make an odd couple," observed Adam, who, after his rest, had joined the group minutes earlier, "the sanguine penguin and an unreal seal. Rather like Prune and Andrew". Then he addressed Kit: "How can you make a virtual seal, a digital construct, into a creature that can live in the real world?"

"It would be a bit of a miracle, if you ask me," said Kit.

79 Confrontation

Nick Peters liked nothing more than going out into the field and getting things done. He could handle Head Office well enough but, truth to tell, he despised the Nigel Vales of this world. Bureaucrats, hiding behind their desks, lording it over those who ventured out into the world, took risks and did things.

That was the heart of the problem. People like Nigel spent all their time trying to minimise risk, covering their arses so that if, heaven forbid, anything went wrong, they could always blame it on someone, anyone else. And that someone was usually a field operative. They picked on people like Nick because Breakers in the field force were less practised in the art of arse-protection. In any case, Nick and his breed were out of the office most of the time because of their work and therefore far less able to defend themselves than the equally practised arse-covering clones who were Nigel's office colleagues.

"I'll want a squad of a dozen Breakers," Nick had told Nigel, "and I want the best. I'm going to end this little affair once and for all. I had planned for Adam and Eve to live on as a warning to anyone else stupid enough to go on a quest for the truth or for anything else but it seems there's been a glitch. Well, there won't be any glitches this time. This time, it's total wipe-out."

"I'll get you the men you want," Nigel had replied, "but finish this today. The Board is in no mood for any delays or excuses. Maintaining the mysland has just about drained all our spare generation capacity. If we don't close it today, we'll have to rely on our main power supply and that will mean problems here. So do the job, no loose ends."

Of course they agreed to his demands, thought Nick. They're all panicking. I could have asked for an army and they would have provided it without a second thought. Well, when this was over, he was determined to have his just deserts.

Ironically, in the Breaker Board Room, the Chairman and his co-directors were reaching very much the same conclusion. When this was over, Nick Peters would surely get what was coming to him.

The team allocated to Nick convened for a briefing in the Breaker theatre, where all training and presentations took place. While they waited, there was much discussion about the possible nature of their mission. Nick, with Grimrose in tow, arrived when all twelve Breakers were present.

"Well men, we have a job to do," said Nick. He smiled. Nigel had done him proud. He recognised amongst the squad some old friends and one or two past rivals. All were highly experienced members of the Breaker field force, at the top of the Breaker profession. They had given him the best of the best. "It's a simple total wipe-out. A bunch of trouble-makers has taken up residence in my mysland house on Poulner Hill. There's seven of them altogether, six men and a woman. Oh, and a dog. The only one who might cause a problem is a wanderer called Kit but he's blind. There's a couple, Adam and Eve. They are the main questors. The woman's feisty but emotionally screwed up. Her husband Adam, well, he's just come out of a spell in hell so he's not much use to anyone. There's an old guy, a bit eccentric, and his nephew, Numpty, who's about as sharp as a woolly jumper. And there's a couple of handymen, an Irish dwarf and his English mate, a long streak of Anglo-Saxon piss. Not exactly worthy opponents but a mess that needs to be cleaned up. As I say, we have clearance for a total wipe-out. Any questions?"

"Does that include the woman?" asked one of the men.

"Especially the woman," Nick replied. "I hope nobody here is squeamish. It is crucially important that we eliminate all of them. Even the dog. Any more questions?"

"I'm not squeamish," said the man. "I'm horny. I'll take the woman. I leave the dog to someone else."

There was general laughter.

"Then let's get on with it. There are three Range Rovers outside. It will take us about fifteen minutes to drive to Poulner Hill. I can open the gates. Two of the cars should drive up to the house; one will wait at the gate in case anyone makes a run for it. I'll be in the lead car. I don't expect any resistance. We go in. Clean executions – two to the body; one to the head. OK?"

Throughout the briefing, Grimrose watched intently. Everything Nick Peters said confirmed to Grimrose that he had made the right decision.

"Come along," said Nick to Grimrose. "You're with me."

"You don't need me for this," said Grimrose, a little too desperately.

"But I do," said Nick. "A shapeshifter should always be at his Breaker's side. In any case, you might come in useful."

Grimrose had no choice but to accompany his master. He had hoped to be able to phone a message to the questors to warn them of the impending attack but Peters seemed determined not to let him out of his sight.

There was a feeling of excitement in all three cars as they headed down the A31.

"Looks like the storm has cleared," said Nick to Grimrose.

He was right. The sun was shining in a blue sky all the way to Bournemouth and beyond.

"Nice weather for a day out," said Nick happily. "When we're done here, we could pop down to the beach for a dip."

They started to drive down Poulner Hill towards the slip road that led to the house.

"What's the matter with the car?" Nick asked the driver.

"I don't know. It feels as though the handbrake is on, but it isn't."

The car was moving more and more slowly, despite the frequent pumping of the accelerator by the driver.

"Don't know what it is," he said as he just managed to reach the slip road and pull in.

"We can walk from here," said Nick. "It's a bit of a hike up the lane but it won't kill us."

The occupants disembarked. The two other Range Rovers, which had also experienced mechanical problems on Poulner Hill, pulled in behind them. All the Breakers checked their weapons. Grimrose watched, frustrated. He considered adopting the form of the creature that had destroyed Sandy and Maizy but decided against it. All the members of the Breaker field force squad were armed with automatic weapons. He'd be lucky to kill one of them before the others shot him to pieces.

"Ready," said Nick. He started up the lane. And then he stopped. He extended his arm, feeling the air.

"What's the matter?" asked one of the men.

"I don't know," said Nick. "There's something there."

"You're seeing things," the man replied and walked past Nick, only to come to an abrupt halt.

"It's an invisible wall," said another of the men, who was gingerly feeling the space that seemed to be blocking their way.

Nick pulled out his phone and speed-dialled Nigel.

"We seem to have a bit of a problem," he said to Nigel as soon as he answered the phone. "There's something blocking our way."

"What do you mean? What is blocking your way?" asked Nigel. It was a sensible question but not one which, in the circumstances, permitted a sensible answer.

"We are at the lane that leads up to the house, but we can't get past an invisible wall."

'Shit!' thought Nigel, 'he must be pissed.' Why had he ever entrusted him with such an important mission? He was messing up again and, this time, Nick was going to take Nigel down with him. The Breaker Board had made it abundantly clear this was a final chance for both of them. "Are you sure you're not imagining it?" he tried.

The profanities that spewed out of the ear-piece of his phone merely served to convince Nigel that Nick was drunk or mad. All he could pick out was the last sentence.

"It's my fucking mysland so why can't you morons at Cadnam control it?"

That was a rather intelligent question, thought Nigel. The intense, localised storm had been a warning. Evidently, they had lost control of part of the mysland. Yet, logically, that was impossible. The mysland was an artificial construct. Real people could exist and operate within it but they couldn't affect the programme. The only way the mysland could be affected was if somehow the code became corrupted or there was a catastrophic power failure and, in either eventuality, the entire construct would automatically collapse. So, assuming Nick wasn't drunk or mad, they were facing an unprecedented and inexplicable problem.

"Have you tried going round it or over it?" asked Nigel, ignoring Nick's profanities.

"My men are working their way round but it seems the house is encased in an invisible dome," Nick replied. He was calmer now. He had realised that, if he couldn't reach the house, he couldn't complete the mission and that would lead to incalculable consequences, all of which would be very bad for Nick Peters. "We need some help here," he added.

"I'll get back to you," said Nigel.

80 The gathering in

Up at the house, Kit had convened a meeting in the Library. Prune Leach and Andrew Rimzil joined Adam, much restored by rest and the Promethean cordial, Eve, Rambler and Numpty, who, with Kit, had been pursuing an animated conversation reviewing all aspects of the quest.

"I suggest we sit down at the main table," said Kit, indicating a beautiful, round, walnut table, embellished with fine marquetry, which stood in the centre of the Library. Fortuitously, there were seven chairs.

"Where's Luke?" enquired Numpty, who always felt the questor team was incomplete without the presence of the golden retriever.

"I expect he's roaming around the grounds," said Eve. "He loves it here. There are rabbits and squirrels for him to chase and lots of land for him to explore."

When all seven were settled in their chairs, Kit spoke: "We are under attack. A squad of Breakers, under the command of Nick Peters, is at the end of the lane. They are heavily armed and their intention is to kill us."

"What!" said Adam.

"Why?" said Eve.

"Fear," said Kit, answering Eve's question. "They are afraid."

"Should we not be taking some precautions?" enquired Rambler tentatively. He was understandably troubled by the thought that, while they were sitting, quietly conversing, at a table in a library, a team of armed men intent on murder was preparing an assault.

"It seems precautions have already been taken," said Kit.

There were blank looks. "There is a protective shield around this property. Nick Peters and his fellow Breakers are unable to reach us, for now at least."

"What protective shield?" asked Eve.

Prune coughed. "It might be something to do with some tinkering Andrew and I have been doing. We had some spare time so we thought we would service the camper van. You know us. Can't bear to be idle. We've removed the exponential drive and the paradox device from the camper van and put them on test. We're using the engines in two of the house cars to run them both in parallel. The test on the paradox device involves running the observation bubble, you know, the one you used to observe the start of the universe. It could be that. The bubble stops anything outside from coming in."

"How long will it last?" asked Eve, cutting to the chase.

"Well, the cars we're using to power the test have full tanks so the test should run for about four or five hours, maybe a little longer. We're not sure how much power the exponential drive will take. That's the main variable."

"I don't know if four or five hours will be long enough," said Kit.

"Long enough for what?" asked Adam.

"Can't you feel it?" Kit replied. "We are on the cusp. I have spent years wandering this country and many others. I have lived through many strange experiences, one or two of which I have shared with you. Occasionally, you realise that a person you meet or an event you witness is really important, out of the ordinary, truly remarkable. Well, that is the feeling I have now, but in spades. It is not any one of us and it is not where we are, but there is something…," He paused, lost for words. Then he said "…imminent, impending, I don't know."

"Not us being massacred, I hope," said Rambler.

The house phone rang. Kit picked up the receiver. It was Nick Peters.

"I don't know what you're playing at and I don't know how you're doing it, but you'd better stop it and let me in. It's my bloody house, after all."

Kit paused and then said something that surprised the questors as much as its intended audience. "Nick Peters, today is judgement day and you are to be judged. How can I put this? Nick Peters, you are a pothole on the road of life. You are a fly in the amber of evolution. You are a haemorrhoid…"

"What the fuck are you talking about?" enquired a genuinely and understandably puzzled Peters.

"It's obvious you have come here to destroy us," Kit replied.

"Were they metaphors?" asked Numpty. Rambler nodded.

"If we were to let you and your friends in," said Kit to Nick, "we would be committing suicide. We would be lemmings rushing to leap over the cliff. We would be Trojans wheeling in the wooden horse. We would be sheep inviting the wolf for dinner."

"Just on a point of fact," Rambler interpolated, "lemmings don't hurl themselves over cliffs."

"What are you doing?" Eve asked of Kit.

He put his hand over the mouthpiece of the phone. "I'm playing for time and I'm trying to throw Peters off balance."

"With a barrage of metaphors?" queried Eve.

"Breakers don't like metaphors. They feel they are inappropriate."

"Well, I'm not surprised Peters is a bit pissed off," said Adam who had remained silent thus far. "A pothole, a fly and a haemorrhoid! Not a flattering choice!"

"It wasn't a choice. I was applying all three," Kit explained.

"Are you letting me in or not?" Nick screamed down the phone. Then, in a calmer voice, he said: "I'm not planning to do you any harm." Finally, he added: "We've got your dog."

"Not Luke," said Numpty loudly, loud enough for Nick to hear down the phone.

"How many bloody dogs have you got?" Nick sneered.

"That's not possible," said Kit, looking to Prune for confirmation.

Prune shook his head. "It is possible if Luke wandered outside the perimeter. Things inside the bubble can go in and out. It's just things outside can't get in. For them, it's a closed system."

"We would want proof of life," Kit demanded.

"I'll give you proof of life," said Nick. "There was a moment's pause, then a yelp, then a whimper. "Is that proof enough, or do I need to cut the whole leg off and post it to you?"

Kit could not make out what Luke was minding to him but he could feel the dog's pain.

"Leave Luke alone," cried Numpty.

"I'll bring the dog with me if you let me in," said Nick. "I just want to talk to you. Come on. I released Adam. It's all over. There's no need for any more trouble. We just need to talk."

Numpty looked pleadingly at Kit, but Kit remained unmoved. "You can talk to us over the phone. You just can't kill us over the phone. So if it's talking you want, go right ahead."

"Are you going to let me in or not?" Nick demanded.

"No," said Kit. "Anyone who can torture an animal is not to be trusted with a human life." Kit then heard another voice on the phone but fainter. "It's Cadnam for you," he heard the voice say. "They have an answer."

"I'll be back," said Nick to Kit. The phone went dead.

oooOooo

"What are we going to do?" asked Adam. "We can't just wait here for the cars to run out of fuel. You say we can get out but they can't get in. If you've serviced the camper van, we could make a run for it."

"The problem with that as a tactic," said Rambler, "is that if we leave here, they can catch us. They will have every exit covered. At least we're safe here while the bubble holds. If we try to leave, we are fair game, so to speak."

"There's nothing fair about this," objected Numpty. "And it's not

426

much of a game. Why are these Breakers trying to kill us? Why does Nick Peters hate us? Why did he hurt Luke? We have to rescue Luke."

"Tell me more about the mysland," said Adam to Kit. "What exactly is it? I mean it seems real enough but you say it's some kind of construct. Is it real?"

"It depends what you mean by real," Kit replied. "If we get killed in the construct, we will be dead. There is the real world and there is the mysland, which is a replica of part of the real world, so there are two realities – but there is only one of each of us so, if we are hurt or killed here, we are hurt or killed. That's it."

"The mysland is really an invention based on a set of rules," said Andrew. "I've studied these phenomena. They are replicas of a small piece of the outside world but, within it, there are a set of rules, programmed by the Breakers, to hold it all together. The main rule is that they have complete control of everything that happens within the mysland boundary."

"So how have we been able to set up a defensive shield? How are we able to frustrate their wishes?" asked Rambler.

"Search me," said Prune. "I bet that's the question they're asking at Cadnam."

"It all depends who makes the rules," said Adam.

"It all depends who's telling the story," said Eve.

"Whoever makes the rules can change the game," said Adam.

"It's the story that gives meaning, only the story," said Eve.

Kit grinned. "It's happening. We need to organise ourselves. Prune and Andrew, you should leave now. There is nothing more you can do here. Leave the paradox device running. Take the van and wait for us at the Elm Tree. I doubt if the Breakers will try to stop you. You're no threat to them and you've already helped as much as you can. Pick up Elsa as well as Optimius when you leave the mysland. I promised Elsa a reward. With a bit of luck, we'll join you in a few hours."

oooOooo

Nigel Vale didn't really understand what the engineers had told him. After all, he was just a manager. But it seemed that the questors and their friends had somehow created an anomaly in the mysland. Because the Breakers' mysland, really Nick Peters' mysland because it was Peters who had determined the dimensions, was so large, the power needed to maintain it had been spread just a little more thinly than was recommended.

As a result, there were one or two tears in the seams of the mysland

and, because the construct was not maintained everywhere at full strength, the questors had been able to use another power source to create, in effect, a mysland within the mysland. This mini-mysland was not under the control of the questors but nor was it under the control of the engineers at Cadnam.

What could be done about it? Probably nothing. Peters and his squad would just have to wait until the questors ran out of power, and Peters would have to pray that the questors' power ran out before Cadnam had to close the whole mysland because its own power reserves had become depleted.

The only possibility of breaking the mini-mysland would be to bombard the defensive dome over Poulner Hill, either in the hope of rupturing the shield or simply to speed up the draining of the questors' power reserves.

With that in mind, and to show Peters that the Breaker Board was determined to see an end to the matter, the Chairman of the Board had instructed Nigel to send a division of infantry, equipped with artillery, to back up Peters' squad and to see what some heavy shelling could achieve.

Nigel had mixed feelings about sending troops. Of course, he wanted the assignment to be successfully concluded but it irritated him that Nick, who really didn't have the best of track records as a Breaker field operative, always seemed to be able to get what he wanted. The more mistakes he made, the more he demanded and the more he got.

On the positive side, the involvement of troops must, to some extent, dilute any kudos Nick Peters would be able to derive from the successful conclusion of the operation.

At the end of the day, what Nigel felt didn't really matter. He had to do what he was told, and he had been told to send the troops.

It took two hours for the troops to reach Poulner Hill. Although he were based only a few miles from the target area, Nestor Gruin, the commander, had to gather his troops, brief his officers and transport the men and materiel. Like Nick and his squad of Breakers, the army found the final leg of the journey down Poulner Hill difficult, with all the vehicles plagued by mechanical faults.

"When you're ready, commander, fire at will," Nick had ordered. "As far as I'm concerned you can raze the house and its environs to the ground. After all, it's what we Breakers do best."

The first shell landed on the topmost section of the dome. The sound of it exploding was muffled by the shield but, in the Library, where the questors were sitting, they heard a thud. They all looked up. Then the barrage began. Thud, after thud, after thud.

"Can the shield hold?" asked Rambler. Kit shrugged. "The power generated by the house cars must be pretty small when compared to the resources available to the Breakers. The real answer is, we don't know. The defensive bubble generated by the paradox device wasn't built to withstand sustained shelling."

"Then we should do something to strengthen it," said Adam thoughtfully.

"We should tell a different story," added Eve. "Or at least add to this one."

"We could change the rules," said Adam. "You said the Breakers didn't like metaphors. Why can't we use metaphors against them?"

"What?" asked Rambler. "Do you mean bombard them with abusive figures of speech? I really don't think that will cut the mustard on this occasion."

"Oh I think we can do better than that," said Kit. "We can call upon an army of metaphors."

"Is that a metaphor?" asked Rambler, who felt he was losing a grip on the conversation.

"No," said Adam. "We can deploy…" he paused, thinking hard, "a Metaphorce."

Rambler was entirely bemused for two reasons. First, Adam had just coined a word which, as far as Rambler knew, did not correlate with anything real but which Adam seemed to think could have a significant impact in their current predicament. Secondly, why had his nephew not asked any questions?

An explication of the Metaphorce was to be furnished shortly. The answer to the question about Numpty's unwonted reticence became immediately apparent, or rather not apparent. Numpty was nowhere to be seen.

81 The Metaphorce

Nick Peters and Nestor Gruin, the commander of the Breaker troops, were astonished when Hector Meap, leader of the Metaphorce, approached them in the Control and Command tent. He was exceedingly smartly dressed, in a sky blue military uniform on which was displayed a kaleidoscope of medals. He carried a scroll of paper in one hand and an ice bucket in the other.

"I take it one of you is in charge," said Hector. "Sorry I can't salute but, as you can see, my hands are full. I'm Captain Meap, leader of the Metaphorce, widely known as the Lion of the North; that's me, not the Metaphorce. The Metaphorce is generally known as the Metaphorce or, occasionally as the Claws of the Lion, which I rather like. I am here to demand a ceasefire. Let the lion lie down with the lamb. Not that I'm suggesting either of you is a lamb. But peace is always better than war, don't you think? Chat rather than splat, I always say. The pen is mightier than the sword, sort of thing, so, if you'll append your signatures to this document, we could all settle down in this rather pleasant spot and get to know each other over a bottle of champagne, which I happen to have brought with me."

The silent, open mouths of Peters and the commander said it all.

Eventually, Nick spoke. "Who the fuck are you?"

"Thought I'd just explained all that but, if your hearing is impaired or even if you are as deaf as a post, or a few million neurones short of a full complement, as in one can short of a six pack or not the sharpest sabre in the armoury, or the lights are on but the house is empty, no offence intended or I hope taken, I'm happy to run through it again."

"Did Cadnam send you?" asked Nestor Gruin. Had the Breaker Board decided to send yet more reinforcements?

"No, of course not! I would scarcely be suggesting a ceasefire if we were on the same side. Keep up."

"Then you can't be here," said the commander.

"Do you mean I shouldn't be here or are you in denial of the blindingly obvious?"

"He means," Nick Peters interrupted, "if you aren't part of the mysland programme you can't be here. You can't exist."

"What is this mysland?" asked Captain Meap, although his voice sounded as though he knew the answer.

"It's a construct, a replica of a small part of the real world," Nestor explained.

"So it's not real," said Captain Meap. "I see. So some figments of someone's imagination in an unreal world brought into being by a computer programme are trying to tell me I don't exist. Bit incongruous and bloody rude, I'd say."

The commander, who indeed had no existence other than in the mysland, was somewhat put out by the captain's reasoning. Nick, on the other hand, simply felt angry. The whole point of a mysland was that this sort of thing, whatever this sort of thing was, couldn't happen. You might as well operate in the real world if entirely unexpected interventions could take place.

"Who sent you?" Nick asked.

"I'm operating under a mandate from the legitimate occupiers of the estate you are shelling," said Captain Meap.

Nick grunted. "Legitimate occupiers, my arse! It's my house."

"Is that a metaphor?" asked the captain.

"Is what a metaphor?"

"You seemed to be equating the occupiers with your anus. Were you expressing yourself and your feeling towards the occupiers in metaphorical terms? I'm thinking some kind of love–hate relationship. You despise them but, at the same time, you reluctantly recognise their usefulness."

"No, that's not what I was saying," said Nick as calmly as he could. "The important part of what I said is 'It's my house'. And, just for future reference, we Breakers don't use metaphors."

"Oh dear!" said Captain Hector Meap, Lion of the North, leader of the Metaphorce, "sadly not a lot of common ground there then."

"Tell you what," said Nick, in his chatty mode, "why don't you bugger off?"

"Can't do that unless you agree to a ceasefire, stop the shelling and let the questors leave the mysland." The captain sounded very serious now.

"And if we don't?" said Nick.

"My men are camped about half a mile back from Picket Post on the top of Poulner Hill. We outnumber you and we are far better equipped. We have the 'Fist of God', a rather quaint denomination and a bit of a metaphor for a bomb genetically programmed to wipe out Breakers and their little helpers."

Nick's eyes screwed up with incredulity. "You're talking complete bollocks. There's no such thing. How could a bomb, which is fundamentally indiscriminate, seek out Breakers?"

"You've almost answered your own question. This bomb discriminates fundamentally. The bomb is equipped with an olfactory sensor which can seek, find and destroy Breakers by locking on to the scent that hangs around the Breaker anus after excretion. However hygienic you may try to be, some smell lingers in the molecules trapped in the hairs. The sensor on the missile is as sensitive as a dog's nose. Indeed, 'dog's nose' was the working title for the device when under development; the name was changed to the 'Fist of God' because it had a better metaphorical resonance. Anyway, brilliant piece of engineering. Never fails."

"I think you're making this up as you go along," said Nick.

"Thought you might," said Hector. "So I've arranged a demonstration." Hector tapped what looked like a button at the neck of his uniform.

There was a whistling sound of an unpleasantly high pitch. What looked like a small silver ball but which, on closer inspection, would have revealed itself as a silver fist swept into the tent and circled the three men once. The fist-shaped missile then ducked down behind the commander, shot up aiming unerringly for the commander's anus, dug itself in and exploded. It was not a large explosion but it shook the tent. The commander fell to the ground, a look of astonishment on his face.

"He doesn't feel any pain," said Hector to Nick. "The Fist of God severs the nerves in the spinal column. God and His Fist are just but merciful."

The commander nodded thanks and acknowledgement to Hector for his kind consideration, and died.

"Petty impressive, eh?" said Hector. "Are you ready to sign? No point in pushing matters any further. Of course, war is my business and war involves killing but I hate to see unnecessary carnage, even if most of the victims are merely constructs."

Nick paused for thought. He had no idea how, but clearly the mysland had been compromised. Not only was he unable to access the house where the questors were holed up but, even if their defensive shield collapsed, his forces were outgunned. If he was to salvage the mission, he would have to think laterally.

"I'll stop the shelling," he said. "Hold your men where they are. I'll talk to my own people. You wait here. I'll get back to you."

With that, Nick left the tent and made his way back down to the entrance to the lane where his own men were either checking their weapons or resting. They had tied Grimrose to one post and Luke to another. Luke had lost a lot of blood from the knife wound that Nick had caused when on the phone to Kit. Grimrose could do nothing to help himself or the dog. Nick had told his men to cut the shapeshifter to pieces if he made any move to change his form or to escape.

When Nick had checked that Grimrose was still safely held prisoner,

432

he phoned Nigel Vale. There was no answer. He then phoned the main switchboard at Cadnam. For several minutes again there was no answer. Eventually someone picked up and he heard a frightened female voice say "Yes".

"This is Nick Peters. Get me Nigel Vale and get him now."

"I don't know where he is," said the girl. "It's chaos here. Everyone's running around. There's a problem."

"I know there's a problem and I'm trying to deal with it. Find Vale and put him on the line. I'll wait."

A few more minutes passed. Then, against a hubbub of noise, Nick heard Nigel's voice. "Have you broken in?" Nigel asked.

"No, I haven't broken in. And I've had to stop the shelling."

"Why?" Nigel's voice sounded close to hysterical. "You must break in and wipe them out. The monitor is showing red. It's still flickering between amber and red but it is more red than amber. The Board is planning to evacuate, leaving the rest of us to face whatever it is that terrifies them. Use everything you've got to break the shield."

"We have a problem with that," said Nick. "I've just left a guy called Hector Meap, Captain Hector Meap. He's the commander of something he calls the Metaphorce and, according to him, his troops outnumber ours and are far better equipped. I've seen a demo of one of their weapons, the Fist of God, and it's pretty impressive. He certainly made the late Nestor Gruin uncomfortable. He's said we must cease shelling or face the consequences."

"The commander is dead! What are you saying?" asked Nigel, with tears in his voice. "Is there nothing you can do?"

Nick paused for a few moments, just to let Nigel savour the utter hopelessness of the situation. Then he said: "I've got the germ of an idea. It's a long shot but, if it comes off, I want a guarantee of promotion, a much higher salary and pretty much freedom to do what I like with the typing pool or whatever you call that cornucopia of pussy hanging around Head Office in Cadnam with nothing to do."

"You pull this off and you can be Chairman of the Board if you want." There was no fight left in Nigel.

"There's nothing I want less," Nick replied with a laugh. "Just make sure the Board understands my terms." With that, he terminated the call.

oooOooo

Nick then wandered over to Grimrose, kicking Luke on the way, not so much to cause the dog pain as to see whether he was still alive. Luke

433

whimpered faintly.

"It's a dog's life," Nick quipped. He then addressed Grimrose: "Now Grimrose, first let me apologise for the way my men have treated you. There seems to be a feeling, not shared by me of course, that you're not to be trusted. Anyway, you now have a chance to silence the doubters once and for all while performing a truly noble service for your masters in general and me in particular."

Grimrose said nothing.

"As you will have gathered, we need to gain access to the house but we are prevented by some kind of shield. My men cannot break through. My field force is being impeded by their force field, you might say. Get it? Never mind! We could of course wait for the questors' power source to run out but I understand from Cadnam that waiting involves an unacceptable level of risk. I have therefore come up with a solution which, centrally, involves you."

Still Grimrose said nothing. What could he say? He was not going to help Nick Peters but to make that clear now would simply bring about his abrupt termination, thus ensuring he could be of no help to Kit and the others.

"I want you to make one more shape-shift," said Nick. "It will enable you not only to enter the property but also to fulfil our mission."

Despite himself, Grimrose's curiosity was aroused.

"It will call for ingenuity and some degree of self-sacrifice, as well as your normal but remarkable shapeshifting abilities," said Nick.

"Well?" said Grimrose impatiently.

"Isn't it obvious? What could penetrate a defence shield and deliver a lethal blow? Come on, it would have to be small, very small, exceedingly small but nevertheless lethal."

Grimrose still looked blank.

"A virus," said Nick triumphantly. "For example, an Ebola virus."

Blankness turned to incredulity, which then turned to horror.

Luke made a noise the equivalent in dog sounds of a groan. He had been listening to Nick and had realised before Grimrose what Nick had in mind.

"You must be completely insane," said Grimrose.

"Well, when I say an Ebola virus, obviously I don't mean a single Ebola virus, I mean billions of them. I realise you couldn't compress your material essence into a single virus. It was tough enough for you to squeeze into a fairy. Please give me some credit."

Grimrose ignored Nick's warped attempt at humour. "Let's leave aside the fact that, if I attempted what you suggest, I would have no way of reverting to my normal form. There would be no intelligence, no will, no 'me' to initiate a reversal. So I'd be dead."

"That's the element of self-sacrifice," Nick confirmed.

"As I said, leaving my annihilation aside, the Ebola virus is not airborne. How do you propose to infect the people in the house?"

"That's the ingenuity. You need to perform a little genetic modification on the virus so it's infectious as well as contagious."

"I'm a shapeshifter not a biologist or a genetic engineer," snapped Grimrose.

"You're so negative," Nick chided.

"Even if it could be done, are you proposing to release an infectious Ebola virus into the atmosphere? Do you realise millions could die?"

"Hold on," said Nick. "What do you take me for? First of all, I would expect the virus to be contained within the defensive bubble the questors have deployed. The virus has a pretty short shelf-life so most of it will have become inactive after a few hours. And, if the questors run out of power and the defence shield fails, it will still be contained in the mysland. We need be concerned only with real people, like you and me and a few of the people at Cadnam. And we can get out well before the virus spreads. Sorry! Of course, you can't get out, now I come to think of it, because you will actually be the virus but every one else should make it."

"What about all the constructs?" asked Grimrose. "They may not be real but they think they are and, if they are infected, they will suffer all the symptoms of Ebola."

"You really are a bleeding heart," said Nick, "which, funnily enough, is how many of the victims of the virus will die. So now you're worried about constructs that don't really exist, or certainly don't exist outside the mysland. I just don't understand you. Cadnam wants to pull the plug on the mysland as soon a possible, so they're all destined for oblivion in days, if not hours."

"Why are you so determined to kill the questors?" Grimrose asked.

"That's the mission," said Nick. "And the last time I checked, shapeshifters had to do what they were told, not ask a lot of bloody silly questions."

Grimrose was about to raise further strenuous objections to Nick's genocidal plan, when he, Nick and Nick's Breaker squad were astonished to see a figure approaching them down the lane. The figure reached and then walked though the impenetrable shield which had blocked the way of the Breakers.

"What have you done to my dog?" said Numpty for it was he, and he was angry.

Nick was so surprised he did not answer immediately.

Numpty knelt down beside Luke and raised the dog's head a little. Luke's eyes opened and he whimpered weakly.

"Did you do this?" Numpty addressed Nick. Numpty might only be a callow youth but the fire in his eyes caused even Nick to hesitate.

'This is one angry retard' he thought to himself. "I shouldn't worry too much about the dog," he said. "He's already well on his way to the kennels in the sky. I should be more concerned about my own welfare."

Numpty continued to comfort Luke. Nick indicated to one of the Breakers that he should cut Numpty's throat, an easy enough instruction to follow since Numpty had assumed a kneeling position. The Breaker produced a hunting knife with a serrated blade and approached the lad.

"Stop!" said Grimrose. "If you want me to fulfil my last assignment, you won't harm the boy."

Nick frowned but signalled to the advancing Breaker to wait.

"Sorry," said Nick. "Did my ears deceive me or did my loyal shapeshifter of many years' faithful service just threaten to disobey me?"

"No," said Grimrose firmly, "your ears did not deceive you. I will not obey you ever again if you harm the boy. Let him go back to the house and face his fate in the company of his uncle and his friends."

"You really are becoming a sentimental old fart," said Nick. "What's the point? They're all going to die one way or another in the next few hours. Wouldn't it be kinder to put this one out of his misery now?"

"I'm not going anywhere without Luke," said Numpty.

"This is becoming sickening," said Nick with genuine revulsion. "Grimrose here is concerned about the feelings of a bunch of pseudo-human constructs and the boy is happy to die for the sake of a dog. I fear my lunch is about to head north and revisit my mouth. What is happening to the world?"

"I will do as you ask," said Grimrose to Nick, "if you release me and let the boy and the dog go without harm."

"It's a deal," said Nick happily. So long as Grimrose was prepared to go along with the Ebola play, there was nothing to lose by acceding to Grimrose's wishes and, since the Ebola gambit inevitably involved the complete dissolution of Grimrose as well as all those holed up in the house, this could be seen as the victor rather nobly granting the condemned man his last request.

When Grimrose had been released, he knelt down by Numpty. "Let me look at the dog," he said gently. Numpty moved out of the way.

"Is there anything you can do?" Numpty asked.

"He has lost a great deal of blood and is close to death but I will try."

"Wait a minute," Nick intervened. "You will need all your will and strength for your last assignment. I can't have you depleting your resources to fix a dog."

"You promised to release both the boy and the dog unharmed. You can't release a dead dog unharmed, now can you?" Grimrose asked and then added: "Don't worry about my capacity to fulfil the last task. Given that I don't have to worry about reversion to my original form, I have plenty of power to help this dog and then do as you wish."

Grimrose cradled Luke's head in his lap. He placed his hand over the dog's ears and looked into the dog's eyes.

"He's dying, isn't he?" whispered Numpty.

Grimrose ignored the question. Beads of sweat appeared on Grimrose' forehead, and a small trickle of blood oozed from his right nostril.

"I'm a little hurt," said Nick. "When I think of the fuss you made about fixing my leg and I now see you putting in all this effort, sweating blood literally, to sort out a dog, well it's rather galling."

Luke's tail gave a slight twitch. Whatever Grimrose was doing, it was reaching all parts of his body.

After a few more minutes, Grimrose rested. "He will live, his heart is strong and his love of life is powerful," he said, "but he will need time to recover fully. The only other help I can give is to mend his leg. The wound was deep and it cut a tendon as well as an artery. It will take a few minutes."

Nick muttered that, given all those within the bubble were going to be assailed with a deadly, genetically modified virus, fixing the dog's leg was pointless and that, given they would all be dead within the hour, telling Numpty the dog would need time to recover fully was a prognosis loaded with irony.

After his rest, Grimrose ran his hand up and down the wounded leg, over and over again. The wound sealed and then healed. Beneath the fur and skin, the tendon bonded. Luke could not suppress a howl because the healing hurt but it was a howl of pain liberally intermixed with hope and joy, as Luke realised he had been pulled back from the edge of oblivion.

"Go now," said Grimrose to Numpty. "Go and take the dog back to the house."

"I don't know how to thank you," said Numpty, a sentiment shared but not articulated, at least not audibly, by Luke.

"No need," said Grimrose. "No need at all."

Numpty and Luke walked up the lane, through the defensive shield and on to the house.

They were watched closely by Nick and his Breakers, one of whom accompanied them to the edge of the shield. As soon as Numpty and the dog had gone through, the Breaker tried to follow, only to bang his face on an invisible wall.

Nick's phone rang. It was Nigel Vale.

"We've checked out this Captain Hector Meap. No such person. As for an army parked a couple of miles back from Picket Post, forget it. There's no one there. If Meap exists at all, he's a confidence trickster. The Board says you should resume shelling immediately and do anything else that is necessary to bring this matter to an end."

"Are you sure?" Nick was unwilling to admit he had been duped. "He seemed to have the Fist of God at his disposal, as Commander Gruin could testify had he not been anally terminated."

"We've scanned every inch between Cadnam and Picket Post. The programme is intact. The only anomaly is the bubble over your house on Poulner Hill. We are still trying to find the fault that is allowing the questors to protect themselves but, so far, without success. That's why you should hit them with everything you've got. The monitors are still flickering between amber and red."

Nigel rang off. Nick turned to Grimrose. "Did you hear some of that?" he asked.

"Enough," Grimrose replied.

"In that case, old boy, you will realise the time has come. You must now do your duty and to fulfil your promise. It's time for you to go viral."

82 The beginning of the Beginning

When Numpty reached the house, all was quiet. He entered and made his way to the Library, where Kit and the others were sitting. He was warmly greeted when he entered, facing a barrage of questions.

"I've had the most amazing experience," said Numpty. "I went down the lane. As I approached the road, I could see a group of heavily armed Breakers, with Nick Peters among them. I could also see Grimrose tied to a post on the right side and Luke, lying on the ground, tied to a post on the left. Luke looked awful."

The others looked at Luke. Adam was patting his dog on the head. Luke's tail was wagging enthusiastically. The dog seemed to be in pretty good shape.

"I walked up to the Breakers. I wanted to see how badly Luke was hurt."

"You walked into a group of heavily armed Breakers?" said Adam.

"I did," said Numpty. "Luke was injured. In fact, Luke was close to death."

Adam concluded that Numpty was exaggerating a little but he let it pass.

Numpty continued. "Then Grimrose intervened. He demanded that Nick should release him and let me and Luke go. They did some deal. Then Grimrose healed Luke. He put life back into Luke. He mended Luke's leg. It was like a miracle."

"Come on," said Adam. "I don't think we believe in miracles any more."

"Really?" said Kit. "You've travelled through time and space, you've visited a Titan, you've seen the birth of the universe, of life and of human consciousness – and you don't believe in miracles."

Adam frowned a little and then shrugged.

"I think we can accommodate the curing of a dog in what we believe," said Eve. "After all, Luke's here and he looks alive and well."

"And we've learned the power of metaphors," said Rambler. "They now seem miraculous to me. I don't know what Adam's Metaphorce did, but the shelling stopped, at least for a while."

"And I know that the only way to make sense of life, to give life meaning, is to find the story in it," Eve added. "It's not so much that the victor is the one who writes the story; it's more that the storyteller is always the victor."

"And we also know that, in the search for answers, we first have to identify the rules of the game," Adam added. "And it's the storyteller who makes the rules."

"But he also has to follow the rules," said Eve. "The storyteller doesn't have absolute power. Stories have their own rules; they have a sense of direction."

"Like evolution," said Rambler.

"Like everything," said Kit. "From nothing to this. From nothing to dust; from dust to life; from life to mind. If it were not so, there would be no stories to tell. There would be no stories at all."

83 Going viral

Nick insisted that Grimrose should make his way to the west side of the bubble that protected the house. Neither Nick nor Grimrose had any idea of the climatic conditions inside the bubble but Nick knew that the prevailing wind was from the west. He reasoned that, if Grimrose began his Ebola infiltration from the west side, and if the wind inside matched the wind outside, the wind-borne virus would quickly spread through the whole bubble.

When they reached the western side, Nick called a halt. "Let's not indulge in any sentimental drivel," he said to Grimrose. "We have a job to do. Best get on with it."

"Before I keep my word," said Grimrose, "there is something I would like to say."

"If you must," said Nick, "but keep it short. And I should point out that, since I'm the only person here, and since my memory for trivia is not the most retentive, the odds of what you say reaching posterity are on the anorexic side of slim."

"Is that a metaphor?" asked Grimrose.

"I doubt it," said Nick. "I don't like metaphors."

"Are you not attributing human characteristics (i.e. slimness) to my words, which are obviously incorporeal?"

"What the fuck are you talking about?" said Nick. "We're not here to debate figures of speech or anything else for that matter. Ebolarise yourself and eliminate the questors."

"I haven't had my say yet," said Grimrose almost petulantly.

"Well get the fuck on with it. We haven't got all day."

"You're swearing rather a lot. That's not like you. Are you under a particular strain?"

Nick tried to control himself. He would happily have pumped Grimrose full of bullets with his semi-automatic weapon but he couldn't because he was relying on Grimrose to pull off his master-stroke. He knew Grimrose would do what he had promised because that's what shapeshifters did. It was ironic that creatures capable of adopting so many and varied guises should be so unalterably single-minded and trustworthy, at least in the dealings with Breakers.

"Not under any particular strain," said Nick. "Just a tad concerned that the entire Breaker world is about to be annihilated by something no one understands and which, it seems, only you and I can prevent."

"So we're a team?" said Grimrose.

Nick didn't answer. Was Grimrose playing with him? Or was there some point to the shapeshifter's questions?

"Because," Grimrose continued, "if this is a team effort, I just wondered which part of the venture was to be undertaken by you?"

"It's my idea," said Nick.

"That's it," Grimrose replied. "That's your contribution. You come up with an idea that involves my utter destruction and that makes us a team. That's a pretty odd kind of a team. That's a bit like saying that the man who drops the bomb and the bomb he drops are a team."

"I just told you I don't like metaphors."

"That was a simile."

"I don't like similes, either. Please could we get on with it."

"Well, I will keep my word and, as you put it, 'ebolarise' myself – but I want you to know I'm disappointed."

"Oh come on!" said Nick coaxingly. "Yes, it's tough. Yes, not only are you going to die but, when your story is told, sadly it will not be a very heroic conclusion. 'Shapeshifter's life ends diffused in a cloud of lethal viruses'. But at least you will play a key part in the salvation of the Breakers. So, yes, it's tough but you have to take a hit for the team. So man up and get on with it."

"There you go again," said Grimrose. "All this team stuff. And I'm not disappointed that I have to die. I'm disappointed with you. I've reviewed the many years we have spent working together. I have gone over every assignment we have undertaken. I have been meticulously fair in attributing credit according to the actual contribution each of us made to our successes and in apportioning responsibility for any failures – and I have reached a balanced view at the end of this rigorous evaluation exercise that you are one monstrous, total shit."

"Gracious me!" Nick mocked. "Language! You must have been mixing in the wrong company."

"You never spoke a truer word," Grimrose replied. "Before I fulfil my promise, I need the answer to a simple question. Why do the Breakers need to stop all the questors from succeeding? Why is it so important that no one should find the truth? And what is the Fourth Beginning?"

"That's one simple question?" scoffed Nick. "Sounds more like three pretty complicated ones. But I'll give you a simple, single answer. It's not for us to ask such questions. All these years, we've been obeying orders."

"Don't you know why?" Grimrose persisted.

Nick paused. No, he didn't know why. But he didn't need to know why. He was fulfilled by doing what Breakers did. Obviously Grimrose was playing for time. "What exactly is your problem?" he asked. "I do what I'm told to do and, when you do me the courtesy of dissolving into a shower of Ebola viruses, I can get back to what I do best."

"And that would be frustrating questors, treading on dreams, undermining relationships, discouraging creativity, promoting insecurity, preaching nihilism, anything to prevent the illusive Fourth Beginning," said Grimrose.

"In a nutshell," Nick agreed. Anything to get to the end of Grimrose's rigmarole.

"Irrespective of the harm you are doing?" Grimrose queried.

"Absolutely," said Nick.

"So you're incorrigible, irredeemable and utterly unrepentant."

"That's about it," said Nick.

"Then I'll begin the transformation," said Grimrose.

Ebola is a peculiarly unpleasant virus. It causes a haemorrhagic fever. The version Grimrose chose to generate had some unique characteristics. It was infectious; merely breathing close to an infected person was sufficient to contract the disease. It was fast working in that, once inhaled, it began to work within a minute or so. It was absolutely lethal in the sense that whoever became infected was certain to die. And it had a life span in the air or in the body of a dead victim of no more than three minutes. In other words, in metaphorical terms, it was a supernova of a virus, immensely powerful but short-lived.

When Grimrose said he would begin the transformation, Nick moved well back, expecting Grimrose to approach the rim of the defensive bubble. Instead Grimrose stood where he was and began to pulsate. With each throb, an invisible cloud of viruses spread out. The only sign of change was that Grimrose himself seemed slightly diminished.

"Are you transforming?" Nick asked. "Have you started? Are you doing it? Shouldn't you stand closer to the rim? You're supposed to be infiltrating the bubble."

Grimrose continued to pulsate.

"Grimrose," said Nick, with a cough. "What are you doing?"

By now, although he couldn't see it, Nick himself was enveloped in the viral cloud. Beads of sweat began to appear on his forehead; the muscles in his arms and legs began to ache; a sharp insistent pain knifed its way through his head. And yet his confidence in his power over Grimrose was so strong he found it exceedingly difficult to accept what was clearly happening.

"Oh no!" he said, with some difficulty as his pharynx became inflamed.

The virus attacks the endothelial cells lining the interior surface of all blood vessels. As a result, the whole body is under attack. Nick felt many things. He felt anger; he felt bitterness; he felt fear. He also felt vomit rising and diarrhoea descending. He felt utterly humiliated. Most of all he felt betrayed. How could Grimrose do this to him? Grimrose was breaking the prime directive for all shapeshifters. He had turned on his Breaker. Why? What had Nick done to deserve such treachery? And for what? So a bunch of questors could survive. So the Storyteller and Kit could have the last laugh. So the Fourth Beginning could start.

After a few minutes, all he felt was the pain. As Grimrose diffused completely in a final throb, Nick succumbed.

So it was that, even as the Breaker and the shapeshifter seemed to be merged together in death, Grimrose finally severed his links with N. Peters and, in the severing, at last found freedom and peace of mind.

84 The Fourth Beginning

In Cadnam, in the now empty boardroom, the monitor flashed red three times and then went a brilliant white. A claxon sounded. A message appeared on the monitor. It said: "This facility will self-destruct in five minutes."

No one saw the brilliant white screen; no one heard the claxon; no one read the message.

oooOooo

The bubble over the house on Poulner Hill began to expand. Its size increased slowly at first and then faster and faster, as though inflated by a giant breath. In fact, seemingly unbidden, the exponential drive and the paradox device had entered into a synergistic relationship. The bubble subsumed Cadnam within its compass before the promised self-destruction could take place. The Breaker Head Office simply dissolved into nothingness. In three minutes, the transparent, translucent bubble had encompassed and absorbed the entire mysland, fitting over the Breaker construct perfectly before gently blowing it away. By the end of ten minutes, the rim of the bubble in the east had reached Europe. In less than an hour, it had spread round the world. The first phase of its development completed, the global bubble settled for a few minutes, and then, with a paradigmatic gear shift, fuelled now by vast new energy resources within itself, paradoxically and exponentially of course, it began to expand outwards.

oooOooo

In the garden area of the Elm Tree pub, Prune Leach and Andrew Rimzil were sitting with the Storyteller beneath a cloudless blue sky. They had told him of their trip into the mysland and how, on Kit's orders, they had made their escape. They were on the third round of drinks when suddenly the sunlight became brighter and warmer. Prune and Andrew looked at each other. The Storyteller smiled. "Don't you just love happy endings?" he said.

"Well," said Prune, standing up and wiping the foam of Guinness from his mouth, "I hope you're right but, whatever the outcome, Andrew and I have to be on our way. We have left Optimius and Elsa in the van and they are both very keen to sample the delights of the Welsh coast and the Irish sea."

445

"A sanguine penguin and an unreal seal," the Storyteller laughed. "Of course, it makes sense. It's a wonderful world!"

"Elsa's not unreal, not any more" said Andrew Rimzil, "and she's certainly not imperfect. We're not sure how she managed the transition but she's thriving outside the mysland. Optimius has many plans for the future and Elsa is totally supportive."

"So the sanguine penguin has won the seal of approval, so to speak," suggested the Storyteller.

Prune Leach groaned and Andrew Rimzil gave the Storyteller a withering look.

"Sorry," said the Storyteller, "but, what the hell, this is a great day!"

oooOooo

In the well-stocked Library in the house on Poulner Hill, now very much part of the real world, the questors sat, at ease and at peace with themselves. They passed the time delving into their understanding of what they had seen and heard; they shared their hopes and fears; they told each other tales of love and life, of joy and disappointment, of success and failure. They began to understand the correct question was not whether the story was true but whether it was right. The teller of stories was not merely the seeker of truth; he was the maker, the creator, of truth, a truth so powerful it swept away all the objections of the deconstructors, just as a sun-warmed breeze effortlessly dissipates the morning mist.

Luke listened attentively for a while, and then, assured that all was well with the world, fell asleep, with his head on Numpty's feet.

The questors continued to converse. Every word they spoke was honest and whole. They talked for hours. They laughed a good deal and cried a little. Adam and Eve recalled all the good times with Bella and finally made their peace with themselves and each other. They found their love was stronger and more durable than Mount Strobilos, stronger far than either of them could reasonably have hoped. Rambler discarded his notebooks on discovering that his mind, now inexplicably capable of exceeding its own limits, was able to touch thoughts that were more expansive than the universe itself. Numpty found himself inspired by a potent blend of courage and confidence that could easily, if need be, put to flight the entire host of hell, both literally and metaphorically. And Kit finally saw himself for what he was.

It was then that the questors realised the truth.

And Kit said what all of them already knew. He said quietly: "It begins."